Oswald: Return of the King

"A spirited and enjoyable canter through Conversion-Age Northumbria, which breathes life into the dry bones offered by the Venerable Bede regarding the hero-figure of King Oswald, stays in touch with modern histories of the period and offers a homage to Tolkien's love of this same landscape and period."

Nick Higham, author of **The Anglo-Saxon World**

OSWALD

Return of the King

The Northumbrian Thrones II

Edoardo Albert

LION FICTION

This book is for my boys, Theo, Matthew and Isaac:
may their shieldwall never break.

Text copyright © 2015 Edoardo Albert
This edition copyright © 2015 Lion Hudson

The right of Edoardo Albert to be identified as the author of this
work has been asserted by him in accordance with the Copyright,
Designs and Patents Act 1988.

Published by Lion Fiction
an imprint of
Lion Hudson plc
Wilkinson House, Jordan Hill Road,
Oxford OX2 8DR, England
www.lionhudson.com/fiction

ISBN 978 1 78264 116 2
e-ISBN 978 1 78264 117 9

First edition 2015

Acknowledgments
Extract p. 259 taken from *The First Poems in English* by Michael
Alexander, copyright © 2008 Michael Alexander. Used by permission
of Penguin Random House UK.

A catalogue record for this book is available from the British Library

Printed and bound in the UK, May 2015, LH26

Contents

Dramatis Personae

Names in *italics* are invented characters

House of Ida (the Idings), kingdom of Bernicia

Oswald Lamnguin (the Whiteblade) King of Northumbria, the combined kingdom of Bernicia and Deira. Son of Æthelfrith and Acha.

Oswiu Younger brother of Oswald; son of Æthelfrith and Acha.

Æbbe Sister to Oswald and Oswiu.

Acha Mother to Oswald, Oswiu and Æbbe. Sister to Edwin, of the royal house of Yffi of Deira; married Æthelfrith, Oswald's father.

Eanfrith Half-brother to Oswald and Oswiu, via Æthelfrith's first wife, Bebba, after whom Bamburgh is named. Only known child of this marriage.

Æthelfrith Father to Oswald, Oswiu and Æbbe through Acha, princess of Deira, and to Eanfrith through Bebba. Became king of Bernicia in 592 and king of the joint kingdom of Bernicia and Deira, Northumbria, in 604. Killed in 616 at the Battle of the River Idle by the combined forces of Rædwald, king of the East Angles, and Edwin, exiled king of Deira, whom Æthelfrith had been pursuing for the previous decade.

Bran Oswald's raven.

Cyniburh Daughter of King Cynegils of the West Saxons. Wife to Oswald.

Æthelwald Baby son of Oswald and Cyniburh.

Rhieienmelth Daughter of King Rhoedd of Rheged. Wife to Oswiu.

Ahlfrith Baby son of Oswiu and Rhieienmelth.

Drest Warmaster to Eanfrith.

Corotic Chief of the Brigantes.

House of Yffi (the Yffings), kingdom of Deira

Edwin King of Northumbria from 616 to 633 when he was killed in battle with Cadwallon of Gwynedd and Penda of Mercia. His story is told in *Edwin: High King of Britain*.

Acha Sister to Edwin. See heading under House of Ida.

Osfrith Eldest son to Edwin through his first marriage to the daughter of the king of Mercia. Killed with his father at the Battle of Hatfield Chase in 633.

Eadfrith Younger son of Edwin's first marriage. Taken prisoner after the Battle of Hatfield Chase and held captive by Penda of Mercia.

Æthelburh Edwin's second wife. Fled with their children to Kent and then France after Edwin's death.

Osric Cousin to Edwin. Claimed the throne of Deira following Edwin's death.

Oswine Son of Osric, so *ætheling* (that is throne-worthy) in Deira.

Coifi Pagan priest to Edwin. Played a large part in the conversion of the kingdom to Christianity.

Acca Scop to Edwin.

Bassus Thegn to Edwin. Became warmaster to Oswald.

James Missionary sent to Edwin. He remained in Deira after Edwin's death.

Paulinus First bishop. Fled with Æthelburh after Edwin's death. Became bishop of Rochester.

House of Icel (the Iclingas), kingdom of Mercia

Cearl King of Mercia. Grandfather to Eadfrith and Osfrith, Edwin's eldest sons, through his daughter.

Penda Warmaster to Cearl. Took throne of Mercia after Cearl's death, although he was not of the House of Icel.

Eowa Brother to Penda.

Wihtrun Pagan priest to Penda.

Hroth Warmaster to Penda.

House of Wuffa (the Wuffingas), kingdom of the East Angles

Rædwald King of the East Angles and patron of Edwin. See *Edwin: High King of Britain* for his story.

Sigeberht Joint king of the East Angles with Ecgric. Abdicated the throne to enter monastery.

Ecgric King with Sigeberht, his kinsman, and then sole ruler.

House of Cerdic (the Cerdicings), kingdom of Wessex

Cynegils King of the West Saxons.

Cyniburh Daughter to Cynegils; wife to Oswald.

Birinus Missionary, sent by Pope Honorius to the West Saxons.

House of Cunedda, kingdom of Gwynedd

Cadwallon King of Gwynedd.

Briant Abbess, sister to Cadwallon.

Cian Bard to Cadwallon.

Hwyel Warmaster to Cadwallon.

Cadafael King of Gwynedd after Cadwallon.

House of Coel ("Old King Cole"), kingdom of Rheged

Rhoedd King of Rheged.

Rhieienmelth Daughter of King Rhoedd; wife to Oswiu.

Monks and people of Iona, the Islands and Lindisfarne

Ségéne Abbot of Iona.

Aidan Monk of Iona, friend to Oswald and Oswiu and first bishop of Lindisfarne.

Corman First missionary sent to the Northumbrians from Iona.

Diuma Warrior monk of Iona.

Talorc Warrior of the Seal People. Accompanies Oswald from Iona.

Gunna Fisherman's daughter.

Glossary

Ætheling A throne-worthy prince.

Angles One of the three main peoples that migrated to Britain in the fifth to seventh centuries. The Angles settled in the east and north.

Bernicia Anglian kingdom centred on Bamburgh.

Britons Original inhabitants of Britain. Ruling families, and possibly much of the populace, displaced by incoming Anglo-Saxons.

Dal Riada Sea-spanning Gaelic kingdom, linking Ulster and Argyll.

Deira Anglian kingdom, centred on York.

Dumnonia Kingdom of the Britons corresponding to Cornwall.

Gododdin A tribe who lived in what is now the south-east of Scotland and the north-east of England.

Gwynedd Kingdom of the Britons in north-west Wales.

Hide The area of land required to support a family.

"Hwæt" The traditional way to begin a recitation or song. Can be translated as *listen*, *hear this*.

Picts The original inhabitants of what later became Scotland.

Rheged A kingdom of the Britons, roughly centred on Carlisle.

Saxons One of the three peoples that migrated to Britain. The Saxons settled along the Thames and to its south and west.

Scop A bard and poet – the keeper of the memory of his people.

Seax A short sword/long knife, worn by all Anglo-Saxons (indeed, it gave the Saxons their name).

Strathclyde A kingdom of the Britons, with its chief stronghold upon Dumbarton Rock.

Thegn A nobleman – that is, a warrior.

Witan A gathering of the chief men of the kingdom.

Wyrd Key Anglo-Saxon concept. Can be translated as fate or destiny.

The Kingdoms of Britain, c. 635

MERCIA   Kingdom ruled by the Anglo-Saxons

POWYS   Kingdom ruled by the Britons

Sea, swamp, or salt marsh

······ Hadrian's Wall

Iona

PICTS

GODODDIN

DAL RIADA

Ad Gefrin

Lindisfarne

Bamburgh

BERNICIA

NORTHUMBRIA

Carlisle

Battle of Heavenfield

Monkwearmouth

Jarrow

RHEGED

DEIRA

Isle of Man

York

ELMET

Isle of Anglesey

LINDSEY

GWYNEDD

Battle of Maserfield

Oswestry

Tamworth

Crowland

MERCIA

MIDDLE ANGLIA

EAST ANGLIA

POWYS

HWICCE

Oundle

Rendlesham

DYFED

Gloucester

Cirencester

London

ESSEX

Bath

Rochester

Canterbury

Glastonbury

WESSEX

Winchester

KENT

SUSSEX

DUMNONIA

Pronunciation Guide

How do you pronounce Æ?

In Old English, Æ (or "ash" to call the letter by its name) represented a vowel that sounded like a cross between "a" and "e". Try saying it like the "a" in "cat".

A note on names

The names in this book are difficult to say. Two conquests – the slow motion one of the Anglo-Saxons and then the lightning bolt of the Normans – have consigned most of the personal names in use during the seventh century to obscure history books. The only exception is Oswald himself, a king whose cult became so widespread and famous that it was able to weather the Norman storm and continue into medieval and modern English, alongside Edwin and Alfred, two other great Anglo-Saxon kings. But of the rest, almost all were swept away, as Robert and Richard and, most of all, William shouldered Leofric and Godwine away from the baptismal font.

Another factor in the loss of Anglo-Saxon names was the conviction among the Anglo-Saxons that a name was personal property and, as such, should be unique to the person and not handed out to later generations, even if related. A notable example of this is that while Cerdic founded the kingdom of the West Saxons, the most long-lasting of all the Anglo-Saxon realms, none of his successor kings ever bore the name of their legendary forefather. As generations passed, and original names became harder to come by, the solution was to combine words in compound forms, so producing names like Godgifu (Gift of God) and Sigeberht (Victory Bright). But while names had to be unique they also, particularly in the case of noble or royal families, had to indicate family relationship. This was done by alliteration and using the same stem. Thus Alfred the Great, the youngest of five brothers and one sister, was the only one whose name did not begin with Æthel. Presumably, once his parents had got through calling on Æthelbald, Æthelberht, Æthelred, Æthelstan and Æthelswith they decided they could not face another Æthel in the hall (Æthel means "noble" – an appropriate name stem for an ætheling) and plumped for Ælfræd (which means "elf wisdom" or "counsel"). Although modern English is the direct descendant of Old English, the sound of the old language strikes the present-day hearer as akin to that of Danish – search on YouTube for readings of *Beowulf* in Old English to hear how it sounds.

To make matters more difficult, many of the names in this book come from Brittonic and Goidelic, the related languages that diversified from the original proto-Celtic, with Brittonic going on to produce Welsh, Cornish, Cumbric and Breton, and Goidelic giving us Gaelic, Scottish Gaelic and Manx.

To help readers (and the writer!), Dr Alex Woolf, senior lecturer in history at the University of St Andrews, has very kindly transcribed the most difficult names into the International Phonetic Alphabet and modern English. Here they are:

Name	International Phonetic Alphabet spelling	English equivalent
Rhieienmelth	χriː nveːld	Hriënveld
Rhoedd	χrɔið	Hroyth
Rheged	χreged	Hreged
Lamnguin	laːvngwin	Lav'ngwyn
Oswiu	Ozwĭɣ	Oswíuh
Ségéne	ʃɛgeːnĕ	Shégénuh
Cynegils	kuːnĕgiːlz	Kúnegíls
Cyniburh	kuːnĕbŭʁχ	Kúneburch
Cearl	Caːʁl	Char'l

Of the Events in Edwin:
High King of Britain

King Edwin, having taken refuge in exile with Rædwald, the king of the East Angles, learns that his host has agreed, under pressure, to hand him over to the man who has been pursuing him across Britain for the previous decade: Æthelfrith, king of Northumbria, and his brother-in-law. Unsure whether to flee or face his fate, Edwin goes out into the night, and in the darkness meets a stranger who promises him that he will overcome his enemy and gain greater power than any king since the days of the emperors. But this promise comes with a price: when the sign the stranger shows him is repeated, he must accede to the wishes of whoever shows the sign.

Desperate, but now with a smidgeon of hope, Edwin agrees and returns to the hall of King Rædwald to learn that Rædwald has decided not to forswear his obligations as host: with Edwin at his side, Rædwald decides to ride out and attack Æthelfrith, even though the king of Northumbria is the most powerful man in the land.

Æthelfrith is taken by surprise, but he just has time to send his young son, Oswald, away with a retainer. However, once safe, Oswald refuses to run further and the boy, twelve, watches from afar as Æthelfrith's small band of men is overrun and his father is executed, slowly, by Rædwald, whose own son died in the battle.

Rather than await the mercy, or otherwise, of her brother, Acha, Æthelfrith's wife, flees into exile with her children, Oswald, younger brother Oswiu and sister Æbbe. Edwin is now unchallenged king of Northumbria and, when Rædwald dies after falling from his horse, he becomes paramount, the High King of Britain. While in exile, Edwin had married Cwenburg the daughter of Cearl, king of Mercia, and she had borne him two sons before succumbing to illness, but he had not remarried. Now, to help secure his kingdom, Edwin contracts to marry Æthelburh, the sister of the king of Kent. As part of the marriage agreement, Edwin, a pagan, agrees that Æthelburh, who is Christian, may continue to practise her religion and that she may bring a priest with her when she travels to Northumbria.

On her way north, Æthelburh is ambushed by a raiding party led by Cadwallon, king of Gwynedd, one of the kingdoms still ruled by the native Britons. Learning that she is betrothed to Edwin, Cadwallon enjoins her to ask Edwin how he betrayed Cadwallon and his family when he sheltered with them during his exile. Speaking to Æthelburh alone, Cadwallon accuses Edwin of raping his sister while he lived in Gwynedd.

Æthelburh arrives in Northumbria, with Paulinus, her priest, and James, a deacon, where they find that Edwin's sons from his first marriage, Osfrith and Eadfrith, are grown men and, naturally, suspicious that any children from this new marriage of their father will compromise their own chances of gaining the throne. Edwin's pagan priest Coifi regards Paulinus with considerable suspicion, but he is struggling with the failing of his own spiritual vision, which before had allowed him to read the patterns of wyrd in the chance happenings of everyday events, from the fall of leaves to the crackle of logs on the fire.

On their wedding night, Æthelburh asks Edwin if he raped Cadwallon's sister. Edwin refuses to answer, but asks his new wife to trust him.

Enraged by the attack upon his betrothed, and Cadwallon's theft of the dowry Æthelburh had brought from Kent, Edwin launches a seaborne attack upon Anglesey and, catching Cadwallon unaware, takes him prisoner. But, at the entreaty of Cadwallon's sister, Edwin spares his life and instead sets him adrift upon the sea, without sail or oar, expecting the ocean to do his work for him.

As Edwin's power grows, other kings grow fearful and the king of the West Saxons sends an assassin to try to kill him. Only the self-sacrifice of Edwin's oldest friend saves the king, but even so Edwin is seriously wounded. The attack happens on the same day that

Æthelburh gives birth to their first child, a daughter, and in pledge for his recovery and for victory over the West Saxons, Edwin offers his daughter for baptism and suggests that he too will follow her into the new religion.

Following his recovery, Edwin defeats the West Saxons and forces them into alliance. That leaves only the kingdom of Mercia as a potential threat to him, but King Cearl is grandfather to Edwin's elder sons and without heir himself. Going to Cearl's hall, Edwin extracts a pledge from the old king that Eadfrith, the younger son, shall be his heir and king of Mercia, while to his elder son, Osfrith,. Edwin promises the Northumbrian throne. However, Cearl's warmaster, Penda, has grown powerful in defence of Mercia, his power increasing as the king ages, and Edwin sees that Penda will not lightly give up that power when Cearl dies.

Returning to Northumbria, Edwin calls a witan, a council of his thegns, to discuss the pledge he made: that he would accept the new faith, brought by Paulinus, should he achieve victory over the West Saxons. Edwin's decision to bring this matter to his people is strengthened by Paulinus giving him the sign that the stranger in East Anglia had shown, and asking him to accept the new religion. Many men speak in the witan, in favour and against the new religion, but the decision is made to adopt Christianity when Coifi, priest of the old religion, stands within the witan and abjures the old gods as unable to deliver to those most devoted to them any true blessings in this life or the next. The decision made, Coifi, in an iconoclastic frenzy, rides to the nearest sacred grove and profanes it.

Edwin and his sons and his thegns accept baptism in the newly built and as yet incomplete church in York, and Paulinus travels around Northumbria with the king, preaching and baptizing.

His overlordship now accepted by most of the kings of Britain, Edwin decides that he must secure the throne of Mercia for his son. While Cearl is happy to declare Eadfrith his heir, Edwin is sure that Penda will not relinquish the crown, even though he is not a descendant of Icel, the founder of Mercia's royal house. So Edwin decides that Penda must be removed. Summoning all the kings to York, that they might do homage to him, Edwin plans to kill Penda and ensure a smooth transition to the throne for Eadfrith. But, unknown to Edwin, Penda has entered into alliance with Cadwallon. For the king of Gwynedd had survived his ordeal by ocean and returned to his kingdom to rebuild his strength. So, when Edwin rides with his sons, in stealth, to cut down Penda, they are themselves surprised by the trap that Penda and Cadwallon have prepared. In the battle, Edwin, High King of Britain, is killed, and Osfrith too, while Eadfrith is taken prisoner.

When news of this reaches Æthelburh she takes her children and, with Paulinus, flees into exile, taking ship to her kin, first in Kent and then to her mother's people in France. James the deacon remains to minister to the people of Northumbria, but Cadwallon ravages the kingdom, exacting revenge for the humiliations suffered by him and his people.

News of the High King's fall travels through the land and eventually reaches a small island off the west coast of Scotland, where a community of monks has established a monastery and where a young prince, in exile, has for a while found peace...

PART 1

Return

Chapter 1

"He's dead."

Oswald stared at the breathless young monk panting in front of him, sweat beading his shaven forehead and braiding into rats' tails the hair trailing down his back.

"Who is dead, Aidan?"

"The king! The king is dead." Brother Aidan's eyes were bright with excitement. He pointed away, over the flat expanse of machair, the grass speckled with buttercup and vetch, to the strand by the abbey. Oswald stood up from his digging and shaded his eyes against the early sun. There, on the beach, the young prince saw figures milling around a beached boat, its sail still flapping in the morning breeze.

"The brothers brought the news," said Aidan. "They were supposed to be bringing us a fine white cow that the king had promised to Brother Fintan in the scriptorium, but when they heard they just jumped in the boat and sailed back here." The young monk turned to Oswald, his face becoming suddenly solemn and his address formal.

"Is it not fine tidings for thee?" he said.

Oswald shook his head, but he could not help smiling. "Is it? I do not know, Brother Aidan. You tell me the king is dead, but which king? There are many on these islands."

"*The* king. The High King. The king who killed your father."

The smile went from Oswald's face. "Edwin," he said. "My uncle."

"Yes, he is dead and his sons either dead or taken."

"Who did this?" Oswald stared intently into the young monk's face. "Who killed him?"

"Cadwallon, king of Gwynedd, and Penda of Mercia."

The young prince nodded once, then stared away into the

east, towards the hills of Mull across the Sound. The monk, in his excitement, shuffled from one foot to the other, then when Oswald said no more he touched the young man's arm.

"Will you be going back?" he asked. "Back to Northumbria? The throne is yours now, I think."

Oswald's gaze turned slowly on his questioner. "My father is avenged, but not by my hand." He held up his right arm. "You know the name Domnall Brecc, king of Dal Riada, gave me when I fought in his warband? Oswald *Lamnguin*, the Whiteblade, but it was not this arm that cut down the High King and," the young man's gaze focused suddenly on the even younger man in front of him, "I do not know whether to weep or laugh."

"Weep *and* laugh," said Brother Aidan, "for that is our life in this world: sorrow and joy joined as flesh to blood. The Lord has taken vengeance on your father's killer in his pride, and the Lord, in his mercy, has spared you the blood guilt of your uncle's slaughter."

A raven croaked nearby, and Brother Aidan looked to the sound. The great black bird took wing and flew towards them, the young monk ducking out of the way and stumbling backwards as the raven settled upon Oswald's upheld forearm in a dry, bone rustle of feathers. The raven ducked its head and croaked its greeting, and Oswald answered in kind, the sound straining his throat muscles as if ripped from the flesh.

"I will never get used to that bird," grumbled Brother Aidan as he picked himself up from the springy machair, brushing grass and clover from his habit.

Oswald tickled the raven's throat and the great bird tilted its head to better direct the man's fingers, clicking with enjoyment.

"Bran pays you no mind," said Oswald. "You should do the same with him."

"I know he pays me no mind," said Aidan. "It's bad enough being ignored by the abbot, but to be ignored by a bird…"

"He's training you in humility," said Oswald. "You are a monk, after all."

"The raven never returned to Noah."

"Doves are stupid birds." Oswald continued scratching under the bird's beak. "Bran is not stupid." Oswald looked around, squinting into the distance. "Have you seen my brother? I must speak to him."

"The last time I saw Oswiu, he was trying to persuade one of the fishermen to introduce him to his daughters."

"But women are not permitted on Iona," said Oswald. "I thought at least here he would be kept from temptation."

"They weren't on the island. They were on the fisherman's boat, waving to Oswiu like a pair of moon-struck maids. Your brother, seeing them, dived in the sea and swum out to their boat; the last I saw, he had dived under the curragh when the fisherman tried to hit him with an oar."

Oswald shook his head. "Will he ever learn?"

"He is young," said Aidan. "Younger even than me, and eight years younger than you; the blood is hot and thick at that age, and if the cold sea won't cool it, then nothing will, save to tup a maid."

"He should learn restraint."

The monk shrugged. "So should we all."

Oswald bent his head to the bird and whispered before launching the raven into the air.

"Bran will find Oswiu."

The young monk watched the bird claw its way into the sky, before settling into a long circling glide, the beat of the slaughter birds as they waited above a battlefield for its red harvest.

"If you were not ætheling, worthy of the throne of Northumbria, Abbot Ségéne would have commanded that bird stuffed. He shudders every time he sees it, and makes the sign against the Eye – but beneath his habit, so that none may see it."

"I thought, of a time, you Irish worshipped different gods to my people. The raven is Woden's; it belongs not to the Tuatha de Danaan or any of the old gods of your people."

"It is still pagan."

"Bran is no pagan – he is a bird, and my faithful friend, so I will stand beside him. Besides," and here Oswald pointed away to the south of the little island, "he is my eyes as well!" Silhouetted against the bright blue sky, the raven flew back towards them, calling his finding.

"How did you find me?" The young man, dark where his brother was fair but in all other ways his younger image, grumbled as he stumbled towards the landing beach, the sole of Oswald's foot hurrying him along whenever he lagged. Beside him, and not nearly as abashed as the young ætheling, the fisherman's daughter walked, rolling her hips and flashing the whites of her eyes at the startled glances of passing monks.

"Bran found you," said Oswald.

Oswiu looked around, scanning the sky for his accuser. "I hate that bird," he said.

"Bran does what I tell him."

"As do we all."

"You do not."

Oswiu flashed a grin back at his brother. "Of course I don't – ow!"

Oswald brandished a birch switch at him. "Hurry up. We have to get her off Iona before the abbot hears you brought a maid ashore."

"I didn't bring her – she came herself, didn't you?"

The fisherman's daughter smiled sidelong at Oswald, who did his best to ignore her. Aidan, tagging behind, thought it best to lag so that the brothers might sort the matter out between themselves.

"You encouraged her."

"I wouldn't say encouraged…"

"Paid?"

"No! Of course not."

"Here, what be you thinking I am?" The fisherman's daughter stopped fast in her tracks and turned to face Oswald, hands on hips, outrage on her lips. Her hair was black, her skin white and still unstained by wind and sun. The ætheling, forced to stop, looked her in the face, steady and long, and blood flushed the girl's cheek and she dropped her gaze.

"I think you are beautiful," said Oswald, "and I know we must get you off this island. Now, hurry." Taking the lead, Oswald strode towards the beach, where curraghs lay upon the strand like seals sunning themselves.

The fisherman's daughter fell in beside Oswiu. "Why didn't you tell me about your brother?" she whispered, staring after Oswald as he led them on.

Oswiu groaned. "Not you as well."

"What do you mean?"

"I dived into the sea to speak to you, and your father nearly killed me with that oar, but one smile from him and you'd do anything." Oswiu stared after his older brother. "How does he do it?"

"God's grace lies upon him." Brother Aidan had caught up. "And he gives of it freely and without thought." The monk too looked after Oswald. "I do not think he even knows – it is as natural to him as breathing is to us."

Oswiu shrugged. "Maybe that is true – you are a monk. But I've seen him in battle, when we sailed with King Conadh Cerr and fought at the disaster of Fid Eoin, when Cruithne cut down Dal Riada, and men were calling on their mothers to save them, and others were falling upon their own swords in despair. Then my brother rallied what was left, and brought us back to our boats, holding the hordes of Cruithne at bay with a sword that flashed brighter than the sun." Oswiu looked at the monk. "Then he came back for me, who was stunned and stupid and too young to have been allowed upon the war boats, and dragged me back to his curragh, and I live and am not dead." The ætheling nodded towards his brother. "That is why men follow him. That is why I follow him, and will never betray him."

Aidan nodded. "That is well. Treachery is ever the greatest threat to ætheling or king."

Oswald stood waiting for them upon the beach by a curragh pulled up onto the sand. Three benches ran across it, a short mast carried a small sail, and its oars lay shipped within.

"That's a big boat for one maid," said Oswiu, hands on hips, looking at the vessel.

"We're going as well," said Oswald. "We're going to see Mother."

*

Out of the Sound of Iona, the sea kicked up a great rolling swell that carried the curragh to the height of each crest before it slid, light as a leaf, into the deep, green valley. Oswiu and Aidan laid to with the oars, the fisherman's daughter – her name was Gunna – tended the sail so that, when the curragh rode up out of the valleys onto the wind-scoured wave ridges, it flung the boat onwards, swift and sure, all but keeping pace with the seabirds that hawked hopefully around them. Bran, disdainful of these pale creatures, remained perched upon the bench next to Oswald, its eyes hooded in sleep, as the ætheling moved the steering oar through the thick water.

Brother Aidan, facing south as he rowed, kept a weather eye to his right, to the south-west, where clouds were massing. The sky had been clear out of the Sound, but as they'd passed the tall stack of rock that was Staffa, its milling seabirds screaming insult at the small passing vessel, he had seen the first massing, and passing the Treshnish Isles he had thought to suggest landing. But Oswald had laughed off the idea and taken a spell rowing, and for a while it seemed for sure that they would outrun the storm. But now he was not so sure. Upon the wave tops, the wind was pulling the water into fine spray. His habit, with the hood up and its wool coated in beeswax, kept him reasonably dry, but Oswald, on the steering oar, was wiping the spray from his face as he peered north, searching through the spume for the low shores of Coll.

"You did not tell me we were going on the green pilgrimage afore we set off," said Aidan, "else I would have asked the abbot's blessing – and his shriving."

"I did not think we were." Oswald looked around doubtfully. "I do not know where we are."

Oswiu, weary, shipped his oar. The boat, light as down, skimmed back into the deep valley and the world was water.

The air slack, Gunna left her tending of the sail and, gathering her skirt around her knees, stepped lightly over the benches to where Oswald sat holding the steering oar at the rear of the boat.

"Leave the steering to a fisherman's daughter that knows the waters round here like her own hair, and you tend the oars." Gunna tied her skirts off around her hips, tipped a staring Brother Aidan such a wink that he flushed red, gave Oswiu a long smile and, once Oswald was in place, nodded to the ætheling. "This is how it should be done."

The curragh, its spine flexing against the water, sprang forward, and Gunna held it along the wave ridges, crooning a soft song to the wind as she steered, the men bending to their labour, and the raven, having opened one eye to check all was well, returning to its rest. Under Gunna's hands, the curragh outran the oncoming storm, leaving the rolling clouds massing on the horizon.

"There be another boat, northways, but it is drawing east, away from Coll, not to it." Gunna pointed and Oswald stood, swaying but steady, to see where she indicated.

It was a large curragh, and it sat heavy in the water, for shivering between the men pulling oars were three or four shaggy, short-horned cows.

"Cattle raid." Oswald turned back to Gunna and smiled. "We have them."

"But there's only three of us, and one woman," said Brother Aidan, squinting against the spray as he counted. "There must be ten men on her."

Oswiu laughed. "I would swap you for Gunna. Besides, two sons of Æthelfrith are a match for ten other men, on sea or land."

"Their boat is heavy laden and slow. Ours is light and fast, and its pilot," Oswald nodded to Gunna, "is the most skilful I have seen."

"Nevertheless, I have seldom heard good of fights conducted at sea," said the monk.

"Neither have I." Oswald smiled. "So we will not fight."

*

It was like a heavy highland cow, driven mad by a swarm of stinging midges, flinging itself about until finally it collapses under its own weight. The curragh, steered by Gunna, danced around the cattle raiders in their larger boat, flicking in and out of their range, drawing their insults and skipping away, pulling the oars from the hands of rowers, pitching men into the sea so that they clung like bedraggled children to the skirts of their mother and, finally, ripping the sail through with a finely judged sword pass.

The cattle raiders, helpless, wallowed in the sea, the animals lowing plaintively in the belly of the boat. Whenever a raider attempted to clamber back into the boat a little pointed jab was sufficient to send him back into the sea.

"It's summer and the sea's warm; why you be trying to get in the boat?" Gunna laughed. Oswald threw a rope over the curragh's stern post and they began towing it towards Coll. The cattle raiders, still clinging to the side of the curragh, offered threats and curses, but the sea soon chilled their insults and sapped their energy. By the time they reached Coll, the cattle raiders were content to crawl upon the beach and collapse upon the sand. There, waiting for them, were the men of Coll, the sons of Feall, fingering blades and staffs and fish hooks.

"Send them home." Oswald stepped from the curragh and stood between the exhausted men, lying groaning upon the beach, and the sons of Feall.

One of the men stepped forward and Oswald nodded to him. He knew him of old.

"They came when we climbed the stacks of Staffa and took our cattle while we clung above the waves. There was no glory in this raid, only thievery, and thieves should die. That is our law."

"It is my law too." Oswald squatted down and grabbed the wet hair of a man lying beside him, pulling up his face, covered in sand. The man coughed, seawater trickling from mouth and nose. "But disgrace is worse than death. Send them back, and soon all the islands will know that these raiders, these brave, bold raiders, were caught by a girl." The ætheling pointed to Gunna. "She it was who stung them, harried them and then dropped them, one by one, into the sea. Let them live, and then never let them hear the end of it!"

The men, the sons of Feall, broke into laughter, while Gunna did again something she had not done for many a month before meeting Oswald: she blushed, flushing all the redder when Oswald came to stand in front of her.

"Never in my days have I seen a curragh better handled, Gunna, fisherman's daughter. I thank you for saving us, and for bringing back the cattle of Coll." And the ætheling made the courtesy to her, in the fashion of his people, and Gunna, tongue-tied, bobbed in front of him as a bird upon the wave.

"Come, Oswiu, we must upon our business with Mother. Brother Aidan, will you wait here for the moment? I'm sure these people would appreciate the blessings of a monk of Iona." Oswald turned and made his way through the sons of Feall, the men parting before him and whispering his name when he had passed, and Gunna, fisherman's daughter, stared after him.

Oswiu tapped her on the shoulder. "I have to see Mother for now, but this storm will last a while, I think, so we shall not be returning to Iona today."

Gunna glanced at him distractedly. "What?"

Oswiu saw her staring after his brother. "Oh, never mind," he said, and stalked off in Oswald's wake.

It was a short walk across the machair to the small house where their mother dwelled. Oswald had expected to see her sitting on her stool outside, sheltered by the white walls, skilled hands weaving while her eyes looked south across the sea, in the direction of Iona. But the machair lay bare save for its summer sprinkling of flowers. Overhead, Bran rolled upon the air, croaking greeting and warning to the ravens of the island, who answered in kind, rising upon the wind to greet their visitor.

"Why are we coming to see Mother?" Oswiu asked.

"To ask her counsel and her blessing."

"She would not say against your claim?"

"Our claim, brother. We are both Idings, sons of Æthelfrith; we each may claim the throne of Bernicia and therefore Northumbria."

"I can see it: the two of us standing in the great council, the witan of our people hearing our claim, and then choosing me over you." Oswiu laughed, and there was no bitterness in his laugh. "As likely as me becoming a monk."

"As likely as us both surviving this." Oswald stopped and turned to his brother. "Think on this: Cadwallon of Gwynedd and Penda of Mercia have brought down the High King, our uncle, the man who killed our father. Not since the days of the emperors has there been a king of such power in these islands as Edwin – I have heard tell that where the king's writ ran, it was possible for a woman with babe at breast to walk alone and untroubled from sea to sea. Now the king is dead, and the law with him. Now there is only the sword, and the men who wield it, taking what they will. The wolves are circling, Oswiu, the ravens picking at the flesh, and we have hardly the men to do more than raid among raiders, to plunder and despoil and make a brief, sorry stay against death." The elder took the younger brother's shoulders and held him. "This world reeks of death, brother, and glory is but a lightning flash before night falls. If we go to reclaim our kingdom, we go as the lightning, fierce and fast, but we must have more men. So again, we go to Mother, for she is family to the kings of Dal Riada, and cousin to Colman, High King of the Uí Neíll. If she will, she can ask of the king many men; enough to make us more than raiders; enough to win us our father's kingdom."

Oswiu swallowed. "Ah, Oswald, there may be a small problem with your plan."

Oswald let go and stepped back, staring at his brother with a sudden, terrible suspicion.

"What have you done?"

Oswiu swallowed again. "I – I don't think we will be getting much help from the Uí Neíll."

"Oswiu…"

"Um, you remember when we sailed with King Colman's warband last year? I was injured in the first raid and stayed at the king's hall to recover while you went off. His – his daughter was very kind to me."

"Oswiu…"

"And – and the baby must be due soon."

"Baby?"

Oswiu closed his eyes. "Yes."

"You – you mean to tell me you tupped a princess?"

"Yes."

"But not just any princess: Fina, daughter of Colman, High King of the Uí Neíll."

"Yes." With each assent, Oswiu's voice squeaked higher.

"The Uí Neíll who promised us many men to reclaim our kingdom."

"Yes." Oswiu's voice had reached falsetto.

"Argh."

Oswiu waited, eyes tight shut, but Oswald said nothing more. He opened one eye. His brother, seeing him, balled his fists.

"I should…"

"Yes, you should."

Oswald quivered, strung between rage and restraint, then abruptly he turned away and marched up the machair towards the white house.

Oswiu, seeing him go, ran after him, but before he could get too close, Oswald held up his hand in warning. No nearer.

So, one brother trailing the other, Oswald and Oswiu, the sons of Æthelfrith, arrived at the house of their mother, Acha.

As the æthelings approached, a woman emerged, a rich shawl wrapped over her shoulders and hair but otherwise plainly clad, and then a moment later a young woman followed her, to stand waiting outside the house, a broad smile upon her face. Seeing her, Oswiu hurried on, catching his brother as they neared the house.

"I did not know Æbbe would be here as well," he said.

"I – I hoped she might," said Oswald, then breaking into a run he surged up the machair, past the outbuildings and workshops and the men, women and children greeting and gaping at the æthelings, to the two waiting women.

"Mother." He made the courtesy to the older woman. "Sister."

Before they could answer in kind, Oswiu wrapped his arms around Æbbe. "Sister! I thought you were in Ulster with our kin there. When did you come back here?"

Æbbe laughed and extricated herself from her brother's embrace. "I was going to send word to you today, only you have come to me!"

"This is a fine chance." Acha put out arms to enclose both sons in her embrace before pushing them away so she could see them, and once again commit their faces to memory, lest this be the last occasion on which she see them in this life. She looked searchingly from her older son to her younger, and then back again. "But I see it is no chance that brings you both here today."

The brothers looked to each other, communicating silently, then turned to their mother.

Oswald, the elder, spoke, as Acha knew he would.

"News came to the abbey today." The ætheling was pale and his mother knew he was struggling to find words. He always hated to tell her ill tidings, so she brought his discomfort to an end by holding her finger up.

"I know. Word reached us today as well. The king, my brother, the man who killed your father, is dead." Acha held her hand to her heart. "I have not seen Edwin for many, many years, not since he fled from Æthelfrith, but he was kind to me when we were children, and he did not pursue us after your father died." Unexpected tears welled from her eyes, and the queen, who had endured betrayal and death and exile dry-eyed, turned away and stood, her body shaking, in tears.

Her children stood about her, uncertain, until Oswiu gestured to his sister: do something. Æbbe stepped forward and put her arm about the exiled queen, and slowly Acha's shoulders stopped shaking. Taking a breath, Acha turned to her children and forced a smile. But seeing them all together, the smile grew true.

"Come, my beloveds, let us eat and be glad, and then take counsel together, for we have much to ponder."

Chapter 2

It was a simple meal, but joyful. The household slaves set up a table and benches outside on the machair, for in this season the night scarce came before the dawn arrived to banish it once more, and the air was mild and the wind kind. The storm that had threatened earlier grumbled upon the horizon but, as if mindful of the meeting that had taken place, it bided away upon the sea, waiting its time. Oswald and Oswiu laughed with the slaves as they set up the supper, for most of them they had known since childhood, the slaves going with them into exile when their father died.

Remembering that he'd left his friend to the hospitality of the islanders – always generous, usually noisome – Oswald sent a messenger to fetch Brother Aidan from the village, ignoring his brother's suggestion that Gunna be summoned as well, and the monk arrived just as the food was being brought out to the table.

Brother Aidan called down blessings upon the meal and their fellowship as the slaves bustled to and from the house, setting up their own table on the machair in among the preparations for the family meal. Oswald was old enough to remember the two false summers and hard winters of his childhood that had brought famine in their train, and the children lying hollow-eyed and swollen-bellied by the side of the road, too weak to hold out hands to beg. Many of his mother's slaves came from those terrible years, when families had come staggering, carrying the young and the old, to the royal compounds that lay a day's journey apart throughout Northumbria, and begged to be taken as slaves, that they might have food and live. Oswald remembered his mother gathering the household slaves together when his father died, in the fever of fear that gripped Bamburgh as it waited upon the arrival of Æthelfrith's slayers, and telling them that those who wished might have their freedom; for the rest, exile and an uncertain future waited. All but a handful – and in the cases of those who stayed it was because of pregnancy or illness – had followed them, choosing exile and to serve the Idings over Edwin, the descendant of Yffi, who would rule over Northumbria for sixteen years.

Brother Aidan raised the cup and it seemed that the sun, low in the evening sky, filled it with light as he sang blessings upon it. They would all, for many reasons, remember this evening together through the remaining years of their lives, but it was not the glow of reminiscence that coloured the memories golden, for the sun itself poured gold upon the evening, gilding the machair and turning the sea into a moving cloth of jewelled blue. Acha sat with her sons across the table from her, that she might see them the better, while her daughter took the cup that the monk had blessed and brought it to Oswald and Oswiu in turn, bidding them, "Drink, give thanks and be glad." Each, in turn, took and drank deep, returning the cup with solemn joy.

"There is great joy for me this eve," said Acha, as Æbbe returned the cup to her. "And great tidings too." She looked to her sons and there was a deep smile filled with soft shadows upon her face. Acha turned and beckoned Æbbe to her side, and the young woman came and stood beside her.

"Give your sister your blessings, my sons, for she is to forsake the pleasures and pains of this world to join herself in eternal union with our Lord, and become abbess of a monastery – King Domnall Brecc has given into our hands land and house for such a one."

Oswald and Oswiu stood and embraced their sister, while Brother Aidan bounced from foot to foot in excitement before welcoming Æbbe as a sister in Christ. Æbbe herself, after an initial flush, settled into their contentment, but as they took seat again, she turned to Oswald.

"I was worried that you would want to make me a marriage that would bring the family warriors and influence – Mother said you would not forbid me, but I had not the courage to tell you before."

Oswald laughed. "We tried that already, when you were fourteen, and word reached us that Rædwald was dead and Edwin no longer had his support. Do you remember, we went, all of us, to the king of Ulster? That was a miserable journey, and I feared more than once that our curragh would founder, and our welcome was hardly less miserable than our voyage, and then Ulster introduced his son." Oswald turned to Acha. "You went pale as death."

"As did you."

"True."

"What was wrong with him?" asked Æbbe. "Remember, I never saw the young Ulster."

"For which I remain grateful; men wake sweating from dreams of battles remembered. You have been spared similar dreams of marriage through never seeing him."

"Was he that bad?"

Mother and son exchanged memories by look, then turned back to Æbbe.

"Worse," they answered.

"But if you had betrothed me, Ulster would like have given you the men to claim Northumbria; would you not have wished that, brother?"

"And then I would have faced my uncle in battle, and he or I would have lived, but either way part of our mother would have died. This way, our hands are clean of Edwin's blood, there is no guilt upon us, and we may call down God's blessing with full heart."

"But now I will never bring any warriors to our family's cause."

"You will hold us in your heart and fill God's hall with your prayers and those of your community, that he may remember us and bless us. What greater aid could we wish for?"

Æbbe smiled at her elder brother, and golden light played upon her face and her hair.

They ate well that eve, taking the fruits of sea and land: cream and rich cheese from the small cattle that browsed the machair, fish and the fatty meat of porpoise, harpooned from a curragh and dragged flopping ashore for butchery. Bran, having made his courtesy to the birds of the island, swooped down upon the machair and, gathering his wings around him like a cloak, high-stepped to Oswald's side and, croaking, announced his presence and his hunger. Æbbe clapped her hands and laughed at Bran's arrival.

"We are all together again," she said.

Brother Aidan, sitting to the end of the table, contented himself with his meat, striving to make himself as invisible as possible while the family talked and remembered and ate, then talked some more.

The meal taken and thanks given, the Idings, the sons and daughters of Ida, first king of Bernicia, sat upon the machair, the sun hanging in the sky at their backs as if refusing to dip his red head into the cooling sea.

"God has brought us all together this eve," said Oswald, "when news has reached us all of the High King's death. We have full bellies..."

"Speak for yourself," said Oswiu, reaching for a hand of cheese.

"...we have bellies that may soon burst," continued Oswald, "a clear eve and gentle wind." He sat up straight upon the machair. "Let us take counsel together. Mother, what say you?"

Acha smoothed her skirts over her knees. She sat, legs bent and knees embraced, upon the machair, the late breeze rippling her shawl, and her children each saw in her then the beauty she had had in her youth, before the hard tidings of her husband's betrayal of her brother, the years spent married to a lord of uncertain temper and the further years of exile had broken her looks and tempered her soul upon the anvil of regret and pain.

"I say that I would not have this eve end. I have my children about me. I can wish for no more, lest it be grandchildren."

At that, Oswiu turned his face from Acha lest she see him blush.

"But the night will come, and it will grow dark, though only for a short time in this season. So we must speak of what will be. My sons, you brought me the news of my brother's death at the hands of Cadwallon of Gwynedd and Penda of Mercia. Know you when he died?"

"It was in October of the year past," said Oswald.

"And what of the kingdom in the time since? Have you any further tale?"

"The messenger brought rumour of great suffering, though whether that be true I cannot say. But it seems that Cadwallon and Penda remain in the kingdom, for the last tale had them still in Deira, ravaging and plundering as they go and laying the land to waste and ruin."

"They wintered in Northumbria?"

"That is what we hear told. And as they go, they burn, setting flames to the great halls that our fathers built and driving those that remain to flight and exile. Those thegns that still hold their land and halls wait upon the arrival of Cadwallon and Penda like men wait upon winter, knowing it will come, helpless to prolong the summer. We have heard that Osric, Edwin's cousin, has put himself to what remains of the witan as king of Deira, but can he rule when Cadwallon and Penda and their warbands roam the land like wolves? I doubt it."

"Wolves require feeding," said Acha. "When there is no more to eat, the pack will return to its den."

"They have not gone yet, and the season draws on. The month for planting is past, the month for reaping draws near. If Cadwallon and Penda remain in the kingdom until harvest, then they are not returning to their kingdoms, but seeking a new one."

"Two kings and one kingdom do not match." Acha smiled grimly. "That is what your father told me after our wedding night and before the feast from which my brother fled for his life."

The family fell into the silence of memory until Oswiu spoke. "The Britons called him *Flesaur*, the Twister, did they not?"

"He loved that name and so did his warriors," said Oswald. "He would have his scop chant it before battle, even though it did not fit into our tongue."

"The men chanted it too," said Acha. "Standing in front of him, brandishing their swords and shields, shouting 'Flesaur, Flesaur' over and again as he handed out the shining gold rings."

"He never gave me a ring," said Oswald. "I was too young. The first time he took me with him in his warband, he died, and I was left, struggling and crying to get back to him, in the arms of Dæglaf."

"He was more generous to his men than his sons," said Acha. "He only gave Eanfrith one ring, and he was your elder by five years."

"I remember that ring. Eanfrith would dangle it in front of me, and when I tried to touch it, he would pull it away, laughing."

"He was cruel to you," said Acha, "but I could not blame him. Eanfrith's mother, Bebba, died when he was four and your father took me as his new wife; each of you was a threat to him."

"I did not feel a threat when he was beating me," said Oswald.

"You fought like a wildcat," said Acha "and the next day Eanfrith was as cut and bruised as you."

"But not the day after," said Oswald. "I could not lie down for a week. But he let me be after that."

"He has let us all be these years since your father's death," said Acha. "He went to his mother's people, the Picts, after Æthelfrith was killed, and made no move against us, but now I have heard tell that he is gathering a warband from among the Picts and those men who went with him into exile. I have sent messengers to learn more, but I think it sure that they will return with tidings that your half-brother will attempt to claim the throne of Bernicia and, if he succeeds, then Deira and all of Northumbria."

Oswald made no reaction, but Oswiu grimaced. "He will ignore us no longer if he wins the throne, brother. We will have to watch for knife and arrow and poison then. We should act now, before he has the power to make our friends over into our enemies."

Oswald shook his head. "Eanfrith has done us no ill – well, not since I was a boy." He turned back to Acha. "Have you any word of where stands the witan of Bernicia? Will they bow to him, or turn their back on him?"

"He is your father's eldest son, and his thegns remember the glory and gold your father brought them. He is eldest, and throne-worthy. They will bow to him if he comes to them first."

"Let us get there before him," said Oswiu, turning urgently to his brother. "We are Father's sons too, and throne-worthy; if it be but a matter of priority, let us gather a few men and horses and sail for the

Solway Firth. It is but a two-day ride from Carlisle to Bamburgh, and we may gather aid from Rheged."

"A few men will not defeat Cadwallon and Penda," said Oswald.

"They would not have to. Get back, raise the witan, swear the thegns of Bernicia to you; then we have an army to beat them."

Oswald shook his head. "Let us say it happens as you wish, brother. We would then have to face Eanfrith and his warband."

"So? If we've already defeated Cadwallon and Penda, we would be able to defeat Eanfrith too."

"Eanfrith is our brother."

"Half-brother." Oswiu glanced at Acha. "The wrong half."

"Brother." Oswald closed his eyes.

The eve was silent. Fires and lamps flickered in the twilight, but no true night would fall.

Oswald opened his eyes and turned to his brother. "I will not fight him," he said and, standing, he brushed the machair from his tunic.

"Mother, I would speak with you. Alone," he added, as Oswiu and Æbbe began to get to their feet as well.

Leaving his brother and sister with Brother Aidan by the white house, Oswald walked with Acha towards the lines of waves breaking upon the beach. They went in silence, reaching the strand without word, and there Oswald stopped.

Looking out to sea, Oswald spoke.

"Oswiu was four when Father was killed. I was twelve. I remember Dæglaf gripping me on the horse as we rode away from where they killed Father, me struggling, kicking, trying to get away, to get back to Father, until Dæglaf slapped me. 'He's dead,' he said. 'I will not let you die too.' And he tied and trussed me like a slave and slung me over his horse. That was how I came back to you: tied up like a boar taken for the hunt.

"I saw your face when you heard the news, Mother. I saw your panic, your fear, your... relief. You were relieved that Father was dead." Oswald looked to where sea touched sky and his mother made no answer. "I hated you then, for I saw him die as I had seen him fight, and I knew no king mightier nor more terrible."

Acha remained silent. The sea answered, waves hissing upon the beach and withdrawing, sucking the sand and spitting it back up again.

"I remember the fear that gripped everyone, the panic as you gathered Oswiu and Æbbe to you and we rode north, always looking over our shoulders lest Uncle be behind us. We came to Dunadd, the stronghold of Dal Riada, and you left us waiting without its walls while you went within to speak with the king. Æbbe cried, asking if you would come out again, and Oswiu too, and I had no words for them; I thrust them away.

"I remember taking ship to Ulster, the cold of that journey and the colder welcome. We were passed from court to court, from kingdom to kingdom, like unwanted guests; we were treated better than lepers, but not by much. And I hated you the more, Mother, for you said nothing. You accepted the silence and the insults; you bore them all and shuffled us on to somewhere new where they could mock us, fatherless children of an alien land.

"And I remember when everything changed." Oswald turned his gaze from the horizon and looked upon his mother and smiled. "We were on yet another curragh, sailing from Ulster back to Dal Riada, and for a mercy the wind was calm and we were dry. The boatmaster put me to row, but Oswiu was too little yet, and he and Æbbe were sleeping with you. I had not marked the other men on board when we set to rowing, for I was yet too wrapped in my anger, but as we plied the oars I saw they were dressed alike, in robes akin to those worn by the priests of the strange god that men worshipped in these island kingdoms. And as we rowed, they began to sing, long and low, chanting out in a strange tongue words I did not know, yet understood. Their chant entered into my rowing, and the music moved my hands and the words filled my heart; the bitterness that had filled me since Father's death and our exile was gone and I looked about me with a hope and a joy I had not known – I had not even known I could know."

Oswald's smile came through tears now. "I said not a word on that voyage, but I swam in the sound of their singing, and when we landed, and their song was done, I asked whence they came and where they were going and what music they sang.

"'Iona,' they said. 'The Holy Island of Colm Cille, where saints walk in the noon and angels tread by night.' I knew then where I must go." The ætheling put his hand to his mother's shoulder. "I am sorry for the worry I must have caused you then, but I could not ask lest you forbid. I went with the monks when they took ship again at dawn, and as the sun set in the west I set foot for the first time upon the Holy Island, and voices upraised greeted me as I stepped off the boat, and a young man, seeing me standing upon the strand, entranced as one bewitched, took me by the hand and led me to the abbey whence the music flowed, and I stood in heaven, unmoving save for my tears."

Oswald, ætheling, throne-worthy prince of Bernicia, the Whiteblade of Domnall Brecc, looked upon his mother, queen in exile, and spoke what was in his heart.

"I would give up the throne. I would put down my sword and put away my claim and be a monk of the Holy Island and there end my days. What say you?"

Acha took his face in her hands. As always, she committed him to memory, adding this face to all the others that she stored in her heart, ready for the day when they might be all that remained to her of her son.

"A fire burned in the sky when you were born, a fire that could be seen by day and night, and men said that it was a great sign. And I, looking at you in my arms, knew that they were right.

"You wish to lay aside your claim to the throne and enter the holy life, like your sister? More than anything, I would that this happen, that you might live and I not have to clean the blood from your wounds and wash your body for burial. Go to the Holy Island, my son, and ask them, beg them, to take you. Abbot Ségéne knows you well – he will not refuse, I am sure."

Oswald smiled, his smile turning into a laugh. "You will not think me frightened?"

"No, never. How could I, who have seen you these many years?"

"It was the news you gave that decided me."

Acha looked puzzled. "What news?"

"Of my brother Eanfrith. With Cadwallon and Penda ravaging the kingdom, if he had not returned to claim the throne I would, of need, have done so myself. But I will not fight my brother, and his claim is God's sign that my heart's wish is true: I will return to the Holy Island and ask the abbot to accept me as a monk." Oswald laughed for pure heart's joy. "Oh Mother, give me your blessing."

"You have it, my son; you have it always."

"*Ark!*"

They both started, then laughed together as the affronted shape of Bran alighted next to them upon the beach.

"He cannot sleep for the light," said Oswald. "Come, let us return to the others. I must tell them my decision."

"Wait." Acha took his arm. "What about Oswiu? If you say that you intend to become a monk of the Holy Island, he may try to raise a warband himself – he is rash enough."

Oswald put finger to mouth in silent thought.

"He will not raise a warband against Eanfrith. Half-brother though he is, he is still our brother. But he would ride first against Cadwallon and Penda, if he could. Therefore, we must delay him." Oswald smiled. "Let me return to the Holy Island with him. I will say we go to ask Abbot Ségéne for his blessing and prayers, and for his intercession with the king of the Uí Neíll, and the kings of Dal Riada and Rheged and Strathclyde, that we might gather an army sufficient to meet and defeat Cadwallon and Penda. It is a long and difficult matter to get so many kings to agree, and it will take many months – time for Eanfrith to win Bernicia for himself. Once we have news that Eanfrith is secure upon the throne, then I can tell the whole of my mission to my brother, and with the ears of the kings of the Uí Neíll and Dal Riada, of Rheged and Strathclyde, I can ensure that Oswiu and his retainers have a land to go to and a king, ring giver, glory lord, to take their service and reward it." Oswald turned back to his mother. "What do you think?"

Acha held up her arm and Bran flew to it, croaking inquiringly into her ear. Apart from Oswald, Acha was the only person Bran would fly to.

"Yes, let us go back."

Chapter 3

"The abbot wants to see me?"

Brother Aidan straightened from the task of scraping clean the hide of a newly slaughtered calf. The beast was white, its skin without blemish, and it would provide four pages of the finest vellum for the scriptorium, as long as he did not damage it in preparation. It was the only task he was trusted with; Brother Fintan, the venerable monk in charge of the scriptorium, had tried Aidan on other duties, from preparing the materials used to make colours through to sharpening styli for the monks who did the copying, but with a sense of inevitability matched only by death, Aidan had found himself directed towards the smelliest and dirtiest job upon the Holy Island of Iona. Surrounded by the cloud of flies that buzzed about him as he did his work, and that followed him to the sea afterwards when he went to wash the blood and fur and fat from his hands and arms, the distracted monk drew his wrist across his forehead to wipe away the sweat, cursed for the realization that he had succeeded only in smearing offal over his face, and then remonstrated further with himself at the knowledge that, in cursing, he had called upon one of the old pagan gods.

Brother Erraid, standing as far away from Aidan as was possible while still delivering his message, nodded. "He sent me to fetch you."

"Are you sure he meant me?"

"Abbot Ségéne said, 'Bring me Brother Aidan.'"

Aidan straightened further, a flush of his own blood adding to the redness of his face. "The abbot knows my name," he said.

"Abbot Ségéne knows everybody's name," said Brother Erraid. "He also knows if he has been kept waiting."

"Oh, yes, for sure." Brother Aidan dropped the pelt he was working on and began picking his way through the fly-coated remains stacked around him.

Brother Erraid held up one hand and pinched his nostrils with the other. "You had better wash first. I will tell the abbot you are on your way."

Gathering his robes around him, Brother Erraid made a hasty retreat to cleaner air, leaving Aidan to make his way to the little bay that served the double function of bath and mortification – although now, at high summer, the water was so mild that he had to stand in it for quite a long time before he lost the feeling in his limbs. In winter, the shock was so great that despite his every effort, he could not keep himself from bleating when it rose up over his bare flesh, and the mortification was all but immediate.

As the abbot had summoned him, Aidan walked straight into the water in his habit – the old, patched, stained one he used for his work – and scraped the blood and fat from his skin with handfuls of sand. Stripping off the habit, he left it draped over a rock to dry and put on the robe – clean if threadbare – that he wore when he joined the rest of the monks of the monastery at their divine work: the singing of the office of prayer. Dripping, but no longer rank, Brother Aidan gathered up his robes and scurried off in the same direction as Brother Erraid.

Barely acknowledging the salutations that followed him as he ran past the men working in the fields, Aidan hurried towards the cluster of low, whitewashed buildings with thatched roofs that marked the heart of the monastery of Colm Cille. The abbey church was naturally the largest building, big enough to take every monk upon the Holy Island but yet still not large enough to accommodate all the visitors when pilgrims came for Colm Cille's day, to ask the saint for his blessings. Then, men stood gathered around the church, its doors flung wide, straining to catch the fragments of chant that floated from the building, lifting each other up to see when the Lord was upraised, behind the rood screen, for the profane, that they might glimpse him.

Alongside the church was the scriptorium, but at this season of the year it mainly lay empty; those monks trusted with taking and copying the sacred anew generally preferred to take their work into the daylight, where they might see it better. The only danger was from a sudden squall that might ruin a day's work before it could be brought under cover, so to that end a monk was placed as look-out, watching west whence sudden storms came, armed with a handbell and a loud voice. Should clouds mass and rain threaten, he was tasked with giving sufficient warning that the writing monks might guard their work. Aidan had been given that job once. It had not passed well. The night prayer had been long, sleep short and the day warm. The first he knew of the storm was when it woke him. Brother Keils had sought Aidan out in the refectory later that day and dumped upon his lap a congealed mass of vellum, wrinkled and swollen.

"Three years' work," he had said.

Now Aidan preferred preparing the skins. At least if something went wrong no work was lost, only his time, and nobody missed that.

Approaching the church, Brother Aidan's heart lurched: the abbot was standing, waiting, outside its door. Redoubling his effort, Aidan ran onwards, coming to a skidding stop just in time.

"A-Abbot S-Ségéne," he panted. "You wanted to see me?"

The abbot held out his hand and Aidan kissed the ring upon his third finger.

"I wish words more than sight," said the abbot. "Come, it is a pleasant day. Walk with me."

Abbot Ségéne turned and headed off along one of the many paths that threaded through and around the monastery, heading towards the hill that stood above the monastery, windbreak and protector against winter storms. Brother Aidan walked a pace behind the abbot, reluctant to walk alongside him despite Ségéne's efforts to slow down enough that he might catch up. In the end, when their progress had slowed to that of the clouds, the abbot stopped.

"Do you think your shadow carries some evil influence, Brother Aidan?" he asked.

"N-no, I don't think so. Do you think it does?" Aidan added in sudden panic.

"No, I do not. Therefore, do not be afraid of casting it upon me; then we may speak and I may do so without creaking my neck."

Putting his hands into his sleeves in the characteristic way Aidan had seen through his years in the monastery – he had come to it as a boy, in fulfilment of a vow made by his father – Abbot Ségéne moved on. Aidan started after him, treading on the machair as the abbot walked the path.

"Oswald, son of Æthelfrith, of the House of Iding and ætheling to Bernicia and Northumbria, is your friend, I believe?"

"Um, yes, I suppose he is, but I don't really know why, Abbot Ségéne."

"Don't you?" The abbot looked at him sidelong. "Well, there are many reasons for friendship, some good, some bad. I shall leave you to discover, in time, the reasons for your friendship. But suffice to say, you are friends?"

"Er, yes, I think so. Through God's grace."

"Indeed. And I understand you accompanied Oswald and his brother when they sailed from here to the Isle of Coll this last seven day?"

"Yes, yes I did, Father Abbot."

"Along with another."

Brother Aidan blushed. "Y-yes," he stammered.

"And upon reaching Coll, Oswald and Oswiu went to visit their mother?"

"Yes."

"Did you accompany them?"

"Not at first, but then Oswald sent for me, that I might share meat with them."

"As well it was not a day of fasting. When you were with them, what did they speak on?"

Brother Aidan licked his lips. "I – I do not know if they would want me to speak of this, Father Abbot."

The abbot continued serenely on towards the hill of Iona. Aidan rushed to catch up with him.

"Your reticence does you credit, Brother Aidan, but as I

understand it, no oaths were taken, no pledges given; thus you can speak without fear of fault."

"They – they spoke about Northumbria, and their half-brother Eanfrith, and whether they should claim back their kingdom."

"What reason did they give for not doing so?"

"Oh, Oswiu wanted to leave at once, but Oswald said he would not fight against his brother for the throne."

"Oswald gave no other reason?" The abbot glanced sharply at Aidan as he spoke.

"No, Father Abbot, he did not."

"Very well." Abbot Ségéne fell silent but gave no indication that he wanted Brother Aidan to leave, so the young monk scurried along beside and slightly behind him as they began to climb up the gentle slope of the hill of Iona.

The abbot stopped before he reached the summit of the hill. On this, eastern, side of the hill they were sheltered from the wind, but Aidan could see, from the froth upon the wave tops, that a stiff wind blew intermittently from the west. Turning back upon the way they had come, Abbot Ségéne looked down upon the monastery, and to the Sound of Iona and the Isle of Mull beyond.

"It is a splendid sight, is it not?" he asked Brother Aidan without looking at him.

"I suppose it is." Aidan had grown up among hills and lochs, in sight and sound of sea. What he saw now, from the hill of Iona, was what he had always seen.

"I come here when I have need of thought and there are too many brothers pressing upon me for word and judgment and counsel."

Aidan, not knowing how to respond, remained silent.

"So perhaps you can tell me why today Oswald Iding came alone into the abbey church and lay his sword before the altar?"

Brother Aidan stared at the abbot's back. Maybe he had misheard Abbot Ségéne.

"He did not take it when he left," the abbot continued.

No, he had not misheard.

Abbot Ségéne turned to face him. "And then he came to me and professed the wish to enter the monastery of Colm Cille and become a monk."

Brother Aidan's mouth opened and shut, but no sound came out.

"Have you anything to say on this, Brother Aidan?"

And slowly, Aidan's mouth curved upwards and his eyes began to shine and, despite the fact that he stood before the abbot, he gave a great cry for the joy of such tidings.

"Father Abbot, that is – that is wonderful! Wonderful!"

"I was afraid you would think that. Have you encouraged Oswald in this wish?"

"He has never spoken of it to me, Father Abbot, but I have long thought that he is happiest in prayer. Is this not most marvellous?"

"No," said Abbot Ségéne. "No, it is not marvellous at all."

"I – I … Your pardon. Did you say it is not marvellous?"

"Yes, I did. We have spent many years forming Oswald and his brother, training them in faith and knowledge and understanding, even though they came to this Holy Island as pagans and enemies. King Domnall Brecc sent word to me, when they arrived at Dunadd, asking counsel: should he give refuge to these children of Æthelfrith, who slew so many of the saints at the battle where he defeated Gwynedd? It was like, he said, taking young vipers into your bed, that the warmth of your body might heat them until they had the strength to bite: for what else could one expect from an Angle other than treachery and evil? He was of a mind to kill them, and snuff out the Idings.

"But I forbade him. Our Lord too was exiled and abandoned. Besides, these æthelings were young, unformed. I sent message back, asking Domnall Brecc to send the young Idings to me. They came, rough and wild, like little eagles and as proud. Like hawks, they needed training, feeding, until they might fly and hunt for themselves. Like hawks, they needed hooding, until their sight was trained and their hearts remade. And like hawks, one responded to the training better than the other. But to Oswald we opened, through God's grace, the path to life, and he, seeing it, took it, and took to it as well as any young novice I have seen. His brother too has entered upon the path, although I fear he is subject to more distractions than his brother.

"Then, made, we sent them out to hunt for themselves, and the Idings sailed and rode with the kings of the islands, with Dal Riada and the Uí Neíll, winning renown, forming friendships, gathering young men, brave men, men seeking glory to their name. King Domnall Brecc gave Oswald the name *Lamnguin*, Whiteblade, and bards sang his deeds in the sea halls of the kings of the isles. And all the time, the power of Northumbria grew, pushing back the kingdoms of the Old North, cousins and kin to us, until Rheged and Strathclyde and Dal Riada acknowledged Edwin High King; a pagan lord to the Baptized. But then God, we hear, sent his word to Edwin, and wrought his conversion out of the forge of his power, and here, on our Holy Island, I offered thanks that the High King too had been given knowledge of life.

"But Edwin is dead. You have heard – we have all heard. Cut down by Cadwallon of Gwynedd and Penda of Mercia, an unholy alliance between one who calls himself the avenger of the Baptized and a pagan. Already we have received messages from Cadwallon, calling on our prayers and the intercession of the Blessed Colm Cille, that he might demand the allegiance of the kings of the Old North, and the islands, and all the Baptized."

Abbot Ségéne stopped. "I lay an oath upon you, Brother Aidan. Speak not of this if you value your soul."

Aidan nodded, his mouth too dry to utter assent in words.

"I too have sent messengers forth, to Dal Riada and the Uí Neíll, to Rheged and Strathclyde. Their kings are proud, and ancient. They will bow to none among them, nor will they kneel to Gwynedd, I think. Rather, they wait. To see what power Cadwallon accrues, whether Deira and Bernicia will submit to him; they wait upon Penda – will he withdraw, or remain? The kings, like all kings, wait when they can and fight when they must or they believe they will win.

"And we, we have a hawk, trained, ready to set wing, ready to claim a kingdom and bring the Angles into the hall of life. But now the hawk refuses to fly." The abbot shook his head. "This must not be allowed to happen. The hawk must take wing. But to hunt, the hawk must hunger. You must give Oswald back his hunger, Brother Aidan, his hunger for glory and renown, for gold and power and the homage of men, that he might take the throne and bring it to the boat that sails safe through to an eternal harbour."

Abbot Ségéne looked closely at the young man staring blankly at him. "You do not understand, do you?"

Brother Aidan shook his head. "I am sorry," he said.

"No, it is I that am sorry. I wish all was as simple as it seems to you: a young man gives his heart to God, and wishes to follow him; that is what you see. I see it too, but I am abbot of the monastery of Colm Cille, and charged with the care of the souls of many, many men, here and far. If Oswald enters the monastery, he will no doubt save his soul, but many others will die without ever hearing the tidings that brought him to salvation. Let Oswald return to Northumbria and claim his kingdom, then I will send him many helpers, that he may claim souls as well as glory, and his glory shall be all the greater, and extend beyond the bards to the highest heaven. Now do you see why he cannot be allowed to become a monk of Colm Cille?"

"But Cadwallon and Penda are great warriors. I have heard tell of their deeds. What if Oswald fails?"

The eyes of the abbot grew bleak. "Few æthelings live to rule. The hawk flies. We cannot know if it will make its kill; we can simply set it to wing."

"But maybe it is God's will that Oswald should be a monk."

The abbot's eyes grew even colder. "Can you discern his will? Do you claim that knowledge, as the druids of old, with their blood casting and runes?"

"No." Brother Aidan held up his hands. "Not I, Father Abbot. But – but Oswald is my friend. I would not have him die."

"Nor would I," said the abbot. "For friendship, for faith and for the effort that has been expended upon him. But you know as well as I: men will follow him, for already the whispers grow loud that fortune – that idol of warriors – favours him. In words, warriors seek glory and gold, but in their hearts they cleave to fortune, and seek any man upon whom fortune's favour rests. Let him but call, and many will follow, even should the kings of the isles and the Old North stand back from him. And I, I charge you with helping Oswald to accept this. I know of a certainty that it is no easy thing to gainsay what you believe to be God's will, but I tell you, and tell you solemnly, that it is better this way. The hawk must fly; you must set it to wing."

Brother Aidan said nothing. Beyond the abbot he could see the monastery laid out before them, the monks busy about their tasks, curraghs drawn up upon the beach, others skimming across the Sound. This was his world, and had been for as long as he could remember. He had hoped his friend would share it with him.

"He will not fight his brother," said Aidan.

"Eanfrith is a pagan. Let us pray that his bid fails. Besides, Oswald is faithful to his friends. Were he to become a monk, he would perforce have to abandon his friends, and one in particular." The abbot looked meaningfully at Brother Aidan.

"I?" asked Aidan, holding his hand to his heart.

Abbot Ségéne smiled. "No, not you, but that damnable bird that cleaves to him. I would no sooner have a raven in this house than I would have a wolf. Make sure he understands that. Better that he accepts God's will and returns to claim his throne."

"God wills that Oswald be king?"

"If Oswald takes the throne, then God wills it." The abbot folded his fingers together. "Our decisions and God's providence are bound together as tightly as my hands."

Aidan nodded. "You said that if Oswald won the throne, you would send him helpers to bring in the harvest. Would you send me?"

"Oswald needs a bishop, who can consecrate priests and teach the new life." The abbot looked at Aidan. "You are not a bishop."

"But the bishop you send will need hands, and legs, to do his work; may I be his hands and legs – I do not ask to speak, for I have not the gift of eloquence and teaching, but I am young and healthy."

"It – it would not be wise for you to go." The abbot laid his hand upon Aidan's shoulder, and there was compassion in his glance. "You are friend to Oswald now, ætheling as he is, but landless: a man without power. Should he come to the throne, that friendship would be dangerous to you, for seldom does a king remain uncorrupted when power passes into his hands. The temptation to take what he desires – be it land, or women, or gold – grows strong, and you would be called to stand, as Samuel stood before Saul, and call the Lord's judgment down upon him, and the Lord's curse. Seldom does a king stand correction, and even less so from a friend of his childhood, to whom he looks for friendship and confirmation in his evil-doing. At such times, a king's wrath is terrible, for it is born from the promptings of the evil one, and it burns with the fury of the damned. Better by far that I not put such a load upon you. No, Brother Aidan, you will stay and he will go, and God's will will be done.

"Now bow your head." Abbot Ségéne placed his hands in blessing upon Brother Aidan, murmuring the words, and the wind took them away over sea.

Chapter 4

"I have learned your tongue well these past years." Cadwallon of Gwynedd spoke without looking at the man next to him at table. The white nights of midsummer were past, and the sun set, and set properly, casting darkness over the land. In the nights without moon, men huddled in the yellow light of the hall, and told tale and battle memory, setting fear and blood into boast and rhyme, that they might be faced anew when the time came.

"You have not learned mine." Now Cadwallon turned to the man beside him. Penda of Mercia stared ahead. Their alliance had brought them glory and gold; it had all but brought him the throne of Mercia. Some of the older and more stubborn thegns still held for an Iclinga – a descendant of Icel – to take the throne, but each victory gained and hoard won brought him closer to bringing the witan of Mercia to his cause.

But it had been a half-year and more since he had rode from Mercia and, meeting Cadwallon, pledged the death of Edwin, High King of Britain. Alliances soured if shared too long.

Penda made no answer as he sat beside Cadwallon in the great hall of York, the hall they had taken from Edwin, with his life and his head. His brother Eowa had taken half their men and gone reiving through Deira and Bernicia these past four week. It had been a hard choice for Penda: allow his brother freedom to gather men to his standard and reward them with gold, or leave Eowa with Cadwallon while he himself went gold gathering. But he had spent many months riding hard between Mercia and Northumbria, gathering support from the thegns of Mercia, reaping the gold of Northumbria; now he needed rest, and to gauge the temper of his ally. He would no more have trusted Eowa with such a task than he would have trusted a hungry young ætheling. Penda smiled grimly. Of course, Eowa was ætheling, throne-worthy by reason of the blood he shared with him. The witan of Mercia, its ties to the old king still not broken, had muttered against him when he stood before it and called upon the grey hairs to call him king. And still they waited. Some had looked to Eowa, known to them since he was a young man and he had gone to seek glory and gold in the old lands across the sea, returning with both, but in measure not sufficient to win a crown. Not quite.

Eowa would be back from his reiving soon. Time to be going home.

"It is the language of mountain and sea, of bird and beast, and of the Baptized. It is holy; there is no wonder that you have not the wit to learn it."

While Cadwallon spoke, from his place in the drink and the dark, Penda looked to where Edwin's head sat, set upon a pole rammed into the hard-packed earth of the hall's floor. Cadwallon had taken Edwin's head; Penda had taken his sword. He fingered the hilt of the blade. He fancied he could hear it whisper to him, in the voice of dead, dry leaves, telling of blood and souls and the music of war. He listened to the sword now far more than he listened to Cadwallon.

"Cian." Cadwallon gestured a man forward from the hall. "Sing to King Penda in our tongue, that he might hear its beauty. Sing him one of the songs of our heroes of old – sing him one of the songs of Arthur." The king of Gwynedd turned to his ally. "In our tongue, we call such men bards."

"We name them scops, but they each say of men who sing what they are told to sing."

"No, no," said Cadwallon. "A bard is the memory hoard of his people, the marker of law and battle and glory; without his tales and his recking, we are people no more, but mewling infants, without benefit of wit or history. Come, Cian, sing."

"I have tales of Arthur, that is true; but lord, I have a new song, a song of victory, not long defeat, that I would sing for you, the author of our new-found glory."

Cadwallon smiled. "You have a song of me? I would hear it." He turned to Penda. "It is a shame your brother is not here to hear it too."

Penda shrugged in answer, and the bard stepped out, but he stayed to the side of the kings; no man wished to have Edwin's head at his back.

"He takes many weeks." Cadwallon paused. "I have heard he rides to Mercia."

Penda, for the first time, looked properly upon his ally.

"Who told you this?"

"Riders heading home to Gwynedd must needs pass by the borders of your country."

"You know this of a certainty?"

Cadwallon stroked a finger across his lips. "Death alone is certain, friend." He turned to Cian, raised his cup and drained it. "Sing! Sing praise."

The bard fingered the harp, pulling notes from it as he sang. Penda, hearing words familiarity had not rendered any more intelligible, took his cup and drank, while beside him Cadwallon listened in rapt admiration, beating out the rhythm with his palm upon the table. The Britons, Penda had learned, could sing and listen for hours in hall, growing increasingly tearful as song turned to lament and beer filled bellies.

But Cian's song was, by his standards, short, although it drew from Cadwallon the gift of a heavy gold ring. The bard slipped it upon his arm, then went to find refreshment for his voice, while Cadwallon too drank, draining cup and then cup in silence.

Penda waited.

Cadwallon pointed at Edwin. "He knew my tongue. He learned it from my father. He learned it from me. Now, tell me, what is your word for us?"

Penda slowly turned to look at Cadwallon. "You are drunk," he said.

"Of course I am drunk." Cadwallon stood up, but he did not sway upon his feet. "See, I stand. He," he pointed at Edwin, "set me upon the sea, without sail or oar, to die, but here I stand, alive and drunk! Here." Cadwallon held out his cup and gestured to a slave. "Give him to drink."

The liquid dribbled from Edwin's mouth and ran down the pole, staining the earth dark. In the dim light of the tapers, it looked like blood.

"My priest doesn't like me doing that," Cadwallon said. "You know, he wants to bury Edwin, give him prayers and blessings. What about your priest?"

"My priests do what I tell them," said Penda.

"You are lucky." Cadwallon swayed a little, then straightened. "But you are pagan. Not so lucky."

"Why so?"

"When I die, I will live forever. When you die, you will be in hell."

"What of my fathers?"

"They will be in hell too."

"Then I am content. I will follow the ways of my fathers, whether it be to hell or Woden's hall."

Cadwallon's eyes narrowed. "I too. In life, your fathers took this land. In death, they burn."

Penda reached for his cup. He had had enough of this conversation. "In death, we all burn," he said.

Cadwallon grasped his wrist. "You did not answer my question."

Penda stared at the hand holding him.

The men, back from the latest raid into Deira, and resting, eating and drinking in the hall, began to fall silent. Eyes turned to the high table.

Penda relaxed. Now was not the right time.

"What question?" he asked, still not looking at Cadwallon.

"What is your word for my people?"

Penda turned his gaze upon the king of Gwynedd, the most powerful king of the Britons, the most powerful king in the land, and he answered: "*Wealh*."

"*Wealh*," repeated Cadwallon. "'Slave.' That is what you name us."

Penda stared at him. "Yes, that is what we name you."

Cadwallon let go his arm.

The hall was silent, watchful. The men of Gwynedd and the men of Mercia looked round for their comrades, all suddenly aware that they ate and drank in the midst of strangers. Fingers inched towards seax and knife, the only weapons men might carry into hall, save for their kings.

Penda laughed. "It is a joke, my friend," he said. "A joke, nothing more. Names mean nothing; it is deeds that count. Look," and he pointed out into the hall, "he is called Nothhelm, which means courageous protector, but I saw him puke his breakfast up before his first battle, and his second, and his third. Names mean nothing without deeds. We have brought down our enemy and put his head before us. That is what counts."

Cadwallon disagreed. His words came thickly, although he still stood without swaying. "There is deep magic in words."

"Maybe in your tongue. In mine, words are just words."

"A word made the world."

"Ha! That is what the scops like to say, but what would you expect of men who wield the lyre better than the sword? Words make worlds, you say? Tell that to me when scops sing songs of scops, and not the kings who fill their bellies with food and who put gold rings upon their arms."

"You should learn my language – it is beautiful beyond all that you know." Cadwallon looked earnestly into Penda's face as he spoke, his gaze frank with the honesty of the cup.

"So I hear when your scop sings; that is enough for me."

"It is more beautiful than gold."

"That is why I see the tears upon your face when your scop sings."

"Do you not weep when your scop sings?"

"No." Penda shook his head. "I do not weep."

"I weep," said Cadwallon, standing upright. "I weep for my people, and the heroes we have lost, and the land and the bright kingdoms that are no more. I weep for Arthur, that he might hear my lamentation and return to lead us once more and drive the Saxons back into the sea, as he did once before – before vile treachery defeated him. I weep, and I swear vengeance."

"Your people have waited for Arthur to return for many years." Penda looked around. "You are still waiting. The Saxons and the Angles, we do not wait for any of our kings of old. They are dead and feasting in Woden's halls, paying us no mind. So we fight, and take your land. If this Arthur does not return soon, there will be no land left to the Britons for him to return to."

"He will come." Cadwallon leaned forward. "He will."

"My lord."

Cadwallon looked around. The words came in his own tongue.

His bard, Cian, sat with harp upon knee, perched upon the table's edge, and he looked with bird-bright eyes at the king. Penda looked too upon the bard, with eyes veiled and hidden.

"My lord," Cian continued, "mayhap Arthur has returned. Mayhap Arthur is here…"

Cadwallon stared at the bard as if stricken with the freezing sickness. His jaw worked but no sound came from his lips.

"For the tales tell that Arthur will cast the Saxons from Logres, but since his day we have known only long defeat, until you, lord, cast the High King down and broke him upon your sword, and put his land to waste. You drive the Saxons from our shores, for has not his queen and her whelps taken ship and fled? Do not his thegns flee before us, abandoning their halls and their gold, until your hands run over and your men cannot lift their arms for the rings upon them?" The bard, in the midst of speaking, stood from the table, and his voice gradually took power and presence, until all the men of Gwynedd in the hall fell silent to hear him, their breath an exhalation of wonder as they turned their eyes upon their lord. Could it be so?

"Lord, King, Restorer, take, I beg, the title you have earned by your deeds. Send word to the kings of the Old North, to Rheged and Strathclyde, to Dal Riada and Gododdin; send word to the kingdoms of the south, to Powys and Dyfed and Ceredigion, to Dumnonia and across the Narrow Sea to Brittany, to all the lands where the blessed tongue of old is spoken; send word that they may know: Arthur has returned!"

The men of Gwynedd rose to their feet. Cadwallon, face pale as death, turned to face them. They looked upon their king – a man they had known through defeat and victory, through campaign and in hall – and they saw, as if unveiled, Arthur, the king of their hope, and they acclaimed him.

Cadwallon received their acclaim and their homage as Cian sang songs of praise and blessing. Penda sat in dark silence upon the high table, and his men withdrew to the rear of the hall.

"So, you are Arthur now," he said, when Cadwallon turned to him.

"I am Arthur," said Cadwallon. The king of Gwynedd looked upon him with suspicion. "You understand our tongue?"

"There is no great need to do so when your men chant, 'Arthur, Arthur, Arthur,' and weep into their beer."

Cadwallon smiled, all trace of his former drunkenness gone. "This is a glad day, a day waited upon since our fathers' fathers' fathers' day." The king paused, and looked upon his ally. "I asked you for your name for us. Now I ask if you know our name for the lands of the Angles and the Saxons."

Penda shook his head. "I do not know."

"Logres. The Lost Lands. But bearing before us the dragon banner of Arthur, we shall reclaim our lost lands, and the Baptized will drive the pagans into the sea."

Penda stared at Cadwallon. "What of me and my people? Will you drive us into the sea too?"

"Even though you be not of the Baptized, yet you are allies. I will give you leave to remain in these lands, so long as you render me homage."

"What form would this homage take?"

"To declare foes those whom I declare enemies, to march with me when I summon thee, to attend me when I call upon thee, and to render to me the gold that thy brother, Eowa, out these past four week in Deira, bears upon his horses and in his wagons. That is homage."

Penda stood, and gestured for his men to follow.

"We will take our leave. The summer is near over, and men hear the call of home, and wives, and harvest. I was your ally when none other answered your call – remember that well, king of the Baptized."

"The kings of the Old North, all the kings of the Baptized, I will call upon them and they will come to me, for Arthur has returned in glory to lead them." Cadwallon grasped Penda's forearm in friendship. "Take the gold your brother has garnered, for you have served me well, though you be pagan and damned."

"What of Eadfrith? You have him still."

"Edwin's son? I have kept him alive since we found him after the battle, insensible upon the ground, lest the men of Northumbria attempt to raise another king against me. But they flee before me as ducks before the hunter; take him, if you want him."

"We will ride then; I will send messengers to call my brother home. Should he return here, send him after us." Penda took Cadwallon's forearm too. The two kings looked into each other's faces and were glad they parted now, before their friendship turned to blood.

As Penda led his men from the hall, he could already hear the messengers being called up to Cadwallon to take word to the kingdoms of the Britons, telling them that their hopes stood realized: Arthur had returned, in the guise of Cadwallon of Gwynedd, and he claimed their fealty. The Mercian grimaced. Maybe they would follow Cadwallon, thinking him Arthur returned. Then the power Cadwallon wielded would be great indeed; sufficient maybe to push the new peoples back into the grey sea that had carried them to this land at the edge of the world. But kings were jealous of power, and shy of sharing glory. Some would come, some would listen, some would plot against the new power, closer at hand and more dangerous than any Angle. It was ever thus.

Besides, he had needs find what delayed his brother. Gold could buy men at witan, and Penda knew his claim upon the throne was not yet secure.

But first there was the matter of Eadfrith, Edwin's son.

"Come." Penda called his warmaster, Hroth, while the men prepared horses, wagons and boats for the journey south. It was a day's sailing down the Ouse, and then hard rowing up the Trent, into the heart of Mercia. The same journey on foot might take three or four days. However, some of the men would return the slow way, taking the roads of the emperors of old with the wagons and those horses that could not be accommodated on ship.

*

The city of York lay in ruins, a haunted place that breathed of the giants that had built it. Penda made his camp outside its tumbled walls, in tents and shelters his men could build in a few hours at the end of a day's march. Cadwallon, though, remained within, laying claim to Edwin's hall and feigning conversance with the city's ghosts, and keeping his captive in an old building near the hall.

Penda, with Hroth by his side, made his way through the weed-choked streets.

"Cadwallon calls himself a Roman," Penda said to Hroth, after they had both started at the sudden explosion of an unknown bird from a dark door. "That is why he prefers to camp in the city of the Romans."

Hroth, a man who spoke little, grunted, but his sword remained in his hand. "The giants are gone," he said.

"Yes, they are gone," said Penda, "but they have left their works." He drew his own sword. These places of the old ones were wraith-haunted; men did not enter them unnecessarily. As such, it was a good place to keep a man prisoner, for few would go to find him among such ghosts, and Penda himself had been but once before, when Eadfrith had been consigned to the dark.

Now, the evening was drawing in and shadows lengthened, flowing out of the empty doors and windows that looked in silence upon their progress.

They came at last to the house, its walls broken down on two sides, and, putting their shoulders together to the stone, pushed the boulder aside. A stench, rank and raw, rose from the pit, and although no strangers to foul smells, they drew back as the evening light flowed down into the dark.

Hroth took the ladder that lay propped against a wall and dropped it into the pit.

But from the dark came a voice, little more than a croak: "If you want me, you will have to fetch me."

Penda looked at his warmaster. The big man shrugged, handed over his sword, tied his tunic up to his waist, breathed deep and climbed down into the dark. He emerged moments later, carrying a bundle that, on laying it down in front of Penda, proved to be a man.

Penda covered his mouth and nose. "You stink."

Eadfrith, son of Edwin, of the house of Yffi, heir to the throne of Deira and Northumbria, staggered to his feet, holding his hands over his eyes to protect them from the light. His skin clung to his bones, but the hair had mostly fallen from his head: he was as a skeleton, walking, but his eyes burned in his skull.

"I stink in the flesh," he said. "But you stink in the soul."

Penda stared at him for a moment, then turned away. "He is no danger. You do not need me, Hroth. Wash him, then bring him."

"Where are you taking me?" asked Eadfrith.

Penda looked back to him. "How long have you been in that pit?"

Eadfrith wiped a trembling hand across eyes that wept at the evening light.

"I do not know."

"I am taking you to your grandfather's house."

"You killed him?"

"He is dead."

"His blood to my father's and brother's."

"You live; they are dead. Men call you 'faithless son'."

"I care no longer for the words of men; I care only to see you dead."

"You will have your chance then, Eadfrith. I will bring you before the witan of Mercia, that they may judge between us: last remaining scion of Cearl, or I, Penda. Wash him well, Hroth, lest the witan choke on his smell." Penda turned to go.

"Wait!" Eadfrith stumbled forward. "You will let me speak my case to the witan?"

"Yes."

"What trick is this?"

"There is no trick. You will speak; I will speak; they will choose. Too long have they demurred, though I bring them gold and victory beyond anything they have known before. Still some mutter for the Iclingas. Very well. Let them see you before them: the last of the Iclingas." Penda smiled. "Wash him, Hroth, but not too well."

Chapter 5

"Gone, gone, gone. All gone."

Coifi, once priest to Edwin, abjurer of the old gods, turned about amid the stumps and poles of what had been the site sacred to Woden at Goodmanham, a day's ride from York. Upon his thin shoulders he had drawn the raven-feather cloak of his priesthood, in his hand he held the bone rattle, but the feathers rustled upon his back as leaves in winter's deep and the rattle mumbled in an idiot's voice.

Dropping to his knees, Coifi sketched the gesture the priest of the new god had made, touching head and heart and shoulders. He held his hands up to heaven, to where all the gods dwelled, whether they be old gods or new.

"Where are you?" he cried.

The heavens, heavy with cloud, grey and dark, gave no answer.

"I have no lord either."

Coifi looked around, struggling to get to his feet, hand going to his sword. As priest of the old gods, he might bear no weapon, but priest no more, it was not safe to venture abroad without sword and spear; not since the death of the king.

A man slid out of the shadows and stood before Coifi. "And it is bitter indeed for a scop to have no lord – as bitter as a priest without a god."

"Acca!" The priest put down his sword. "What brings you here?"

"Like you, blown before the storm, and seeking harbour. I was told you might be here."

"Who told you?"

"Oh, the local people. They still talk about the day you rode here and put fire to the gods! You seemed a god to them yourself that day, Coifi – I have spoken with them, through some tedious nights when

I needed shelter and they insisted on telling me their tales. Come, I have found you; you are summoned. Let us go."

"Who summons me?"

"Have you not heard? There is a new king in Deira."

"Cadwallon?"

"No, a king of the Yffings, a true king of Deira: Osric, cousin to Edwin, has arisen and called the witan to acclaim him lord, and they have done so, casting off the promises they made to that interloper as easily as a man casts off the dreams of the night when the morning comes. He calls you to him."

"Why does he want me?"

"To call the favour of the gods down upon him, that he might strike down Cadwallon and win the throne."

"But Osric was baptized with all the thegns; he follows the new god of Paulinus."

"Paulinus has fled, with the queen and her children. Mayhap they will return some day, but Wuscfrea is still a child: he cannot claim the throne. No, only Osric is ætheling, a throne-worthy man, and he calls you to come to him. He has returned to the ways of our fathers, casting off the promises he made to the new god, for that god has failed us, and given victory to our enemies. So now he summons you to sacrifice to the old gods, to Woden and Thunor and Tiw, to call their blessings back upon us that we might tear the hearts from our enemies and hear the weeping of their women."

Acca stopped and passed a trembling hand over his forehead in a gesture the priest remembered well: it signified a particularly poignant moment in his tale. But Coifi, looking more closely, saw that this time there was no art in the movement, no sidelong eyeglance to see whether the audience were following where his words led, be it into the hall of Hrothgar or the fen fastnesses where monsters stalked; Acca was not acting, and little that Coifi had seen over the past year disturbed him so much.

"It has been terrible, Coifi, terrible. When the news came that the king was dead – and then the rumours that Eadfrith yet lived and was coming with men, or no, that Cadwallon and Penda rode upon us, ready to burn and plunder – then I fell into such a state that I have not known: it was as if I walked yet slept, moving with eyes open and wits dead. I saw the queen and her children take ship with the priest of the new god, and if my wits were with me I would have run to them and begged to sail too, but I stood and watched as stupidly as an ox chewing the cud while it waits the slaughterer. I saw the other priest, James, gather his robes and his people about him, the ones he had taught to sing in the language of the new god, and, loading people and whatever they might carry in wagons, set off north. I hear he lives yet, in Catterick, with his people about him, singing his new song and skulking in the woods whenever Cadwallon's raiders come seeking provision and treasure.

"Maybe I should have done as he did – hidden and waited. But I could no more live without a lord than you can live without a god, Coifi, so I set out in search of a hall and a lord. I have ridden and walked the kingdom, and everywhere I have gone I have seen the devastation wrought by Cadwallon and his men: they strip the food from the living and what they cannot take they spoil, falling upon hard-won halls as rats and leaving a waste where all that can be heard is the wail of women as they wait for death." Acca placed his hands upon a lean belly.

"I starved, Coifi, starved. Stumbling from hall to hall, driven out when men learned that I was Edwin's scop. I felt my stomach swell and my flesh fall away, until I could scarce raise my harp or pluck a song from memory. Mayhap I would have died if Osric had not found me, lying abandoned by a spring where in better days our good lord Edwin had placed brass cups that travellers might refresh themselves and none dared take them all the days of his reign. But the cups were gone, long gone, and I had not the strength to raise water to my lips, but only to take my mouth to the water. And that was when Osric found me, lamenting Edwin's passing, and he heard my voice and remembered me. I had not known any strength remained to me, but when he said he remembered my singing I raised myself to my feet and raised my voice – weakened though it was by hunger, I was pleased to hear it sound all the purer – and told our hope: that Osric, ætheling, of the House of Yffi, would deliver us from our tormentor and save us from his depredations. Osric, hearing me sing, said he would take me as his scop as long as I would bring to him another of Edwin's household: you."

Acca stared at the priest, clad in his old raven-feather cloak and bearing the bone rattle that told the working of wyrd.

"Cadwallon has promised to drive us into the sea, and many say it would be a better fate to die there than to starve in our own homes when the winter comes. He has left us nothing, Coifi, nothing. When Penda sailed south, taking poor Eadfrith with him, we hoped that things might improve, but Cadwallon's fury grows worse – any who cross him he kills. The witan passes messages in secret, and called upon Osric to deliver us – and he promised me that he would be my lord if I brought you to him. Will you come?"

Coifi squatted, drawing his cloak around his thin shoulders. Acca was not alone in hunger – since Edwin's death he had scarce known a full belly. He had wandered, alone, sleeping in the hollows under hawthorn and blackthorn, snuffling roots and small creatures, sometimes taking shelter and sup with isolated houses where news of the king's death bought a meal, or a shake of his bone rattle produced a dry bed for the night. He had not known it, but his wandering had an end in view, and he knew it when he topped the ridge over Goodmanham and saw the dark crowns of the trees of Woden's sacred grove. There had been a time when those trees hung with sacrifice, things bright and golden, things of blood and bone. Now they hung empty, save for their fringe of leaves, but the memory of sacrifice hung dark upon them, and he felt its weight upon his back as he squatted upon the earth.

"Coifi?"

The priest dug his finger into the earth. If he dug deeply enough, surely he would find the blood he had spilled into this dark earth, the offerings for victory, for a son, for deliverance from illness or enemy or hunger. He had made all these offerings and more, and in his latter days he had sacrificed on his own behalf here, asking the gods to give back what they had taken from him: his sight. Once, the workings of wyrd had been clear to him, the weavings of the fate singers revealed in rattle bone and leaf fall, in smoke rise and blood spill, but his vision had dimmed, leaving him a haunted, hunted creature, searching always for the track that eluded him, as a hunter lost in the woods, slowly coming to the knowledge that that which he had once hunted was now hunting him.

The gods no longer spoke and when the priest of the new god had come with Edwin's bride, Æthelburh, and he had seen the way the king listened to him, Coifi had tried to learn Paulinus's ways and the ways of his new god. Guthlaf, Edwin's warmaster, had come to him, promising gold and gifts if he spoke for the new god in front of the witan, and Coifi had taken the promise, for the gods had abandoned him. He still remembered the wild, fierce delight when he tore down the poles sacred to them and set flame to their sanctuaries under the trees – Acca had said the villagers thought him a god that night, and it was true: a god he had felt himself, raw with power. Then, the promises of Paulinus and his new god seemed to bear fruit, and as Edwin's power waxed, his own wealth grew, though he yet shied from the water that Paulinus wished to bathe him in.

But then the king had died; the promises of the new god failed. Where was the new life? Where was the victory he claimed, over death? Edwin had abandoned the gods of his fathers to follow the new god, and his vows had proven empty and his teaching false.

"The gods no longer hear me." Coifi looked up at the scop. "They stopped listening to me long ago, but I made to others, made to myself, that they heard still, for though I might see no longer, mayhap they smelled my offerings and heard my prayers. But now…" Coifi gestured around him. "They have gone from here. I drove them away and I do not know where to find them."

"Osric would have the gods of our fathers return."

"Tell me where to find them, then I will bring them. Until then, leave me be."

Acca shook his head and, squatting himself, he looked into the shadows beneath Coifi's raven-feather cloak, finding the man's face there.

"It seems to me there is little to tell between a scop and a priest: we each tell kings what they wish to hear. I sing praise of their past; you promise victory to the future. Osric shows bright and bold to the witan, promising to drive Cadwallon from our land, but inside he is fear full. Cadwallon killed Edwin, a king Osric never dared to challenge; how should he now face him? Yet he must, and he seeks heart filling in the songs of his deeds and in the promise of the gods. Will you not give it to him?"

"I cannot. The gods do not speak to me."

"Nor did Osric stand in the shield wall against Lindsey, nor wield sword against Æthelfrith, but those that did are dead, and I am the memory of this people, and I make it anew, that we might live. The gods listen, Coifi, even if you do not hear them. Osric seeks their aid; promise it to him." Acca held out his hand to the priest. "Osric will bring the old gods back. Will you not clear their paths, that they might return?"

Chapter 6

Coifi looked up from the bloody entrails of the ram, his hands dark with its blood. The bone handle of the sacrificial knife felt slippery in his grasp, for the animal had struggled against its death, taking three men to hold it down with its throat turned, that he might pull the blade across the artery and spatter the spurting blood across the strewn willow. He had seen nothing there, only meaningless daubings of blood. Then, his voice drying in his throat and words falling from his mind, he had taken the knife and cut the beast, laying its inside open, so intent that he scarce noticed the usual stench of spilled intestines. And there, in among the twisting segments of stomach and intestine, he had seen it: the will of the gods laid out in blood and gristle.

"Victory!"

Coifi pointed with trembling hand to what he saw, and the waiting men, the great voices of the witan, gathered around him and looked to where he indicated and saw there only death.

"Victory," Coifi repeated. "It is there, I see it. The gods have spoken to me again."

Osric shouldered the thegns aside and peered into the animal's body. He looked at the priest, kneeling beside the sacrifice.

"You are certain?"

"Yes," said Coifi, and as he spoke he felt the warmth of that certainty spread through his body, as a man come in from the storm feels the hall heat seep through his skin. "Yes," he said, "I am certain." And Coifi, abjured priest of the old gods, felt the knowledge deep inside him, and knew that he was a priest once more.

Osric stood straight and looked around at the gathered men. They had come at his summons to the old sacred grove at Goodmanham, riding in the darkness of the new moon along tracks that they knew from childhood, and now they waited upon the fall of blood and the favour of their old gods – the gods they had forsaken and whose aid they sought anew.

"The gods hear us!" Osric turned so that all might hear. "The gods hear us! They remain faithful to us although we were faithless to them. Here now, make pledge to them so that they will know we cleave to them once more, and forever, keeping to the ways of our fathers and forsaking new gods and new ways come over the whale road. The gods hear us; let them hear you!"

And the gathered men put up a roar, beating their chests and striking sword hilt to shield edge, such that the gathered rooks upon the trees took to the air in protesting clamour.

Osric raised his arms for quiet. The rooks slowly settled once more upon the treetops.

"The gods hear us, and they are the gods of our fathers, the gods that helped us drive the Britons, the *wealh*, from this land and make it ours. Edwin, my cousin, was a great man and a great king, but he forsook the ways of our fathers and adopted the god of his queen; the same god that the Britons follow. Is there any wonder he fell to the Britons, when he followed the same god? Edwin, my cousin, was a great man and a great king, but I have not forsaken the ways of our fathers and the gods have not forsaken us! Cadwallon, the despoiler, sits in York, bleeding our land and taking our gold; let us go there and face him, our gods against his god, the ways of our fathers against the ways of his fathers." Osric smiled broadly. "And we all know whose fathers won, don't we?"

The men cheered, and even Acca, who considered it his task as Osric's scop to rouse the men to battle, raised his fist in salutation. Only Coifi remained silent and still, crouched over the sacrificial ram. The gods spoke victory, but a sudden dread gripped his heart: did the gods speak true? Fear gripping his heart, Coifi looked for counsel and saw Acca applauding with the others as the men ran to their horses. He signed him over.

The scop approached, smiling, but the smile dropped away as he saw Coifi's face.

"What is wrong?" Acca hissed, pretending to inspect the dead ram.

"I – what if the gods lie?"

"Lie? Why would they lie?"

"Why do gods do anything? The fate singers weave wyrd, the gods raise kings and bring them down, and we know not why."

"That I know. But lie?" Acca looked around to make sure no one was listening. "Lies make bad stories, and if there is one thing I am certain of, it is that the gods tell the best of tales. Besides, why would they lie when we come back to them? This also I know: a tale needs an audience and a teller; the gods need our praise as we need their favour. They do not lie: it would be as if I, finding a lord, refused to speak or, worse, turned weasel words against him; all men would surely call me cursed then, and declare me outcast; can the gods do different? No." Acca put his hand on Coifi's shoulder. "Do not fear, but trust in the gods of our fathers and they will give us victory."

*

Cadwallon looked out at the men encamped beyond the walls of the city. The old ramparts of York that the emperors had built in the days of their strength were still intact in many places, and he had had his men fill the gaps with rubble and bricks pillaged from the remains of the imperial city. The makeshift barricades amounted to little more than unsteady mounds, yet the Saxons stayed outside the city walls, content to yell insults in their uncouth tongue at his men, while more men arrived, swelling the small army into something more formidable. If he had had his whole forces with him when the Saxons had first appeared then he would have attacked immediately, but the best part of half his army were out in the field, bringing in supplies for the men and, more importantly, for the horses. The longer they stayed in one place, the further afield the foraging parties had to roam, but Cadwallon was loath to leave York. Here, among the glorious ruins, he knew himself for what he was: a Roman, defending the empire against barbarians, the leader of the Baptized fighting the pagans.

"Where did these men come from?" He turned to his warmaster, Hwyel. "They must have buried themselves in the woods; surely we received submission from all the thegns in Deira?"

The warmaster shaded his eyes against the summer sun. "They hid in their halls, lord, and covered themselves with lies: I know many of the shields that lie against tent and pole. Thegns who swore themselves to us, who submitted to you and to whom you gave rings – they are faithless."

"Just as well I did not give them too many rings then, and those of little worth." Cadwallon shook his head. "After I killed Edwin, they came to me as supplicants, pleading for their halls and land. Do you think I did wrong by giving them rings, Hwyel?"

The warmaster shrugged. "In battle, men's hearts are tested, and when the blow comes they ring true or they break. There are no lies there. But when the wolves and ravens have fed and men come before the king, then words turn in upon themselves, and men who pledge prove false, while others who say nothing may show true. We had too few men to take and hold this kingdom then, lord; we must needs call on others to hold it for us."

Cadwallon laughed. "And now here they are." He pointed to where the men grouped thickest, around the boar banner. "That is the mark of Osric. So it is he who leads them against us. I wonder if they would follow Osric so readily if they knew how he came to me and covered my hand with his tears as he pleaded for me to leave him his hall and his lands. 'I have a son, bare off the breast, at last, after so many daughters; would you take his father's land before he has had chance to walk it?' That was what he said, and I had to dry my hand afterwards, so wet did he leave it with his tears. Do you think those men would follow him if they knew how he had pleaded with me?"

"Is there a man there who did not come before you and plead suchwise? Shame draws them together, and holds them fast against us."

"It is not just shame. See." Cadwallon pointed to the pole set into the ground by Osric's banner. "That is the sign of the demons they worship and call gods – see the skull upon it and the marks?

They have abjured their baptism; pagans once more, their state is worse than the one they started with, for Edwin – may he be cursed for this – gave them the truth of life, and they have spurned it. Paulinus the priest opened the doors of heaven for them, and they have turned their back. Now, only the pit and its abominations await them." Cadwallon smiled. "Praise be to God; he has tested them and found them wanting, and, casting them off, has delivered them into our hands to visit his vengeance upon them." The king clapped his hands. "I would have had to search them out, hall by hall. Now, they come to me. All I have to do is wait and they will deliver themselves into my hands. God favours me."

"Why do they not attack?" asked Hwyel. "These walls would scarce stop them and we have not the men to man the gaps."

"The Saxons fear this place, for it carries still about it the power of the emperors of old. Penda could scarce bring himself to walk within; these men are no different, for they have had hold of this city for our lives and the lives of our fathers, and yet they left it untenanted and empty, the haunt of wraiths."

"But Edwin built his hall here and the church he raised for Paulinus still stands, though it has yet to be roofed; he did not fear this city."

"He told me he spent much of his childhood here, exploring the ruins. He knew it, and did not fear it. But those men are not his; they were not with him at Hatfield Chase, when we brought him down, Edwin and his sons. They are thegns of the king's march, not of his household, the ones who come when summoned but do not remain with him. They fear the city's ghosts."

Hwyel grinned. "They should fear us more."

Cadwallon struck his warmaster's shoulder. "The men will be ready?"

"They will be ready."

"Good. Of course, we could wait, but although the kings of the north will come, I do not know when." Cadwallon turned to his bard, who stood silent on his other side. "They will come, won't they?"

Cian nodded. "Oh, they will come, lord, for God blesses the new Arthur. It is the time of fulfilment, when the old prophecies come true. Men not born will curse the chance of their birth: that their mother's womb had not brought them forth that they might see this day."

"The messengers. You have sent them forth to the kings of the north: to Rheged and Strathclyde, to Gododdin and the Picts; to Dal Riada and the Uí Neíll; and to the kings of our land, the kings of Powys and Ceredigion and Dumnonia and our peoples in Brittany?"

"Yes, they have all ridden or taken ship." Cian smiled. "I sent them forth with words to call the kings to us, to remind them of the prophecies of old and to see in you their fulfilment. But they have only been gone this past week; it will be a week more before the first return to us, and others will take longer. I do not think they will come to us before the year turns. Ah, but next year, when the seas grow gentle and the sun warm, then they will come, answering your call, and with such an army, united as none have united them before, you will cast the Saxons into the sea and the lost lands will be ours once more."

"When we have dealt with Osric, send further word to the kings: let them know again that Arthur has returned in me." Cadwallon looked to his warmaster and his bard. "You will have work in the morning, the best work. For you, Hwyel: war. And for you, Cian: the songs of war, the renown of men. Then, with none left in Deira to oppose us, we will quit this city."

"Home?" asked Hwyel. "We have been gone from Gwynedd many months now."

But Cadwallon gestured to take in all the land around York. "This is our home, Hwyel. Too long have we allowed ourselves to shrink back into the hills that we know; these lands were lost in our hearts as well as by the sword. Now, to take them back, we must put them in here too." Cadwallon held his hand to his chest. "Do you not think I too miss the mountains of our birth, the meadows of Inys Mon and the teeth of Tryfan? But these lands are our lands, and we must find a place for the water meadows of the Ouse and the wolds of Ebrauc if we are to hold them." He turned to his bard. "Sing these lands into our hearts again, Cian: help us to love the meres and the marshes and the meadows. Will you do that?"

"I will do that, lord. I will sing such a song that all the Baptized will come here, as on pilgrimage, to where the new Arthur first led his army against the pagans, amid the willow meads and marshlands of the old kingdom of Ebrauc."

*

Coifi woke from nightmare into nightmare. The nightmare of his sleep had been one of loss, searching in the fall of twigs and the swirl of water for a wyrd that danced beyond his sight, playing at the edge of vision but ever and again slipping away when he turned to face it. The nightmare of his waking was one of finding: men screaming, falling into tents and shelters; the Britons, in among the Angles, but armed and awake, cutting rope and bringing down tent and shelter and setting brands to them that the men within might emerge clothed in flame. Black-cloaked, rattle-boned, Coifi gaped at the chaos around, then scrambled back as a man fell, face first, to the earth in front of him, his shoulder near severed from his side by the blow that had killed. The man's killer looked down at Coifi and for a moment their eyes met, and the man, dark-haired, blue-eyed, thought on death for the priest before turning and dealing it to another who advanced with sword and shield.

Still on his back, the priest scrabbled backwards, pushing with feet and hands, trying to get away from the chaos that had engulfed his waking. Hands reached under his arms and pulled him along, heels rattling over the ground, and he looked up to see Acca above him, face straining.

"This is no place for us," the scop said as the two men fell into a thicket of stinking, half-rotted rushes, standing in a waterlogged hollow.

Mud-smeared, they stared out from their hiding place at the battle in front of them. Only now was the sun edging over the horizon; Cadwallon's men had fallen upon Osric's camp in the shadows that presaged dawn, when men slept heavy and the night lingered, creeping from the city and attacking in silence. Osric had posted guards, of course, but the best men, the most experienced warriors, had been with him on the evening before, planning their own attack and drinking until the moon rose. Those same men, bleary and red-eyed, emerged to the slaughter. For until this morning, Cadwallon had always employed his horsemen to lead his attack, the riders following the streaming dragon banner and launching volleys of javelins against the shieldwall of his enemies before sweeping back for more missiles and sending them afresh into the lime and leather shields.

But this time, the Britons had attacked before dawn on foot, in silence, cutting the few unsuspecting guards down before engulfing the sleeping camp in flame and death. From their hiding place, Coifi and Acca saw Osric's boar banner surrounded and pulled down; they heard the roar that announced his death, and the panic of the many, fleeing and being cut down as they ran, and the courage of the few, fighting to the end beside the bodies of their lords.

They saw and they heard the ravens gather overhead, announcing the flesh feast to their fellows. Other birds came too: crows, red kites; all the scavengers of the battlefield, while at the margins of the field human scavengers gathered, ready with sharp knives to dispatch the wounded and harvest buckles and blades; anything that could be stripped from a corpse.

Battle turned into rout, became pillage and slaughter. Among the men who lived, some fell into paroxysms of laughter or held their arms up to their god; others collapsed in exhaustion and slept where they lay; men vomited and voided bowels, and raped and rested, and the quiet of exhaustion was broken by the croaking of ravens and the cursing of scavengers by warriors too spent to defend their gains.

By day's end, little remained save the naked corpses of the Angles. The men of Gwynedd had gathered their dead and taken them, slung over horseback or upon wagons, back into York, but there were none to gather the dead of Deira. Eventually, on the morrow or the day following, their kin would hear tell of the disaster that had befallen

Osric and his followers, and wives and children and parents would come, searching the slain for husbands and fathers, but on that first night, the only watchers of the dead were the night scavengers, and two waiting, fearful men.

Coifi and Acca had not spoken during the long, terrible day, as the bog they hid in grew sticky with men's blood and the flies clustered thick on them. The priest saw the slaughter overlaying the sacrificed ram; its blood had flowed as the blood of Osric's army had flowed. The scop made no song for the day, and never after spoke of it, save to list the names of the men who had died.

They did not speak as they crept away in the dark of the night, making their way east without word, towards the sea. They spoke only when dawn fingered the horizon towards which they walked, and they searched for a hiding place.

"The gods lied." Coifi spoke in a flat voice, devoid of feeling. Where his heart had been, there was only void.

"No, no," said Acca, taking his arm. "The gods promised victory, but they did not tell you when, did they?"

Coifi made no answer, but he did not deny the scop's suggestion.

"Victory will come to us, but not with Osric," said Acca.

"If not him, then who?" asked the priest.

"Eanfrith." Acca squeezed the priest's arm tighter. "Æthelfrith Flesaur's eldest son, from Bebba of the Picts. He will give the gods their victory."

"Where is he?"

"Eanfrith has returned to his ancestral home, the fort named for his mother, Bamburgh, and holds it now. Bernicia is his. Cadwallon has scarce ranged against it. Let us go to Eanfrith and take a new lord, for he keeps to the way of our fathers too, and the gods will give him the victory they promised, for he is truly throne-worthy in a way that Osric was not – did you hear the tale of how he begged Cadwallon to keep his hall and his land?"

"The son of the Twister? He has returned?"

"So I hear, with many of his mother's people."

"No one can take Bamburgh if it be held."

"With the rock as his base, Eanfrith can gather men to him and raise an army to face and defeat Cadwallon. Victory will come, Coifi. The gods have promised it – but they did not tell us how long it would take."

Coifi laughed. "It is a fine morn when a scop tells a priest to heed the promise of the gods; before the morn is out, the priest might tell the scop to wet his throat with wine." The priest pointed towards the crimson horizon. "It looks to be a day of fire, and we have neither drink nor food."

"The shades drink not, nor do they eat, and a death skulking in hiding will not take us to the All-Father's hall, so I would be glad for the wine should you have it. For now, I fear we will shadow the shades this day, but when night comes we may find ship or boat – whether the master knows or not – to take us up the coast to Bamburgh. What say you, priest?"

"I say that those willows look a good place to hide, and there may be water there too."

"Wine is better than water for the throat."

"And a lord is better than both." The priest shook his head. "We have lost two lords, Acca. Let the third keep us."

"I learned many new words from Paulinus, but there is only one I still use: amen."

Chapter 7

"How long are you going to spend on your knees while our people are dying?"

Oswald did not look around. He had heard the approach to where he knelt in the nave of the church, but monks and novices and pilgrims came and went often during the Great Work of the monastery, the daily singing of the Divine Office. Some pilgrims came but across the Sound from Mull; others had crossed great expanses of sea. Oswald had travelled up and down the west side of Britain and around to the west of Ireland, where the sea surged in untrammelled ridges and, some men said, there was no end to water, while others told of lands of fire and ice that emerged, steaming, from the cold northern waters. But he had never gone further south than the Narrow Sea, and some of the pilgrims brought tales of the wonders to be found in lands where the sun was so fierce that it burned men's skins. In truth, his mind had wandered from prayer into travellers' tales when the words of reproach broke upon him.

Oswiu stopped behind Oswald. All around, pilgrims added their prayers to the Great Work of the monks, the chant reaching to heaven. Oswiu ground his teeth in frustration. The news had arrived with the latest round of pilgrims and messengers – Oswiu made it his practice to meet each curragh when it beached – and he had thought that this, at last, would rouse his brother into action. But all Oswald did was remain on his knees.

Oswiu bent down and hissed into his brother's ear. "Did you not hear? Do you not care what happens to our people?"

If he had not been so angry himself, Oswiu would have noticed the tension that pulled his brother taught as a lyre string. He reached down to drag Oswald up only to find his wrist caught, crushed in a grip so strong it might have broken rock.

"I will hear the Office finish, then we will speak. For now, hold your peace."

Oswald heard his brother grunt with the pain of bruised bones, then, when he let go, he heard Oswiu make his way through the pilgrims to the door. The Great Work soared forth, fending off God's wrath and calling down his blessing, but try as Oswald might he could not hear it with heart undivided.

He rose to his feet and followed his brother from the church. Oswiu was waiting for him outside, his back turned as he stared across the Sound to Mull. But from his posture, Oswald saw that Oswiu was looking far beyond the next island, over the sea and across the spine of mountains that divided the country to the grey sea-washed land of their birth. It was strange how Oswiu pined for it, for he had been only four at the time of their exile, while Oswald had been twelve and all but a man, yet it was the one who had known the lands of their birth less who yearned for them more.

The elder brother sighed, but so quietly that Oswiu did not hear. "You miss home."

Oswiu turned around. "Yes, I miss home," he said. "Don't you?"

"I've made a home here," said Oswald. "I would not return."

"Well, I would. This is not our land, Oswald. It is not the land our fathers won – it is not the land our father won."

Oswald shook his head. "No, it is not." He stared back into memory. "You were a boy then, barely walking, but I remember Father winning that land. I remember his battles."

"Then why don't you want to win it back?"

Oswald stared at him. "Because I remember the winning of it. Because I remember Father."

"Our father was a great warrior and a great king."

"Yes. Yes, he was a great warrior and a great king…"

Oswald remembered their father: warrior, king, a man whom men feared and revered. That was how Oswiu called him to mind when they spoke of Æthelfrith, but Oswald recalled other aspects of their father too, such as the still, resigned calm that took their mother when their father, in his cups, thrust aside his concubines and turned his eyes to his wife; or the shouts and wails of the monks – monks like these among whom they lived – when Æthelfrith sent his warriors to slaughter the ranks of religious praying for his defeat before the Battle of Chester. The monks dead, or fled, Æthelfrith turned his attack against the armies of Powys and Gwynedd, defeating the Britons and making him, for a while, the most powerful king in the land. Before his voice had broken, Oswald had seen hundreds of men die. Before his voice had broken, he had killed men too; for after the Battle of Chester, where he had been an excited but protected eleven-year-old held behind the shieldwall, his father had brought him to the group of broken, beaten men who had survived the encounter but not managed to escape. Most were booty, as valuable as sword and buckle, to be sold at the slave markets that sprang up following a battle; traders arriving from far and wide with the news of war and captives. But Æthelfrith had a different use in mind for one of the captured men.

Taking his son by the hand, Æthelfrith led him through the aftermath of the battle, describing its course, explaining to him how the Northumbrian shieldwall had pushed the Britons back through its sheer man weight – "These Britons are, man for man, smaller than us, and lighter; use that against them" – and showing where a hollow in the ground had caused the men of Gwynedd to stumble and fall, opening a gap in their lines through which Æthelfrith, with his household warriors, had poured, peeling open the lines of the enemy like a skinner stripping a cow.

Æthelfrith brought the marvelling boy to the cowed group of prisoners. The battlefield scavengers, man and beast alike, were working at the corpses, but the king's own warriors had stripped all the most valuable items from the bodies already and laid them in a great glittering pile at the feet of Æthelfrith.

"I will give many rings this evening in camp, and in hall when we return there, and one," the king clapped his son on the shoulder, "I will give to you, Oswald."

"To me? But – but I didn't do anything. I just watched the battle."

"I will give you your first ring because you killed your first man."

"But I haven't killed anyone, Father."

Æthelfrith laughed, his face still flushed with the memory of battle. "No, but you will." He pointed to the group of prisoners, lying slumped on the ground. "Pick one of them and kill him."

Oswald looked at the men who stared, uncomprehending, as Æthelfrith spoke their fate in a tongue they did not understand.

Misunderstanding his expression, Æthelfrith ruffled his son's hair. "Yes, you can kill any one you want, although if it were me, I would save the fit ones, as they'll sell for more to the slavers, and pick one of the wounded. We all but have to pay the slavers to take away the wounded, so getting rid of one or two of them would help."

Oswald stared at faces that avoided his gaze, staring blankly at the sky, muttering under their breath oaths against a god that had failed them or comrades that had fled. He had been given the power of life and death over them – at his hand, one more would be dead. He looked up at his father, who smiled encouragingly at him.

"It's not easy killing a man," said Æthelfrith. "They're like wild boars: they squeal and they struggle – though not as much as boars – and this lot," he gestured at the captured men, "don't look as if they have any fight in them. I wager I won't even have to hold yours down. Now, who's it going to be, lad? That one over there, with the red hair and squint? Or him, old one eye? Or maybe you fancy one of their priests? We killed most of them, but there are one or two left over – you can always tell a priest by looking at their hands: soft they are, like a baby's."

"I – I can't."

Æthelfrith looked down at his son, then ruffled his hair again. "It's the choosing that's hard, Oswald, but believe you me, in the shieldwall you don't get to choose who you kill; they just come up against you, and most of the time you don't even remember how many there were afterwards. Oh, I know you'll hear men boasting in the hall about the number of men they killed, but believe you me, in the shieldwall there's no time for counting kills or remembering faces; it's just block, stab, push, block, stab, until your arm feels like it will drop off and the sweat's like as not about to turn your mail to a heap of rust if the battle don't end quick. Look, I'll pick one for you, a little one, 'bout your age – they're easier to kill then: less fat and muscle in the way."

The king pointed into the group of prisoners and one of them, a boy little more than Oswald's age, was hauled out. Æthelfrith looked him up and down.

"He's so scrawny, the slavers will want me to pay them to take him away. Go on, son, he's yours; kill him, and I'll give you your first ring. What's more, I'll give you my own sword to do it with." And Æthelfrith drew his sword, the blade he'd named Splitter on account of the ease with which it sliced men's bellies apart, and handed it, hilt first, to Oswald. Æthelfrith turned around to his men.

"Here, come watch: Oswald's about to make his first kill."

The men, those who weren't too exhausted or too drunk, put up a cheer, and the more mobile among them formed a rough half-circle around Oswald. The ætheling remembered feeling the sword's weight in his hand, marvelling at how it lay balanced upon his palm, but not looking, never looking, at the boy he was about to kill.

The men waited, and their wait grew past expectancy to encouragement to clapping, and Æthelfrith, seeing them grow impatient and not wanting his son disgraced, pushed Oswald forward. The boy stumbled and, in stumbling, looked into the face of the boy he was about to kill.

"Oswald, Oswald, Oswald," the men chanted, for they were fond of him, calling him their luck and their fortune, and carrying him upon their shoulders before and after battle. Hunlaf, Æthelfrith's warmaster, saw the glance from his king and, slipping behind the boy who was about to die, pinioned his arms to his sides, taking care to stand with his arms extended. Hunlaf had seen too many killed by a sword piercing through one man to stab another to stand anywhere within range, even if it was a boy who was about to thrust the sword.

"Oswald, Oswald, Oswald." The chant grew louder. Æthelfrith leaned in towards his son.

"Go on, lad," he said. "Aim for the belly – no bones there to turn the blade."

Oswald stared at the boy. The boy was staring at him. His eyes were grey. The boys lips were moving, but he could not hear what he was saying over the chant, and he would not have understood him if he could hear.

"Oswald, Oswald, Oswald!"

The boy closed his eyes.

Oswald pushed the blade and, as it met resistance, the boy's eyes flew open and, almost embracing, he fell forward against him as he pushed harder. Hunlaf, not needing to be asked, pushed too, running the boy forward onto the blade until its red tip emerged from his skinny back.

Face to face, almost cheek to cheek, Oswald heard the boy's last sound. He did not know its meaning, but it had remained with him until, coming to the island of saints, he had heard the sound again, at the end of the monks' Great Work, and known it for a word: *amen*.

The king looked down at the dead boy lying at his son's feet. "He died well," Æthelfrith said. He turned to Hunlaf. "Make sure he is buried well – get one of their priests to do it, then throw him in after the boy." The king grinned. "A gift for our gods!"

Oswald was shaking. He could feel his hands and arms trembling, but they seemed a long way away from him, and there seemed nothing he could do to stop them. But then his father clapped him on the back, a blow fierce enough to all but fell him, and the shaking stopped. Æthelfrith squatted down by his son and stared him full in the face.

"I shook for two days after I killed my first man," he said quietly to Oswald. "And that was after I'd thrown up everything that was in my stomach and voided my bowels too. You did well – you did better than me: my father had to push the sword for me; I hadn't the strength." The king leaned in closer to his son. "It gets easier. I don't know if it should, but it does. And killing is part of being a king. It's best done in battle, but sometimes you'll need to kill cold, like you've just done, and that doesn't get much easier." The king drew a ring from his forearm, a thick, heavy gold ring, and pushed it onto his son's arm, up to near the shoulder, so slender was Oswald's build as yet in comparison to his father's. "You've done the hardest thing a king has to do, Oswald."

Standing up, Æthelfrith raised Oswald's arm.

"My son," he cried. And the men cheered, and Oswald, the tears still wet on his cheek, smiled at their acclaim, while at his feet the dead boy stared glassy eyed at the grey sky.

Oswald shook the recollections of his father from his mind. Oswiu revered the memory of Æthelfrith and neither he nor Acha, his mother, saw fit to tell him otherwise. But the memories of Northumbria cast dark shadows over him; in truth, Oswald did not want to return there.

"What news?" he asked, for though he did not want to return, he must needs know what had happened.

Like an eager dog, Oswiu brightened at the interest shown by his brother. "The witan of Deira declared Osric, Uncle Edwin's cousin, king, but when he went to besiege Cadwallon in York, Cadwallon and his men crept out from the city in the night and killed Osric and most all his army. Now Cadwallon's anger falls upon Deira, and he is burning and killing all the thegns that remain, for he said that he had their oath before, and they broke it, so now he will lay waste their land and their homes."

"Did they?"

"Did they what?"

"Did they pledge themselves to Cadwallon?"

Oswiu shrugged. "I do not know. Some will have done, to save their halls and their land. The rest…" He shrugged again.

"God's disfavour lies upon those who break oath: maybe that is why he allowed Cadwallon to kill Osric, if Osric had pledged himself to Cadwallon."

"I don't think Osric cared what God thought; after Edwin died, he brought back the old priest, Coifi, and had him sacrifice to the old gods for victory."

"But Osric was baptized, wasn't he? Surely all Edwin's thegns accepted baptism from Paulinus."

"So they say. They all followed him into the pool that Edwin had built in his church in York, one after the other, *in nomine Patris et Filii, et Spiritus Sancti*." Oswiu shrugged again. "Maybe it didn't work?"

Oswald stared over the Sound towards the mountains of Mull. "When the Israelites broke their covenant with God, he sent the Babylonians to punish them, and they were carried away into slavery; now you tell me Northumbria has broken pledge and abjured God – is it any wonder God's punishment follows?"

"What did Edwin do wrong then? God punished him."

"I – I do not know," Oswald said, a note of helplessness in his voice. "I have thought much on this and I do not understand it." He shook his head. "If Uncle Edwin had lived, then Northumbria would be safe and there would be no question of what I should do." Oswald turned to look at his brother. "If our uncle had lived, it would have been convenient for everyone for me to become a monk, thereby removing a threat to the throne, and it would have been God's will."

"But he didn't live," Oswiu pointed out.

"I don't know why." Oswald squeezed a fist with frustration. "I don't understand it."

Oswiu looked at his brother. "You mean, you usually do understand things?"

Oswald looked startled. "Don't you?"

Oswiu laughed. "No, hardly ever. I just do what you tell me – then I know things will work all right."

Oswald shook his head. "Such faith. Brother, you should place your trust in God, not me."

"But don't you see, Oswald? God gave me you as a brother so I could have someone to trust. Maybe your job is to understand, and mine is to trust you and do what you say. So what should we do about Osric, and Cadwallon?"

"I – we will speak of this later. As to Cadwallon: what word is there of Eanfrith?"

"He has returned with men from Pictland, and claimed Bernicia for his ancestral right, taking Bamburgh. There he remains, making only short trips for supplies, and those mostly by boat, sending men to take birds, eggs and seals from the Farne Islands or Lindisfarne, and waits for Cadwallon to come to him."

"That is a good strategy. Even if he had an army ten times the size, Cadwallon could not take Bamburgh. Our brother learned well from Father."

"I never liked Eanfrith. He ignored me."

Oswald smiled. "He must have been the only person who did. You were the loudest boy I have ever heard."

"But do you think he will be able to defeat Cadwallon? Penda has taken his men back to Mercia, but young warriors flock to Cadwallon, and his army swells. I have heard rumour that he sends messengers to the kings of the Britons, anointing himself their High King and proclaiming that he is the answer to their prophecies of long ago, that a king would arise from among them to cast the Saxons into the sea."

"We are not Saxons," said Oswald.

"They call us all Saxons," said Oswiu, "as we call them all *wealh*."

"We do not call the monks of Iona *wealh*, or the warriors of Dal Riada, or the Uí Neíll."

"It would be stupid to do so, as we are their guests. But you have not answered, Oswald. Will Eanfrith defeat Cadwallon?"

"How many men did he bring from Pictland?"

"Enough to take and hold Bamburgh, but not enough to march against Cadwallon."

"And with the ear that you put into other people's conversations, have you heard rumour of whether young men ride to join him?"

"None from Dal Riada or the Uí Neíll. There may be some from Strathclyde and the Gododdin, but I have not heard so."

"And what of God or the gods? In whom does Eanfrith place his trust?"

"Paulinus has gone south to Kent. I have heard tell that the other priest, James, remains, quietly praying and teaching around Catterick, but that is far from Bamburgh. The Picts have their gods; Eanfrith most likely sacrifices to them."

Oswald nodded, and turned his back on the Sound to look back to the abbey church. It was a long, low building, thatched, with white walls and small windows, and he had known no happiness greater than that which he had found within it.

"I pray he will succeed," Oswald said quietly. "I fear he will not."

*

"Abbot Ségéne, there is a messenger to see you."

The abbot looked up from where he kneeled in prayer, although in truth he realized that the prayer had turned into anxious thought about his community.

"Oh, it is you, Aidan," he said as he struggled to his feet, his knees cracking as they straightened. "Who is he from?"

"King Cadwallon," said the young monk.

"Cadwallon?" The abbot looked for confirmation and Aidan nodded.

"Yes, Father Abbot."

"Bring him to me," said Abbot Ségéne. "I will hear his message. Oh, and Brother Aidan…" The monk stopped in mid stride. "Stay with us. I want you to hear what this messenger has to say."

"Yes, Father Abbot."

While Brother Aidan hurried off to fetch the messenger, the abbot stretched and bent his knees, working hard to keep his face impassive as twinges of pain shot up and down his legs. He tried not to think what the saints would have said about the fuss he was making from legs aching through kneeling, when they would stand for hours in the winter sea, or fast for a month and a day, or cast themselves upon the waves in a curragh with no oars, that God might take them where he would, be it to the depths of the sea or new islands upon which to make their cells and live in communion with the Lord of sea and sky, wind and wave.

Abbot Ségéne grimaced. They might have thought little of such pain, but could they have brought the Irish, a people so far beyond civilization that even the empire never reached it, to the faith if they had not been able to walk anywhere because of failing knee joints?

He would ask one of the brothers to bring him a stool, that he might pray sitting down. After all, the apostle had said to pray always – he did not specify what position in which to do so.

Brother Aidan led a travel-stained and weary man into the abbot's cell. He made the courtesy and Abbot Ségéne nodded in acknowledgment.

"I hear you come from Cadwallon, king of Gwynedd."

"And king of Deira, and Bernicia, of all the lands north of the Humber, the High King, the prophesied one, *dux bellorum*, the once and present king: Arthur, the deliverer, who will drive the Saxons back into the sea and take back the lost lands for us and our children and our children's children." The messenger recited the titles and promises with the faintly distracted air of a man who has rehearsed the words over and again through days of travelling.

"Really?" said the abbot. "Cadwallon was plain king of Gwynedd when I last met him, a title to satisfy most men. But I see he is not most men. Now, what is the message you bring from him?"

"My lord, King Cadwallon presents his greetings and wishes you to be informed that he is, through God's blessing and by his divine signs, the deliverer long promised to the baptized people of this land, to rid them from the pagans that have taken what was once theirs, to unite the many kingdoms of the Baptized into one great kingdom. He furthermore asks your prayers and blessings upon him and his people, that God's grace may further flow upon him, and he asks that you send him relics of the holy Colm Cille, founder of this monastery, that he may bear them before him in battle and, with the saint as his standard bearer and protector, meet the remaining armies of the pagans and utterly defeat and destroy them. He furthermore asks that you use your good offices and send messengers of your own to the kings of the Britons, to Strathclyde and Dal Riada, to the Uí Neill and the Picts, announcing that the deliverer long promised by God and his saints has arisen among us, and that they should accept him as High King over them all, and pledge themselves to his cause, that together they may drive the Saxons from this land and know a unity and peace unknown since the days of the emperors." The messenger, message delivered, gasped for breath, but underneath his panting he bore the unmistakable relief of a man who had unburdened himself of a heavy load of words.

The abbot nodded slowly. "This is news indeed. What is your name?"

"Pedrog, Father Abbot," said the messenger.

"Of the Ceredegion?"

"Yes." The young man smiled at the abbot. "You know them?"

"Of course," said Abbot Ségéne. "What man alive has not heard of Clinnoch and his feats?"

"I – I thought it was just among the sons of Ceretic that his fame had spread."

"You will find it has spread much further than that. Now, you will stay with us, taking food and drink and rest."

"Er, the king wanted me to return with your reply as soon as possible."

"And you will, you will. But is it possible for a man to travel far and fast on an empty belly, with thirst cracking his lips and weariness turning his limbs to stone? No, of course not. Therefore you must remain with us for a while, eating and drinking and resting, and then when it is time to return to the king, you will travel all the faster. I wager a well-fed and well-rested Pedrog will arrive much sooner than a Pedrog who takes boat now and falls ill upon the long journey home. Now, I will find a monk to take you to your quarters – we live simply here, but it is better than an open curragh – and then to the refectory; you are fortunate not to arrive on a day of fasting, but even if we had been abstaining from food, we should have found for you to eat." The abbot turned to Brother Aidan. "Take young Pedrog and find a monk to look after him, and then return to me here."

While Abbot Ségéne waited for Brother Aidan to return, he thought through Pedrog's message once more.

"Come," he said, when the young monk, red faced from rushing, appeared at the door to his cell again. "Let us walk. My knees are cracking and my legs grow weary from lack of use. Besides, I think better when I walk."

The two men, Brother Aidan following a slight but respectful distance behind the abbot, walked over the machair down towards the Sound of Iona. Keeping the sea to his right, the abbot led them along the path towards the northern tip of the island.

"What do you make of this, Brother Aidan?" the abbot asked when he was sure they were away from the ears of any but sheep and gulls.

"There has long been a prophecy, said to have come from Merlin, that Arthur would return and lead his people to final victory against the Saxons. I heard the bards sing of Arthur and his return when I was a boy, and my father before me."

"But it is one thing to hear of a prophecy and another to live in the time of its enactment. We must ask this Pedrog what the signs were that convinced Cadwallon that he is the fulfilment of prophecy and the hope of the people. For myself," the abbot turned away and looked out over the grey-backed sea, "I am not so certain."

"Why are you not certain?" asked Brother Aidan. "Cadwallon has defeated the High King, he has taken Deira and killed Osric its new king. The rumours are that he rides north to Bernicia, to take that kingdom from Eanfrith. Should he succeed, he would indeed be king of all the lands north of the Humber and south of the Tweed, and not even the emperors of old ruled there. Does that not make him Arthur?"

"Arthur is the hope of a defeated people to whom we are cousins; a people who would rather fight among themselves than unite against the Saxons. You know the tale of Urien of Rheged, the last great king of the north? He drove the sons of Ida back, expelling them even from their stronghold at Bamburgh, until they waited in fear for the turning of the tide around Lindisfarne and their final destruction, for Rheged was camped on the shore with a great army of allies – the kings of Strathclyde, of Elmet and the Gododdin. But then, in the night, King Morgant, rather than acknowledge Urien of Rheged as his lord and High King, sent an assassin and killed him, and the morn saw the last great army of the Britons dissolve in suspicion and skirmishing, and the sons of Ida, watching from Lindisfarne, could not believe what their eyes told them when they saw the hosts of the Britons marching away and leaving them alive. So the Idings reclaimed Bamburgh and one by one defeated the kingdoms that were on the point of defeating them. So it has ever been among the Britons since the emperors left – one king turning upon another and calling in the Saxons to do his killing for him and thinking himself superior for his baptism, when God calls upon him, by reason of that baptism, to be more than a barbarian. Arthur is their hope, but he is not my hope." The abbot turned back to Brother Aidan. "Do you know who my hope is, Brother Aidan?"

"Oswald," said the young monk.

"Yes, Oswald," said the abbot. "Let him claim the throne, and then we might send among the Saxons men to win them to eternal life, and through them the pagan barbarians, their kin, who live across the North Sea. That is my hope, and it is a great hope, and Cadwallon is no part of it."

"But what message will you give to Pedrog to take back to Cadwallon? Surely you will not say that?"

"No, of course not. Oswald may be my hope, but hopes are often times dashed in this world, and kings fall by the way more readily than a horse casts its shoe. Should Cadwallon prevail, should he for a while reign as High King, it would not do for him to know that he had not the support of the Holy Isle. But for myself, and for the Blessed Colm Cille, our father in faith, I will not give it. But I will prevaricate." The abbot smiled ruefully at Brother Aidan. "For the sake of your soul, brother, I hope you are never burdened with the rule of a monastery, for what you think of as an outpost of the kingdom of heaven is mostly a foundation of this earth, and an abbot spends more time on rustled sheep and importunate kings than he does upon his knees."

"Who would want me as abbot?" asked Brother Aidan.

"You would be surprised," said the abbot.

Chapter 8

"Have the kings answered? Any word from the abbot of the Holy Isle?" Cadwallon rode with his men north, the hooves of their shaggy horses loud on the cobbles of the old road, but still the king's mind turned to his messengers, dispatched four weeks ago or more, and the answers they would bring. But none had returned.

"It could be they went first to York, where we were, missing us upon the road," said Cian. "Only when they have gone past us and received word that we have gone will they know to turn north and follow us upon the old road."

Cadwallon twisted in the saddle to look back along the road, but all he saw were his own men, in column, with the ox wagons of their camp followers forming the long, drawn-out tail of an army on the move.

To the east, the sea glittered under the late summer sun, moving as easily as a horse under saddle. To the west, the land rose in ascending ridges to the humps and whalebacks of the Cheviots. Many of the hills were garlanded with tumbledown fortifications, the walls of the forgotten men of the hills, a people so old that even their name was forgotten: all that remained were the stones they had set in rings about the mountain tops, the rock flashing pink where a scrambling sheep displaced a boulder and revealed the fresh quarried colour beneath. This was the land of the Old North, a land so old that even Cadwallon, who knew his family back to before the days of the emperors, felt young in its shadows.

"You can feel it, can't you, Cian?" Cadwallon's gesture took in the hills and lush plain they rode through, its fields worked into careful strips by the peasants who stopped their tasks to watch the horsemen riding past. "There is a strength still in this land that the Saxons haven't understood. It is only a matter of time before the kings rise up together, and cast the invaders back into the sea."

Cian wiped the sweat from his forehead and flicked it onto the cobbles. "On a day like this, I would be cast into the sea myself."

Cadwallon laughed, and the bard gave silent thanks for the joy of the king, for he had been grim and silent since the messengers were so long in returning.

"But to answer your question, yes, there is power in this land. Talk to some of the peasants – I do it, lord, so men such as you do not have to – and you will learn that there are places they will not go, for they believe the wraiths of the Old Ones, who lived here before reck of kin, haunt those barrows and mounds still, waiting to take the living down with them into the cold earth. There are hills they will only pass upon the east, for to the west lies a door that leads under hill to silent halls filled full of the treasure of the first walkers of this land – yet none would touch such treasure, were it laid out in front of them, for it comes at cost of wits, and kin, and soul. Even the rock upon which the Saxons make their fort is old beyond any reckoning, and I have heard some say that once it looked over great plains to the east as well as the west, a land rich in game and fish from its many lakes. But a great flood came and took the land, and it has been sea ever since, and the land that once was lies beneath it, lost to men. Yes, this is an old land, lord, and a strong one. One day, and that day draws nigh, it will remember its strength and its pride, and cast the newcomers back into the sea."

"That is what I think," said the king. "May the Lord grant that the day come soon." But as he spoke, he looked back again, and still no messenger appeared upon the road.

"They will find us at Ad Gefrin," Cadwallon continued. "I have heard men tell of Edwin's palace in the shadow of the hills – they say it is the most marvellous hall in the land, longer than many boats laid stern to prow and higher than a tree, with gold pillars and silver tapestries. I would see this marvel – before I burn it."

"We must be close. There's one of our scouts." Cian pointed ahead: a rider approached from the west.

Cadwallon signalled his warmaster closer and Hwyel urged his horse on until it walked alongside the king's mount.

"Take the wagons and enough men to protect them, and keep on the north road until you reach Bamburgh – Eanfrith will be there, skulking on the rock. We will meet you there, but first I have to attend to a task of my own. Cian will come with me; he will have something to sing about after today."

So as the wagons made their slow, ox-pulled, way north, Cadwallon rode with Cian and a hundred men towards the line of hills in the west. It seemed as if every summit was ringed with fallen walls, and the men rode in silence, the antiquity of the hills silencing them. The king, for his part, talked with Cian as they rode, pointing out the thick sprinkling of white upon the hills.

"There are many sheep here, and cattle. Edwin built his palace that he might have somewhere to gather the render of the hills, and looking around us that render must have been rich indeed. I will have it for my own soon. After all, the people of the hills are of our kin, not Edwin's."

Cian shrugged. "May that be so. But in my experience, the men of the hills hold no one kin if he has not been born in the shadow of the mountains and sucked their stone teats in infancy. It may not be so easy a matter to gather their render."

"They cannot be harder than the men of our own hills – never have I seen greater innocence than that on the face of a peasant when he assures you he really only does have one sheep, and that an old, colicky beast good for one summer more before being put into mutton. Holding a sword to a few throats uncovers all manner of things that they would have hidden. These will be no different." Cadwallon sat up in his saddle and stared ahead, then pointed.

"There, what do you see?"

Cian shaded his eyes against the sun that was swinging low in the sky. To his gaze, it seemed as if the sun itself had come down from the sky and blazed from the walls of the great hall that had appeared as they breasted a rise and looked down into a long, low valley between the hills.

"Edwin's hall, Ad Gefrin."

Cadwallon reined in his horse and looked upon the hall.

"They are right; it is a marvel," he said, but quietly, that no one might hear.

*

Many weeks' walking, a few days upon wagons and even fewer upon a horse, which coped with having two men astride by moving slower than they could walk, had brought Coifi and Acca to within sight of Ad Gefrin. Here, in the shadow of the hills, they hoped to find Eanfrith. Acca had insisted on singing as they walked the final miles. For his part, Coifi went in silence, his bedraggled raven-feather cloak drawn tight around his shoulders despite the warmth of the season. He turned eyes to hilltop and the motion of cloud shadow, he heard the call of meadow pipits and skylarks, the distant bleat of sheep, grazing the high meadows of the hills, and he had no peace, for all of these were signs of wyrd, of the weavings of the fate singers, and he could no longer trust the meaning he saw in them, for the victory he had seen in the sacrificed ram had proven a defeat.

"I am glad you are happy," he grumbled, as Acca launched into the tale of the Battle of Tears, "but when are we going to get there? My feet are sore and my legs ache."

Acca laughed. "You mean you have been so busy searching for signs of wyrd that you did not see what lies ahead? There it is, the golden hall of Ad Gefrin, palace of Edwin." And he pointed to where it glowed in the late sun.

Coifi stopped and shaded his eyes against the glare, then turned to Acca.

"The golden hall is burning," he said.

"What do you mean, burning?" said the scop. "It's the sun shining upon it."

The priest passed a trembling hand over his eyes, then looked again. "It burns," he said, turning a frightened gaze to the scop. "In its wyrd, it burns. I see the flames."

"You mean like you saw Osric's victory?"

Coifi stiffened. "You said the gods did not say when victory would come."

"And in the same way there's no telling when the palace will burn. It's made of wood; wood burns."

Coifi looked doubtfully back towards Ad Gefrin. "I – you may be right. I do not know when."

"Of course I'm right. Let me tell you, the palace will be standing long after we've gone into the shadows; who would burn it? It is beautiful, magnificent. Not even the emperors of old built like this." Acca pointed. "Look at the door columns, how the animals carved there climb upwards, and the gold of the pillars." The scop stood with his hands on his hips, his lyre hanging on his back, breathing deep. "Ah, it is good to be back. I gave some of my greatest performances here. Did I tell you about the time I sang the tale of the Scyldings for Edwin and everyone here – this was after Paulinus had been standing in the river for a month and then took fever – and they all cheered so loudly I thought the roof might split open, and the king gave me a golden armband as thick as my thumb. That was my favourite of his gifts, his many gifts, to me." Acca passed a hand over his face. "I had to sell it to that outlaw of a shipmaster to gain us passage up the coast – a journey I made in better times for a handful of clams and a promise to sing to the crew as they rowed." The scop shook his head in disgust. "I would have sung as many songs as they wanted, making light work of the rowing for the crew, but all that whoreson wanted was gold, and of course you didn't have any gold to give him, so I had to pay, hey, Coifi? Coifi?"

The scop turned to see the priest staring back the way they had come.

"Er, Acca..." Coifi pointed and the scop followed his finger to a column of riders approaching fast, their spearheads glinting in the slanting sunlight.

"No," said Acca. "No, no, no. This cannot be; it is not fair. We have come so far."

"I don't know about you," said Coifi, "but I'm going to wait for them here. There's nowhere to hide and they'll have seen us already. If we run, they'll only come after us." And he flopped down, in a heap of bedraggled black feathers, by the side of the track.

But the scop continued to stare at the approaching riders. "I – I think they are Britons," he said. "Their shields are rectangular, not round like ours."

Coifi shaded his eyes to look. "It will be Cadwallon and his men, come to burn the palace of Edwin."

"No, it can't be," said Acca, but as the riders drew nearer, he saw the dragon banner flying from the leading horseman.

"Wyrd," said Coifi. "The fate singers have drawn the thread of our lives tight, Acca. It will take but a single cut to sever them. Sit down, enjoy the sun of our last day – there is nothing else we can do." The priest lay back, staring up at the blue bowl of the sky, and for the first time since Edwin's death, he felt content. He was going to die soon, he knew that, but he did not mind. He was tired. He would rest. That was enough.

Acca slumped down on the grass beside him. "That it should end like this: cut down by men ignorant of my craft when in sight of a palace fit for the finest songs and tales I could tell. When I die I'm going to tell the gods, or God, what I think of how I have been treated, but I will make my lament so beautiful that the gods themselves will shed tears for the waste of my talent."

"The gods may, but men won't," said Coifi. "Men forget, and those who call on you to sing their praises one day will not remember your name the next. Our time is over, Acca. We are better off leaving this world."

"You speak such truth, Coifi. If I were but spared, I could tell of the sadness of this middle-earth in words that would have even the most blood-soaked lord drowning his beard in tears." The scop sighed, and looked towards the riders. They were close now, and to men sitting upon the ground they loomed large upon their mounts, although they rode beasts that were little larger than ponies. "But it is not to be."

At a command from the man who rode alongside the dragon banner, the troop of horsemen came to a halt by the two men sitting upon the grass. He rode over to them and, looking down, pointed his spear at them, speaking in a tongue they did not understand.

Acca looked up, shading his eyes against the low sun.

"I do not speak your tongue, stranger. If you are going to kill us, it would be meet for you to tell us your name in a language we can understand. But for our part, that you know who it is you will kill this day, I am Acca the scop and this is Coifi the priest."

The man lowered his spear and looked carefully at Acca, then Coifi.

"I have heard of you," he said, the words coming from his mouth with the swinging intonation of the Briton.

"You've heard of me?" said Acca, brightening suddenly. "This is happy tidings; at least my killer has heard my fame. Tell me, was it for my verses on the Battle of the River Idle, when Rædwald and Edwin slew Æthelfrith the Twister, that you know me? Or perhaps for my elegy for King Edwin, although that is but new…"

"I know you for Edwin's bard and Edwin's priest and soothsayer."

"We call it scop in our tongue," said Acca.

"And I call you bard in mine. This is a fine chance, for we ride to Edwin's palace, where you be bound on foot. Come, we will take you there, for I would have a bard of your people on hand to tell the tale of what I will do there this day."

"And what will you do there this day?"

"Burn."

At that word, Coifi scrambled to his feet. "I saw it," he said, his body trembling. "I saw you, raising fire as on the day when the heavens fall and all ends."

The rider laughed. "So I have heard of you and you have seen me. This is a fine chance indeed. Well, know you that I am Cadwallon, heir to Arthur, High King, and I will drive you and your people back into the sea whence you came." Cadwallon leaned down closer to Coifi. "Can you see that, seer?"

"I – I see fire and flame, and twelve riders and a great stronghold atop a rock by the sea; I see knives flashing, and a raven flying against the moon. I – I see…" The priest's voice trailed away and his eyes rolled up into his skull, leaving only the whites, as the strength drained from his limbs and he slowly collapsed.

Acca shrugged. "He does that sometimes when he sees the wyrd; trouble is, when he wakes up he usually can't remember what he saw before he passed out."

Cadwallon signalled to one of his men. "Take him," he said. "Tie him over a horse – I don't want to lose him." Then he called Cian forward and gestured Acca closer. "This is my bard. The two of you will have much to talk on. And later, I would hear you both. It has been many years since I heard a song battle."

*

Acca sang that night in the fierce blood light of the burning palace. He sang of the death of kings and the passing of all things with the voice of a gull lamenting the sea, and the men who listened, although most did not understand the language of his song, heard the sadness of it and tears glittered on their cheeks by firelight.

Cian sang too, an exultant song, of the downfall of enemies and the fulfilment of promises, of laments heard in the distance rather than sung within camp, a song to make the heart pound and the blood race. Cadwallon heard the two men sing as he sat, face turned towards the burning palace. Coifi watched too, looking from the flames to the hills that surrounded the palace, and he saw shadows moving there – so many that he could not tell if they were the living hillmen, come to watch the destruction of the palace that took their food render each year, or the dead, come to welcome new shades to their number.

While the fire yet burned, Cadwallon, laughing, gave the winner's wreath to Acca for, as he said, "It is right he should lament what I have burned, for it was indeed the most beautiful building in the land, and if any but Edwin had caused it to be made, I would have taken it for my own." At his words, Cian stalked into the night, accompanied by the laughter of his king, while Acca, wreath-crowned, sang on long into the night, until men, craving sleep, threw stones and sticks to silence him.

Coming to rest beside Coifi, Acca took off the wreath and held it for the priest to see.

"This is what they give for a song battle. Twined leaves! I would prefer a thick gold arm ring, but still, did you see the expression on that scop's face when the king gave the wreath to me?"

"I saw, but I fear he will look the happier tomorrow, when Cadwallon has us killed."

"Oh, don't worry, Cadwallon won't kill us – he wants us to tell the news of his victory. Tomorrow he rides to Bamburgh, where Eanfrith waits. There is no taking such a stronghold, no matter how many men you have, for it has a well dug deep into the living rock, and space enough to store supplies for more years than an army could lay siege. Eanfrith will simply wait upon the rock, and Cadwallon knows there is nothing he can do to bring him down – which is why he lets us live, Coifi. He told me, after he gave me the wreath, that he wants me – wants us – to go to Eanfrith and to tell him that he, Cadwallon, will accept him as his client king of Bernicia, so long as he comes to make his submission to him, and pledges his fealty."

"Why should Eanfrith listen to us?"

"He knows us, of course. I was scop to Æthelfrith, his father, before Edwin became king, and I remember Eanfrith well – sings like a crow, but a remarkable head for beer – and you were priest too then, were you not? He will remember us and receive Cadwallon's message."

"He might receive it, but he won't like it."

*

"He wants me to do what?"

Eanfrith sat upon the judgment seat within the great hall of Bamburgh. Looking around, Acca saw that the men who had accompanied Eanfrith from Pictland, men painted after the manner of their people in swirling designs, filled at most half the benches in the hall.

"He wants you to submit to him, and then he will accept you as under-king, to rule Bernicia, while he takes Deira for himself, to add to his own lands. For he told me that the men of Deira broke their faith with him, but King Cadwallon said to tell you that he has no quarrel with the men of Bernicia, for, as is told among men, you have ever kept your word."

Eanfrith leaned forward in the judgment seat and Coifi, standing silently beside Acca, saw a terrible eagerness in his face. He too had noted the few men the king had with him, and how plain the clasps and buckles of their belts and clothes. These were the leavings of a king, the men who could find no place in a lord's hall; oft times, they would slip between brigandage and serving whatever lord would feed and shelter them for the night. It was no army, and if Eanfrith had not the stronghold of Bamburgh, he would never have stood against Cadwallon's hardened men.

But Acca and Coifi had been there, riding alongside the Britons, when they came under Bamburgh rock and looked up in wonder and awe at the stronghold above them, to be reached by a single path that wound down the rock to a fortified gate upon the side that the sea washed. Stone walls topped the rock, and further wooden stockades sat atop them; a weakness in most cases, for wood might burn, but the walls were set so high above the surroundings that even a fire arrow might fail to reach them, and the greater quantity of burning material necessary to set such a sturdy structure ablaze could never be set to it.

Cadwallon, staring up at the rock, whistled through his teeth. "You say they have a well up there?" he said, turning to Acca.

"Yes, lord," said the scop. "King Æthelfrith had it dug through the rock to sweet water far below."

"I don't suppose it ever runs dry?"

"Never."

Cadwallon looked up at the rock again. "Take my message to Eanfrith. Tell him that to show good faith I will withdraw my men and meet him with but my own household, at a place of his choosing."

"My choosing?" Eanfrith repeated that part of Cadwallon's message. "He said I could choose where we are to meet?"

"Yes, lord, that is what he said."

Eanfrith nodded, and looked to the man standing next to the judgment seat. His warmaster, Acca supposed.

"He treats me as a king, worthy of speech. That is more than my mother's own people did."

The warmaster shook his head, and looked warningly at Acca and Coifi.

"Oh, do not worry about them. I remember them from my father's time, when they served him. They are faithful."

"If they are faithful, why do they serve Cadwallon?" asked the warmaster.

"Er, excuse me," said Acca, "we do not serve Cadwallon – he captured us as we neared Ad Gefrin, where we sought you, King Eanfrith, as the true king of Bernicia. He spared us not to serve him, but to bring you his message, for he knew that you would receive us, as you have."

"There, you have your answer, Drest. All kings need reliable messengers. It is not surprising that Cadwallon should choose two men known to me to carry his message. The question is, what shall we do?"

"I would not go to him," said the warmaster. "Here, we are secure: he cannot come against us; he cannot out wait us; he can do nothing against us. But should we come down from the rock...."

"You saw his army arrayed around us. We cannot stand against him – we have too few men. My – our – only chance is to make peace with Cadwallon; after all, he has done what he wished and taken revenge on Edwin. He cannot rule Bernicia himself, not from Gwynedd, so he will need someone to rule it for him, and how much better a man with claim to the throne, a son of Æthelfrith, a man like me?" Eanfrith turned to Acca and Coifi. "What do you say? Can he be trusted?"

The priest shrugged his shoulders. "Can any man be trusted?" he said. "But I am alive, when I had not thought to be."

"For myself," said Acca, "I would say he is a man of discernment; he has shown great interest in the songs and tales I had to tell him, favouring me even over his own scop – a man of meagre talent named Cian – so it seems to me that the rumours of the hatred Cadwallon holds against our people must be false, for would a man who hates us wish to hear our stories? Far be it from me to counsel a king but, as with Coifi, I am alive and had not thought to be. Make of that what you will."

Eanfrith pressed his hands together, squeezing the blood from his fingers. Outside the hall, the wind, blowing in from across the grey sea, drew tears from the eyes of the men who stood watch on the walls. Cadwallon had withdrawn his men through the day, the army striking its tents and breaking down its shelters, loading wagons and riding south until, by noon, there were none left investing the castle, but only a long, slow-moving tail of ox-drawn vehicles, leaving.

From the rock, the sentries had heard the curses of men who, arriving the day before, had set up camp in expectation of many days, if not weeks, to recover from the exertions of the journey only to be told to pack up the next morning. Cadwallon's dragon banner had gone first, leading the column, and the king himself, unmistakable in the fine armour he wore, followed soon afterwards, leaving the rearguard to hurry along the camp followers.

"Send out scouts," said Eanfrith. "Let us see if they have gone. If they have, then we know Cadwallon speaks the truth, and I will meet with him at a place of my choosing."

"I've already done that," said the warmaster. "They have gone indeed, and look set to keep on going. There is nothing to suggest that Cadwallon means to return."

"There, what did I say? It is meet for him to accept me as co-king and ruler of Bernicia, for there will be gold to be paid – he and I know that – but this will be gold that comes without men's lives lost and warriors slain; its only price will be the time it takes to negotiate with him, and the hostages Cadwallon asks for."

Acca could not help notice that when Eanfrith spoke of hostages, his eyes flicked to him and Coifi.

Eanfrith, king of Bernicia, whose writ did stretch beyond the walls of the castle in which he found refuge, turned to Acca. "Take word to King Cadwallon of Gwynedd, lord of Deira, High King of Britain, that I acknowledge him my lord and my High King. Tell him that I will meet him…" Eanfrith looked round to his warmaster. "We need a place out in the open, where he can't hide any men from sight. Where do you think?"

"Upon the beach, where the boats pull up for market. There is nowhere to hide men there. And if there is need of help, then you can call it from the castle."

"You'll come with me, won't you, Drest?" asked Eanfrith.

"It would be better that I remained here. Then should the talking miss its mark and weapons be drawn, I could bring help quickly."

"Any fool can answer a call; I need you with me when we face Cadwallon."

"I – it would be better otherwise, but if that is what you wish."

"It is what I command, Drest. It were well that you remember who is king here."

The warmaster nodded, a tight, controlled nod, and Eanfrith turned his attention back to Acca. "Tell Cadwallon we will meet him on the beach tomorrow. Tell him I will bring twelve men with me – that is the customary number for negotiations between kings – and they may be armed, but with sword and knife alone; no shields. And tell him, as further surety, to bring you to the meeting as well, in addition to his men, so that we may have there the messenger who brought us together, that he may speak if there be any misunderstanding as to what was agreed between us. There, do you understand?"

Acca's lips moved silently as he rehearsed the message under his breath. A scop schooled in recalling the history and tales of his people found little difficulty in committing such a message to memory, and he repeated it to Eanfrith's satisfaction.

"What of my friend Coifi?" asked Acca. "Where will he be?"

"I will bring him with me," said Eanfrith. "Do not fear."

*

Coifi, watching from among the tired sentries, saw the sun rise on the morrow, and men essay from the gate with the light to set up tents and shelters upon the beach. He had no appetite with Acca gone, and Eanfrith had not called upon him to read the future in the blood of a sacrificed animal, for which he was grateful.

But as the day rose, Eanfrith did call him, not to prophesy but to propitiate, giving the priest a white goat for the knife and the flame. "I would give cattle, but we have none here upon the rock, for they would eat more than they milk with the dry hay that we have. But I give you this goat for the gods, with the promise that I will give many more, and cattle too, when I have secure hold of this kingdom. And tell the gods that I will cleave to the ways of our fathers, and not go seeking after new gods from far away."

Coifi had told the gods this as he held the goat down, using his knee to hold it immobile upon the stone altar while he held the knife ready. Edwin's priest, Paulinus, had used this altar for his sacrifices, and Coifi had stood with the others, watching and wondering at what he did and the strange language in which he did it, but now he took the altar and made blood sacrifice, a sacrifice the gods would understand. Drawing the knife across the goat's throat, he emptied its life upon the altar and smeared the stone with red, chanting to honour the gods and call their blessing down upon the day, and the king.

Now, as the sun climbed towards the sky's summit, Coifi followed Eanfrith, his warmaster Drest and ten sword companions, as they made their way down the steep, rock-hewn steps to the gate. The door warden opened the gate and they stepped out upon the beach. The tide was out, and sand stretched level and gold to either side of the rock upon which the stronghold squatted, commanding land and sea and sky.

From the south, riding up the beach under the dragon banner, were twelve horsemen and one other, perched uncertainly upon a following, braying mule.

Cadwallon had come, and he had brought Acca too.

Coifi was glad to see him coming and happier to see him alive. He had not realized, until the parting that had been forced on them the night before, how much he had come to rely upon the scop's presence and his spirit. Seeing him approach, however uncertainly he balanced upon the mule, brought unexpected lightness to his heart.

The walls of the stronghold were lined with men, but as they marched out to the tents and shelters, Coifi realized the mistake Eanfrith had made by ordering his warriors to keep watch on the proceedings: his forces were on display and Cadwallon, approaching on horseback, could not fail to count them. But with the stronghold at Bamburgh, it barely mattered how many men there were: a handful could hold the castle against an army. But to take and hold a kingdom... That was a different matter. That needed men, and there were precious few on display at Bamburgh. Coifi shook his head. Cadwallon would drive an even harder bargain now.

Cadwallon and his companions reached the tents first, dismounting and picketing the beasts on the beach, bridles loosely tied to posts. Coifi knew that Eanfrith would rather have been there to receive Cadwallon, but custom dictated that when two kings met, the senior should greet the junior, rising from his seat to welcome him, but then being again the first to sit. Coifi saw Eanfrith whispering to his warmaster Drest as they approached the cluster of tents. Beneath their feet, the sand was hard packed, ridged and dark. If the negotiations were not over within six hours, the kings would find the sea lapping around their ankles. Coifi smiled. However great his power, a king could no more turn back a tide than he could turn back wyrd.

Wyrd.

Coifi heard the word, deep in his spirit, the weaving of the fate singers, the will of the gods, the workings of forces and powers he did not even know the names for, and the unfoldings of the human heart. And as he heard it, he fell into it: wyrd engulfed him, swallowed him into vision in a way that had not happened for many years – not since he had sat beside Mul and learned from him to fly in vision and walk in dream. The priest's eyes rolled black into white, his limbs collapsed as if the threads holding them were all cut at once, and he fell upon the dark sand. Drest, ever alert to unexpected movements, poked Eanfrith and pointed.

"Leave him," Eanfrith said.

Drest nodded agreement. "I will see to him when we return." He would not lose a man to look after the priest.

But the Britons, dismounting by the tents, had also noticed Coifi's collapse.

"Your friend is ill." Cadwallon pointed Acca's gaze to where Coifi writhed upon the sand, in the grip of his vision.

Acca started towards the priest, then stopped and looked back, but Cadwallon waved him on.

"Go to him." The king looked straight at Acca. "It were best that you remained with him. Do you understand?"

The scop swallowed. He stole a glance towards Eanfrith and his men, nearly come to the meeting, then back to Cadwallon. The king of Gwynedd stared at him, and he quailed under his black eyes.

"Go," said Cadwallon.

Acca scurried across the sand towards Coifi. His path took him past Eanfrith and his men, but they ignored him, intent upon the men of Gwynedd who had formed in welcome around the tent of meeting.

When he came to him, Acca found Coifi lying still upon his back, face upturned, unseeing, to the sky, and drool leaking from his mouth and trickling down his chin.

The scop chafed his hands, bending low over the priest.

"Coifi," he called. "Coifi, can you hear me?"

The priest's eyes rolled back. "Acca?" The priest's voice was distant, as if it came from beneath a great lake.

"Yes, yes Coifi, it is me."

"Has it happened yet?"

"Has what happened?"

"Eanfrith."

"What about Eanfrith?"

"Has Cadwallon killed him?"

Acca sat back on his haunches. He stole a glance towards the tent. Most of the men had disappeared within, but others remained outside, in mutual, silent, suspicious guard. There was no sign of anything untoward.

"Yes," said Acca.

"Oh." Coifi reached up for Acca's arm. "I – I saw. Wyrd showed me. I should have warned him."

"It would not have done any good," said Acca, stealing another look towards the tents. "Eanfrith would not have listened to you."

"I could have tried..."

As the priest spoke, the tent suddenly boiled. Acca saw men spilling from it, some clutching wounds as they fell to the ground, others falling upon the men outside. It was over in little more time than it had taken Coifi to speak, and with barely a cry. Only when the defeated men lay scattered over the sand, some dead, some dying, did any great sound reach Acca: the cries of the wounded, cut off suddenly as men, moving among them with knives, finished them off. Acca watched, waiting to see who would emerge from the tent. He knew – of course he knew – but he had to see.

Cadwallon pulled the flap of the tent open and walked out. In his right hand he held Eanfrith's head, his eyes still wide with the surprise of his death. From across the sand there came the moan and wail of the men watching from Bamburgh, seeing their lord killed almost before their eyes. Mounting his horse, Cadwallon rode towards the castle, still holding Eanfrith's head. He rode alone and unafraid, and none emerged from the gate to meet him, although many men waited there to come to their lord's aid. But now Eanfrith was beyond aid, and fear filled the hearts of his men.

Cadwallon pulled his horse to a stop beneath the stronghold.

"Your king!" He held Eanfrith's head up. "That was his mistake. I am your king! I and no other, and I will suffer no one to rule alongside me. When you crawl away from this rock, back to the places which spawned you, tell your peoples this: Cadwallon is High King of Britain."

The High King pulled his horse's head back, and it reared, kicking against the air. From the rock, the men watched in silence. Although many held spears, none thought to throw them, nor the few bowmen to loose their arrows, and Cadwallon urged his horse back across the wide sands to where his men waited, surrounded by the corpses of Eanfrith's men. But before he reached them he stopped beside Acca and Coifi.

"You brought Eanfrith to me as I asked, so you will live." Cadwallon circled around them, his horse excited and snorting at the smell of blood, pawing the sand. "Live, and think on this: I have killed the æthelings of Northumbria. When I have killed Oswald, all will see there is no strength left in the Idings, and then I will drive the Saxons into the sea and take back our lost land." Cadwallon laughed. "It was so easy – Eanfrith truly believed I wanted him to be king under me! He was still talking of how much he would pay in tribute when I slid my knife between his ribs – I feared he would keep talking, but that at least silenced him, and of his men only the warmaster fought. So I thank you again. You have served me well, though you did not know so."

Cadwallon and his men rode off across the sand, heading south along the broad path left by the low tide. The priest and the scop watched them go.

"When I asked, Eanfrith was not dead, was he?" Coifi asked.

Acca did not look at the priest. "You told me once that the fate singers will not change their weaving, neither for men nor for gods. It would have made no difference."

Coifi watched the riders diminish into the distance.

"I had worried the tide might return and catch the kings as they talked. It has bare turned and Eanfrith is dead." He turned to Acca. "I saw wyrd. It spoke to me as it has not spoken these many years, since I sat at the feet of Mul and learned to dream-walk and spirit-fly. Wyrd spoke to me, and I lay witless upon the ground and Eanfrith died." The priest shook his head. "I asked the gods to hear me, but for what end? The ætheling is dead and Cadwallon has all Northumbria under his sword. Would that they had never spoken, and we might have died alongside Eanfrith, rather than be left, lordless men once more, to wander as wraiths upon this middle-earth."

"I would not have died," said Acca. "Not for Eanfrith." He shook his head. "He had not the wit of his father, nor the courage of his mother, but was as a man led by fears and the counsel of others.

Without Drest by his side, he would not even have taken Bamburgh, though there was none there to hold it against him. Did you not see how few men he had? Few indeed must have gone with him into exile, and fewer followed when he returned. Such a man could not be king long, and we did well not to die alongside him, for he had not given us rings to make us his men; all we had from him was the hospitality of a night, and that is owed to any visitor." Acca turned to Coifi. "Besides, there is one more, and him I remember from when he was a boy: bright, brave and a lover of my songs. Oswald is ætheling too, and now surely he will return."

"He would be foolish to come now, when Cadwallon can turn all his army against him. For many will hear of Cadwallon's victory, and young men, hungry for gold and glory, will flock to him. I fear that Oswald, should he come, will meet a fate no different from that of Osric and Eanfrith."

"Do you see that, or do you fear it?"

Coifi shook his head. "Everything has become as it was: unclear, as on an autumn day when the sea mist rises. But I fear it, Acca. Oh, I fear it."

Chapter 9

"What should I do, Aidan? What should I do?"

Oswald had sought out his friend, as he cured the stinking hides of cows for the scriptorium, and told him the news: Eanfrith was dead, and Cadwallon ravaged Northumbria, driving thegns from hall and land, and leaving those dead who would not flee.

Aidan scrubbed his arms in a bucket of seawater. The warmth of summer was past now, and some trees were tinged with the colours of autumn, but a memory of warmth lingered yet in the sea, lessening its normal chill. Washing gave him time to think as Oswald paced up and down, telling him what had happened.

"What should I do?"

Brother Aidan straightened, and brushed the water from his forearms.

"First, before you do anything else, we should pray for Eanfrith, your half-brother."

Oswald stopped his pacing as if suddenly stricken. "Of course. I am sorry – I gave him no thought, although he is dead. But," and here Oswald looked to his friend, "I have not heard that Eanfrith was ever baptized, for he took refuge with his mother's people when Edwin killed our father, and the Picts are, for the most part, pagan still. *Can* we pray for him?"

"We can pray for everybody," said Aidan. "There is a tale, of when Patrick first came among my people, telling them of the life that awaited them should they open their hearts to it. For when Patrick stood before the people then, the king and all his household gathered around the heights of Tara, they put this question to him: what of our fathers, and our fathers' fathers? For if we adopt this new life and this new god, what will become of them? May they enter into this new life, although they be already dead and without benefit of the baptism you offer us? For if they cannot come where we go, then we will not enter in without them, for we are their sons and they are our fathers, and it would not be meet that we separate ourselves from them. And then Patrick, the holy apostle, spoke to the assembly of the people and the kings of the land, and he told them that he would open the gates of heaven to our fathers and our fathers' fathers, for the sake of those hearing him, and for their children and their children's children." Aidan turned to Oswald. "So we can pray for Eanfrith, your brother."

The two men knelt on the rocks by the sea, and the waves joined their rhythm to the ancient words of commendation, as Aidan and Oswald asked God to receive Eanfrith into his halls.

Aidan got to his feet and held out his hand. "Let us walk. And walking will remove us from the stink here." Oswald got up and the two men walked along the shore, leaving the tannery behind.

"There are times," said Oswald, "when I have wanted to speak to you, but the smell has driven me away before I could find or call you."

"A monk should work undisturbed, but I am sorry to have not heard your call."

"Why do you do this?"

"The abbot has asked me. And if not me, who? I have no other skills, whereas the other brothers can all contribute to the monastery, whether it be by writing or cooking or carpentry." Aidan smiled. "My greatest talent is my lack of a sense of smell. There have been times when I have returned, believing I have washed the stink from arms and clothes, only to see the brothers flinch from me. I have heard that some suspect I do this deliberately, to persuade the abbot to ask some other brother to take over this task, but the truth is I think I have cleaned myself, and I smell nothing unusual." Aidan looked at Oswald. "How do I smell now?"

"A little ripe," said Oswald.

"Oh, no. I thought I had cleaned all the smell away. I should go back and wash myself properly."

"Would you wait until after we have spoken?"

"Can you speak to one who smells as I do?"

Oswald smiled. "Yes, Brother Aidan, I can; for a few minutes in your company and I no longer notice the smell, but only my delight in your company. Now, you have not answered my question: what should I do? My heart tells me that God wants me to put away the sword and enter this monastery, where I have found a peace and fellowship I have known nowhere else, but now I have received news of Eanfrith's death. I had told my brother I would not return to Northumbria as long as he lived, for I would not fight Eanfrith for the throne. But now he is dead, and Oswiu came to me and laid my sword, that I had given into his keeping, on my lap.

"'There is no one else,' he told me. 'No one else men will follow. You are ætheling of Northumbria, king of Bernicia by right of our father, king of Deira through our mother. All the thegns that yet live will follow you and fight for you, and they must, or Cadwallon will cast them from their halls and from their land. For what he has done to Eanfrith proves he fights not as other kings fight, for glory and gold and to spread his rule through subjecting other kings to his mastership. No, Cadwallon fights to drive our people from the land and back into the sea; he fights to reclaim the land our father and our father's fathers took and made their own. There is no one left to do our fighting for us but you, brother. Will you lead us?'

"That is what my brother told me when we received the news, and then he left me, and I came to seek you out." Oswald walked across the machair alongside the monk. "What should I do, Aidan?"

The words of Abbot Ségéne returned to the monk. The abbot was a holy and subtle man, but Aidan knew well that his displeasure was not something to be incurred lightly. There had been one brother who had earned Ségéne's disfavour and he was banished from the community within a week, his head shaved to show he was a monk no longer.

But Oswald was his friend.

A shadow passed above them and Aidan raised his eyes to see Bran flying silently overhead.

"You know that the abbot will not accept you into the community if you bring Bran?"

"So he has told me." Oswald smiled. "I asked him to show where, in book or the traditions of the saints, it forbade a raven entry into a monastery, and he had to admit that this was nowhere the case. After all, even Father Noah took a raven with him upon the ark, and trusted him with first finding land after the Flood."

"But the raven didn't return."

"True, but Bran is his descendant, and God has sanctified all the creatures of the ark, marking them with his favour, for he saved them from the Flood. This is what I told the abbot, and he could not gainsay it."

"You said that to Abbot Ségéne?" asked Aidan, incredulous.

"Did I do wrong?"

"Not wrong, exactly. But I would rather die than go against Abbot Ségéne, so you had better get your sword ready, Oswald, for you will have to kill me after I have spoken what I have to tell you."

The monk stopped and Oswald too came to a halt. Brother Aidan sighed. "This is as like heaven as I believe anywhere to be on this earth. I would not leave it, so I can understand why you would join us. But the abbot has spoken to me, telling me to dissuade you from your wish. I think he wished me to speak as a friend, offering counsel, but I will speak in truth, telling what he told me, and then placing myself at his mercy. For Abbot Ségéne would not have you as a monk, Oswald, but rather he wants you to be king, that you might bring the word of eternal life to your people and thus win them to a hope that, with Edwin's death, lies in danger of being extinguished. That is what the abbot wishes; that is what he asked me to counsel you. I have spoken straight, not using false words to hide my meaning, as men do before kings, so that you may know the truth of things and make your decision."

The monk looked at the young prince standing before him. "What will you do, Oswald?"

The ætheling made no answer for many minutes, but thoughts rolled behind his eyes, and his face moved as with a great struggle.

Then he turned to Brother Aidan. "I will go before God and ask him, that he may decide. I will go on the green pilgrimage, into the desert of the sea, and seek his answer there."

"The abbot will not want you to do that," said Brother Aidan, "for many make no return from the green pilgrimage, and he would deem it a waste to lose you thus: neither king nor monk, but drowned among the waves."

"Nevertheless, it is what I will do, for I must know what God wills, or whether he would take me from this life and raise up another to deliver Northumbria from Cadwallon. You have a boat?"

"It is a little thing, a coracle, good for bays and inlets but not the open sea."

"It will suffice. I seek an answer, not an exile. Come, take me to your boat."

Brother Aidan stared into Oswald's face and saw there a light such that he had only seen in a few men before; he would not be gainsaid by any power of the earth and few indeed of the heavens.

The two men walked in silence back to the inlet where Aidan worked the monastery's tannery. The monk lifted the coracle from where he had stowed it upon the rocks and dropped it into the sea, where it bobbed light and high, riding like a duck.

"You are certain of this?"

"Yes."

"I will wait for you here."

Oswald stepped lightly into the coracle, settling himself into it and taking the paddle.

"Give me your blessing, Brother Aidan," he said.

"I give it you. I give it right gladly," said the young monk. He watched, not moving, as the young prince paddled out of the inlet and onto the wave-ridged waters of the Sound of Iona. He watched as the coracle bobbed out of sight behind the headland, and for once he took heart from the dark shape that followed it: Bran would not leave his master, even when he took to the waves.

Brother Aidan did not move for many hours, but prayed, his lips moving and the mumble of prayer as constant as the breaking of the waves. The hours of the Office, the Great Work of the monks of the island, came and went, and he knew he should be attending to the work, but he remained where he was. In part, this was for fear of what the abbot might say should he ask where Oswald was and Aidan, bound by obedience, would have to tell him; but the greater reason was the conviction, deep in his soul, that it was the rope of constant, unceasing prayer that held Oswald to this life, and if he should cease, then God would take Oswald as he ventured out upon the green pilgrimage, and not return him.

Oswald, Iding, ætheling of Northumbria, would-be postulant monk, paddled the coracle north up the Sound, the light vessel skimming over the water. Bran flew above him, croaking, then swooped down and settled to bad-tempered grooming of his feathers while clutching the side of the coracle. Every so often a wave would break upon the side of the coracle and sprinkle the raven with salt water, whereupon he would begin his grooming again, but only after a black-eyed stare at Oswald.

"I know you would not be here," Oswald said to the bird, "but I will not ask you to leave." He dipped the paddle into the green water, shallow above submerged rocks, pushing the coracle out into the deeper water of the Sound. "I will be glad of company, I think."

That he held a paddle at all worried Oswald. Many monks set out on the green pilgrimage without paddle or sail, trusting in God to take them where he would, and accepting that that might be beneath the waves and not over them. However, those monks were dealing solely with eternal matters and the salvation of souls; by the very fact of going out on the green pilgrimage they had left all temporal matters behind. But for him it was different.

"When I heard of Eanfrith's death, it was as if some enemy had made me slave – I felt the chains fall upon my heart and my limbs." Oswald spoke as he paddled, and Bran the raven listened, his glittering black eyes unblinking. "That was why I came to Brother Aidan to speak: for I had thought to escape the chains of my birth and to leave over the sword, the stink of blood and the screams of men, for the Great Work of the monks and the peace of Iona."

The raven croaked and Oswald laughed.

"Yes, I know you think me foolish, a wide-eyed boy transfixed by what he has seen, as a lad is when he sees a warrior, shining in battle array, for the first time. I know they are men, with men's faults; I have heard gossip and rumour, seen anger lay plans for vengeance behind honeyed words, and lust stoked in imagining."

Bran bobbed his head, as if agreeing with Oswald's assessment.

"But I have also heard the Great Work, raising prayer to heaven; and books written and made to carry wisdom and beauty to the future; I have seen saints, Bran, walk in the form of men. That is what I would be part of, an unworthy part no doubt, but I can see nothing better for my soul."

The coracle was emerging from the Sound and here the waters grew choppy as the Atlantic swell split upon the islands of Iona and its far greater parent, Mull. Oswald steered the vessel west. He had in mind the two small islands that lay in the ocean west of Iona, the haunts of seabirds and seals. Only rarely did the men of Mull or the surrounding islands visit, and that was when the birds nested, to harvest eggs. Now, the breeding season was past, and the islands would be quiet. He might land there, and think and pray.

Bran was finding the swell of the open sea not much to his liking. He side-footed his way around the edge of the coracle until he stood behind Oswald, using him as a shield against the spray that broke more regularly now over the boat. For his part, the young prince felt the cold of water and wind settling into his bones. He had not thought to fetch the waxed cloak and hood that men wore when on the sea, and his own clothes were wet and clung to him. The fierce joy of escape that had settled over him as he took the coracle and paddled away was beginning to ebb, leaving the cold of the open sea.

If God took him, it would be a cold death.

Living amid the islands and seaways of Dal Riada, Oswald had seen many bodies taken from the sea. Even the most sunburned of men emerged from the water pale, as if the sea had washed their souls clean as it took their lives. He hoped it would wash him clean too.

Bran croaked. Oswald awoke from the stupor of coldness and saw what the raven warned of. In the west, the black and rolling face of a storm approached, rising over the sea. Oswald looked back. He was far from Iona, in the middle of the passage to the islands. The sea, already disturbed by the approaching squall, began to whip up around the small boat, flecks of foam curling off wave tops. He looked ahead, to where the long whaleback of Rèidh Eilean and the hump of Stac Mhic Mhurchaidh broke up the advancing waves; he might possibly be able to land on Rèidh Eilean; with the sea running high and rising, any landing on the steep sides of Stac Mhic Mhurchaidh was impossible. But the storm was coming fast, the line of rain moving across the ocean towards him and preceded by an advance guard of squally, gusty winds; Oswald measured distance and time against his own ability to paddle into the teeth of the approaching wind: there was no landfall there. His only chance was to fly before the storm and let it drive him on, using the lightness of the coracle and its ability to ride lightly over the waves to escape the green martyrdom.

Digging the paddle hard into the water, Oswald began to propel the coracle back towards Iona, while Bran croaked and, seeing where they were heading, took to the air, riding the gusty winds with ease. Looking up at him, Oswald laughed with a wild, free delight, the joy that sometimes came on him in battle, when he knew death was very near and yet to laugh in its face was the simplest, most natural thing to do. Now too death approached; the Lord was about to put him to the test, and Oswald welcomed it.

"I have no wings," he yelled up as the raven swooped overhead, croaking its joy in the face of the oncoming storm, "but I am flying too!"

And in truth, he did seem to be flying as the coracle swooped and soared on the backs of the waves, riding high over the tops, plunging low into the depths, where green hills of water surrounded him and only the glimpse of Bran above told of a world that was not water.

Oswald and the raven fled before the storm.

Brother Aidan, feeling the winds bite and pull at his habit as he prayed, knew that a squall was approaching. He looked to the west, at the dark skies there, then gathered his habit around his knees and rushed across the neck of land at the top of Iona to see if there was any sign of Oswald upon the sea. Standing on the machair, now exposed to the full force of the wind, the monk squinted out to sea.

There, bobbing up upon a wave crest, was it a coracle or a seabird, riding the ocean? The dark shape disappeared as quickly as a bird into a trough only to re-emerge as the wave swept in and, closer, he saw the motion of arms, driving a paddle through the water, and knew it for Oswald.

But the storm was behind him, a curtain of rain drawing forward across the sea, and Aidan knew all too well that the coracle would not ride out such weather. His lips moving in prayer, Aidan urged Oswald onwards. He could see the raven, circling above the coracle, but its calls were lost in the rising wind.

Focused as he was on the ætheling's approach over the sea, Aidan did not hear the approach by land until a hand touched his shoulder, and he all but squealed in shock.

"Brother Aidan, the abbot sent me to ask if you know where is the ætheling, Oswald." The novice, a boy bare old enough to scrape a few hairs from his chin, looked innocently at the monk. He, in his turn, had been so intent upon delivering his message from the abbot that he did not notice Aidan's surprise.

"Brother Aidan?"

The monk raised his hand and pointed out to sea. The novice, a boy raised as much on sea as he had been on land, for his folk were island people, followed Aidan's direction and saw the coracle, and the storm chasing it, and without a word he gathered his patched robes around his knees and ran back to the abbot. He understood all too well what he was seeing.

Aidan remained where he was, the wind lashing his shaven scalp and whipping the hair that hung from his crown down his neck. His prayers increased in pace as the race drew nearer, the words skipping from his tongue but as swiftly pulled away by the wind.

Through his prayers tumbled images: the Lord calming the waters, the still voice after the storm. And through the running words came the thought, unbidden but irresistible: *Will you not calm these waters, Lord, that your servant might live?* But the storm advanced faster than the coracle, drawing closer to it, and unless the wind changed, there seemed no chance that Oswald could out-run it.

"Where is he?"

Brother Aidan, despite his prayers, had no difficulty in hearing these words, for they were uttered by a man accustomed to being heard. The abbot had come himself, keeping pace with the young novice, and Aidan again pointed out to sea, and Abbot Ségéne turned his eyes to see the storm close down upon the coracle as night falls upon the land.

The abbot's shoulders slumped. "We are too late," he said. He looked at Brother Aidan. "You knew?"

The monk nodded. He could not speak.

"We will speak on this later. It makes no odds now." The abbot drew his hood over his head as the first squalls of rain reached them. "Come."

Brother Aidan made no move. He could not speak.

"You wish to remain here for a while?" asked the abbot.

The monk's answer was his silence.

The abbot nodded. "I cannot find it in my heart to care where you are now," he said. "Why did you not stop him?" He chopped his hand down. "Do not answer. Stay here. Watch for him. Bring me his body when – if – it comes to shore. We will bury Oswald at least."

Without further glance, Abbot Ségéne, with the young novice trotting behind, made his way back along the track towards the monastery. The rain came, and blotted them from sight. Aidan remained where he was, staring blindly out to sea, his lips moving in the silent prayer that they had not ceased uttering, even when the abbot berated him.

The wool of his habit could no longer shed the water falling upon it, but Aidan barely felt the water trickling down his body. Indeed, he barely felt his body at all; he was reduced to a single prayer: *Lord, let him live. Lord, let him live.* The squall – one of the short, fierce Atlantic storms that, once passed, left the day washed sea blue – began to lessen, for he was able to see more than a few feet in front of his face. What he saw, though, offered no comfort, for the sea churned in a chaos of froth, stirred by the competing winds that swirled within and around the squall. In truth, Aidan was no longer searching for the coracle but for a corpse, arms outstretched in the characteristic position of the drowned, as if the body was embracing the sea that had taken its life.

The croak was the first thing he heard, the raven's croak, and Aidan spun around, searching for it, then saw Bran overhead, wings spread then angled downwards as it landed near him. The bird lowered its head and croaked again.

"Where is he? You know, don't you? Where is he?"

Bran croaked once more, lowering his head and pointing, and then, as if losing patience with the short-sightedness of the earthbound, he took wing again, pushing up through the last of the rain and out over the headland, over the spray of waves breaking on the isle's northern reach.

Aidan followed the bird with his sight – *Lord, let him live. Lord, let him live* – watching the dark shape flap firmly onwards until it reached a point not far from shore, where it began to circle.

And there, amid the slowly settling wave spume, Aidan saw the dark circle of the coracle, still afloat upon the water. But the monk could see no man shape moving within the coracle, wielding paddle; only the boat itself and the raven above, circling, croaking its call.

The monk did not hesitate. Taking off his habit, he dived into the sea. It was late summer and the season had been warm. The sea did not strip the heat from his body immediately, as it would in winter, but even as he tried to swim out to the coracle through the churn around the isle, he could feel the strength being pulled from his body. He would not have long in the water before strength failed him and he embraced the sea in his dying.

Aidan was an island boy – he had learned to swim near as soon as he had learned to walk. But most of his swimming had been confined to sheltered bays, to striking out for islets and their haul of birds' eggs, not to breaching the remnants of an Atlantic squall. He felt as if he had been in the water forever, but glancing back, the isle seemed barely further away than when he had first plunged into the sea. However, even if he was making little progress towards the coracle, it was spinning towards him, swooping up and down the waves as easily as a sea duck. The coracle span towards him, then dipped away as the waves parted them, and Aidan struck towards it again. But the receding water pulled it back, before a fresh wave sent the coracle scudding past him, and this time the monk saw it scud through the line of breaking waves into one of the little coves of the isle. Making a final effort, Brother Aidan turned back to land and struck out, adding his own strength to the waves attempting to push themselves up the beach.

So it was that almost together monk and coracle landed upon the Holy Isle, Brother Aidan crawling up onto the narrow beach, the boat rubbing over the sand and finally settling.

Bran landed upon the sand and croaked, lowering his body and pointing his beak at the coracle.

Aidan scrambled to his feet and rushed to the boat.

But as he did so, a face appeared above the rim of the coracle. Brother Aidan slowed and then stopped.

Oswald turned his face to the monk and it was the face of one who has seen death and yet lives: pale and bedraggled, his skin as white as those who had given their lives into the ocean's embrace, yet a slow fire burned in his eyes.

"You are alive?" Aidan asked. Even as he spoke them the words seemed fatuous, yet until he heard Oswald speak, he would not know if what he saw was a man truly living or a wraith returned from the sea.

"I – I do not know," said Oswald, and his voice sounded as from one far away, although in truth he was but a few feet from the monk. "I had thought I must die, but now…" He stared at Aidan, as if only just remembering him. "But now, unless this be heaven, and it seems too wet for that, and you be Peter, a Peter who bears the appearance of my friend Aidan, then I must be living, and the Lord has given me his answer."

"I am not Peter," said Aidan.

"Then I am Oswald, Iding, son of Æthelfrith, nephew to Edwin, by my blood ætheling to Bernicia and to Deira, and I will return to Northumbria to claim my throne."

Chapter 10

"I should make you clean out the pigs for the next five years!" Abbot Ségéne could scarce keep the smile from his face, try as he might.

Brother Aidan hung his head, but that was as much to keep his own smile from showing too obviously as to hide his shame.

For his part, Oswiu, who had been called from his station at the isle's landing place with the news that his brother had been lost at sea, only to find him again, dripping but definitely alive, remained unusually silent. When word had reached him, he had felt the world lurch beneath him, as if the very earth beneath his feet was breaking. But piercing through the shock, there was also a thread of triumph, that now he would no longer be measured against his brother and found wanting. Both feelings clashed, then were washed away with relief when they found Oswald alive.

"For the next ten years!" said the abbot.

"Then I shall clean them out with him, for it was my doing that I took boat for the green pilgrimage, not his." Oswald was making no effort to keep the smile from his own face.

"I expect you to be giving out gold rings for the next ten years, not swilling pigs," said the abbot.

"And then?" asked Oswald. "Ten years is long to reign – few kings do."

Abbot Ségéne clapped him on the shoulder. "Let us concern ourselves with what will happen when you return to Northumbria rather than the events of ten years' time: '*nolite ergo solliciti esse in crastinum. Crastinus enim dies sollicitus erit sibi ipsi: sufficit diei malitia sua.*'"

The ætheling looked at him blankly.

The abbot shook his head. "If we had had longer, I would have had you speaking Latin. 'Take therefore no thought for the morrow:

for the morrow shall take thought for the things of itself. Sufficient unto the day is the evil thereof.'"

Oswald nodded. At those words, he saw himself thrashing against the restraining arms of his father's retainer as, across upon the far shore of the River Idle, King Rædwald of East Anglia, with Edwin at his side, slowly killed his father.

"But now that you have decided – and, my son, I truly believe that the decision is wise and one blessed by God – we must decide what to do. You will need men, horses, weapons, supplies, ships, passage from the kings through whose lands you will travel…"

Oswald held up his hand. "No, Father Abbot. What I need more than all these is speed. The campaigning season draws to its close, and we have not even begun our preparations; therefore no rumour can possibly have reached Cadwallon of what we plan to do. We must act now, before the turning of this year, before word can reach him and before he can prepare his men. I must come upon him as the storm came upon me at sea: unprepared and alone." The young ætheling smiled. "When I went upon the green pilgrimage, I hoped that God would give answer to the question in my heart; not only did he do that, but he gave me my strategy too."

"But you will need *some* men," said the abbot. "Cadwallon is scarce like to give up the throne to you on your own. And even if you should find him unprepared, you will not find him alone."

"I will send my brother to Dal Riada to bring from there those of our old retainers who now serve the king, and whatever other men would follow me on this venture. There will like be some. I had thought to ask the Uí Neíll, for they have many young men eager for battle and gold, but Oswiu's, er, friendship with Fina of the Uí Neíll precludes that." Oswald shrugged. "It will be enough. God wills it."

The abbot held up his hand. "In my experience, it is unwise to state too strongly that God wills what you want, for our hearts are dense and our desires dark; the evil one ever seeks to bend them to his ends."

But Oswald shook his head. "Father Abbot, I went out upon the green pilgrimage and the storm took me and I was as one dead.

But God brought me from the storm; he brought me back from the dead. He wills that I should return and save my people." There was no doubt in the ætheling's voice, and those hearing him believed.

"It may be as you say," said Abbot Ségéne, "yet nevertheless, God requires us to act too when he wills something: you will seek as many men to accompany you as possible?"

"Of course," said Oswald. "But we will not require many, for by accomplishing this with few, we will bring greater glory to God's name, and spread his fame through all the land, that my people, and the people of the other kingdoms of the Angles and the Saxons, will know him. But that I will leave to my brother; Oswiu will gather those men who will follow us. For my part, I must seek the blessing of our mother."

"Can't I come too to see Mother?" asked Oswiu.

Oswald looked at him. "If this was an ordinary warband, where we fail or triumph according to the strength of our arms and the chance of the day, then of course you would need to go to Mother to seek her blessing and to bid her farewell, lest the warband fail. But this is no ordinary war party. We will not fail, but my heart tells me that speed is our greatest weapon. You must prepare the men, while I prepare our mother." He smiled at his younger brother and took hold of his shoulders, so that all Oswiu's doubts melted in the radiance of his regard. "Will you do that for me, brother?"

Oswiu shrugged. "Don't I always?"

"I would ask you to return here from visiting your mother on Coll, Oswald," said the abbot. "Before you go on to Dal Riada I will have gifts of my own for your – for our – venture."

"I would wish Oswiu to bring the men he gathers here first anyway," said Oswald. "We should depart upon this venture from this Holy Island."

"I will go as soon as I find a boat to take me," said Oswiu.

Oswald pointed to where the coracle lay, bottom up, upon the beach. "I already have a boat to take me," he said.

"No, no, no!" The abbot held up his hand. "You have near broken my heart once today. You will not do so again. I will send a curragh for you, a vessel fit for the sea, not this eggshell you set out upon the green pilgrimage in."

"I jest," Oswald shuddered. "I would no more set out again upon the ocean in that coracle than I would go against your will, Father Abbot."

Abbot Ségéne rolled his eyes. "If that is supposed to give me surety, it doesn't. It seems to me you have done little else than go against my will in all the years you have lived on the saint's island."

"Now *you* jest, surely. I have always sought to follow your counsel; it is only that there were times when God's will was not yours, Father Abbot."

Aidan stifled a gasp. For him and the brothers, Abbot Ségéne knew God's heart as intimately as a mother knows her son. Oswiu, for his part, covered a smile, for he had spent much of his time upon the Holy Isle evading Ségéne's will, and he could scarce help but enjoy his brother's discomfiting of the abbot.

A dark shadow passed over the men and they looked up to see the raven circling. Seeing them, the bird croaked its greeting. Oswald held out his arm and the raven settled upon the machair, bouncing to a stop upon the springy turf before high-stepping towards the ætheling, who bent down so that Bran might claw his way up his arm and sit upon his shoulder. With talons dug firmly into Oswald's cloak, Bran dipped his head and croaked again, black eyes fixing each man in the watching ring.

"At least," said Abbot Ségéne, "I will be rid of that benighted bird!"

Bran turned his head to the abbot, his black eyes cold.

"I sometimes think he understands what I say," said the abbot.

"He does," said Oswald.

"Very well: then listen to this, unfaithful cargo of Noah. Keep watch upon Oswald. Fly high and bring him warning of enemies, speak to the wind and the sun, talk to the mountains and the marshes; be his eyes and search far. Do this and I will call you blessed among God's creatures and a worthy cargo of the ark. What say you, raven?"

The bird regarded the abbot with its black eyes, then dipped its head and croaked out its reply, to the amazed laughter of the men.

"It truly does understand what I say," said Abbot Ségéne.

"Yes," said Oswald, "he does."

*

"Mother."

Oswald took Acha's hands in his own. She had seen the curragh coming, racing across the sea road, blown by a steady, following wind, and Æbbe, her eyes keen, had seen the dark circling shadow above the boat and known that Bran flew above the curragh, so her brother sailed upon it. They had laid hands alongside the family slaves, pulling the long table out upon the machair in front of the white house to take advantage of the warm, late season weather, and each had set to with baking and cooking, so that Oswald arrived to delicious smells.

"Oswald." Mother embraced son, then held him away from her, so that she could see his face more clearly and again fix it in memory. Each time she saw him, he had changed: and now her searching eyes saw that the lines of uncertainty that had marked his face before were gone.

"It is my turn," said Æbbe, stepping beside Acha. Oswald reached out to her, and sister and brother held each other, while Acha took in the sight of them, her two eldest children, hale and whole and grown. She had buried three others in the years between these two and Oswiu, two girls and a boy, and she held their memory tightest of all, for she knew that she alone in this middle-earth remembered them. She had buried them in the days when she still followed the old gods, wrapping their little bodies in the finest cloth, giving to the grave richly jewelled spoons and brooches, but taking from it, as the earth closed over them, no hope. For only warriors, heroes slain in battle, were taken to Woden's hall to feast and fight alongside him through the ages until, with the gods, they would face the monsters of the encircling darkness, and fall to them in the final death. For the newborn and the child, for the woman taken in birthing and the crone withered with age, there were only shadows, drawing down towards the dark until they fell away into silence.

Such was the belief of her fathers and her mothers, and Acha accepted it with dumb grief as she had buried, one after the other, her babies who had died young. But fleeing the death of her husband and the vengeance of her brother, Acha had taken her children for refuge among the islands, and there learned a hope she had not known: life, life for all, babe and greybeard, warrior and woman, king and slave. And in hearing, Acha knew it for the answer to a hope she had not known she had cleaved to, even as she buried her three lost children. In her heart, in her soul, she commended them to hope. Acha held them among the saved, for from each she had kept a part, hair or nail, and this she blessed and, apart from priests and monks and any man, these she baptized.

"You have not brought your brother?" Acha asked.

Oswald shook his head. "I ask your pardon, Mother, but we have need of speed, and I sent him to gather men to our cause." The ætheling let go of his sister, and abruptly knelt before Acha. "I ask your blessing. I ask your blessing as queen of Bernicia, as queen of Deira, of the house of Yffing, married to the Idings, bridge between two kingdoms, widow, mother."

Acha looked down at her son. Although he knelt, his face was upturned to her, and the sun caught it, as so often it seemed to catch Oswald's face. In truth, the lines of uncertainty had gone from his skin and his eyes were clear of the doubt she had seen before, when they had come together to debate what to do after Edwin's death.

"What have you seen to make you so sure?" she asked.

"I – I went on the green pilgrimage, and God, in storm and wind and land beyond hope, showed me what I must do. Though I wished for the peace of the Holy Isle, God has called me to take the sword in defence of our people and to claim the throne in his name." The young man smiled, but tears glittered in his eyes. "I would have been more happy than I can say to be Brother Oswald, a monk of the Holy Isle, but I will be Oswald *Lamnguin* once again, the Whiteblade, and go to seek my throne."

Acha took his face in her hands. "Are you certain of this?" She looked into his eyes, and looked away. Her breath caught in her throat and her heart lurched, for fear tugged at her bowels: the mother fear, too often realized, of laying her child into the earth's long embrace.

"I am certain," said Oswald. She knew he spoke truly, but still she could not bring her gaze back to his face. Letting go, she turned her back upon her son and gazed out over the sea. Tiree lay close to the south-west, a short pull across the Sound. North-west, barely visible, were the first of the Outer Hebrides: Sandray, Vatersay, Barra. And then sea. Rolling, grey, green, blue. But even the sea, first and masterless, had quietened at the command of her heart Lord. If he had chosen Oswald, she could not hold him back for mother fear.

Acha turned back to her son, still kneeling upon the machair. Oswald, seeing her framed with the sun, saw her as the queen, the queen twice over, that she was: tall and fierce and dark. She seized his face between her hands and turned it up to her.

"You will live; you will take the throne and cast down your enemies and the enemies of our people; you will fill their mouths with dust and the throne that is yours will be yours, my son, my son. My son." Then, placing her hands upon his head, Acha breathed her blessing upon him.

Oswald rose. "Will you come to me? Mother, after I have taken the throne and an Iding rules once more in Bernicia and an Yffing in Deira, will you come to me, and Æbbe too, and make your home again in the east lands, between the mountains and the sea? I would give land to you, Æbbe, good land to hold, that you might make a holy house and hold the kingdom in your prayers, that we might live. And you, Mother, you could remain with Æbbe if that is your wish, or you could stay with me, queen once more."

Acha brushed a strand of hair back beneath her scarf. "Ah, after all these years, you still take me by surprise, Oswald. I had not thought to be asked that and now I do not know what to say." She shook her head in thought. "A king must needs wed: for children, for young æthelings to tumble their rivalry in the sun and for maidens to marry the æthelings of other kings. It would not do to have such as me, your mother, about you when you wed. Nor would I ask our slaves, who followed us into exile when I offered them their freedom, to move once more when they have made new families here, and children. Besides, I have lived many years here, within sight of the Holy Isle, and I have grown used to seeing the sun lay the red road of its setting upon the sea. This is where I had thought to die and be lain to rest, and I am content that that should be so."

"Give them again the choice they made when we fled: freedom to stay, or go. For love of you, they followed you into exile; let them choose once more. But Mother, come when I call and I will make for you a new Holy Island. Abbot Ségéne has promised to send me a bishop and monks when I win the throne, and I will give over to them the island that is not; the place which takes pilgrims dry-shod then sets them back to shore." Oswald smiled as he saw his mother grasp his riddle.

"Lindisfarne," Acha said.

"Yes, Lindisfarne," said Oswald. "A new Holy Island, daughter to the Blessed Colm Cille's house in Iona, an island and mainland, a place apart and yet part of the whole: what better home for the monks that the abbot has promised me! With them, Mother, my sister, we can tell the people, our people, the news of hope and bring them life." Oswald looked to his mother and saw she still hesitated. "Besides, you said you have grown used to watching the sun set? Come with me and watch the sun rise!"

Acha smoothed her hands down over the front of her dress. She looked to her daughter, who nodded her assent with bright face and ready eyes.

"Very well," Acha said. "Win the throne and we will come. But only win the throne first, my son, and in winning it, see to your brother, for he is rash and prone to anger, and if there was one thing I learned from your father of war, it is that killing is better done with cool head than hot heart. Now," said Acha, turning to where the table sat upon the machair in front of the house, "you will stay and eat with us…"

"Mother, I should ..."

"You will stay and eat with us," she continued, undeflected, moving to direct the slaves about their task. Oswald glanced at Æbbe, who smiled at him with the shared understanding of siblings.

"I think you're staying to eat with us," she said. "Besides, you have to give us a little time: we have to finish weaving your banner."

Oswald looked at her in surprise.

"Oh, yes," said Æbbe. "We have been weaving your banner this past two month. While the days were yet long we set to, weaving long into the white night, and even now, when the days grow shorter, we spend our time weaving."

Oswald glanced at Acha, busying herself with preparations around and about the table now. "Why, if she knew this would happen, did she hesitate to lay her blessing upon me?" he asked.

"Don't you know? We weaved against the weavers, brother. We sewed against the fate singers, and breathed our prayers into the thread. When the time comes for you to fly your banner upon the field, Oswald, know that our prayers lie within it and upon it."

*

Oswald, belly still full from the feasting of the day before, stepped back onto the strand of the Holy Isle. Although the wind, blowing keenly from the north-west, had served to clear his head on the voyage back from Coll, his legs felt heavy as he walked upon land again.

Bran, perched upon the curragh, opened a heavy eye, but when he saw that the boat was being pulled up above the tide line, he closed the eye again. Raven had eaten as well as man at the feast and, belly full, insisted upon riding Oswald's shoulder back to the boat, where he had climbed upon a bench, tucked head under wing, and promptly fallen asleep. Oswald, when he was not pulling an oar, had joined him in dozing, but land had forced the ætheling awake in a way that it had not wakened the bird.

Meeting Oswald, Brother Aidan pointed towards Bran. "I would swear that he is snoring," he said.

Oswald, squinting painfully against the sun, nodded. "He is," he said. He looked around at the few small curraghs ranged upon the beach. "I take it Oswiu has not returned yet?"

"Ah," said Aidan. "He has."

Oswald stopped and looked around. "But there are barely any new curraghs here, and those that are are small."

"That would be because he returned with barely any men. Maybe a dozen?"

"Twelve? Is that all?"

"No, not twelve." Oswiu straightened from where he had been inspecting the hull of an upturned curragh further up the strand, in company with a tall, wind-weathered man. "Fourteen. I counted."

"Fourteen." Oswald blew air through pursed lips. "I expected the Uí Néill to speak against men riding to our cause, but I did not think their enmity would lie so heavy against us, nor for it to stretch so far across sea. Even at Dunadd, stronghold of Dal Riada, you could not find more men to come with us?"

"Twins." Oswiu shrugged. "I heard while I was at Dunadd, putting our case to the Lord of the Isles, that Fina gave birth to twins. A boy and a girl." Oswiu could not help but grin at his elder brother. "How many children have you got?"

Oswald shook his head, partly in disgust, partly in discomfort. He was in his fourth decade now, old for a man still to be without child. But Oswald knew the ways of his people, and the ways of monks too. After his youth, when the desire to be a monk on the Holy Isle had first grown within him, he had abjured the early tumblings of his youth. Besides, that part of him which thought still upon thrones remembered that only children born after a king assumed the throne were considered truly throne-worthy by the witan: any children born to him beforehand would likely be overlooked in favour of younger siblings born once he had become king.

This was the way of his people, but tales and his own judgment told him that it was a path towards war, for an older prince would seldom stand aside for his junior, even if the younger had more claim by reason of being born while his father sat upon the throne.

The elder, through his years, would have made alliances and forged friendships against such chance, leaving the witan to plunge into recrimination and bloodshed.

Better not to risk raising any æthelings while his own fate remained unsure. But now that Oswald had given over the thought of being a monk of the Holy Isle, he would have to think on a wife and children. But not now, not yet. First, the throne.

"There was something else I heard at Dunadd." Oswiu moved closer to his brother. "A messenger, from Cadwallon, had recently left to return to his master. While I kicked my heels and waited upon the king, I learned that this messenger had spent many hours with the king. The messenger had come to tell the Lord of the Isles of Cadwallon's victory over Osric at York, and of his killing of Eanfrith at Bamburgh – although surely all the kingdoms of the north have heard tell of that already – and to announce to the Lord of the Isles that Cadwallon has proclaimed himself the answer to the prophecies that speak of a king of the Britons that will drive the Angles and the Saxons and the other sea-comers from these lands. Cadwallon has proclaimed himself Arthur, returned, and as such claims the allegiance and the men of Dal Riada and Rheged, of Strathclyde and the Gododdin."

Oswald breathed out slowly. "Will he receive it?"

"That I could not find out. At least, not for Dal Riada. The Lord of the Isles gave his answer to the messenger in private, and then the messenger rode forth, and none have yet learned what answer the Lord of the Isles gave. But at least he did not order me bound when I came asking for men to ride with us. But nor did he give me aid, and he forbade his men to join our cause. Those that I brought are all lordless men, Oswald, either abandoned for some fault of theirs or so faithless that they live when their lord has died." Oswiu grimaced. "I would not trust most of them in the hunt, let alone in battle, but they are all that would come."

"I had best see them. Where are they?"

"I had the monks build a shelter for them, away from the pilgrim accommodation. Looking at them, I thought it likely some pilgrims

would return rather poorer than they had come if the men were
billeted near them."

"If that's what they're like, we had better get moving quickly.
When would they be ready to go?"

Oswiu looked at his brother. "We're still going? You're not going
to give up?"

Oswald looked surprised. "No. Why should I?"

"I – with just fourteen men… I didn't think it would be enough."

"It won't be. But others will join us, and by the time we face
Cadwallon, there will be enough." Oswald grinned. "Besides, what
is the worst that could happen?"

"Er, we could die," said Oswiu.

Oswald's smile grew even broader. "Exactly," he said.

Oswiu shrugged. "If you say so." He led his brother from the
beach. "This way."

The men were indeed, as Oswiu had said, lordless, and in some
cases probably outlaws too. Oswald saw in their eyes and their
demeanour, the way they lay stretched out upon the ground or
squatted upon stools, the veiled violence of men who have dealt
death as much through the concealed knife as in the shieldwall;
they walked on either side of the line that separated warriors on the
battlefield from the scavengers that raided it afterwards, stripping
corpses and dispatching the wounded that they might be preyed
upon more easily. They were not the men he would have chosen
to accompany him back to Northumbria, but they were the men
he had.

"I am Oswald," he said. "Who here speaks for you?"

The men shifted, looking among themselves, until one finally
looked up from where he sat upon a stool cleaning under his nails
with a knife.

"No man speaks for me," he said. "So I will speak for myself. If
any man hears and thinks I do not speak for them, let him say so
now or answer later to my knife." The man got up from his stool.
His cloak was patched but had once been rich, and the buckle that
held it upon his shoulder was heavy gold, inlaid with scarlet garnets.

But the pattern told of more garnets that were now gone, prised from their sockets by the knife the man held lightly in his hand, to pay for boat passage or meal or horse. "I am Talorc, once of the Seal People, but now I have no people and I seek a lord who will repay my sword with gold and avenge my death in blood." The cold-eyed man stared at Oswald. "I have heard tell of you. *Lamnguin*. The Whiteblade. Are you that lord?"

Oswald returned his stare. "No," he said.

Talorc held his gaze a moment longer, then made to turn away.

"No, for I will pay for your sword in glory."

Talorc paused, then turned back to Oswald.

"And my dying?"

"I will give hope not blood to your dying." Oswald's lips twitched. "Dying usually produces enough blood on its own."

"Depends on how you die," said Talorc.

"Kings do not die in bed." Oswald stood in front of Talorc, and the men about him shifted upon the ground, pulling themselves straighter, sitting upright. Some stood. "Nor will you. But if you die with me, it will be a death that the scops sing of, and not the mean and lonely end that you are all drifting towards, cut down in some ambush when men you cheated find you alone and lordless. But know this..." Oswald, although he spoke still to Talorc, took in all the watching men with his words. "Should you prove faithless, I will lay such a curse upon you that men will turn their faces from you and no hall will suffer you to enter, but you will wander, alone and accursed, until the ravens pick your body and the wolves chew your bones, and hell itself will refuse you."

And as Oswald spoke, Bran, finding himself earlier alone upon the beach, flew about his head and then settled upon the ground beside him, adding his own croaked warning to the doom that Oswald had pronounced. The men still upon the ground, seeing the great bird, made the sign against the evil eye as Bran turned his black gaze upon them, scrambling to their feet so that they were no longer at the same level as the bird. Whispers rose among them, nudges of shared knowledge.

"Woden's messenger."

"The slaughter bird."

"The doom bringer."

Oswald held out his arm, and in a rattling flash of black feathers Bran flapped up onto it, and with claws grasping the ætheling's thick wool sleeve, the raven pointed its beak towards the watching men and coughed its own warning.

Talorc stared at Bran. Holding his fingers over his chest, he made warding-off gestures, seeking protection against the bird's influence, while his lips moved in throated invocation.

"Are-are you a spirit walker?" he asked Oswald.

The ætheling stared back at him and made no reply.

Talorc licked his lips. He looked a man caught on the edge of a cliff, with enemies behind and the fall before. His gaze flicked to the other men gathered around, landless, lordless men all, and then back to Oswald.

"I-I will follow you," he said. "To death."

Oswald held him fixed in his gaze. "And beyond," he said.

"And beyond," Talorc echoed.

Oswald nodded once, sharply. "We sail when the tide turns. Fill your bellies while you may, for we will travel fast and hard." Then the ætheling raised his arm and Bran climbed into the sky, cawing, while Oswald turned and made his way to the monastery, Oswiu walking by his side.

As they walked away, aware of the watching eyes following them, Oswald knew that his brother was bursting to talk, but he kept peace until they were far enough not to be overheard, and even then spoke without turning his head.

"What is a spirit walker?" Oswiu asked.

"I have not the faintest idea," said Oswald.

Oswiu almost stopped in surprise, then scurried forward after his brother. "You don't know?" he hissed.

"Of course not. Do you?"

"No, I don't know what a spirit walker is, but I thought you must – you said you were one!"

"I did not say I was a spirit walker. But I did not say I wasn't, either."

This time Oswiu did stop. But they were now out of sight of the men.

"You lied," he said, incredulity raising the pitch of his voice. "You lied."

Oswald, not stopping, shook his head. "I did not. I allowed Talorc to think what he wanted to think."

Oswiu caught up with his brother. "I can't believe it. My brother lied."

"I did not lie," snapped Oswald. "I did not say anything."

"Those are the best sort of lies." Oswiu clapped his brother on the shoulder. "Next thing I know, you'll be taking part in a boast battle."

"I did not lie."

"As you say, brother." Oswiu looked up. "Where are we going?"

"To see the abbot. I would have his blessing before the tide turns and we sail. Besides," Oswald flashed a smile at his younger brother, "he might know what a spirit walker is."

*

"A spirit walker?" Abbot Ségéne looked up from the small desk that, apart from a stool, was the only furniture in his cell. "Why do you want to know what a spirit walker is?"

"Ah…" Oswald glanced at his brother. "Oswiu?"

"We heard one of the men mention it – he seemed to think they were powerful," said Oswiu.

The abbot inclined his head. "I have heard of them. Among the Painted People, there are some tribes, the Seal People, the Sea Eagles, whose priests claim to be able to take the skins of their tribe's animal and walk, in spirit, with the seals or the sea eagles and thus talk to their gods. Generally, these spirit walkers have an animal companion with whom they converse and into whose bodies they claim to be able to place their spirit."

The brothers exchanged glances.

"It is nonsense, of course. The spirits they speak with are most likely demons, sent to lure them into evil. You say one of your men is a spirit walker?"

"No," said Oswiu, "not one of our men…"

"That is good. To have such a one among your company would be to open yourself to the influence of devils such as those that plagued the Blessed Colm Cille. And," the abbot stared across his desk at the brothers, "you are not Colm Cille."

"That is true," said Oswald. "But for that reason, we ask for you to give us the saint's blessing, for we leave with the tide."

Abbot Ségéne smiled. "I will give you more than that: I will give you the saint himself."

The æthelings looked to each other, then back to the abbot.

"You cannot mean…"

"Could you…"

The abbot stood up, flexing his knee slightly from the stiffness of sitting for so long, then pointed the way to the door of his cell.

"I had not thought you to be leaving so quickly. But I have prepared my gifts. Come." The abbot led the brothers to the church, quiet now in between the hours of the Great Office of prayer, and took them to the rood screen, which separated the sanctuary from the nave.

"Wait here," he said. Leaving them, the abbot slipped through the gate in the rood screen.

Oswiu looked to his elder brother. "What do you think…" he began, but Oswald held finger to lips, and Oswiu returned to silence and waiting.

The wait was short. Abbot Ségéne came back through the screen, carrying a small wooden casket wrapped in rich, gold-woven cloth. He held the casket out to Oswald.

"The Blessed One will go with you," he said.

Oswald fell to his knees, and after a glance Oswiu followed him.

"This – this is more than I could have hoped for," said Oswald.

"God always gives more than we hoped for," said the abbot. "Take these relics of the Blessed Colm Cille, as blessing upon you, as fortune in your task, and as promise of fruitful success."

The abbot gave the casket into Oswald's hands.

Oswiu looked up at Abbot Ségéne. "What relic is it?" he asked.

But the abbot shook his finger at Oswiu. "Suffice that I have given you a relic of the Blessed Colm Cille – a relic for which many kings have begged and gone away unsatisfied."

"Truly, I know not how to thank thee," said Oswald, holding the casket to his chest.

The abbot put his hands upon Oswald's shoulders and stared into his face.

"Win," he said. "Take the throne that is thine, and bring thy people to the knowledge of the Lord, and thou will have the blessings of heaven, and of all the monks of this Holy Island." The abbot placed his hand upon the crown of Oswald's bowed head.

"I bless thee, and call down heaven's favour upon thee, through the prayers of Colm Cille, in the name of the Father, and of the Son, and of the Holy Spirit. Amen."

Then, turning to Oswiu, the abbot blessed him too, before embracing both men with his smile.

"That is my gift, my greatest gift, to you. But I have another gift that may prove of value in the task that lies ahead." The abbot led the æthelings from the church and there, standing outside, was a group of five young monks. But these were monks dressed as Oswald had never seen before: they carried shields upon their backs, swords hung from the belts about their waists, and, glimpsed beneath the rough wool of their habits, the dark rings of mail gleamed.

"You may know Brother Diuma and some of these other brethren, but they have been away from this Mother House for many months, helping to, er, resolve some minor points of difference that one of our daughter houses was enduring with a local king." Abbot Ségéne gestured and the foremost of the monks stepped forward. "God turns all things to the good – even the murderous depredations of the Fenians, the sons of death. When young Diuma here led his gang to steal a gift we had sent to the king of Ulster, he expected to find gold and jewels and the riches that are human slaves, did you not?"

"I did, Father Abbot," said the monk, bowing his head.

"But what he found instead was the saint, Blessed Colm Cille himself. And the saint was not about to let a group of young hotheads take his relics and make mockery of them. So what happened, Diuma, after you had slaughtered or captured all the monks I had sent to convey the saint to the king of Ulster?"

The monk, head still hung, said, "I went to take the saint for myself, for he was clothed in the richest gold and cloth."

"And then what happened?"

Brother Diuma looked up at Oswald, and for a moment his eyes appeared as black as the water at the bottom of a well.

"He struck me blind. The moment I touched the saint, with my heart full only of the foulest avarice, the sight left my eyes and I was left fumbling in the dark, more helpless than a child. Those of my men who touched the saint were similarly struck down. The rest, seeing us afflicted, abandoned us and fled. We were left to the mercy of the monks we had not killed – the ones we had bound to take as slaves. I expected my end, and cursed the day that I had thought to raise my hand against God's favourite, Colm Cille. But the monks, when they had freed themselves, treated us gently, save for only one or two blows, and led us, a line of blind men, to Ulster, where they fed us and kept us, saying to questions the Ulstermen asked only that we were afflicted pilgrims, joined to their party that we might more safely make the pilgrimage to the Holy Island." Brother Diuma shook his head at the memory. "I did not even know where the Holy Island lay, nor why men called it holy, but when we arrived here and set foot upon its shores, our sight was returned to us, and we saw, first of all, the house of the Blessed Colm Cille and the brothers processing around it in prayer, and I and my fellows resolved at once to join this community and put our souls at the service of the Blessed Colm Cille." The monk glanced at Abbot Ségéne. "It was Father Abbot who decided that our swords should be put to the service of Colm Cille too. So we have served these past five years, sometimes in prayer and doing the Great Work, other times on our feet and doing war on the enemies of God. Is that what you call upon us to do once more, Father Abbot?"

"It is. I place you and your men in the service of Oswald, Iding, ætheling of Northumbria, from this day until he releases you, God takes you or I call you. Do you understand?"

Brother Diuma bowed his head.

"Very well," said Abbot Ségéne. "But I must lay one further condition upon you. You are to tell no one that you are monks of the Holy Island, in the service of Colm Cille. You must seem as the other men that follow Oswald in this venture: lordless, landless men, seeking fortune and glory and gold. Do you understand?"

"I understand," said Brother Diuma. He stood up. "We must needs change our clothes then." He rubbed his hand over the stubble of hair that had begun to grow back over the front of his head, where the monks that traced their lineage back to Patrick and David and the ancient saints of Britain shaved their hair. "And wear hats."

"Yes," said the abbot. "Now prepare your brothers. You leave with the tide's turning."

As Brother Diuma signalled his small group to follow, Oswiu turned to his brother and held up his hands. First, five splayed fingers, then ten, then two.

"Seventeen men. Is that enough? I have heard tell that Cadwallon's army is as much as two hundred men, most horsed."

Oswald held up another finger. "You forgot one, and that the most important: Colm Cille."

"But the saint, being in a box, is not going to wield sword for us."

"He will do better than wield sword: he will fire hearts and strengthen souls; he will give courage and endurance and the capacity to choose true. That is worth more than any number of men."

"I hope so, brother; I hope so. For the saint will have to stand surety for the Uí Neíll and Dal Riada, for those of our own men who came with us into exile and whom we gave into the service of the kings of Strathclyde and Rheged."

Abbot Ségéne touched Oswiu lightly on the shoulder. "The saint has never failed us – he will not fail you."

"But just in case, you're making sure your help is hidden, so if Cadwallon wins you can bless him High King of Britain with a straight face and no fear of a dagger being slipped between your ribs!"

The abbot's face grew stiff, but he made no answer.

Oswald touched his brother's arm. "Abbot Ségéne has already given us so much. You cannot expect him to risk everything on this one throw of the stones."

"Why not?" said Oswiu. "We are."

"Because the abbot must see to the care of the Holy Island…"

"And we to the lives of our people!"

Oswald shook his head. "I understand what you are saying, but let us not take our leave of the Holy Island in hot words and bad blood, brother."

Oswiu closed his eyes. A shudder passed through his body as he breathed in, trying to calm his heart. As he did so, he heard footsteps, running footsteps, coming towards them, and he opened his eyes to see Brother Aidan, robe gathered up around his knees, rushing towards them.

"Father Abbot, send me with them," he said, skidding to a halt and taking in the three men with his supplication. "Please."

Abbot Ségéne shook his head. "You are no warrior, Brother Aidan, and the monks I send with Oswald know how to wield a sword better than they know how to sharpen a pen."

"But they will need someone to tend them, someone to cook, to feed the horses."

"Speed too they will need, more than anything, and you are no horseman, Brother Aidan."

"Then I will run alongside them."

"Then they will call you the king's hound – would you wish to be called a dog in song?"

"Men have been called worse, Father Abbot."

Abbot Ségéne nodded. "That is true, Brother Aidan." He stood in silent thought for a moment, then shook his head. "My decision stands."

"But…"

Abbot Ségéne shook his head. "No more, Brother Aidan. When

your father gave you into my keeping, he did so in the knowledge that you were his only child, and I undertook to keep you here safe, preserving his blood. By releasing you, I would be going back on my pledge."

"But…"

This time Abbot Ségéne said no word, but merely raised an eyebrow. Brother Aidan turned a beseeching gaze to Oswald.

"Will you not speak for me?"

Oswald went to his friend. "We go to kill, or be killed, old friend. That is no task for you."

"If you die, I would die alongside you."

"I know you would. But I would that you live." Oswald put his hands upon Aidan's shoulders and looked into his face. "I give my mother and my sister into your keeping. Will you look after them when we are gone, and be as a son to them, should we die?"

"You know I will, Oswald."

"Then I am well content." Oswald leaned forward and kissed Aidan's brow. "Pray for us."

"Without cease or end."

Oswald smiled. "Thank you, my friend." He turned to Abbot Ségéne. "We are ready."

"Go, with my blessing." The abbot raised his right hand, and in the gesture so familiar from the Great Work of the community he drew it down to the nadir, then to the extended arms of the cross whose shape he redrew whenever he laid his blessing down upon people and place.

"*In nomine Domini, et Filii, et Spiritus Sancti.* Amen."

Chapter 11

"My father near enough drove the Idings back into the sea whence they came. Now you come over sea, from the Holy Island no less, to seek my aid in claiming back the throne of Northumbria." The king, seated upon the judgment seat, ran his fingers through his beard. "Though I have not heard the priests tell of it, I think God must jest with us sometimes."

"What is jest for one may be insult for another, King Rhoedd." Oswald, standing before the high throne of the king of Rheged in his stronghold at Carlisle, held out his hand in token of friendship. "In the years of my exile I have sailed with the men of Dal Riada, in cattle raid and war party; I have ridden with the Uí Neíll as they warred with the men of Ulster and Connacht…"

The king of Rheged snorted with suppressed laughter. "I hear that it was not only horses that were ridden when you stayed among the Uí Neíll."

Standing at his brother's side, Oswiu flushed at the jibe, but gave no other answer. For his part, only the whitening of his knuckles betrayed Oswald's anger at the king's all-too-accurate insult, but Rhoedd had held the throne of Rheged for many years – he saw the bone show under flesh.

"But it is a fair chance, if chance it be, that brings you to Carlisle at this time. It is late in the season to hazard the coasts of Strathclyde, but the wind has stayed fair and I hear tell from the portsmen that your curraghs came ashore with little damage and more horses than you have men. And a great black bird." The king stroked fingers through his curling beard once more. "A strange party indeed to bring before me. But I have stranger ones with me, waiting upon my answer, and I would hear what you have to say of them before I hear the rest of what you have to say to me, Oswald, Iding, the

Whiteblade. Oh yes, I have heard of you, and from mouths that bring strange tales to my ears. Now we will eat together, but you," and here King Rhoedd pointed at Oswiu, "you will keep your rutting ways for the Uí Neíll. We will eat and you will hear and I will hear and then I will decide. What say you, Oswald, Iding?"

Oswald took a breath. As he did so a young woman, her hair covered with a rich scarf, approached the judgment seat and whispered to the king. Although the words were too quiet for him to hear, the way the maid glanced at them as she spoke suggested to Oswald that his party of men featured in her words. The maid looked once more, then as rapidly away, her face flushing slightly at the eye touch.

King Rhoedd stroked the maid's forearm, then put a finger under her chin and lifted her face so that the light caught her beauty. He looked to the brothers standing in front of him.

"This is why I told you to keep your rutting for the Uí Neíll. This is my daughter Rhieienmelth. Is she not fair?" And he lifted her head further, so that the girl must need raise her eyes to the æthelings standing before the judgment seat.

The brothers glanced at each other, then, as elder, Oswald spoke.

"Rhieienmelth, maiden of Rheged, you are indeed fair," he said, and then he made the courtesy to her.

"Her mother bore me nine children, and six sons, before the tenth took her in his birth," said the king, "and Rhieienmelth has her mother's hips. She will make a king a fine wife. But I will not have her worth lessened by some overeager ætheling who should be out tupping slaves and whores."

King Rhoedd took her head in his large, thick fingers and, not without resistance on Rhieienmelth's part, turned her face this way and that so the brothers might see her the better.

"A king though. A king would be a worthy husband to Rhieienmelth."

"She is not a horse."

King Rhoedd's glance, as sharp as a bone needle, swung to the speaker. "What did you say?"

"She is not a horse." Oswiu took a half-step forwards. "We turn a horse's head that the buyer might see its teeth and eyes, inspect the line of its jaw and the slope of its brow. But your daughter is not a horse."

"You are right. She is not worth as much to me as a good horse – not until she marries. Then she will be the price of five white mares. What say you to that, ætheling?"

Rhieienmelth, her head free of her father's strong fingers, nevertheless turned her face to Oswiu, and he saw her glance for the first time.

"I say to you not five hundred white mares would I accept for such beauty."

King Rhoedd held the young man's gaze for a tense, trembling moment, then slapped his hand to his thigh, the thick fingers making the sound of flesh cleaved upon the butcher's block.

"With a tongue like that, the Uí Neíll must have been easy meat for you! I was like that too in my youth, when my blood was hot and my words warm. In the hall they say it's a man's arm that gets a girl into bed, but I say it's a man's tongue. Come, we will feast tonight and you will tell me of the girls you've known, and Rhieienmelth will serve us. But hands off, you hear."

Oswiu lifted those hands. "Or you'll cut them off?"

The king laughed, slapping his thigh with the same dead-meat thud.

"How did you guess?"

The king was still laughing as they left his presence, the æthelings both conscious of Rhieienmelth's gaze following them as they withdrew.

"How did you do it?" Oswald asked from the side of his mouth as they went, conscious of the king's men laying sprawled around the hall or sitting on stools at table, bent over games of stones.

"You're asking me how I did it? You never ask me how I did it!"

"That's because I'm usually the one who does it. But this time you did. So how did you do it?"

"Oh, it was nothing. Just a bit of talking, banter – you know how it is."

"No."

"Pardon?"

"No, I don't know how it is. Tell me."

Safely out of earshot, Oswiu stopped and turned to his brother.

"Look, I take it you want me to be honest?"

"Yes."

"It was an accident. I got cross about the way he was moving her around, like she was an animal." Oswiu's eyes grew slightly distant as he remembered. "I have never seen such beauty, and he was treating her as if she was a piece of horseflesh to be put on display. It made me angry."

Elder brother stared searchingly at younger brother.

"It wasn't like that," Oswiu protested.

"I did not say it was."

"It was just – I did not like how he was putting her on display. Like I said, it made me angry."

"Maybe you should get angry more often. At one point, I thought he was going to sell us all to slavers. Now we will get some idea of what's going on. Not the help I had looked for, but better than I had feared. Come, let's tell the men. At least we'll eat well today."

*

Princess Rhieienmelth brought the drinking cup around the hall as the men sat eating and drinking, moving with the practised ease of a woman trained and accomplished in the art of raising warriors' spirits, while at the same time giving nothing of herself as hostage to slander. But to Oswald's eye, she lingered a moment longer with his brother than she did elsewhere, and her eyes met his more frankly over the upturned cup than they did with the other men gathered in the hall. Oswald glanced at their host. If he had noticed, it was likely that King Rhoedd had seen too. But the king was engaged in serious consideration of his cups, draining one after the other – wine, rich and red, come via the trading ships that plied their way up and down the Irish Sea, from the kingdom of the Britons across the Narrow Sea where some had fled in the chaotic days after the emperors, when his forefathers took the whale road to these islands.

As he too drank, Oswald took thought on the dark-haired princess who moved with swan grace around the hall. King Rhoedd's stronghold was the Roman city of Carlisle. Its walls still stood, high and complete, and the king's hall was the emperor's fort, a building of stone, cold and draught-ridden to Oswald's mind, but magnificent with age in a way that no wood building, prey as they were to the yellow flame fire, could be. As the king had said in his greeting, Rheged and Bernicia were enemies of old: kingdom of Britons and kingdom of Angles. But he and his brother had found refuge and friendship among the Britons; more importantly, they had found the truth of the belief the Britons professed.

As Oswald turned his cup between his fingers, seeing the light spread and catch through the thin-ground horn, he thought on alliances, and enemies, and marriage – and the wayward habits of hot-blooded brothers. Marriage would cool Oswiu's blood and, watching the way the princess and the ætheling weaved around each other, the elaborate game of glance and look away, the idea grew in the watching: before he left this court, he would propose an alliance between Rheged and Northumbria, to be cemented through the marriage of his brother and Princess Rhieienmelth.

But as the idea formed in his mind, it jabbed him in his loins. For he saw Rhieienmelth and knew she was beautiful, and he desired her too. Coldly, though, the calculations of power and wealth and prestige flowed through his mind: Rheged had once been great under King Rhoedd's father, Urien, but then he was assassinated, and Æthelfrith's, and then Edwin's, power had waxed, while the ancient kingdom of the Britons had waned. As king of Northumbria – should he claim the throne – he must needs wed the daughter of a more powerful throne: one of the kingdoms of the Angles or the Saxons could provide a wife. But by marrying his brother to the daughter of the king of Rheged he would make much of his northern border secure. Oswald gazed at Rhieienmelth, and for a moment she caught his regard, unveiled, and she glowed with it, but then he veiled his eyes and hid his thoughts, and she, unsure, turned her face away from him.

Oswald stared into his cup, dragging his eyes away from the woman he had decided would one day be his brother's wife. The decision was made.

Rising above the hubbub of conversation, many-accented and many-tongued, King Rhoedd's bard chanted, telling the tale of the king's ancestors through the generations, singing him back to men who had walked this land before the emperors came across the sea and whose descendants still ruled this corner of it even now, when the emperors had long departed. It was called the tale of names, and in all the halls of the Britons and the Picts and the Gaels, the tale of names was told before any other tale of the evening. The tale of the names of the kingdom of Rheged was long indeed, and Oswald let the sound of them wash over him as light through breeze-blown leaves. He looked around the hall, its walls hung with tapestries and cloth – by their appearance taken long ago from beds and boats – in an effort to keep the sharp west wind reaching its fingers through the gaps where frost's fingers had prised the mortar.

Pulling his cloak around his shoulders, Oswald reflected that the effort had failed. But he was not alone in feeling the wind cold. Other men sat half-hooded, which was the limit that a man might cover himself at king feast, further along the table. One played at the food set in front of him as if it was of no interest, but the other two cut into their meat with gusto, slicing lamb from bone, skewering it upon their seaxes and taking it with teeth. Seaxes. They were no Britons then. Oswald bent his ear towards them, but they ate without conversation.

"I promised to give answer tonight, and so I will."

King Rhoedd stood up, swaying, his eyes unfocused as they scanned the hall for the man he sought. Oswald expected the king's gaze to alight on him, but the king's eyes moved on, until they came to the man sitting half-hooded and uneating at the table's end.

"Messenger of Cadwallon, stand."

The man stood up, pushing his hood back, and Oswald saw a man dark haired and dark eyed, with white skin save for the scars that marked face and forearm.

"Messenger of Cadwallon, you brought word from the king of Gwynedd, welcome word, that he had cast down the king of the enemies of our people of old, Edwin of Northumbria, and that he had killed the unworthy men who pretended to take that throne, and that he, Cadwallon, now sat upon the throne in the ancient stronghold of Bamburgh, impregnable, indomitable. We applaud that word – we applaud it!"

And King Rhoedd of Rheged raised his men in great acclaim, so that their cheers resounded from the stone walls of his hall. Oswald saw that the other two men, who had been eating so hungrily, sat back from the table at the cheer, but did not join it. Rather they gazed warily around, as one might who finds he has taken shelter among thieves and brigands.

Rhoedd held his arms up for silence, and his retainers fell back into the muttering and quiet conversation that passed for quiet in hall.

"But if that was news beyond expectation, the message you then brought from Cadwallon was beyond hope: after all this tale of years, after we have fought the long defeat and seen our lands taken from us, and strangers walk our hills and lay in our halls, Arthur has returned. Beyond hope, beyond expectation, you tell us that Arthur has returned – and his new name is Cadwallon. That is, indeed, beyond our hope and our expectation – but we are glad, are we not, my men, my warriors? We are most surely glad." And the king raised his arms to raise the acclamation once again.

"Arthur, our king of old, you tell us, calls our homage to him; he calls us to acknowledge him High King, to bend our knee to him and open our hands to him; to send him gifts of gold and silver, and warriors, bold, bright, eager for glory: all this we would do, and do gladly, for Arthur, our king of old. We will do it, and do it right gladly, for this new Arthur, this Arthur Cadwallon, when we are sure that he is indeed Arthur returned; that he has taken ship back from the Blessed Isles and returned to mortal lands to wear the crown and wield the sword. And, indeed, we are all but convinced – for as Arthur did of old, this new High King has driven our foes from the land and taken back our ancient strongholds. So we promise and pledge that we will send men, full fifty warriors, mail-clad with bright swords and linden shields, to him where he awaits, at the far end of the Emperor's Wall. We will send the men you ask for, messenger of Cadwallon, and if he be indeed Arthur returned, then they will join with him in driving the ancient and hated foes of our people from this land. Logres will be lost no more!"

The men cheered and the messenger came and knelt before King Rhoedd of Rheged.

"Now you have given your answer, I must go at once, for my king – our king – waits upon your answer. When, lord, will your men arrive that King Cad– King Arthur may begin to drive the enemy from our land?"

"They will come quickly. Tell Cadwallon, tell Arthur, not to move – my warriors will be with him in ten days."

The messenger made the courtesy, and throwing his hood over his head he all but ran from the hall. King Rhoedd watched him go, his eyes narrowing once the man had disappeared from sight.

"I have no king, and certainly not the son of Cadfan the False," Rhoedd said. He looked to Oswald, sitting near him, and the grin he showed him bore not the slightest trace of the wine he had bibbed through the day. "But it does not do to tell him that, Iding." The king gestured Oswald closer.

"The kings of Gwynedd were goatherds and shepherds when my fathers were kings. I will not bow before them and accept their bastard issue as king, not save I have no recourse." Rhoedd took Oswald's forearm with his thick, meat fingers and stared him fiercely in the eye. "You are my recourse. Cadwallon sits upon the Wall and he will not move now for ten days. Ride, meet him, defeat him, kill him. Speed is everything, but do not ride so fast that you overtake his messenger. And if you lose, and die, then I will say my men were on their way but could not overtake you, and I will bow on creaking knee before him and wait the time when he sleeps to slip the killing knife between his ribs. Such did Morgant when my father Urien stood poised to drive your people from Bernicia. He was the last Arthur, and he was my father: Cadwallon is not his match."

Rhoedd squeezed the bones in Oswald's forearm until they creaked, but the ætheling did not flinch.

"You will do this or you will die."

"I will do this and I will not die." And here Oswald, in turn, leaned to Rhoedd of Rheged. "And when I send word that I have cast down Cadwallon and taken the throne of Northumbria, I will send for your daughter, for Princess Rhieienmelth, that she may wed my brother Oswiu."

The king shook his head. "You."

"No."

"We will make good friends to you."

"I know. That is why I want my brother to marry your daughter."

"It is not enough for Rhieienmelth."

Oswald peeled Rhoedd's fingers from his arm. "Rheged is not enough for me," he said.

Rhoedd stared at Oswald through hooded eyes. "If I should agree, what bride price will you pay for her?"

"If I win, I will be king of Northumbria, master of the islands, overking to Lindsey and Elmet, allianced to Dal Riada and the Gododdin. If I win, you may name your bride price."

And King Rhoedd of Rheged smiled the long, heavy-lidded smile of the gold lust.

"Then I accept your proposal, Oswald, Iding. May the alliance between Northumbria and Rheged be long and fruitful." The king paused. "But for now it will remain words between us. The cup of its closing we will drink when Cadwallon is dead and you sit in the judgment seat at Bamburgh."

Oswald nodded. "Very well."

"Good, good." The king pointed down the table. "There are others here who want to see and speak with you, ætheling."

Seeing the king marking them out, the two men approached Rhoedd and Oswald, and made the courtesy.

The ætheling saw two men, travel-worn, their faces and bodies bearing the unmistakable signs of long journeying and short commons in skin drawn tight around skull and finger.

"Who are you?" Oswald asked. "There is about you the air and presence of the land of the mountain passes."

The darker of the two men – and Oswald saw that beneath his travel cloak he appeared to be wearing a dark, feather mantle – looked to the fairer, but he did not return the glance. Instead, he stepped forward.

"I am Acca, renowned through the kingdoms and among the thrones as a scop of surpassing skill. I am Acca, who sang the lay of the lords of Northumbria, who told the deeds, dread deeds of battle, when Æthelfrith cut down the kings of the Old North and made himself master of Northumbria. I am Acca, who served your father and who remembers you, a boy, hanging on my words. I take it you remember me?"

Oswald stared at the man. If he had indeed been scop to his father, then he should remember him, but his memory of the days before exile were dim. He seldom sought to revisit them, and when he did it was as if he saw them through mist.

"I – I do not remember your face or bearing…" Oswald began.

"B-but you must. I am Acca – all know me."

"It is many years since we fled Northumbria, and memory grows cold if it is not stoked. But – I think I remember your voice."

Acca beamed. "Of course you would remember my voice. Give me but leave to sing one of the songs of Northumbria and you will surely recall better."

Oswald held up his hand. "Later, if King Rhoedd wills, but now, I am eager for news of Northumbria. How do my people fare with Cadwallon ravaging the kingdom?"

"They fare ill, lord," said Acca. "Cadwallon takes from all, so that his men grow fat, and what he does not take he spoils, leaving for the wolves and ravens and rats. Already I have seen the fat bellies of children with no flesh on their bones, and it is yet autumn. By the spring, many will die. It seems Cadwallon spoke truly when he said he would cast our people back into the sea or lay them to rest under the ground: the kingdom resounds with the lamentations of women and the groans of the old and the wailing of children. They wail for food and for justice against the men who steal from them, but most of all they wail for a king." Acca paused, aware that many people around him in the king's hall had stopped to listen, but, giving no sign that he was aware of the scrutiny, he bent his knee before Oswald.

"Will you be our king, lord? Will you return to us? Will you save your people?"

Oswald glanced around. Far too many people were looking curiously at the scene playing out at the king's table, and even though many in Rheged did not understand the language of the Northumbrians, enough did for Oswald to be sure that news of his conversation with Acca would spread. Everything depended on speed and secrecy – he had to find some way of making Acca shut up.

Oswald leaned across the table. "What will buy your silence?" he asked quietly.

The scop, still on one knee, looked up alarmed. "Silence, lord?"

"You must stop speaking of me. I cannot force your silence here, in Rheged, but I will buy it."

Acca shook his head as if he did not understand what he was hearing. "I live to sing, to riddle, to tell tales and fix memories in the hearts of men. I can no more fall silent than a bird can fail to greet the sun."

Oswald leaned closer, dropping his voice. "How much?"

And this time, Acca leaned to him, modulating his voice so that it pitched to the same level as the background conversation in the hall, and fell away into it.

"I am a scop without a lord, a singer without a hall, a voice with no one to hear. Give me a lord, a hall and men to hear my voice, and I will keep silence."

"You will have those, and gold, and a tale worth telling, Acca, scop to Edwin, my father's killer."

The scop glanced up sharply at Oswald. "Ah. You knew."

"Yes, I knew. But my father's killer was my uncle also, my mother's brother, and when there is time I would hear more of him.

But who is this other man who stands silent beside you? Though your face and voice are present in my memory now, I do not think I know him."

"He is Coifi. As to what he is, I will let him explain that. It is – complicated."

Oswald turned to the dark, intense man beside Acca. Meeting his gaze, the ætheling saw it jerk away, as if following the flight of a swift through the air.

"Who are you, Coifi, and what do you want of me?" Oswald asked.

"I – I do not want anything of you," Coifi said, his head and eyes twitching as if searching for something that played at the corners of his vision. "I was Edwin's priest, his rune-reader and wyrd sight, until his new wife came with her priest from across the sea. Then Edwin forsook the ways of our fathers and, as I wished to please the king, I forsook them too, casting fire and spear into the sacred grove at Goodmanham. But the new god Edwin took betrayed him, and he gave no answer to me when I sought him, so I tried to return once more to the old gods, the gods of our fathers. But they have abjured he who abjured them. I am no priest and I am no man and I am no thing, Oswald, Iding, but a clutch of black feathers and a bone rattle." Coifi let his travel cloak fall from his shoulders and Oswald saw the raven-feather cloak, the cloak of the high priest of his people, and the rattle, juddering its white teeth as it made its clacking noise.

"Hey!" King Rhoedd slapped his hand upon the table. "I will have none of that here; we are of the Baptized in Rheged."

Coifi turned his black eyes to the king.

"I too passed through the water and ate the salt, king of this land. I too am of the Baptized. But the new god left me as he left my lord and now I wander far from the gods and they all turn their hands against me, cursed, outcast." And the priest of no god tore his nails down his cheeks until blood leaked from the wounds and his eyes turned up into his skull as his limbs slowly gave way beneath him.

But before he could fall, Acca took hold of the priest, holding him under the arms as he called for a slave to bring wine. Looking to Oswald, Acca said, "Lord, he has not recovered from Edwin's death; he but needs a new lord to serve and his wit will return to him, and the wyrd sight that tells men the ways of the fate singers. Will you not take him as your priest, lord? Though he served your uncle, Coifi would be faithful to any true king of Northumbria."

"I am of the Baptized too, Acca," said Oswald. "Did you not know this?" Seeing the shock on the scop's face, he added, "I see you did not. But I and my brother and my mother and my sister, we all of us are among the Baptized; I have no need for a priest of the old gods, for we follow them no more."

"You have taken the god of the Britons?" asked Acca.

"I have taken the God of sea and storm, of life and death, Acca; the God of my hope. Beside him, Woden, Lord of the Slain, and Thunor, thunderer, all the old gods, are like the children that come to be raised in an ally's court – mewling creatures, howling after their parents."

Acca struggled to hold Coifi's head upright as the slave attempted to pour wine into his mouth. "Lord, we have travelled together, through battle and hunger and cold and storm, through the death of kings and the slaughter of the innocent. I would not leave Coifi alone, lordless."

The priest spluttered as the wine caught in the back of his throat, but the catching brought his sight slowly back.

Oswald regarded the man carefully, then turned his gaze to Acca.

"I see the love you have for your friend. Very well. Although I have no use for a priest of the old gods, from what you tell me of the hunger that stalks the people, I will have need of an almoner. Will he be that?"

Acca looked at his friend, saw the vacancy that still filled his eyes, and said, "Yes, he will."

Coifi, coming to himself, struggled to put his feet back beneath him as the slave continued trying to pour wine into his mouth.

"Get away from me," the priest said, pushing the slave away. He looked to Acca. "I will what?"

"Be almoner to the king of Northumbria."

"What's an almoner?"

"An almoner is, er… Sorry, what is an almoner, lord?"

Oswald nodded. "Why would you know? My God, when he walked this middle-earth, was a poor man and he fed the poor. He asks us, who have our bellies full, to feed the poor, and among the kings of the Britons there is a man whose job it is to do that: feed the poor. You tell me there is famine among my people." The ætheling turned his gaze upon Coifi. "So, Coifi, priest of the old gods, faithful servant to my uncle, Edwin, will you take that office from me and serve it truly, not keeping back what is destined for the poor but giving freely and with both hands, that they may live?"

Pushing himself free of Acca's support, Coifi faced Oswald.

"I will do that, lord," he said. "I will be your almoner, and never take what you deliver to me to give."

"Very well. Then if you can, find horses to ride with us, and if not, follow as you can. We leave with the light."

As the two Northumbrians returned to their places at the far end of the table, Oswald saw Princess Rhieienmelth moving softly through the hall, passing the cup to retainers of the king. Her eyes met his, and he knew that she had been watching what had passed upon the high table, and he felt blood rush to his neck. Oswald dropped his gaze. His throat felt tight and he fumbled for his cup of wine.

Oswiu, returning from where he had been checking on their horses and preparations for the morrow, saw the glance pass between his brother and Rhieienmelth, and his eagerness to return, to see her dark beauty again, of a sudden fell away.

Again. It was always the same. Even though it was he who had defended Rhieienmelth from her father's treatment, yet she turned her eyes to his brother, as dazzled by him as all the others were. It would not be so bad if Oswald was even trying to win her for himself – but he wasn't.

Oswiu slid onto the bench next to Oswald.

"The horses are fed, watered, ready for harnessing."

"Good," said Oswald, not looking at his brother but rather playing with his seax, cutting his meat into thinner strips.

"You'll need a wife, you know. When you have the throne," said Oswiu.

Oswald cut his meat even thinner. "I know," he said, still not looking at his brother.

"What about her?" Oswiu nodded down the hall. "Princess Rhieienmelth. She is fair."

"No," said Oswald, his voice suddenly thick. "Not her."

"Why not?" asked Oswiu.

"Because you will marry her."

"I – what did you say?"

"I have spoken with King Rhoedd. If we win the throne, you will marry Princess Rhieienmelth and through that marriage secure the north."

"You didn't think to speak to me?"

"No." Oswald looked to his brother. "Did you expect me to?"

"You – you might have said something."

"I thought you would be pleased – she is very fair."

"I know, I know, but…" Oswiu looked down the hall and saw Rhieienmelth share words with one of her father's old retainers – one of the men too old to fight, who sat around the fire of winter, all too eager to impart their experience to young men too arrogant to know they needed it. "She is, isn't she," he said.

"Yes, well…" Oswald stood from the bench. "I shall take some air for now. We ride at dawn."

As Oswald, Iding, left the hall, he felt many eyes upon his back, and many hopes upon his shoulders, and many desires within his heart, and he did not know which were the heavier.

Chapter 12

"So, you aim to defeat Cadwallon with..." King Rhoedd stepped back from Oswald's horse and cast a calculating eye along the line. "... twenty-two men."

Bran, perched upon Oswald's saddle, his feathers fluffed against the night chill, croaked.

"And one raven." Rhoedd ran his fingers through his beard. "I fear our families will never be joined."

Oswald, checking the harness of his horse in the grey light before sunrise, patted the horse's shaggy flank. The beast would have to ride fast and hard for the next two or three days, but there was a thick layer of muscle under the coat and its round belly bespoke that it had fed well on good grass. It would carry him, as would the other animals they had at their disposal – some brought by boat from Iona, others bought on landing – and the final few, gifts from the king of Rheged. The ætheling turned to the king.

"It will be enough," he said.

"Even without Penda, I hear that Cadwallon has an army of near enough two hundred men – most horsed. He will have ten warriors for each of yours."

Oswald pointed down the line of men, each preparing mount and weapons in his own way.

"Each of my men is worth many of his – it will not be as uneven as you fear."

"Even if it were true, do you truly believe that one of your men can meet so many of his?"

Oswald looked the king of Rheged in the face.

"Yes," he said.

Rhoedd shook his head in disbelief.

Oswald laughed. "It is mad, is it not? We ride to claim a throne

160

with fewer men than you have in your kitchen, lord. But we have other, and greater, warriors fighting for us in the fields of heaven." The young prince patted his own horse, satisfied that it was now ready. "Besides, we will like as not have more men with us by the time we face Cadwallon." Oswald looked to his brother. "It is time to raise our banner," he said. "I have returned to claim what is mine – let all know."

From his saddle, Oswiu unrolled the long banner of purple and gold that Acha and Æbbe had woven for them, then fixed it to a pole. There was no wind in the still before dawn, and the banner hung limp from the pole, but Oswiu thrust it into the ground.

"Will you carry it, brother?" asked Oswald.

"Yes, of course I will carry it." Oswiu looked to the king of Rheged. "When the men of Bernicia see this banner, they will know their king has returned, and they will follow us, hurrying to home and hearth to fetch sword and shield, then mounting horse and following behind as fast as they may. The news will spread through the land, in whisper and call, and men will listen and come to us. So, I think when the time comes to face Cadwallon, there will be more of us."

"There will be enough even if none heed the summons," said Oswald.

"No doubt, no doubt," said Rhoedd. "But what if I supply a few more? That would not hurt, would it?" And at his signal, Princess Rhieienmelth, upon a white mare, led a group of ten warriors from where they had been waiting in the darkness within the old walls of the city.

"They will go with you, if you would have them, for these are landless, lordless men who have come to my court seeking glory. Would you give it them?"

The princess led them to the æthelings, and as she approached, her eyes went to them, and she saw Oswiu smile at her approach, his smile broadening as if in token of some secret knowledge on his part. But when she sought Oswald's eyes, he dropped his gaze from her, then stared with unblinking concentration at the men who followed her.

"This is a mighty gift," said Oswiu, when Rhieienmelth brought her horse to a halt beside them.

She inclined her head in response to Oswiu's praise, then looked to Oswald. "Does this gift please you, lord?" she asked.

But still he would not meet her eyes, instead walking past her to inspect the men who sat silently upon their horses. Oswald made his way down the line, asking each man his name, examining horse and armour, and calculating by movement and mien the effectiveness of each warrior, before returning to where Rhieienmelth now stood beside her father.

"They will help indeed," he said. "I thank you, king of Rheged."

"Don't thank me; win for me," said Rhoedd. "Win, so I don't have to bend the knee to that upstart cur Cadwallon. Win, so that I can find a husband for my daughter."

"Father! You don't mean…"

"Yes," said the king, taking Rhieienmelth's arm and patting it. "We settled it last night. If Oswald succeeds and claims the throne, you will marry Oswiu."

"Os – wiu?"

At first, Rhieienmelth's gaze, alive with excitement, had turned to Oswald, but now she turned to her father, puzzled.

"Yes. Oswiu." The king looked at her, then laughed. "You didn't think I was going to say Oswald, did you? You're not even my eldest daughter, though you're fair enough. You didn't think you'd be marrying a king, did you?"

Rhieienmelth flushed. "I-I…" she stuttered.

Oswiu flushed too, for he had seen her gaze skip to his brother when she thought she was to marry him, then the way her face fell when she learned who was to be her husband.

"For my part," said Oswald, "I should have been glad, more than glad, to wed a princess so fair, if it were possible." He glanced at Rhieienmelth, then looked away. "But it is not possible. My brother will be a fine husband to you." He stepped back from her and looked to Oswiu. Oswald went to take his arm to lead him to his future bride, but his brother was like stone in his grasp. Oswald looked to him and saw his brother's face, ferocious and stricken, before a mask of calm slipped over it.

"Bring my wife to me then, brother," said Oswiu.

Oswald stepped back, uncertainty overcoming him. But before he could decide what further to do, Rhoedd stepped forward.

"It should be her father that introduces Rhieienmelth to her future husband," he said. And holding his daughter's hand, he led her forward to Oswiu.

Rhieienmelth slowly raised her eyes to his. Oswiu, seeing her beauty, felt the breath catch in his throat.

"I – I know I am not my brother," he said. "But will I do?"

"Yes," said Princess Rhieienmelth. "Yes."

"Of course he'll do," said Rhoedd, slapping his great thick hand against Oswiu's back. "This boy is going to be the second most powerful man in the land."

"We must go," said Oswald. "It is getting light."

In the east, across the mountains, the sky was lightening, and although the shadows still pooled thickly upon the ground, the night was drawing to its close.

"We must not let the lovers keep you, eh?" said Rhoedd. Rhieienmelth blushed furiously. Oswiu, however, smiled and, letting go her hand, winked, before climbing lightly upon his horse. Urging it forward, he grasped the banner from where it stood in the ground and let it flow out.

"Let all hear and know: the king has returned!" Oswiu circled the group with the purple and gold banner streaming behind him. Coming back to where Rhieienmelth stood, he bent down to her. "And his brother will come back for you," he said.

"Lead off, Oswiu," called Oswald, and the young ætheling, bearing the flag of the Idings, the purple and gold of Bernicia, urged his horse forth, its hooves clattering over the stone of the old road of the emperors, and following behind came Oswald and his men.

Rhieienmelth watched them ride away, the figures gradually diminishing in the distance until only the gold and purple of the banner might be seen, and then that too vanished.

Safely out of sight, her father spat on the ground.

"Pah," he said. "Got rid of them."

Rhieienmelth turned to him. "But Father, you've promised me to Oswiu."

"He'll be dead in two, three days' time – him and all of them." King Rhoedd of Rheged's eyes looked at her with sudden calculation. "But telling them I'd marry you off made sure they'd leave with nothing but a promise – best we can hope is that, in dying, they kill so many of Cadwallon's men that we can pick up the pieces. Then I'll find you a proper husband – someone who'll pay me real money for you."

"But the men you sent with them…"

"Troublemakers! Best to get rid of them. Best to get rid of them all."

*

"Giants built this."

Talorc the Pict looked to see where Brother Diuma was pointing. The Wall ran to their left, climbing hills and ducking into valleys, its stones gleaming in the rain that drove in from the west. At least they were riding east, so the wind and wet was at their backs, and glancing behind the Pict thought he could see the end of the storm beyond the billows of dark cloud.

"I said, giants built this," Brother Diuma repeated. "We have them in our own country – they raised great circles of stones there." He indicated the Wall. "These ones were better masons though – see how they made the stone smooth, so it all fits together. The circles back home are all rough, like teeth pulled from the jaw; not soft like these. Makes me think the giants must have moulded them like butter. What do you say, Pict?"

Talorc rode on in silence, not glancing at the warrior monk. But Brother Diuma jagged his horse over, so that Talorc had to either rein back or have his horse step over the rain channel that followed the road's edges, which was now black and full with water draining from the surface. He reined the horse back.

"I asked what you think, Pict," said Brother Diuma.

"I think I have never heard a man speak so much to so little account," said Talorc, resting his hand easily upon his saddle, but with it positioned to draw sword or knife in one smooth motion.

The monk stared at him, the rain now blowing in his face as he had turned his horse to face Talorc, flowing down his cheeks and dripping from his nose.

"What did you say?"

"I said, I have never heard a man speak so much to so little account. Is that clear?"

Brother Diuma stared at him. Then his mouth twitched, and a smile, broad as the day's rain, spread across his face.

"And I," he said, "have never before met a man willing to tell me that to my face. It is true, when the wind blows from the west and I feel the rain upon my back, I feel as if I am back home and I talk as I did as a child there, when they called me little gull, on account of how I would never stop squawking. Now I'm squawking again." He drew his horse back and ushered the Pict into motion, and then rode again beside him. "My people always said you could get more conversation, and better, from a seal than a Pict. Is that true, do you think?"

Talorc rode in silence.

"Course, I talk a lot, especially when I am wet, cold and riding to my death. But then I reckon that's why Abbot Ségéne sent me out from the Holy Island to do his death-making and trouble-breaking: on account of the fact he couldn't bear to hear my talk all the day around the abbey. Mind, I kept quiet there, on the Holy Island, because the peace of the saint lies upon it and the words, they seem to dry up, even for me. But when I'm away from it, it's like my mouth is trying to make up for lost time; I even talk when I'm asleep."

"I heard," said Talorc.

"Was I talking last night?"

"Interminably. If we had more men, you would not have woken."

Brother Diuma laughed. "Maybe. I'm not so easy to kill – half the kings of Britain and all the kings of Ireland have tried at some time or other, and I'm still alive, while most of them are dead."

"Kings don't live long."

"Our days are as grass, as a flower of the field we flourish, and the wind passes over and we are gone, and of our passing there is no trace." Brother Diuma pointed again at the Wall. "But they left more than a trace, so therefore they cannot have been men, but giants, stone giants, and this like enough their bones."

"Bones do not make a wall across the land – they are carried away by wolves and ravens."

"Maybe it is one giant, and he was wading through the Irish Sea when he tripped on the land and fell, and his head went into the North Sea, and he drowned."

"Have you ever been to Aquae Sulis? London? Have you seen the forts the emperors of old built to guard the Narrow Sea?"

"Have you seen islands of ice, floating in the sea?"

The Pict turned to stare at the monk. "What has that got to do with this?"

Brother Diuma grinned. "Nothing at all." He turned in his seat and called behind. "Did you hear that?"

"Yes," came the answer in a number of voices, in tones ranging from delight to disgust.

Brother Diuma turned back to the Pict. "I had a wager with some of your men last night that I could get you to speak more than three sentences today. I think I have won."

Talorc grimaced. "So you don't think giants built the Wall?"

"Could be," said Brother Diuma. "Then again, it might not have been giants. It could have been the Fair Folk."

"The Fair Folk don't build walls," said Talorc.

"How do you know?" asked Brother Diuma.

"I – I know," said the Pict.

"Well, let us hope they know, and give us a good night's sleep. Yesterday was miserable."

The Pict sniffed the wind. "It will be dry tonight," he said.

"Good. My people always said, if you want to know about the weather, ask a Pict."

"What else do they say about Picts?"

"Never answer their questions."

Talorc glanced at the monk, grunted and turned away. Urging his horse on, he passed two plodding horses and their bedraggled riders before catching up with Oswald and Oswiu.

The purple and gold banner trailed down its pole, clinging wetly to the wood. But even so, when they rode past farmsteads or villages, people came out to stare, and to listen with wonder and the first flush of hope as Oswiu again took up his call: "The king has returned. The king has returned. Come to him – come to Oswald, Iding, Æthelfrith son, king of Bernicia, lord of Bamburgh; bring your spears and your swords and your shields and come follow him."

The children would run alongside them, asking questions, calling out, while the men watched, silent-eyed and watchful, but their fingers tested the edge of knife and the point of spear.

"We go to Heavenfield. Come to us! Come to your lord! Come to your king!"

Even if a village was small and mean, yet still Oswiu called out the summons as they passed through it, and the faces stared up at the passing men. In some, hope was kindled, but in others all fire had gone out, and they stared, dull as ash.

"We stop at Heavenfield?" Talorc asked Oswiu.

"We do," replied Oswiu. He glanced back at the following line of men. "Did he win his bet?"

"Yes," said Talorc. "He did."

"Brother Diuma could make a rock talk."

"I am not a rock."

Oswiu nodded. "Yes, so I see."

"I will kill him."

"Please do not. We do not have enough men as it is – we can't do without you as well."

"But why would you miss me if Brother Diuma is dead?"

"Because I've seen him fight. You would not get anywhere near him, not in a knife fight, and that is the only duel you might have while you are part of a warband."

"You have not seen me fight."

"I do not need to – I have seen you walk, and ride. You would not win in a knife fight with Diuma, but you would have mastery with sword and shield, for you weigh half as much again as him, and strength, as you know, counts more than anything else in such a contest."

"Then I will fight him with sword and shield."

"When we have won the throne you may do what you want, but not before." Oswiu reined his horse back a little so he rode closer to the Pict. "But why would you want to? If we take the throne, my brother will give you and your men gold and glory beyond anything you have seen. Why risk that fighting a man who must give his gold and glory to his abbot?"

Talorc stared at Oswiu. "Is that true? The monk will get no gold – none of the thick arm rings or the buckles crusted with garnets?"

"Nothing," said Oswiu. "Look at him – all he wears is his habit and his mail, and that is just iron."

The Pict turned in his saddle and stared in wonder at Brother Diuma who, seeing his stare, waved. Talorc turned back to Oswiu.

"Why does he fight then?" he asked.

"Because Abbot Ségéne asks him to fight. Because he is good at it. Because it is God's will." The ætheling pursed his lips. "Not sure which of those is the truest."

*

"Will you sing for us?"

Oswald asked this of Acca as the men gathered around the fire they had piled in the corner of the old fort. The years had pulled the roof from that corner, allowing the smoke to escape, but the Pict had been right: the rain had blown past with the evening and now stars shone through the tattered streamers of cloud, trailing into the east.

Acca looked round at the assembled men. Only Oswald and Oswiu among them spoke the language of the Angles and the Saxons fluently – the others could mostly understand simple sentences and commands, but few could manage anything more.

"Lord, they will not understand," he said.

Oswald gestured to take in the men resting upon saddles and sitting with backs against stone, while the horses shifted restlessly at the entrance to the fort, sheltered by a rapidly repaired fence from the depredations of the wolves that howled mournfully in the hill distance.

"They do not need to know the words to hear their music. Sing to us, Acca."

The bard nodded and got to his feet. Outside, the wind moved through the hills, sending its cold fingers in through stone gap and thatch break, but the fire blazed bright and the men, warmed by it, gathered tight to the flames.

"I will tell a tale of a man who came over sea to deliver a king's hall from the monster that plagued it, carrying off men and treasure and food, so that all life and hope was lost. I will tell a tale of a man who defeated the monster and brought hope to the people." Acca picked up his lyre and strummed it, the six strings resonating through the stones.

"*Hwæt!*"

There had been little conversation before, but what there was died away to silence. Acca looked around at the fire-lit faces. And he began to chant.

> "*Wé Gárdena   in géardagum*
> *þéodcyninga   þrym gefrúnon*
> *hú ðá æpelingas   ellen fremedon.*
> *Oft Scyld Scéfing   sceapena préatum*
> *monegum maégþum   meodosetla oftéah*
> *egsode Eorle   syððan aérest wearð*
> *féasceaft funden   hé þæs frófre gebád·*
> *wéox under wolcnum·   weorðmyndum þáh*
> *oð þæt him aéghwylc   þára ymbsittendra*
> *ofer hronráde   hýran scolde,*
> *gomban gyldan·   þæt wæs gód cyning.*"[1]

---

1 These are the opening lines of *Beowulf* in Old English.

The red, fire faces stared in silence at Acca as the sound syllables clashed through their bones and into their blood.

"*þæt wæs gód cyning,*" Acca repeated the last half-line. "That was a good king."

And through the hours of the night Acca told the story, to men who heard its sound but knew not the words, and with the story's end they fell into the sleep that takes men, old in war, on the eve of battle: the deep, death sleep, that lies upon them as if in preparation for the long sleep that some will take on the morrow.

But Oswiu drew his brother outside before sleep took them. They stood by the shifting horses, knowing that the animals' breathing would serve to mask their guarded speech.

"Even if men would come to our call, the rain we have had would slow them. We should wait, let them reach us, then go on."

Oswald looked past the steam of the animals' breath to the starlit hills beyond. Out of the ember light, his eyes soon adjusted to the moonless night. The last shreds of the day's clouds trailed into the east, but the sky to the west was clear and full of stars.

"If I knew they would come, I might wait. But we do not know if any will answer our call. They came when Osric called; they came when Eanfrith called; and they died. Now, maybe they wait rather than spend blood and hope on an ætheling who is little more than a name from the past for them." Oswald turned to his brother. "I would not blame them if they did. But now word spreads and if we do not ride, word will reach Cadwallon before we do, and he will be warned, and forearmed." Turning back to the starlit hills, Oswald shook his head. "We have risked all upon this roll of the bones, brother, and our hope, what there is of it, lies in speed and surprise. And the saint. We will not wait."

"Very well." Oswiu looked up at the stars. "Like as not we will die in the next few days, brother."

"If we do, I am glad that you will be by my side. But we shall not die; we will live." Oswald turned to his brother. "We will live."

Oswiu shrugged. "We live, or Cadwallon. Kings rise, kings fall; fortune favours one, then turns from him and who can say why?"

"It is not fortune. God, not the fate singers, orders things according to his will."

"Maybe. In some things. But in battle, brother, I do not know. I have seen too many battles turn upon a man's slip or another's cowardice; brave warriors cut down because their belly griped the night before or the rain came in the morning. Is that God working?"

"How else would you have God work?"

Oswiu shrugged again. "I don't know. Something more obvious, maybe."

"The Lord is subtle beyond our knowledge, brother, and works his will in ways we do not see, as well as the ways we do see."

"I wish sometimes he would remember that we do not see as clearly as he. You sleep, brother. I will take the watch. I have much to think on myself."

Oswald looked at his younger brother. "Rhieienmelth?"

"As it happens, yes."

Oswald nodded. "I will sleep then. Call me when the sky brightens. We must ride with the dawn. By the day's end I would have us at Heavenfield."

*

"You should see this."

Oswald, shaken awake, saw his brother leaning over him.

"Is it light?"

"Come," whispered Oswiu, threading his way through the men sleeping upon the fort's floor.

Shaking off sleep, Oswald followed, emerging from the darkness of the fort into a sky that was showing grey in the east.

Oswiu pointed. Gathered around the fort, sitting in small groups or standing silently, were many men. When they saw Oswald emerge, those who had been sitting rose to their feet. Those who were standing made the courtesy.

"W-who…" began Oswald. But before he could form the whole question a man stepped forward from the group and bowed to him.

"Lord, you called, and we have come," he said, his voice thick with an accent that Oswald could not immediately place, but one that spoke to him of his childhood, spent in this land of the mountain passes.

Oswald looked to him, and to the silent, watching men.

"Who are you?" he asked.

"We are the men of the high pastures and moors, the descendants of the people who lived here before the Romans came and cut a line across our land and our world. We were here before the Idings came, over sea, and took the rock at Bamburgh. We were here before the hills themselves rose from the land, and some say we shall still be here when the hills fail and the sea takes back the land. I am Corotic of the Brigantes, and I have come to serve you."

Oswald indicated the other men. "What of these?"

"They will as I say."

The ætheling scanned the watching men, taking in weapons and postures and attitudes in practised glance.

"These are not fighting men," said Oswald, for they bore no shields or swords, but carried only spears – the mark of a free man – and knives. In the clash of shieldwalls they would not survive long.

"We do not fight as you do. But give us leave, and we will be your eyes and your ears, and we will still take many men from your enemy before ever you set eye upon him. For even now, Cadwallon rides upon the new road from York with all his host about him; it is a great army. No such army has ridden this land since the days of the emperors. Give us leave, and we will lead many astray, into the marshes and meres, into wood and forest, never to emerge."

The eastern sky glowed with the first sign of dawn. In its light, Oswald stepped forward to face this man who offered aid beyond all hope.

"Why do you wish to help me?" he asked. "I do not know you; I have no call on you or your people."

"Your fathers called to us, from beneath the Hill of the Goats, where they built the great palace, and we heard and came to their call. Each year we came, with sheep and goats and cattle, and received the blessings of the king. But then the new king came, and he burned the great palace, and he took when it was not our time to give, and he sent his men into our high places, the places where only our people go, and put sword to our people when we would not give when it was not the time for giving. There are no blessings in this king; we would have a new king: we would have you."

Oswiu, standing beside his brother, leaned in so that he could whisper to him.

"I was on watch – and I did not fall asleep – but I did not see or hear them approach. I only realized they were here when Corotic came to ask to see you."

"Remind me to set a different watch tomorrow," Oswald whispered back.

"Get one of these."

Oswald looked Corotic in the face. The brightening sky showed his face was painted with the swirling shapes of animals and, joining his eyes, the face of a bird was inked upon his brow and shaved scalp.

The ætheling held out his arm and coughed Bran's name in the language the bird understood, and the great black raven came immediately, settling upon Oswald's forearm, his sharp claws digging into bare skin.

A sigh, soft as the dawn, went up from the watching men as they saw the bird turn towards Oswald and dip its head in greeting.

"It is true." Corotic looked from man to raven and back again. "We are the Raven People, the people of the high passes. We will follow you, Raven King, and do what you will have us do."

Oswald scratched Bran under the chin and the bird turned its head to bring his finger into contact with new areas of skin, roughly gurgling its delight.

"Very well," he said. "I will be your king, and you will bring tribute, once each year, to the palace beneath the Hill of the Goats, as your fathers did, and I will build again the palace of Ad Gefrin to receive your tribute, as my fathers did.

"Do as you have said: harass and harry Cadwallon and his army. I would wish he did not know of our presence, but that cannot be helped."

"But he does not know you are here, Raven King. He hurries north to meet the kings of the north. They have sent word that they will take him as their king, their king reborn, and he goes to meet them where the north road crosses the Wall."

Beside him, Oswald heard the breath hiss through Oswiu's teeth, and it was all he could do to stop the despair showing on his face too.

"Which kings march to Cadwallon's flag?" he asked Corotic.

"We have heard no warbands crossing our hills, nor seen ships sliding down the coasts, and yet Cadwallon goes to greet the kings of Rheged and Dal Riada, of Strathclyde and the Picts and the Gododdin." The chief of the Brigantes, the Raven People of the high passes, scratched the tattoos that scored his face. "That is the news the messengers brought Cadwallon; that is why he rides, yet we do not see the armies that he goes to meet."

"How do you know that was the message Cadwallon received?"

"Not all the messengers returned to him. Some were lost in the hills."

Oswald turned to his brother. "If the kings of the Old North join with Cadwallon, then we have no hope – there will be too many."

Oswiu shook his head. "We saw Rhoedd a bare day ago – could he have betrayed us so soon?"

"The king of Rheged is a man of no truth," said Corotic. "He speaks, and he lies."

"But we heard him send Cadwallon's messenger off," said Oswald. "More likely, Rhoedd plays still for time, waiting to see who will prevail, then sending his main force, pleading late arrival, to claim his share of the plunder and a share of the winner's gratitude. Mayhap the other kings do the same. But even if they have sent armies, they have not yet met with Cadwallon, have they?" He turned to Corotic to ask the question, and the chief shook his head.

"No, Cadwallon's army is still his own alone. The other king, Penda, returned to his lands in the south this half-year past."

"Then if we can meet and defeat Cadwallon before reinforcements arrive, it will not matter how many men Rheged and Strathclyde, Dal Riada and Gododdin send: Cadwallon will be dead." Oswald turned to Corotic.

"I ask you, therefore, to harry Cadwallon and his army, but do not delay it. We will meet him where he expects to meet the kings of the north, where the north road crosses the Wall."

"We will as you ask, Raven King." Corotic made obeisance to Oswald in the way of the men of the mountain passes, and then, as silently as they had come, they withdrew, melting away into the shadows of the dawn so that, try as they might, neither brother could follow their progress once they had first merged into shadow.

"We could get caught between Cadwallon and the kings of the north," said Oswiu. "If we are, we will be cracked like a hazel nut between two stones."

"Yes," said Oswald. "Yes, we will be. So let us get there fast, and set men to watch the northern roads, so that we know if any warbands approach while we wait for Cadwallon. It is a day's ride to Heavenfield. It lies north of the Wall. We will camp there tomorrow; then we will not be caught between spear and Wall if Cadwallon rides as fast as we do – but I do not expect he shall, for he will be bringing wagons and supplies too, to feed and feast the kings he goes to meet, and gifts and gold to give them."

"Gold." Oswiu grinned. "That will make some of our men fight all the harder."

"Make sure they know of it, then. Tell them they are fighting for their share in a king's treasure – such wealth they will likely never see again."

"Nor will we, if we have to share it out among them all."

"If we win, they will deserve it. If we win, there will be more gold than we will know what to do with."

Oswiu laughed. "I think I could find ways of using it, brother."

Oswald nodded. "I'm sure you could." He turned to the east. The sky was light now, only the western horizon still clinging to night's cloak. "Time to wake the men."

As Oswiu went to rouse them, Oswald scratched under Bran's chin.

"Raven King…" he said quietly to himself.

Chapter 13

Oswald reined back his horse as the little shaggy pony, bred for the moors and hills, approached, Corotic's legs dangling almost to the ground.

"Where is he?"

The chief of the Raven People pulled his pony to a halt. Before he spoke, he made sign at the raven that perched upon Oswald's saddle. For his part, Bran paid his votary not the slightest attention, turning his back upon the man and staring, with black eyes, north to where moors rose up beyond the Wall.

"King Cadwallon and his army ride north on the road of the emperors. They move slowly, for he has many wagons with him, but he will reach the ford of the River Tyne by this evening."

"Too far for us to reach him today."

"But you will be able to come down upon him on the morrow, if you ride hard."

"Yes. We must make time." But as Oswald made to urge his men on, Corotic raised his hand.

"Wait," he said. "Cadwallon sends out scouts. Some we caught, and they will not return to him, but others still ride, searching for you. It were best, if you wish surprise, to ride north of the Wall, for the king's scouts will surely expect to find you upon the road south of the Wall."

"But are there any roads there?"

"There are no roads, but there are paths, if you know where to look." Corotic put his hand to his chest. "We know where to look. We will take you on paths that wind between crags and through valleys, on ways that hide in defiles, so even if one of Cadwallon's scouts should come this way, he will not see you, and the king will not be warned of your presence."

Oswald looked at the man perched upon his pony. He had met Corotic a bare half-day earlier, he had no knowledge of him, no man he knew vouched for the chief of the Raven People, and yet by accepting his advice he would be trusting all upon the man's word.

"Very well," he said. "Lead us. We will follow."

The chief of the Raven People looked up at Oswald, and deep in his dark eyes there was understanding of how great was the risk the ætheling took in trusting him.

"I will lead you myself," he said. "Then if I be false, slay me."

Oswald smiled, but there was no humour in his eyes. "Do not doubt it." Then, turning back to the following column of horsemen, Oswald pointed at Corotic.

"We will follow this man – he takes us on paths our enemy does not know, so that we may pass unseen."

Corotic pushed his horse from the broad Roman road that marched in step with the Wall from sea to sea, and pushed it over sheep tracks towards the nearest gate tower. In the days of the emperors, there had been a guarded door there, through which traders might come and go, taking the baubles of empire to the tribes of the north and returning with the gleanings of barbarians. The tumbledown walls near the gate tower showed that a village had taken root there, ready to take first pickings of the traders' wares when they returned from the north, but now the roofs were gone and the walls were going, wearing down into the earth that bore them.

Oswiu, riding with the rearguard, pushed his horse forward to come up beside his brother.

"Are we wise in trusting Corotic?" he asked Oswald, as they sat watching the column of horsemen ride past.

"I was twelve when I last saw this land. You were four. I have little memory of these places. Do you?"

Oswiu looked around and shrugged. "To me, one bit of the Wall looks the same as all the others."

"Then we have need of guides – and Cadwallon has done nothing to make these people bend their knee to him. And the Blessed One will protect us from treachery."

"And if he does not, then I will cut Corotic's throat. Slowly."

"You will have to do so after I have finished with him. He may not have a throat by then."

Oswiu laughed. "Very well. You have led us this far – I would be a faithless follower and false brother if I did not follow further. Let us see where the chief of the Raven People takes us. Besides," and here he leaned closer and ran a finger down the side of Bran's neck, "he is scared of your bird."

The raven twisted his head appreciatively, putting Oswiu's scratching to those parts of his head and neck that he considered most needed attention.

Oswald nodded. "I do not blame him. In truth, sometimes I think even I fear him."

Bran opened one black eye, then the other, and stared unblinking at Oswald.

"I see what you mean," said Oswiu. His laugh was only half a laugh.

The slaughter bird croaked, dropped its head and rose with creaking feathers into the air, its call resounding over Wall and moor as it climbed into the sky. Up ahead, at the front of the column, Corotic heard Bran and started upon his pony, head jerking round as he looked for the bird. But as he saw it circle above them, Corotic relaxed.

Reaching the tower, the space where the gate had once been was yawning open to the north. He waved the column of riders on.

"Come, come; follow." And he led them away from the Wall, onto the narrow paths and ways beyond it.

*

Oswiu pointed back behind the column of riders picking their way along what even a sheep would have had difficulty calling a path, to the west.

"The sun will be setting soon." He sat down in his saddle. "I don't know about you, Oswald, but I would prefer not to still be riding on what our guide considers paths when it is dark. We would all break our necks before we even give Cadwallon his chance."

"We will make camp soon," said Oswald. "Corotic told me he was heading for that ridge yonder – with the remains of a tower upon it. The emperors kept watch, it seems, even beyond the Wall. It will be a good place to rest, for a scout on the south side of the Wall could bare see it, and the tower will allow us to light fire without giving ourselves away. The men will need to eat well tonight."

Oswiu nodded. "Tomorrow is the day, you think?"

"Yes," said Oswald. "Yes, I think it is."

Oswiu nodded. He tried to smile but his mouth felt suddenly dry.

"Nervous?" asked Oswald.

"Me?" Oswiu's voice squeaked high. "Me nervous?" he repeated, a register lower than his normal voice. And now he smiled, wide and clear. "Of course I am nervous."

"Good," said Oswald. "I am too." He looked around, as if searching for something or someone, then seemed to see it. "Go on with Corotic and make camp – I will meet you there shortly."

"Where are you going?" asked his brother.

"There is something I must do," said Oswald. "And I know who to ask to help." He pulled his horse's head round and made his way down the column of men to the rear where, seated upon two old ponies, rode Acca and Coifi.

"Come with me," Oswald told them. "I have need of your help."

Turning to watch from his place at the head of the column, Oswiu saw his brother ride with Acca and Coifi towards and into the only copse of trees in this bare, wind-blasted land. The trees found shelter in a dip of land, and beyond rose the ridge with the watchtower atop it.

For riders without wagons, it was a quick matter to set camp. The horses were tethered, after being led to water – the watchtower had drawn its supply from a stream that ran beside it – while other men set to making fires in the shell of the building. At least it would stop the wind, Oswiu thought, although as with all his people he disliked sleeping in the stone buildings left from the days of the emperors. The monks of Iona insisted that men had built those buildings, but Oswiu found that all but impossible to believe: surely giants must have been responsible for laying the Wall from sea to sea?

Camp set, Oswiu went in search of Corotic. The chief of the Raven People sat away from the warband, his back against his pony, eyes searching the moors. The setting sun filled the land with shadow, but as Oswiu approached, Corotic pointed.

"Your brother returns – with a tree."

Oswiu turned to see Oswald leading his horse and the two ponies belonging to Acca and Coifi, with – he squinted but, yes, he saw true – a tree slung over the beasts' back, and the two other men helping to hold it in place as they approached the camp.

Going to meet them, Oswiu stopped in front of his brother as he laboured to bring the animals and their burden up the slope.

"You have brought a tree," he said.

"No," gasped Oswald.

Oswiu stepped back. "It looks like a tree. An ash tree. Although you've cut off its branches."

"Will you help?" said Oswald.

"What's it for? We have enough firewood."

"I – I will tell you later."

With Oswiu going behind and pushing the animals, they managed to bring the tree up into the camp and dump it onto the ground.

"Now will you tell me?" said Oswiu.

"Dig," said Oswald. He gestured to Acca and Coifi and the men nearby. "Help me dig a pit."

"What is this for?" asked Oswiu again.

Oswald's eyes burned. "I will tell you later. Now dig."

Oswiu shrugged. "Very well. If you insist."

While he joined the others digging, Oswald and Coifi worked upon the tree, sawing the nubs of branches smooth, then lashing a length of wood to the main trunk.

"How deep do you want your hole?" Oswiu tapped his brother and pointed at the pit they had dug, already some four feet deep.

"That is enough. Here, help me."

Oswald started hauling the tree towards the pit and, when its end overlapped the hole, he and his brother, with Coifi and Acca helping, pushed it upright, until it juddered down into the pit. Throwing his arms around the tree, Oswald held it from toppling.

"Fill it," he cried, holding the tree fast. The men shovelled the earth back into the hole, pushing and trampling it down until the tree stood fast, raised up upon the ridge beside the tower of watch.

Oswald lay his hands upon the rough wood of the tree, embracing it. Oswiu stood back and looked up, and saw.

"It's a cross," he said.

Oswald kissed it. "Yes," he said.

Corotic, chief of the Raven People, stood before the cross, staring up at it.

"The tree of the world," he whispered. He looked to the man standing next to him, Talorc the Pict, and the Pict, looking up as well, nodded.

"Yes," he said.

Brother Diuma, with his fellows, knelt before the tree and prayed.

With his right hand upon the wood, Oswald turned to face the men he had brought with him, some over sea, some from Rheged, others who had joined them as they rode beside the Wall.

"Tomorrow," he said, "tomorrow, we fight. So now, while we all yet live, we kneel before this tree." And Oswald bent his knees until they found the earth at the tree's foot, and those of his men who yet stood, they bent their knees too.

"Now, as we kneel together, men of Bernicia and Deira, of Rheged and Iona, men of the mountain passes and men of the islands, I ask the true and living God, the God who hung upon the tree, in his mercy to save us from our enemies, to give us victory, for he who sees men's hearts truly, knows we fight to save our people."

One by one, the men came up to the tree and laid their hands upon it, and as they did so, Oswald placed his hands upon their heads and breathed upon them. Last of all was his brother.

Oswiu knelt before the tree and bowed his head, feeling the

weight of his brother's hands upon him, and then he looked up and saw Oswald looking down upon him.

"Tomorrow," Oswiu said, "tomorrow you will take the throne. Tomorrow you will be king." He pointed to the east. "See, the new moon rises."

But Oswald made no answer. And as he lay down to sleep in the dark shadow of the tower, Oswald felt the doubt of fear gnaw his bowels; for he had seen no sign, no token that he did God's will. And sleep was long in coming.

Chapter 14

"I told you the kings would come." Cian, bard to Cadwallon, stood before him in the hall at Hexham.

"They have taken long enough." Cadwallon sat alone upon the judgment seat that he had his men carry wherever he went. It was of wood, carved, inscribed and painted in the richest colours, and upon its back and its side and its legs it told the story of Arthur: the twelve battles he won, his betrayal at the hands of his nephew and his withdrawal from this world to the island of the blessed. And lest anyone should fail to understand the significance of the judgment seat, it bore upon it, in writing of gold, "Here sits Arthur, of old, come again."

Cadwallon gazed around the hall. It was a mean, low place, meant merely as a wayplace on the journey north, and that was how he was using it. Another day's ride and he would come to where the road crossed the Wall: that was where he would meet the kings of the north and accept their homage to him as High King of Britain, Arthur reborn.

"Bring me wine," he said. He was tired. The day's march had been plagued with ills, from wagons catching wheels and breaking axles, to troops of men taking off into the low forest that lined sections of the road and not returning. Scouts had been sent to search for them, but none had returned yet, and with the night drawing in he began to wonder when they would return.

"Is there a moon tonight?" Cadwallon turned to Hwyel, his warmaster, who sat silently at the bench, hollow-eyed.

"No," said the warmaster. "It is dark. Tomorrow it rises."

"Do you think they went home? The missing men."

The warmaster turned to him, and for a moment Cadwallon thought on how Hwyel had come to look so gaunt when they had

had the fat of the land the past year or more. It was more than a year, wasn't it? Cadwallon grimaced. He could not remember how long it had been since he had defeated Edwin.

"What did you say?" Hwyel asked.

"The men who went missing today. Do you think they went home?"

"Maybe. They have been long from their hills."

"As have we all. If we catch them, kill them."

"That will not encourage men to stay."

"No, but it will make them stop to think before leaving." Cadwallon looked around, then beckoned a slave over. "Where is my wine?"

The slave, a boy barely old enough for there to be hair above his lip, looked around, but there was no one else in sight.

"Th-there is no wine, Lord," he said.

Cadwallon's blow caught the side of the boy's head and sent him crashing against a bench.

"I said, bring me wine."

The boy cringed back, out of range, holding hand to mouth, nodding.

"There is no wine." Hwyel held up his cup. "Only this foul ale."

"Bring me wine," Cadwallon yelled after the boy as he ran from the hall. Those men who sat in hall barely turned a glance to the raised voice. The king glowered out at them.

"Bring me wine!"

Hwyel stood up.

"Where are you going?" Cadwallon turned to his warmaster.

"To sleep. Somewhere quiet." But as he passed by his king, Hwyel muttered, under his breath but not quietly enough, "There is no wine."

Cadwallon surged from the judgment seat, pushing his warmaster back so he fell across the high table, knife held to the man's throat.

Silence, sudden and absolute, seized the hall. All movement ceased, all conversation.

"Tell me, warmaster, how do you know there is no wine?"

Cadwallon whispered the words in Hwyel's ear, but in the hall silence all heard him speak. "Have you drunk it?"

"I know because the steward told me when we arrived that there was no wine." Hwyel put his hand up and slowly pushed the arm holding the knife to his throat aside.

Cadwallon straightened up. The warmaster pushed himself off the table.

"There should be wine," said Cadwallon. "There should always be wine where Arthur is."

"Yes, there should be," said Hwyel. "There are many things as should be in this world, lord, but aren't." The warmaster turned the crick out of his neck.

"There will be wine at Corbridge," said Cian. "Won't there?" he asked, checking with the warmaster.

"I have not received report from the steward of the vill there; but there should be."

Cadwallon sat back in the judgment seat. "Give me some of that ale, then."

Warmaster and bard exchanged glances.

"We meet the kings of the north on the morrow," said Cian. "Mayhap it were better to do that with clear head?"

The king turned his face to the bard, and Cian saw it, gaunt and hollow-eyed, as Cadwallon had seen Hwyel earlier.

"I cannot sleep without wine or ale. Do you understand?"

"I understand, lord," said Hwyel. "I understand." The warmaster turned to the bard. "Give him ale and sing to him, and send him a slave afterwards."

While they spoke, Cadwallon looked around the hall. There was something missing…

"Where is Edwin?" He looked to the warmaster. "Where is he?"

"I – I think he is still in a wagon; this is a short halt."

"Bring him out, bring him out. I would speak with my brother in war."

A minute later, one slave placed the sack containing Edwin's head upon the table in front of the judgment seat while another filled Cadwallon's cup with ale. Eyes fixed upon the sack, Cadwallon drank, and grimaced.

"It is as foul as you said, Hwyel." He held the cup out again. "Fill this and open that."

The slave untied the rope, and the sack fell open.

"Stand him up."

The slave carefully set the head upon the table, face turned towards Cadwallon, and then, with gentle hands, he smoothed the hair away from Edwin's face.

"Why did you do that?"

The slave started back, and looked up at the king.

"Why did you do that? I saw you. Why did you do it?"

The slave opened his mouth, but no words came from it.

"I can see your tongue. You are not dumb. Why did you do that?"

The slave looked from side to side, his eyes as wide as those of a deer when the hounds trap it against a cliff.

"Let us try something else. What is your name?"

"Ber-Bermar, lord."

"So, Bermar, now we know you have a voice, use it. Why did you clear the hair from Edwin's face? He is dead, you know."

Bermar swallowed. His eyes tracked, then settled. He straightened and looked the king in the face.

"He was my king. I honoured him, insofar as I was able."

Cadwallon swallowed in turn. His face, already pale, went paler.

"I could have you killed," he said.

"I know," said Bermar.

The king brought the cup to his lips and drank. Then he grimaced and stared at it. "This really is vile." He looked at Bermar. "Bring me more."

As the slave hurried from the hall on legs that threatened to give way, Cadwallon stared at Edwin.

The head sat upon the table, slightly tilted, eyes closed but mouth open. The skin had grown dry and leathery, drawing tight over the bone beneath, but the face was still recognizable.

"How did it end like this?"

Edwin, dead, made no answer.

Bermar returned with the ale, but Cadwallon barely noticed him, simply holding his cup for it to be filled. Cian, his harp tuned, began to sing one of the beautiful songs of home, but Cadwallon did not hear it, although the music brought silence to the hearth-sick men in the hall.

"I worshipped you, Edwin. When you came to Father's hall and I saw you, all I thought was that one day I would be as you were. All men's hands were turned against you, yet you stood unafraid before Father and proclaimed your name, and the blood price Æthelfrith had lain upon your head, and you challenged Father to take it." Cadwallon drained his cup again, and held it for more.

"I would have stood beside you, then and there, sword to sword, against my own father if he had taken the blood price and raised his hand against you. But my father was as taken as I; he took you into our hall and into our family, and you betrayed us!" Cadwallon flung the contents of his cup over Edwin's head. Ale dripped down his cheeks and ran in streams over dry lips into a mouth that drank no more.

The king held out the cup. Refilled, he drank from it, his gaze upon Edwin's face. Cian sang on, but the music did not enter Cadwallon's heart.

"I thought all would be well when I killed you, when I avenged my family on yours." Cadwallon drank again. His eyes were still fixed upon Edwin, but his gaze was blurring now with the familiar mist that filled his evenings, and without which sleep would not come.

"But they are coming now, Edwin. The kings of the north. Finally, they have heard my call; they have answered. They will acclaim me High King, Edwin – kings over which you were never lord. And then, maybe, all will be well." Cadwallon's head dropped, then started back up again. His eyes lost sight, then gained it again, and Edwin filled the king's vision.

"You will see me as High King, old friend, brother in my heart. You will see me raised higher than you ever were, and then I will put you in the grave and close your eyes with earth and stuff your mouth with dirt, so I hear your voice no longer and see your face no more. It is not long now, dear brother, not long now." Cadwallon gestured Bermar to him. "Wrap him up and take him away. Do it carefully, mind. He was a great king… a great king."

Cian and Hwyel laid the king in his bed as men fell asleep on bench and floor around the hall.

"There is a fey mood upon the king," Cian said to the warmaster as they moved him.

"It lies upon us all," said Hwyel. "Have you not felt it?"

"I put it down to hearth longing; we have been from our hills and rivers too long, old friend." Cian stood up. "I have tried to warm my heart to this new land, for on the face of it here is not so different from home, but I have failed. The names that lie upon the land are strange and I do not know its song."

"It lies upon the king's heart too," said Hwyel. "He has tried to make himself love it, and in doing so has twisted his heart, putting away the sweet memories of home and covering them with remembrance of blood. For there has been little but blood and gold in these new lands, and while I love the gold as much as any man, for the glory to shine you must sing it from your hearth fire, among your own people, not here, amid strangers."

"He has waited many months for the kings of the north to accept him. Now they have, do you think he will allow us to return to our own land?"

"Yes," said Hwyel. He leaned down and smoothed the hair from Cadwallon's face. "Yes, when the kings have come and bowed before him, he will be satisfied and we will go home." He smiled at the bard. "It is not so long to wait now, is it?"

"No," said Cian. "No, it isn't."

*

Cadwallon sat slumped in the saddle. Hwyel, riding beside him, pointed ahead.

"The Wall," he said.

"Go away and die," said Cadwallon.

Hwyel grunted with laughter. "I told you the ale at that vill yesterday was foul."

Cadwallon shook his head, then winced. "It was either that or lying sweating and staring into the dark on my bed through the night," he said.

"When we have met the kings of the north, and they have accepted you as High King, then we could go home," said Hwyel. "It would be good to see the mountains and valleys of Gwynedd again." He looked to the king riding beside him, head hung and eyes squinting against the daylight. "The dreams of home are good dreams."

"Yes." Cadwallon lifted his head and though he winced again, this time his gaze took in the world around him. "Yes, once this is done, once I am acclaimed High King, then we can go home. Maybe I would sleep there..." He peered blearily ahead. "Did you say you can see the Wall?"

"Yes. There. Follow the line of the road. It dips down ahead, to the River Tyne, but then the ground rises beyond, and there, on the hill crest, that is the Wall."

Cadwallon squinted ahead. "Yes, I see it. I think. Your eyes are sharper than mine, Hwyel."

"After the ale you drank last night, a mole might see better in the day time!"

"It's the white line, is it not? The one where the hills rise up beyond the river."

"Yes, that is it. Though the Wall shows white in few places today. Some local people told me that in the days of their fathers and their grandfathers, much more of the Wall was white, so that it shone in the day and glowed by moonlight. But now it only shows white where recesses and cracks in the rock preserve the colour."

Cadwallon nodded. "Maybe, when the kings of the north have accepted me as High King, I should have the Wall painted white again. After all, we are Roman, and Briton too." The king looked to his warmaster. "We should call a moneyer to us and have new coins minted, of gold, with my face and name upon them, and I shall call myself…" The king paused. "What did the emperors call themselves in Latin? I used to know, but I have forgotten."

Hwyel shrugged. "I know not the letters of our own tongue, let alone those of the emperors."

Cadwallon shook his head, then winced yet again. "Ach, it will come to me." He peered ahead, following the road line as it rose up from the river towards the Wall. "You have the better sight, Hwyel. Can you see any camp ahead where the kings wait for us?"

The warmaster stood in his saddle, shading his sight. "No, lord. The road and its surrounds are clear as far as I can see."

"They should have been here." Cadwallon squinted ahead, as if not believing his warmaster. "Is there any with sharper sight among the men?"

"There are men with younger eyes than I, lord. They could see further and clearer, but see for yourself: there are no smoke tracks – they alone should reveal a camp, for we are not meeting a warband but an embassy. They will not be seeking to conceal themselves."

"They must still be on the way." Cadwallon slumped into his saddle.

"We could send scouts ahead," said Hwyel. "They could tell us if the kings of the north approach but are still beyond the Wall."

"Yes, do that," said the king. "But order them to be back before nightfall – we have lost too many men in the dark."

"I will do that, lord."

As the warmaster peeled back along the line of horsemen to select his scouts, Cadwallon rode on. The ache in his head thrummed, but he felt the pain receding. The hills ahead reminded him of the mountains of home. Not that they were as gaunt as the teeth of Gwynedd, scree-sloped and bare, but the rise and fall of them, like a churned sea, carried echoes of the land of his fathers.

As sharp and clear as a seagull's call, Cadwallon heard in memory the chant of the priests as they had laid his father, Cadfan, into the ground of Anglesey. He saw again the monk mason, carefully incising the stone, and he remembered how carefully he had committed the words, written in a tongue that he had never had time to learn, to his memory: *Catamanus rex sapientisimus opinatisimus omnium regum* – "King Cadfan, most wise and renowned of all kings". And suddenly, Cadwallon was filled with a terrible fear that his own body would not lie next to his father's in the holy burial place of his people, but would be scattered upon hills far from his native home. He glanced up at the sky.

"Do men who die far from home wander in spirit, lost in shadows, searching their way back?" he asked. Kings fought, and had priests to do their praying for them. When he had ridden from Gwynedd many months ago, Cadwallon had left the monks of three monasteries praying for him, and promising to keep praying for him until he returned, but now he asked the question of God directly. The priests told him that when a man died, he faced God's judgment. But how could a man face God unless he stood upon the ground that had borne him, that had fed him and raised him? Surely the dead returned home before facing God?

But God gave no answer to his question. Cadwallon watched the scouts urge their horses on, horseshoes sparking on the road stone as they galloped ahead of the army. Turning, he looked back along the column of his army, the men riding in line, spears raised, points glittering in the sun. The king smiled. Such an army had not been seen in this land since the armies of the emperors marched upon the Wall. But now, once he had been acclaimed High King by the kings of the north, there would be a new emperor.

"Imperator!" Cadwallon smiled. That was it. He knew the word would come back to him. His father had been "Rex", but he would be "Imperator", and place his face upon the gold coins of his reign. He looked around for Hwyel, to tell him, but the warmaster was busy further back in the column. Never mind. He would tell him later.

*

With the day stretching to evening, Hwyel led the column of horsemen across the River Tyne, their animals' legs splashing across Styford, while the wagoners drove the mules into the water and, with the warmaster's permission, left their wagons in the shallows for a while so that the wooden wheels might swell and tighten against their iron rims. The wagons were heavy and ran slow behind struggling teams of oxen, for they carried the accumulated plunder of Deira and Bernicia: gold and garnet, torc and ring.

Beyond the ford, the road ran north into the rising hills, the Wall surmounting the distant ridge, but it was too far to go in failing light. Cadwallon ordered camp to be made on the north bank of the Tyne. With the light failing, he called Hwyel to him.

"Where are the scouts? Have they come back yet?"

"No, lord," said the warmaster.

"Find out what has happened to them." Cadwallon stared north, to where the broken line of the Wall skimmed the hills. "They should have returned – it will be dark soon."

While the warmaster set lookouts to watch for any sign of the scouts, the king went to the tent that had been set for him, the red and gold of his banner fluttering in the evening breeze. Around the royal shelter the men rested by fires. The camp was quiet, and Cadwallon noted a sullen air – there were few jokes, and no songs were raised to chase away the aches of a day in the saddle.

It was the camp of a hearth-sick army, far from home. But soon they would turn south and west, riding the roads of the emperors until, of a fine morning, they would see the sun gild the hills of home. The camp would be happy enough when the army turned for home – and then there would be no shortage of men to help the wagoners push the wagons through fords and across breaks in the road.

Cadwallon took to his tent. Slaves set food for him, and drink, but after the price he had paid for the previous night's drinking he took ale sparingly. Besides, he felt in his bones that he would have no difficulty in sleep tonight.

The warmaster returned as the king was finishing his light supper, coming into the tent with one of the scouts.

"Tell the king what you saw."

The scout made the courtesy and glanced questioningly at Hwyel.

"Go on," said the warmaster.

"Lord, I crossed the river with the other scouts in the early afternoon. The road of the emperors continues north there, to the Wall, so we rode upon it but saw nobody save for drovers moving sheep down from the high hills. When we came to the Wall, we found the gate lying open and broken, and beyond the road – for we could see far from the towers of the fort that guarded this part of the Wall – the road to the north seemed empty. However, that was still the way most likely, we thought, for the kings of the north to take, so two of my fellows set forth upon it, resolved to ride north for a further two hours, but leaving themselves time enough to return before dark." The scout suddenly stopped his report and turned to Hwyel. "Have they returned yet?"

"No. Get on with it."

"We decided that one of us should ride east, following the road that lies south of the Wall, and another – I – should go west, lest the kings of the north be approaching from either of these directions. It was late afternoon by then, and the shadows were lengthening, but the sun was in my eyes as I rode into the west. Then, as the sun touched the horizon and I resolved to turn back, I saw it, lord. A camp – it was a camp – but one lying to the north of the Wall, maybe a mile north of it. I could see fires, but the rising land obscured much of it, so I cannot tell the number of men there. It was yet light, so I resolved to ride closer, in the hope that I could see more before I must return. I thought that if I could see a banner, I might tell who camped north of the Wall; I might tell if it was the kings of the north, come to do homage to you, lord." The scout licked his lips and risked a glance at the warmaster, who gestured him on.

"I pushed my horse hard, that I might get close enough to see something before night fell, and I did, lord; I did. For in the centre of the camp, there was set a great cross."

Cadwallon sat forward.

"A cross? You are sure?"

"Yes, lord, I am sure. The sun was low, and its light threw the shadow of the cross across the land toward me, and I saw it laid out upon the ground. It was a cross. Seeing that, and knowing that if I did not return soon I would be alone in the night in this land, I ran my horse back here. I hope I did right, lord."

Cadwallon stood from his stool.

"You did right indeed." The king smiled and, taking a ring from his arm, gave it to the scout. "Take this. And then eat and drink, for you must be weary."

When the scout had gone, Cadwallon turned to Hwyel and his smile was broad. The king took hold of the warmaster's shoulders.

"They are here," he said. "They are here! For only the kings of the north would set a cross over their camp as they make ready to go down to meet the answer to God's promise to our people. They have come to me, Hwyel! They have come at last!"

Chapter 15

"I've seen him!"

"What? Who?" Oswiu, shaken awake, saw his brother's face above him, lit with ember glow.

"Rouse Brother Diuma and Talorc; wake Acca and Coifi and Corotic; wake everyone! I've seen him."

And in the glow of stoked embers, Oswald, Iding, ætheling of the throne, stood before his men and told what he had seen.

"Sleep was late coming – and I was not alone, for I heard men turn and speak – but when sleep came, I dreamed, and I saw him: the Blessed One, Colm Cille. He stood as tall as the clouds, and beneath his face all darkness was banished. His cloak covered near enough all our camp, save for that part where the pack horses are tethered, and he spoke to me, saying, 'Be strong and of a good courage; behold, I shall be with thee.' And it seemed to me I knew these words of old. Then the Blessed One leaned to me and spoke again, saying, 'Ride forth this night from your camp, for the Lord has granted to me that your foes shall be put to flight; that your enemy, Cadwallon, will be delivered into your hands, and that after the battle you will return in triumph.' Then the vision – for vision I take it to be – ended, and I awoke and summoned you to me. What say you?"

Brother Diuma stood. "Those words that in vision you knew of old: they are the words the Lord spoke to Joshua, when he stood upon the bank of the Great River, looking over upon the fields of the land promised." He turned to look at the other gathered men. "For those here who do not know, God went before Joshua as he led his people into the land promised, and cast down his enemies and took the land." The monk turned back to Oswald. "I say the Lord has spoken to you this night. I say we ride with the night. I say we ride to victory!"

And as one, the men rose and acclaimed the monk's words.

As the acclaim died away, Brother Diuma sent one of his monks to the horses, and he returned with a rolled bundle of cloth. There, in the firelight, Brother Diuma unwrapped it and, with another monk, held it taut.

"This is the banner of the Holy Island, the flag of Colm Cille. Abbot Ségéne told us we could only fly it if we had a clear sign from the Blessed One that we should: we have that sign. Tomorrow, we shall fight beneath the flag of Colm Cille."

Oswald went to the monk. "That flag will be worth twenty men to us," he said.

Brother Diuma smiled and shook his head. "Fifty," he said.

*

As the moon set, and the first glow of dawn lit the east, Corotic led the column of horsemen south, to the Wall and the fast road that ran alongside it to Cadwallon's camp upon the bank of the River Tyne.

Crossing south of the Wall, Corotic put them upon the road. It ran east, and the glow of the moon's setting and the fire of the sun's rising drew its path across the shadowed land.

"You have led us well," Oswald said to Corotic. "I would ask one thing more of you, if you would give it."

Corotic sat astride his pony. "I would give it, Raven King," he said, "Lord of the Tree."

"Block the road south of the Tyne. Cut trees, roll stones, do whatever you can to make it impassable to wagons. Cadwallon carries with him the treasure of my people, and yours. I would not have him escape with it."

"I will do that, lord, and my people will wait in the woods and marsh there. Any of Cadwallon's men who flee from the road into the wild places will not leave them."

Oswald made the courtesy to the chief of the Raven People. Bran lowered his head and coughed.

Corotic nodded, turned his pony and angled it south, towards the river.

"Farewell, Raven King," he said. "After this, we will return to our hills."

"You will be ever welcome in my hall, Corotic of the Raven People."

"And you in our hills, Oswald of the sea lords."

The ætheling watched the small figure on the pony until he was lost in the shadows of the twilight. Then he turned to the road.

"Ride!" he called. "Ride, to death and death's glory!"

And the horses sprang forward as if the wind had seized their hooves, and the men laughed, for the madness of the hunt, the wild, death hunt, had taken them, and there was no fear but only the pounding of heart, and blood, and bone.

*

Cadwallon woke with the dawn. Few birds sang the chorus at this season, but the first stirrings of light woke him, and he rose from where he lay, and went out into the pale day. Cian, the bard, and Hwyel, the warmaster, found him standing in front of his tent as the camp made its first stirrings. The wagoners, exhausted by the passage across the ford, slept deeply by their oxen.

The king looked about him and breathed the damp air. He turned to Cian and Hwyel. "This reminds me of home. The air tastes of it, and there," he pointed, "the hills – they remind me of home too. When the kings come, when they have accepted me, we shall return." Cadwallon's eyes narrowed and he pointed again. "There, can you see them? Riders."

Cian and Hwyel turned to look, squinting eyes to bring things far from them into sharper vision.

"Yes," said Hwyel. "Riders."

"They fly a banner," said Cian. "Two banners, maybe three."

"Can you see them?" asked Hwyel. "Your eyes are better than mine."

"No, not from this distance. But they ride swiftly – they will reach us maybe before the sun rises."

"It does not matter," said Cadwallon. "I can tell you whose banners they fly: Dal Riada, Strathclyde, Rheged. The kings of the north come; they come to me at last! We must make ready to welcome them."

*

"They have seen us."

The road was wide enough for two, even three, men to ride abreast. Oswiu rode beside his brother at the head of the column. The horses were breathing hard from their gallop to beat the dawn, but light filled the eastern horizon, betokening the arrival of the sun.

Oswald gave no answer, but urged his horse on, and it responded, despite the sweat slathering its flanks.

They could see the camp ahead, the orange glow of fires that Cadwallon had made no effort to conceal, and the stirrings of men moving from tent into the open. Judging the distance remaining, Oswiu knew Cadwallon would have more than enough time to form his men into a shieldwall before they could reach the camp. Then, they would be reduced to riding in circles around them, helpless save for shouted insults, while Cadwallon gathered his horses, fresh after a night's rest, and made ready to cut them down on their exhausted beasts.

"We should dismount, form a shieldwall," shouted Oswiu, forcing his horse up level with his brother. "Advance like that."

But Oswald turned his face to Oswiu, and he smiled the death smile.

"We ride," he said. "We ride them down – for he knows no Angle fights on the back of a horse, and he expects no attack from the kings of the north on their horses. We ride, brother; we ride!"

*

"Set the judgment seat there, upon the road. I will meet them in the north road, the road of the emperors, upon my throne, with you, Hwyel, on my right hand and you, Cian, upon my left, that you might see and hear what happens here today and sing songs and tales of it in our halls and in our land. Gather the men. Have them stand in welcome upon either side of us."

"What about the wagoners?" asked Hwyel.

"Would the kings wish to meet them? Let them sleep – they have less wit than their oxen – and we have the contents of their wagons to give as gifts to the kings of the north. Never will they have known a king so generous in gold – but that befits Arthur, returned to his people."

The sun still trembled below the horizon. There was not enough light to see the banners the riders flew, and as they approached, the road bent behind rock and past a wood, taking the horsemen from view. Cadwallon looked to where the road emerged again. From there, it was an all but straight course to the ford over the river, where they waited. Hwyel pushed men forward, pointing to where he wanted the judgment seat placed, while grumbling warriors – warriors always grumbled when they were woken unexpectedly early – stumbled from the camp. Most carried swords and spears, but they were going to greet the embassy of the kings of the north, so they left shields propped against tents, and mail draped over saddles to drip out the morning dew.

*

In the shelter of tree and wood, Oswald raised his hand, slowing the column but not stopping it, and bringing the men closer around him.

"Today," he said, "we fight like the men of the north; we fight on horseback, we move, we ride, we give the enemy no chance. I do not know why, but he has not formed shieldwall nor raised his horsemen against us – he waits, as a pig for slaughter. Let us not disappoint him!"

"One word," said Oswiu. "Leave the wagons! There will be gold for all – after the battle. Cadwallon's men will try to save their treasure; cut them down, but let their gold fall – we will return and pick the field of slaughter clean."

"God has given Cadwallon into our hands," said Oswald. "We shall not drop him. Now, ride!"

Pulling his horse's head round, Oswald heeled it forward. The animal breathed hard, and he slapped its sweat-soaked flank.

"Last effort," he said. "Last effort."

Flying above the column, Bran croaked, and Oswald looked up at the dark shape of the slaughter bird.

"Today you will eat well, old friend," he shouted. "You will eat well indeed."

The road turned past wood and rock, then swung south towards the river, cutting across low grassland. Now, nothing remained to conceal them from Cadwallon and his army, only the last remnants of night, and as they emerged into clear sight, the first gold appeared in the east: the sun was rising.

"Raise the flags!" yelled Oswald, and the purple and gold of the house of Iding unfurled behind the riders, as did the banners of the Holy Island, and Rheged, and Dal Riada.

Looking ahead, with nothing to check his view, Oswiu saw Cadwallon's men spreading out on either side of the road, forming a line. There were so many of them, while there were bare two dozen riders behind him. But he saw no shields nor helmets. And what was that they were putting in the middle of the road?

"Ride," cried Oswald, taking his animal from trot into a canter and eating up the distance between him and Cadwallon. "Ride!"

*

"See!" said Cadwallon, pointing at the approaching riders. "See how eager they are to meet their High King, Arthur returned. I would do the same if I heard that he had come back. I would drop all that I was doing and rush to see him. Now they do that for me."

"They fly their banners now," said Cian. "Look! Can you see which kings have come, Hwyel?"

The warmaster peered into the dawn light. The banners streamed behind the riders, offering little of themselves to the waiting party, but as the breezes of sunrise began to cut across the land, the flags danced sideways in the crosswind, revealing glimpses of colour and pattern.

"That is Dal Riada," he said. "I think also they fly the flag of Colm Cille, lord! That means the Holy Island has blessed you as

High King! All the kings of the north, and of the islands, will surely follow you now."

"And Rheged as well," said Cian. "I saw its colours, I'm sure. But what is the flag they all ride behind? I do not think I know it."

Cadwallon, seated upon the judgment seat, squinted.

"I know that flag…"

"They ride fast," said Hwyel, as the distance between them and the riders rapidly narrowed. His hand went to his sword hilt, and he looked round for his shield, but it was far from him, left propped against his tent, where he had left it when rushing to organize the warriors into line.

"They do not seem to be slowing down," said Cian.

"I know that flag…" said Cadwallon, slowly rising from the judgment seat.

"They are coming very fast," said Hwyel. It could be a display of horsemanship, a tribute to the new High King; then the column would split into two, streaming past on either side of the judgment seat where the king waited upon them, that he might see their skill. It had better be that. Hwyel's glance took in the men to either side of him – they were unarmoured and unprepared. As long as the riders did not lower their spears, he knew they were safe, and it was merely display on the part of the kings of the north.

Cadwallon pointed, and his hand trembled.

"That is the flag of the Idings. The kings of the north and the Holy Island ride behind the flag of the Idings."

The spears of the riders went down, pointing at them, where they waited.

"It's an attack!" screamed Hwyel. "Swords! Shields! Make a wall, make a wall!"

Cadwallon's hands shook. "No," he said. "No, it cannot be. The kings said they would acclaim me. Surely the Holy Island has not turned against me…"

"Get back!" yelled Hwyel, pushing Cadwallon. But the king stared, transfixed and unmoving, at the approaching riders, as one under enchantment or curse.

The warmaster yelled at Cian, "Get him safe!" Then he turned to the men, fumbling with swords and spears, confusion spreading from the centre into the lines. "Form a wall, a wall!"

The bard pulled at the king, but Cadwallon would not move; his eyes were held to the riders, now but twenty yards away. The road rang beneath their hooves, and floating above the confused orders and shouts from their men came the ululating war cries of the warriors of the islands.

Cian embraced the king, pulling him bodily backwards, seeking to push him behind the cover of the judgment seat. He glanced over his shoulder, and saw the lead rider approaching, leaning past his horse's head, spear couched under his arm, its point steady as the horse galloped closer. And Cian turned and faced the rider, spreading his body between the warrior and the king.

*

Oswald leaned forward, spear held tightly in a loose arm, his body doing without thinking what its training told it – the shaft grip firm, so the spear would not fall from hand; the wrist and elbow and shoulder loose, so the impact would not wrench him from the saddle. He could see the confusion spreading through the line. As he had taken them from trot, to canter, to gallop, and the waiting line of Cadwallon's men had not moved or reacted, Oswald had wondered what enchantment lay upon them, that they did not react, but then the thinking ceased as the thrum of hooves entered into his body, and his heart beat in time with the gallop, and his vision narrowed to the man sat upon the throne in the centre of the road: Cadwallon. By his dress, the gold of his buckles and the gold of his rings and the rich colours of his clothes, Oswald knew him. The king of Gwynedd sat upon a throne, waiting for him, and did not move as they approached, but sat still. The spear pointed at his heart measured the moments before his death.

A man, arms spread, appeared before Cadwallon, shielding him with his body, and the spear passed into him. The horse rode past him and Oswald saw, as he let the spear go, Cadwallon behind the man who had taken the spear meant for him, holding him, but looking up at the rider rushing past. And as he passed he screamed death at Cadwallon.

*

"No!" Cadwallon fell backwards as Cian fell against him.

"No!" Cadwallon screamed as he saw the rider go past, reaching for his sword now that his spear pierced Cian's shoulder.

"What are you doing? Why are you doing this? I am Arthur, Arthur."

Cadwallon spun, seeing the flags of Dal Riada and Rheged and the Holy Island, as the riders burst through the line of his warriors then turned back on them, men slashing with sword from horseback as his men tried desperately to form into wall.

"Run."

Cadwallon looked down and saw Cian yet lived, though blood leaked from his mouth.

"Run, lord."

Hwyel grabbed Cadwallon's arm and he dropped Cian, the bard falling to his knees. He tried to reach for him, but Hwyel pulled the king back towards the wagons and the river.

"Fall back!" he yelled. "Fall back!" Then the warmaster seized the king and slapped him, once, twice, across the face. "Wake!" he shouted. "We need you! We can still win – there are only a few of them."

Cadwallon shook his head.

"I – I do not understand," he said. "Why have they betrayed me?"

Hwyel bared his teeth, snarling as a rider came close, and he thrust with his sword, deflecting the blow that would have struck down the king, then pulled him away, back towards the wagons and horses.

Horses.

If they could get to the horses, they could get away.

"To me!" he yelled, waving his sword. "To me! Protect the king."

And in the confusion and panic, those men closest to him, hearing his call, came to him, fighting their way to their king.

*

"Where is he? Where is he?" Oswald looked around, searching for sight of Cadwallon among the knots of fighting men and the swirl of horses. Already, he could see some of Cadwallon's men running from the battle, the dogs of panic chasing their heels as they escaped towards the distant wood. Others, though, staying together with swords pricking outwards, were starting to back towards the wagons pulled up on the river's banks. Glancing to the wagons themselves, Oswald saw the wagoners struggling to hitch oxen to their vehicles, the beasts, upset and anxious, lowing and pulling, shoving against each other, until an axle broke, sending the wagon's load crashing over the ground. From the chests and sacks spilled a golden vomit and, at its sight, many a wagoner abandoned team and wagon and fell upon it, attempting to stuff gold and silver into tunic and trouser.

Some among the retreating men saw this – the looting of the treasure they had fought for by men who did not even have the honour of carrying weapons – and they broke too, running towards the treasure wagons, the gold fever greater even than their desire for safety.

But elsewhere, the many men of Cadwallon's army were beginning to rally, their superiority in numbers allowing the chance to catch breath and realize how few attackers there were.

"Oswiu!" Oswald pointed at the wagons. "Break them!"

Oswiu reined back his horse and in a glance took in what his brother had seen.

"Talorc, to me!" With the Pict by his side, Oswiu rode to the wagons and, slashing the wagoners out of their way, pulled over the traces of first one, then another and another wagon.

The plunder of Deira, the gold and silver of Bernicia was spilled upon the grass and dropped down into the mud beside the River Tyne, and the men who had fought for it and killed for it saw it fall. With no command from their king, they broke from the small knots of fighting men and went running to it, only to be cut down by the horsemen crossing the slaughter field.

*

Hwyel saw the gold flow and the gold fever spread, but he grabbed each man that went past, pulling him back into formation, slowly building a line of spears and swords with the king at its centre, that pulled back and back, towards the milling, semi-panicked group of tethered horses.

"My treasure…" said Cadwallon, for he too had seen the gold spill from the wagons.

"Leave it," said Hwyel. He pulled the king along with him. "We'll come back for it, when we come back to kill them."

As he knew would happen, in the milling confusion of battle, the attacking horsemen veered towards the easier targets, slicing down upon the necks and backs of running men, their mounts as much as themselves turning away from the bristle of swords and spears that backed and backed and backed towards escape.

*

Oswald saw them, a band resolutely holding together, as they reached the horses and began splitting apart as, with hope of escape, discipline loosened and men began grabbing animals and mounting them.

"No," he shouted, and pointed. "They are getting away." He drove his horse towards them, screaming for others to follow, and he saw, from eye corner, Brother Diuma, face bright, swinging in beside him, and Oswiu and Talorc leaving the fight among the spilled guts of the wagons.

*

Hwyel set Cadwallon upon a horse, then swung up on another next to him. He pulled the beast's head round, seeing men still upon the ground with no animal to ride, for the tethers had been pulled loose and many an animal, panic stricken, had broken free. Beyond, forming up once again, he saw the enemy approaching. For a moment he thought on the fact that he still did not know who they were, but the thought was gone – it mattered not for now.

"Line!" he yelled at the men on the ground. "Form line and protect the king!" Then, taking the bridle of the king's horse, he kicked his own beast into motion and ran it towards the river. Hwyel looked around. There were a handful of men with him, leaning on their horses and urging them towards the ford; all that was left of the army that had destroyed Edwin and taken Deira and Bernicia, and made Cadwallon the most powerful king in the land. All reduced to this.

Hwyel kicked his horse harder.

"Go," he cried, to his king and his men. "Go!"

*

Oswald saw the men mounting behind the screen of swords and spears lined in front of them. He pushed his horse past the jabbing wall and then pulled it round, hooves slipping in the churned earth, after the horsemen riding towards the ford. But the spears had caught Talorc's horse, hamstringing it and bringing the Pict tumbling to the ground, from where he rolled and, screaming the high war cry of the Painted People, he flung himself shield first at the line of men, breaking it apart with his bulk. Only Oswiu managed to follow, but he was enough – the rest of his men could stay and finish off the routed remnants of Cadwallon's army.

Leaning forward, hands light upon the foam-flecked animal, Oswald urged it after Cadwallon. His beast was weary and Cadwallon's horses were fresh. Seeing the way the gap between him and the men he was pursuing widened, Oswald realized, with the sudden sickness of defeat, that he would not be able to catch them. Already they were splashing into the river, not even slowing, though the waters were running higher than they had the evening before. Oswald pushed his own horse after them, but he well knew his only chance of catching them lay in Corotic having done as he had promised, blocking the road south.

*

Cadwallon felt the horse move beneath him, and the familiarity of its motion began to bring him back to himself. The fog that had clouded his mind began to clear – the fog that had descended when he had realized that the banners of Dal Riada and Rheged and the Holy Island followed the flag of the Idings.

Treachery. He had been betrayed. Cold and sick and hopeless he felt, as one who has lost everything, and the king looked around and saw what was left of his army, and knew that that was so. He had lost everything. Only his life remained.

"No!"

Cadwallon looked to Hwyel and saw the warmaster reining back his horse. Ahead, trees and boulders lay across the road, and amid the branches and behind the rocks he could see figures moving and the tell-tale movements of arrows being nocked to bowstring. The warmaster circled his horse, looking for another path.

"That way." Hwyel pointed to where a path branched from the road, heading west and south. He pushed his horse down the way, leading as Cadwallon followed.

*

"Where does the path go?" Oswald reined back his horse and leaned down to Corotic, who had run up to the point at which Cadwallon and Hwyel had left the road.

"It goes to the Devil's Water," said Corotic. "There is no crossing that river until it runs up into the hills."

"They may take to foot. Corotic, hold the hills. We will follow on horse. Do not let them escape."

The chief of the Raven People pointed upwards, and Oswald looked to see Bran circling above, the winds carrying him down towards the Devil's Water.

"Follow him," said Corotic. "He sees where Cadwallon flees."

Oswald nodded, then glanced to Oswiu.

"How is your horse? Can it still run?"

"I'll get off and run on foot if I have to." Oswiu pointed down towards where Cadwallon and Hwyel were receding. "That is no road and they will hardly be able to do more than walk their animals along it. Besides, the Raven People will cut them down if they try to move up into the hills. Let's go."

*

The horses struggled along beside the bank of the Devil's Water. The path became a track that dissolved into tussocks and marshgrass. Hwyel looked back the way they had come and saw their pursuers making their own slow way along the path. There were only two of them on horses, but looking up at the hill that rose to their left he saw movement flickering between the copses and gorse – archers were making their stealthy way around the flanks of the hill. The river ran to their right, heading south now, far too wide and fast flowing to ford with horses. On the far bank, the land rose to bleak moorland heights. Scanning the ground, Hwyel could see no sign of movement – the river that was blocking them was also stopping their pursuers getting to the far bank.

Hwyel nodded. Yes, there was hope. Now he just had to convince Cadwallon. He pushed his horse up alongside the king.

Cadwallon rode without looking left or right, still caught in the despair of his betrayal by the kings of the north.

"Lord, if we can ford this river, we will be able to escape onto the high moors."

The king turned his gaze to Hwyel and his eyes were black.

"There is no escape from this, old friend."

"But you did it before, lord, when Edwin set you adrift, alone and without oar or sail on the sea. You survived and you brought Edwin down. You can do it again – if we get away."

The king turned his gaze away. "The Holy Island prays for the Iding. Who prays for me?"

*

"Leave the horses."

Oswald dismounted and Oswiu swung down beside him.

"They are blown – we will be faster on foot." The ætheling pointed to their left, where the land ridged up before falling rapidly down to the Devil's Water. "We can cut over here, and take them as they come round the loop."

Sword slung over his back, Oswald began running up to the spine of the ridge, pulling himself up the steeper slopes, blood drumming in his ears and breath harsh in his mouth. His brother ran with him, leaping from tussock to crag, pulling their way upwards, until they came to the top of the ridge.

There, below them, ran the Devil's Water, the water rippling and disturbed by the pebbles and gravel at its bed: a ford. But Cadwallon and Hwyel had not yet reached it; they were still downstream, leading their horses through the willow breaks and reed beds that choked the near bank of the river. They were near come to the ford, though, and once across, they would be away on clearer ground and with fresher beasts.

Oswald turned to his brother.

"Now it is us, alone."

Above their heads, a raven coughed.

"All right, not quite alone." Oswald pulled the sword from where he had slung it over his back and turned to face the river. "They ride the Devil's Water – now let us send them to the devil."

And he began to run down the slope, letting his weight pull him downhill. And Oswiu followed.

*

Hwyel heard it first: the sound of water on gravel and rock; the sound of shallow water, where the river might be forded. Then he saw the water, beginning to run glitter.

"We're almost there, lord," he said, pulling his horse along.

But in answer Cadwallon pointed.

Hwyel scanned the slope.

"Lord, there are only two. We can beat them, and then get away. If you will but fight." The warmaster pulled the king's sword from its scabbard and pushed it into Cadwallon's hand. "Fight!"

But Cadwallon let the sword drop from his fingers.

"Fight!" Hwyel glanced over his shoulder and saw the two men were near enough on them. "Please…"

The king turned his face to him, and it was as pale and stretched as a dead man's, and his eyes were blank mirrors.

The warmaster whirled, and parried the first strike, pushing the blade past his shoulder, but the second sword, coming from the other side, bit deep into his side, scraping past bone rib into the lung beneath. Hwyel staggered sideways, trying to defend against the follow-up cut, but the first blade cut into his unprotected thigh, and he fell. Staring up at the sky, he saw the man who was about to kill him.

Hwyel coughed. He tasted the blood; the man over him saw it. They both knew what it meant. The first blow had pierced his lung and he was already drowning in his blood. He looked up into the face of the man above him. His eyes asked the question. The man nodded, and drove the sword through Hwyel's chest and into the ground beneath him.

*

"Why don't you fight?" Oswald pointed his sword at Cadwallon, but the king of Gwynedd did not look at it. His eyes, blank as stone, stared past Oswald into a receding distance. Cadwallon stood with his hands by his side; he had made no move when Hwyel died.

"Your warmaster died defending you, and you did nothing."

At that, the king brought his gaze to the man standing in front of him.

"Who are you?" he asked. "Are you Arthur?"

"I am Oswald, Iding, son of Æthelfrith."

"Oh. I thought you might be Arthur. I thought I was Arthur. I was wrong."

Oswald pushed his sword closer to Cadwallon, so that its tip touched his chest.

"Why don't you fight?" he asked again.

The king's eyes closed, then opened again. "I would not live in a world where my own people betray me," he said.

"Then don't."

Oswald drove his sword into Cadwallon's chest, then as quickly pulled it forth. The king's eyes opened wide in surprise as his hands flew to his chest, then slowly he stepped backwards, once, twice, before his legs gave way. Cadwallon fell to his side, jerking in spasm, and rolled into the river. His legs thrashed upon the bank for an instant and then became still. Oswiu walked forward and looked down at him.

"He's dead," he said, and using his foot he pushed Cadwallon's legs into the river. "As you said, let the Devil's Water take him to the devil." The king of Gwynedd, the master of Northumbria, the new Arthur, bumped out into the stream, his face turned to the sky, and around him the river ran red for a while before the blood was washed from him. Then, the willow fronds trailing over him, Cadwallon floated away.

Standing on the bank, the brothers watched him go.

"Father told me once that the hardest thing a king has to do is to kill a man cold," said Oswald. "He was right."

Chapter 16

Above Inys Mon, the island of Anglesey, the clouds were rushing. Cian, his right arm hanging useless by his side, stood looking east across the Menai Strait, to where the mountains of Gwynedd bulked, the first snows of winter whitening their summits. Gathered about the bard were the people of the island, waiting in silent sorrow.

Cian turned to the woman standing beside him: Briant, abbess, sister of Cadwallon. She bent down and stroked the stone that lay at their feet. Below the slab of granite, locked in the earth's long embrace, lay Cadfan ap Iago, her father, Cadwallon's father. Her fingers traced the inscription incised into the rock: *Catamanus rex sapientisimus opinatisimus omnium regum.*

"He would have wished to lie beside you, Father," she said. "But that was not God's will. He fell far from here and we could not find him. He is lost to us. Will you search for him, Father, in God's great hall, and keep him with you?"

Briant stood up, her knees aching as she did so. The cold of the winter was settling into her bones and she did not think she would ever be warm again.

The first drops of rain fell upon the stone.

"I will join you ere long."

Briant stepped back among her sisters. A hand found hers and she grasped it without looking to see who it belonged to. She knew who it was, and she was grateful for the warmth of the fingers that wrapped tightly around hers.

Cian began to chant, his voice rising alone amid the watching people, rising up to the rushing clouds. He told of the kings of Gwynedd, their victories and their long defeat, his voice as clear as the rain-washed sky. He told of Cadwallon, king of Gwynedd, of the fury of his wrath and the glory of his power.

He sang of his passing.

> *"From the plotting of strangers and iniquitous*
> *Monks, as the water flows from the fountain,*
> *Sad and heavy will be the day of Cadwallon."*

And as the song of Cadwallon died to silence, the clouds gathered above Inys Mon wept too, darkening the grave of his father with their tears.

PART 2

Mission

Chapter 1

"Men of Deira, who will you have as your king?"

Oswiu stood in the centre of the great hall that Edwin had raised amid the ruins of York, a building of wood among brick and stone, and yet to his eyes it appeared no whit less noble and beautiful a building than the works of the emperors – and it kept the rain and snow out, which the houses of stone, their roofs long decayed, did not. Around him, seated upon benches, was the witan of Deira, the thegns and reeves who had survived the depredations of Cadwallon and Penda, and the sons of the many who had not. Oswald sat at the high table, watching the assembly with careful eyes, while beside him sat a monk clad in a rough wool habit, his forehead shaved and his eyes equally watchful, and scattered through the hall were some of the surviving thegns of Bernicia – men who had already acclaimed Oswald king, their relief at surviving Cadwallon at least equal to their joy in having another Iding upon the throne of their land.

Taking boat from Bamburgh, they had sailed down the coast, a passage of sails telling the good news to the settlements that lined the grey road, running to shore whenever winter storm threatened, waiting for the clouds to blow past, then setting to again, wrapped deep in waxed cloaks, fur turned within to keep out the bitter winds. The treacherous waters of the Humber had near claimed them, for the storm-clad seaways of Dal Riada had taught them the ways of rock and reef more than mud and sand, but the tide came and floated them clear, and they were away and up the Ouse, the labour of rowing against the river for once embraced by all as proof against the winter wind. And as they pulled, they proclaimed, telling the death of Cadwallon and calling men to witan at York, that they might acclaim a new king.

Now, with the witan gathered, Oswiu rose and spoke the claim of his brother.

"He is the deliverer, who slew the scourge that bled your lands and took your fathers and your sons and lay them out upon the ground. He is son of Æthelfrith, he is son to Acha, he is the true son of Bernicia and Deira."

Upon the high table, the monk who sat beside Oswald leaned to him.

"It were best your brother had not spoken of your father – these Angles of Deira have no love for the Twister."

Oswald, conscious of the eyes and ears turned to him, made no answer, but remained impassive, watching as Oswiu turned around the hall. Outside, the first winter storm to pass the hills to the west sent sleet and hail rattling against gate and thatch. Within, the fire burned, shedding yellow light upon the shadowed faces. He could see his brother was sweating. Oswiu had expected that the men of Deira, relieved at their deliverance, would rise as one to acclaim Oswald king after a few choice phrases and the recitation of his claim. It was proving more difficult than he had anticipated.

"So, men of Deira, I ask you again: who shall be your king? Shall we be united, as we were before, Bernicia and Deira making one kingdom?"

"Hold! Hold, I say!"

Oswiu turned to see a grizzled warrior, his belly generous with beer and meat, rise to his feet.

"Who are you?"

"I am Bassus," the warrior said. He waited, as if expecting Oswiu to speak, but the ætheling, sensing the expectancy that filled the hall, gave way to him.

"You do not know me? Then, I have but lately returned from Kent. I am Bassus and I live, but should not. For alone of the warband that rode forth with Edwin from York nigh two years ago I returned, sent from the battle that claimed him with word for Queen Æthelburh that she should flee, taking their children with her. Well I remember that bitter voyage; well I remember the grief of the queen and the silence of the children, their faces turned to the sea, that men might think their tears but the splashing of the waves."

Bassus paused and turned around the hall, seeking its mood. Then he turned to Oswiu.

"This is not the way of our people, the men of Deira. You would have us proclaim your brother king when we have not heard the claims of others. You would have us one kingdom, but you name your own land first." He held up his hand to silence the murmurs rising from around the hall. "Mayhap this Oswald, the Iding, has the greatest claim on the throne – I do not doubt that he is throne-worthy. But we must speak on this, hear other voices and other rights, and then decide. This is the way of our people; this is the way of Deira. It is as well for you to remember that if you wish to rule here."

"I will remember." Oswald stood. He looked to Bassus, and the warrior made the courtesy to him.

"We are strangers here and we do not know your ways. Tell them to us and we will learn. But think on this, men of Deira. When Osric claimed the throne of Deira, I did not come. When Eanfrith claimed the throne of Bernicia, I did not come. Only when their claims failed, and Cadwallon laid them out in the dust, only then did I come and, against all hope, against all expectation, I brought the despoiler of your kingdom down. Bassus, know this: I did not want this throne. It was thrust upon me. So if there are any with greater claim, let us hear of them; let *me* hear of them. If there be such a man I would gladly step aside."

The monk sitting beside Oswald glanced up at those words, and a murmur passed through the hall. That a man might be throne-worthy and yet not take the throne: that was a song no man had sung before.

"Tell us then of the children of Queen Æthelburh – my cousins. In truth, they must indeed be throne-worthy and I would hear more of them." Oswald sat down, and the witan turned back to Bassus.

The warrior nodded to Oswald. "I thank you, lord. There are many here who would hear of them, of Wuscfrea and Æthelflæd. The queen took them over the Narrow Sea to her mother's people in Francia, to the court of the great king there, and Princess Æthelflæd

grows in beauty; she will soon be old and wise enough to marry."
Then Bassus shook his head. "But of the boy, of little Wuscfrea, my
news is less good." He looked around the hall. "He died. Of the
sweating sickness. And the queen laid him among her people."

A gasp, a moan passed like a whisper through the men, for many
there remembered Wuscfrea – remembered him toddling after his
elders, calling to them until finally one would sweep him up in his
arms.

"That is why I returned. With Wuscfrea dead, the queen had no
more need of my protection."

Oswald spoke. "I would have raised no hand against her or her
children, for Edwin raised no hand against us when we were in exile."

"That might be so, lord, but if you were the queen, would you
have left the children where they might be claimed? Should you come
to the throne, king of Deira and king of Bernicia, your reach would
be long and many a king might seek to win your favour through foul
means as well as fair."

"Mayhap if I were their mother I would do as Queen Æthelburh
has done. But are there other æthelings of whom you would tell?"

Bassus nodded. "There is one, lord. But before I speak of him, it
is the custom of our people that all the men sitting at the high table
be known to us, and there is one beside you who is unknown to me,
and to many in this witan. Would you tell us of him first, and then
I will speak of those that are throne-worthy."

"Very well." Oswald rose to his feet. The man beside him stared
levelly out at the hall, his face calm with the serenity of seasoned
fighting men before battle.

"This is Corman, bishop, monk and priest of the Holy Island
of Colm Cille; he is the man sent to me by the abbot of the Holy
Island, that we might seek the favour of the God of the Blessed One;
the God that we, the Idings, now follow."

Bassus stared with frank curiosity at the monk, who returned the
scrutiny without sign of strain, but with a small smile.

"We already heard tell of your new god, lord, for the queen
brought a priest from her country; he returned to Kent when we

fled, and he is now master of the stone house men built for the new god there. I do not think he will return. As for this new god, he brought Edwin few favours."

At this, a murmur went through the hall, with some men nodding their accord, while others shook their heads in disagreement. Those who most obviously disagreed turned to the back of the hall where, reluctantly it seemed, a strange figure stood from the bench where he had been sitting. He was dressed in a white alb with a cloak thrown over it against the winter cold, held in place by a simple brooch over his heart, but it was his hair that caught Oswald's attention, for his head was shaved at the crown and sides, leaving a circle of hair like a torc placed on the head.

"Who are you who seeks leave to speak to the witan?" asked Oswald.

The man cleared his throat as if nervous, but when he spoke his voice was smooth and warm, although it carried tones strange to Oswald's ear that spoke of ancient peoples and unknown places.

"I am James."

A whisper passed around the hall at the name. Oswiu, listening, heard men say to each other that they thought him fled, or dead; that he had surely been killed in the year of chaos when Cadwallon and Penda wrought destruction through the kingdom. But those who knew him of old, seeing him again, assured others less certain that he was who he claimed to be.

"Your voice sounds strange to my ear," said Oswald.

James flushed, and those who knew him in the witan smiled at the sight, for surely no other man ever blushed for so little cause.

"I – I try to speak like you, but it is not easy; your tongue sounds harsh to my ear, like crows." James flushed again. "I do not mean it has no beauty, b-but…it is very different from the language of my people."

"Who are your people?" Oswald looked around the hall. "It seems many here know you, but I do not."

"I am of a land in the south, where the sun has its home in summer and the cicadas sing. The blessed Pope Gregory sent me with many others to tell the news of our salvation to the angels of this land – for the pope saw some fair youths of your race for sale as slaves and, seeing them, asked from where they came, and hearing they were of the race of Angles he cried, 'Not Angles but angels,' and resolved at once to send to them the blessed news of life. I was among those he chose, the least and least worthy of them. When Bishop Paulinus came with Queen Æthelburh to marry King Edwin, I came as well. But when Bishop Paulinus took the queen and her children to safety, I stayed to minister to the people, that the light of God's word might still shine in these dark lands." James smiled shyly. "It is winter, and I have been here through many winters, yet still it is a wonder to me how long the sun hides his face at this time of year."

Oswald nodded. "I would hear more of this bishop; but first, tell us how you still live when so many have died."

"After the bishop left, I went from York, taking those who would come with me – in truth, there were not many – and we went north. We heard the great devastation that Cadwallon and Penda were wreaking, killing all who opposed them, so I sent the few people who were left with me back to their homes and I continued north, walking the old road, until I came to a place called Catterick. There I found a river, and a cave where I might make shelter, and there I stayed, praying always that the storm would pass. Over time, people heard that I remained, and they came to seek me out, and I prayed over them, and some were healed, and I cast out demons in the name of the Lord, and ministered to them." James flushed again. "It was little enough, but I hoped, with God's will, to keep word of him in this kingdom. Now, with those who would ravish Northumbria cast down, I would be happy to speak forth again, and carry God's message to the people."

"That is good to know." Oswald glanced at the man sitting beside him. "What say you of this, Bishop Corman?"

The bishop did not stand up. He looked down the hall to where James stood, inspecting him. James flushed once more – to the barely concealed chuckles of the men around him.

"I say: when you heard a bishop had come again into this

kingdom, why did you not come to do homage to one who stands in line of the apostles?"

James's blush deepened. "I – I…"

"What office do you hold?"

"I – I am a deacon."

"A deacon. Not even a priest – and yet you spent many years with Bishop Paulinus here. He did not think to ordain you? Is that not strange?"

"I – I did not think myself worthy to be ordained priest."

"No. No indeed. And finally, I ask by whose authority you minister here, alone, in this kingdom?"

"It was Bishop Mellitus who sent us with Queen Æthelburh, but he died many years ago and I have not heard who is bishop in his place now."

Bishop Corman raised an eyebrow. "So you have no authority for your ministry either. I, on the other hand, come to this country with the blessing of the Holy Island and under the protection of the Blessed One, Colm Cille."

James shook his head. "I – I… Who is Colm Cille?"

Bishop Corman raised his other eyebrow.

"You, who call yourself deacon, know not the Blessed One?"

"N-no."

"Then you are not worthy of the office you claim to hold, and I can only give thanks that the previous bishop had the wisdom and foresight not to ordain you priest, no doubt aware that you would only bring disgrace to that holy office. You say you found a cave? Return to it."

James the deacon stood, his mouth agape, his face and neck bright with blood.

"I – I," he gasped. "My lord…" He directed a pleading glance to Oswald.

"Bishop Corman," began Oswald, "perhaps he could remain; I would hear of his home…"

"My lord," Bishop Corman said, in tones that suggested he called no man lord. "When I agreed to come to this pagan land to tell the news of salvation, Abbot Ségéne assured me I would have full authority over the priests, monks and deacons in the kingdom. Unless this man lies and is no deacon, then I have rule of him, and I say for him to return to his cave and leave the mission to those who carry the blessing of the Holy Island and Colm Cille."

Oswald, for once unsure how to respond, glanced to his brother, but Oswiu shrugged.

"I will go, lord," said James. "It is true: the bishop's word should be as my own will, merely uttered and done." He gathered his cloak around his shoulders and, taking his staff from where it lay under the table, James made his way through the throng of men to the door of the great hall.

In the watching silence, the creak of the door sounded loud as the door warden swung it open, and from without there came a swirl of wind-driven snow. James the deacon went out into the storm, and the door warden closed the door behind him.

As men turned to speak to each other, whispering and glancing at the high table and Bishop Corman, Bassus stood up.

"Lord, if the witan acclaims you, will you be our king? Or will it be this stranger?"

"Let me speak!"

The witan, poised between Bassus and Oswald, turned to see Acca rising from his place by the fire. The scop had put all the training of his years into the shout, and it brought all attention to him. Now that Acca had the attention, he used it. He pointed at Bassus.

"You, Bassus – were you there when Cadwallon cut down Osric and left the fields outside this city covered in the bodies of the dead? I was there. Were you there when he put fire to Ad Gefrin? I was there. Were you there when he murdered Eanfrith under flag of truce? I was there. For a certainty, you served Edwin well and faithfully, but were you here, this past year, when fear and famine stalked this land? I was here.

"And were you there when Oswald brought down Cadwallon and delivered us from his wrath? I was there, Bassus. I was there! And I tell thee, there can be no worthier king for us than this man, son of Æthelfrith, son of Acha: true Iding and true Yffing. If you have another who is throne-worthy, then speak now." Acca looked around the witan, seeming to catch every man's gaze with his own.

"I was there," he said again.

The witan turned to Bassus, but the old warrior did not sit down.

"I do not doubt that Oswald is throne-worthy, but we men of Deira do not rush to acclaim when thought and counsel call us to wait and consider. There is another we must give thought on, another man who is throne-worthy, and though he has not called on me to speak for him, yet will I do so, lest any man later accuse me of holding silence when I should have spoken."

Bassus paused and looked carefully around the assembled men, searching for one face among the many, until his own face lightened with a smile.

"Ah, he is here." Bassus paused as men shifted, whispering names one to another. "Our forefather, Yffi, had two sons, and from his eldest came Ælle and then Edwin. Yet the children of Yffi's younger son are throne-worthy too, and from that line came Osric, whom you were glad to call king, and from that line there is another most throne-worthy. He held his land and his hall when Cadwallon razed the kingdom; a valiant lord and a wise one, for he knew well when to fight and when to hold his peace. So I call upon the witan to think on the claim of Oswine, son of Ælfric, son of Yffi. Should he be our king?"

At the name, many men nodded, though whether from having their guess confirmed or in agreement, Oswald could not tell. He looked around the hall, seeking the identity of this man who would be king, but no man rose from his seat.

"Where is he? Is he here?" he asked.

Then slowly, reluctantly, as if prodded to his feet by the glances of the men who knew him, Oswine rose.

He was young, younger than Oswiu, with fair hair and clear eyes.

"I am Oswine," he said. "And I would not be king."

At this, a murmur ran through the assembly. Many men cried no, for Oswine had a most kingly bearing, and his word was known from his youth as true, and his arm was told to be strong. And more, he had grown up among the men present at the witan: he had ridden on hunt and in war with them, he had suffered through the year of fear and famine, he was their own best selves reflected to them.

Oswald held up his hand, and quiet slowly returned to the witan.

"I too would not be king," he said to Oswine. "And our names alone attest that either of us may yet be called to be king – unless there are others throne-worthy that Bassus has yet to speak on?" He looked to the warrior, to see him shake his head. "Then it is for the witan to decide between us. For myself, I would know more of you. How did you live when so many died with Osric? When your king called, did you not answer?"

Oswine stiffened at the question and the line of his mouth tightened.

"When King Edwin called the witan to consider whether we should hold with the gods of our fathers or take the new God that his priest Paulinus proclaimed, I was there. I was yet a youth and spoke not, but I listened, and heard Guthlaf, the king's warmaster, tell on this life of man as like unto a sparrow flying into a hall in winter storm, and finding there light and warmth and fellowship, but fleeing hence into the dark and the unknown; for such was our state, with no knowledge of what befalls us before we are born nor after we die. Then I heard Coifi, priest of the old gods, speak, and he abjured the gods he had served, for they had failed him who had served them most faithfully.

"I heard all this, and in my heart I welcomed this new knowledge, and when the witan gave voice that we should adopt this new God, my heart rejoiced. When many here followed the king and his sons into the water of new life, I was among those who went afterwards, and I emerged as a man cleansed, gasping, like a babe but full made.

"I answered Osric's call, but when in fear and uncertainty he abandoned our new God and sacrificed blood to the gods of old, I could not – I would not. So I withdrew, returning to my hall with my people, and I was spared and saved, as one who remained true to his pledge to our new God – and yours. That is why I yet live and did not die, and if any man call upon me, I will answer with sword and shield." The young man looked around the hall, but none rose to his challenge; rather, many turned their faces away, remembering the ease with which they had abandoned their oaths, and hiding their shame.

"But now, if no man calls upon me, I would speak for myself in front of the witan." Oswine paused, and the assembly leaned to him, to hear his words.

"I would not be king. Though Bassus proclaims me throne-worthy, my heart tells me no. You must find another." Oswine stopped and looked to the high table, where Oswald sat with his brother and Bishop Corman on either side of him. "There he is."

And then, at first one by one, then in groups, and then all that were left, the men of the witan rose to their feet and acclaimed their king.

*

When all the witan had given pledge to Oswald, and he had laid his hands upon their bowed heads, giving gifts of gold and weapons – for great was the hoard that they had recovered from the wagons of Cadwallon – then Acca rose and sang his claim to the throne, telling the story of the Idings through the generations, from their forefather, Woden. The tale was new to many of the witan, for few now remembered the days when Æthelfrith, Oswald's father, had ruled in Deira, taking the throne from Edwin's father, Ælle, by slaying him at the marriage feast that had been made to celebrate his marriage to Edwin's sister, Acha. Still, the tale of that day had come down the years, and some among the witan bowed to Æthelfrith's son with ill grace. Yet Oswald made no sign that he saw such hesitation, but gave gold as generously to those who gave oath with tight lips as to those who pledged themselves with full hearts.

Oswiu remained beside his brother through all that time, a smile as broad as the Sound of Iona upon his face, and when the last man was done and he was returning to his bench in the hall, he whispered to Oswald, "Did you think, when we waited wet and starving outside

the hall of Dunadd to know if Domnall Brecc would receive us or
return us, we would ever come to this day?"

And Oswald, without turning his head, said, "Your cheeks were
so wet, I thought it was raining."

"I was a boy."

"So was I." Oswald saw the last man return to his place, then
turned and smiled at his brother. "No, I did not think this day
would ever come."

Then Oswald rose to his feet.

"Men of Deira, I have given gifts of gold and silver, jewels and
weapons cunningly wrought, but I have one more gift to give, and
this to you – to us – all. I had not thought to give it before, lest some
among you say I sought to win favour with the witan that was not
my due. But I have a blood guilt of my own that I must pay; for my
father raised his hand treacherously against your king Ælle, slaying
him when he brought his daughter, my mother, for marriage. As for
me, in truth I am my father's son, but more, much more, I am the son
of my mother Acha, lady of the Yffings. I pray that she will return to
the land and people that bore her, and be queen here once more, for
she still lives." At that news, murmurs spread through the witan, for
many stories told of the beauty and generosity of Queen Acha.

"And though my mother was given in marriage to Æthelfrith, yet
she spoke always of her brother Edwin, sometimes when he was in
exile, more when it was we who were in exile, and Edwin made no
move against us, but let us live in peace.

"Men of Deira, know this. My father was a great warrior, but my
uncle was a great king and still I hear men speak of the peace and
plenty of his days, when a woman with babe in arms might pass
from sea to sea without fear or harm. King Edwin fell and we, his
kin, the sons of the man who had driven him into exile, we avenged
him. We killed the man who ravaged this land, burning halls and
bringing ruin, and we watched as the water carried his body away;
he will have no resting place. But now I bring back to you your king,
that he might have a resting place among his people, and we may ask
his blessing, who lives now in God's great hall."

And Oswald signed to his brother, and Oswiu brought forth a richly worked chest, covered in gold cloth, and placed it upon the high table. Then together they took the cloth from the chest, folded it and, kissing it, lay it beside the chest. A silence of great awe filled the hall. Oswald opened the chest, but in a way that no one but he might yet see what it contained. Then, laying reverent hands upon it, he brought forth from the chest the head of King Edwin and placed it upon the gold cloth, that all might see. A great cry went up from the assembled men, and tears sprang from many eyes, but yet they gave thanks to see their king returned to them.

In silence, the men of the witan gave reverence to their king of old, and when all had passed before his face, Oswald rose again and spoke.

"Let us take the High King forth and lay him to rest in the church that he built here in York."

And Oswald and Oswiu placed the mortal remains of their uncle back in the chest and covered it again with the gold cloth. Then they led the men of the witan from the hall, and when the doors were opened, they saw that the storm was past and the world was made white and still, waiting.

They carried Edwin to the church. Its stone walls were set firm and high, but its roof remained incomplete, for it had not yet been finished when the king fell. But they placed the chest upon the altar, and bowed before it, and each man laid his hand upon the cloth that covered it. Then Oswald set guards upon the church, that Edwin might rest there undisturbed until the church was made whole, and the witan returned to the hall that it might feast the new king.

*

"We have eaten."

A satisfied roar answered Oswald as men settled over tables, stomachs full, wiping grease from their mouths.

"We have drunk."

A louder roar answered him. Bassus stood, holding his cup high, and announced, "We are still drinking!" before draining the cup in a single long draught, to the acclaim of the men around him

"Not all of us have Bassus's head – nor his belly!"

The old warrior laughed and held out his cup for refilling.

"Tomorrow, many of you will return to your halls and your fields – although some may be riding more slowly than others – so now, as the night nears, we will hear tales and songs and riddles." The loudest roar of all greeted that, for the men of the witan loved nothing as much as stories of warriors and monsters and gods, except mayhap a new riddle, tough and made to chew over as the fire burned low and the shadows swelled.

"But before I call on Acca, I would have another speak to you. In exile, I lived long on the Holy Island, in the kingdom of Dal Riada, and I saw there... I saw wonders." Oswald's voice trailed away and the men closest saw his gaze fade into memory.

"When I left the Holy Island, the abbot promised, if I should survive and win the throne, that he would send us a bishop, to teach and bless, that we might have knowledge of God and the life he brings forth. As soon as news reached the Holy Island – for the abbot had sent monks too, monks who fought alongside me at Heavenfield and they returned with word – the abbot sent a bishop with his blessings and the blessings of the Holy Island. Now, while we still have ears to hear, I ask Bishop Corman to tell us of God's wonders and his beauty."

Oswald resumed his place at the high table, and the hall, while far from silent – it had eaten and drunk too well to be silent – assumed an air of expectancy.

Bishop Corman rose to his feet. He looked at the watching men, the great shaved dome of his forehead catching the rushlights and reflecting them.

"Today, we laid King Edwin to rest, and we pray he takes his place in God's great hall, before the Holy One. Today, I stand before you, bishop and teacher, in line of the apostles, and I tell you now, that if you do not accept the teachings I bring and change your lives, leaving aside the wretched stories of gods and pagan kings of old, you will burn."

In the firelight, the bishop's eyes burned indeed, and deep

shadows moved across his face. The background conversation in the hall died away and eyes, glinting, turned to the man standing at the high table.

"You will burn as your forefathers burn; the men who drove the saints from this land and filled it with idols and sorcery. You will burn and the cold rain of hell will chill you and you will have no rest but the rest of the damned, which is to curse the living. You will burn as Æthelfrith burns; for God alone is king, and he does his justice on the living and the dead."

A sound, like to the growling of a dog, rose through the hall, and men began to stand.

But before they could speak, Bassus strode forward and stood in front of the high table.

"You tell me my forefathers burn?"

The bishop looked at him and his eyes were cold. "They burn."

"I will not hear my father and my father's father traduced in such manner – if they burn, I will burn with them." Then the old warrior turned and strode from the hall.

"They b…" The bishop made to call after the departing warrior, but before he could finish the phrase, the wind rushed from his belly. Gasping, he looked up at Oswald. "You – you struck me?"

"Oh, shut up," said Oswald. The second blow knocked the bishop out.

Oswiu looked over the prone man to his brother. "Well, that went well," he said.

"You shut up too," said Oswald.

*

"You cannot speak to these men in such a way."

Oswald sat beside the bed to which they had taken the bishop – he had Oswald's own bed, for only the king had a room of his own, and as yet he had no wife to share it with.

"You struck me." Bishop Corman looked at Oswald with unfeigned loathing, although it was mixed with unbelief that such a thing might happen.

"Yes. Yes, I did, and I will again if you speak in such manner."

The bishop struggled to sit up, although his head still spun from the blow he had received. He swung his legs to the ground, made to stand up, then when his legs gave way held his arm out to Oswald.

"Help me, you idiot," he said.

Oswald gave him his arm and Bishop Corman used it to pull himself to his feet.

"Most kings would have killed you for that insult," said Oswald.

Corman stared at him. "Abbot Ségéne will damn you for yours," he said. "To strike a bishop is to strike the apostles themselves."

"If I had let you continue speaking, there would have been no chance for the message of the Holy Island to be accepted in this kingdom. I know these people, bishop."

"I know them too," said Bishop Corman. "I told the abbot there was no point in sending me. They are ungovernable; their souls are barbarous and obstinate; I would as well preach to a kingdom of donkeys."

Oswald shook his head. "I do not understand. If you did not want to come, why did Abbot Ségéne send you?"

Bishop Corman drew himself up. "Because I am a bishop, and you have need of a bishop for the benefit of your soul and to teach and guide your kingdom. And because I speak the tongue of your people."

"Yes. But how do you know it? You are not an Angle."

"I know your speech because when I was a child, men came to my village when my father and the other men were away, and they burned it and took the women they wanted, and the children, leaving those too old or too young spitted by their homes. I was sold; my mother too, but I did not see her again. I learned your tongue from the man who bought me, in between blows and whippings; but I watched and waited, and became useful to him, for he was as lazy as he was stupid. In time, he learned to take me with him whenever he went to a beach market, for I had a gift for tongues and could make myself understood to the traders who came over sea. He loved to drink too, emptying cup after cup, and I learned to hide from him then, until the sleep came upon him, and he fell down to snore."

Bishop Corman paused and his face was taut with memory, withdrawn. Then he saw Oswald looking at him and a grim smile lightened his face.

"That was how I escaped him. The traders were of my own people. I made the best deal for him, and he drank most of it. When he slept, I took the rest and bought my passage upon the traders' ship, and came at last to the Holy Island. So, you see, I too know your people well, King Oswald. They are as I feared: too mired in their old ways to receive the joyful news I bring."

The bishop rubbed his jaw, then winced. "You did right in asking for God's word to be preached here, but this is stony ground: the seed will not take root among your people. I will return to Abbot Ségéne and tell him what I have found. But you have my blessing." Bishop Corman smiled, and for the first time there was warmth in his eyes. "You will need it."

Chapter 2

"Men of Mercia, who will you have as your king?"

Eowa, brother of Penda, turned about the witan gathered in the great hall at Tamworth.

"My brother has returned with victory and gold, gifts and weapons. He has killed Edwin and thrown back the Northumbrians; he has ravaged the East Saxons and brought back their tribute, to lay it at your feet. Now come, acclaim him as king!"

But the witan remained watchful, waiting, eyes going from one man to another to see who would speak first. Eowa began to turn to one of the men he had primed with gold and promises, but before he could rise, another stood.

Penda.

"Time." Penda looked around the hall. "That is what you asked for when I brought the witan together before: time. True, I had destroyed our enemy, Edwin, and brought glory to our kingdom, but you wanted time, and I gave it to you. I gave it to you because I understood your hesitation; because I shared it.

"It is true: I am not Iclinga. My father was not descended from Woden, and as for my mother – well, you all know what she was!"

Laughter rippled through the hall, its spread fuelled by the tension that lay near the surface of the gathering.

"And it is true, it is a grave matter to choose a king who is not Iclinga. That is why, when the witan asked for time, I gave it, and gladly, keeping only the title I had already, that of warmaster, and taking war to the East Saxons. There I forced their kings to submit to us. Men of Mercia, I have given you time, but now it is time to decide."

Penda moved from his place at the high table and walked into the centre of the hall, and all eyes watched him. The grace of his movements had not been lost to the greater muscle that now sheathed his limbs, for, as a warrior will, Penda thickened, in arm and neck and waist. He moved with the ease of youth, but to that he had added the weight of experience.

"Time draws on. A kingdom without a king cannot long endure; see how fell our ally, Cadwallon. Too long he lingered from his own lands; he should have returned when we did, and then he would yet live. But now Northumbria has a new king, men of Mercia, there is time no longer. Choose a king, or the Northumbrians will choose one for you.

"I will make it easy for you." Penda looked around the hall. "I heard the whispers. Yes, I heard them: men saying there was a true Iclinga among us, the grandson of King Cearl. No matter that he was the son of our enemy, King Edwin. No matter that I defeated him in battle and brought him back, hobbled and bound, as hostage. Still men whispered that they would hear this man, this son of our enemies, speak for king."

Penda stopped. Men craned forward from where they sat to hear his next words.

"Very well. Let it be so. Let him speak."

Whispers fluttered around the hall, taking wing at Penda's words.

"Men of Mercia, if you would have above all others an Iclinga as king, then I have brought you one. Eowa…" Penda turned to his brother. "Bring him in."

And amid the hum of excitement, Eowa left the hall, while Penda calmly returned to his place at the high table. Eowa returned leading a man, still hobbled and with hands bound, whom he pushed to the centre of the hall; the final push sent him sprawling.

Eowa stood beside him.

"This is Eadfrith, son of Edwin of Northumbria and Cwenburg, daughter of King Cearl. Men of Mercia, would you have him speak?"

At first there was silence. Then someone laughed. And another.

"Yes, let him speak." The voice held as much humour as interest. "Let him."

"Speak, Northumbrian. Speak."

"You heard them." Eowa kicked Eadfrith sharply in the ribs. "Get up. Speak." He bent down, and whispering, but so all men could hear, said, "You never know, you could end up king."

Laughter followed Eadfrith as he staggered to his feet and stood, swaying, before the witan of Mercia. His face and body bore the marks of hard use and little food; the muscle that had sheathed his bones had wasted away, and within his skull his eyes burned with the fever of hunger and hatred. Yet they burned.

"You laugh." Eadfrith, son of Edwin, looked around the assembly. Fingers pointed to him, faces turned to neighbour in whispered joke.

"I would laugh too, if I were not tied and hobbled. Then, when I had laughed, I would pass wager: how long can he stand, when all about throw their cups at him." At that, a cup sailed through the air and struck Eadfrith on the face, covering his face with ale.

He stopped and stuck out his tongue, taking upon it the dripping ale.

"That tasted good," he said. "Anyone else like to give me their ale?"

Men laughed, and one stood. "Give him a proper drink," he said.

The man nearest Eadfrith lifted his cup to the Northumbrian's lips, and Eadfrith drank, and drank, to the accompaniment of hands slammed upon table tops.

"That was very good," he said, and his smile then might almost have been recognized by one who knew him of old.

"I am to speak. I did not expect that. You did not expect that. After the battle where my father and brother fell, I expected only to die. Yet I still live. Many here are cousin to me, as I to them. Many here are Iclinga, as I am. Many here ask why the son of a Briton should rule them, as I do. For our forefather Icel took the whale road with his warriors and came to this land and made a kingdom for himself, with his sword and his strength, and he passed it on to his kin, that they might live. And live they did, and they grew strong, taking the land and making it theirs, and my grandfather, King Cearl, was the greatest of them, uniting the families of Mercia, making it strong. So strong that no king moved against him, even when he grew old and the strength of his arm failed and the light of his eye grew dim. Yet he still ruled, and well, and the other kings were glad to call him friend."

Eadfrith paused and looked around the hall. The men were listening to him closely; only Penda appeared to be paying him no mind.

"For my part, I was glad to call King Cearl grandfather. And he, for his part – and many of you heard his words – he was happy to call me heir, and acknowledge me as king after him. But... he died. King Cearl died, far from here, when he went with his warmaster, not in a warband but in an embassy, to see my father. King Cearl was old, that is true, but he was healthy. I hear the men with him burned his body rather than bring it home. No doubt it was the time of year – hot weather makes even dead kings smell. I heard he fell from his horse then fell into a fever. It can happen."

The hall was silent. Even the slaves had stopped their work and were staring at Eadfrith.

"But then – a great chance this, don't you think? – the warmaster, before he could return home, meets the army of Gwynedd, also far from home, and together they enter into alliance and meet... well, me. The men of Northumbria."

"It was the army." Penda's voice cracked across the hall. "It was no group of men we met out hunting, but the army of Edwin. What was it doing, coming to meet the men of Mercia, on embassy to Edwin?"

Eadfrith looked up the hall to where Penda, now standing, leaned forward over the high table.

"You ask why the army of my father rode to meet King Cearl? I will tell you, a straight answer, a true answer, unlike the answers you have given to this witan.

"We were coming to kill you."

A long, low breath breathed through the hall.

"We were coming to kill *you* – not the king, nor any other men of Mercia save those who stood around you – for reason that we knew you would no more allow King Cearl's will – that I, his grandson, succeed him on the throne – than you would allow an old king to whom you owed your honour and your duty and your love to stand between you and the throne." Eadfrith paused and stared up the hall at Penda and his eyes burned.

"We failed. You killed my father, you killed my brother, but I yet live and while I do, sleep lightly, warmaster; sleep lightly."

"I have heard enough," said Penda, and his face flushed as no one had ever seen it blood before, not even in the crush of battle. "You are not throne-worthy."

"You may have heard enough," said Eadfrith, "but you are not the witan – it has its own voice: let it speak. Would you hear more of what I have to say?"

And he turned, taking in the faces of the men around and the men far back, in the shadows and corners.

The answer came back, first in murmurs and whispers, then in hands on wood and feet on the hard-packed earth.

The witan would hear more.

Penda, hearing its voice, gave way before it, settling back behind the table. But as he sat he looked to his brother and Eowa, nodding, withdrew slowly from where he stood and started to make his way among the witan, touching one man upon the shoulder, whispering a few words to another, catching the glance of a third. Among those he encountered, some turned away, but others thought and nodded, or gave assent through a narrowing of eyes and a sidewards glance.

Eadfrith, for his part, spoke.

"And what of this great alliance your warmaster forged with the Britons? You have heard, we have all heard, that Cadwallon is dead and his army scattered, few to return to their own land. A new king sits on the throne in Northumbria, an Iding of royal blood. With bare enough men to fill two benches, he defeated the army of Gwynedd and killed Cadwallon. Now, what of this alliance between Mercia and Gwynedd? Does it still endure? And for why should we, whose forefathers came over sea to take kingdoms in this land, enter alliance with the sons of the men we took the land from? But, of course, some here fall from both sides of the bed…

"Now this man, warmaster sworn to protect the king, who returned without even the body of my grandfather that he might be buried in his own land, this man without Iclinga blood, asks the witan to make him king. I say no. I say there is one before you who is Iclinga; one who, in your hearing, King Cearl called his heir; one who would be true king of Mercia!" Eadfrith raised his arms.

"I! I! I!"

The murmur swelled, and mixed in with it, few at first but rising, were cries of, "Yes."

"Hold!" Splitting the building roar and dividing it, a man rose near the centre of the hall.

"I am Ulferth and no man of Penda." He spat upon the rush-covered straw. "That for the Britons and his mother was a little black-eyed slut of a Briton, but his father was a good man." Ulferth looked around. "We need a king – we have left it too long. Let the gods decide it."

And, taking his cloak from his shoulders, he flung it out over the floor. The hall died to eager silence as the witan realized what Ulferth proposed.

"Look at him," said another, pointing at Eadfrith. "He can bare stand."

"I will fight," Eadfrith hissed. He pointed at Penda. "Will he?"

In answer, Penda rose. "I will fight," he said.

"One shield," said Eadfrith. "To the death."

"One shield," agreed Penda. "But I will not kill you. Not yet."

"I will kill you," said Eadfrith.

In answer, Penda turned away and took the limewood shield and sword – an old but sturdy blade – that had been brought to him. As Eadfrith had neither sword nor shield of his own – his weapons had been despoiled after the battle – he was given them. But as they were not his own weapons, custom dictated that Penda could not fight with the sword and shield he bore into battle.

The two men took station, each with a foot upon the corner of the spread cloak. Men gathered, standing on benches to see, while boys, slave and free, wormed between legs and under tables.

Eadfrith hefted the shield upon his left arm and gripped the sword with his right hand. He looked at Penda, standing loose and ready at the far corner of the cloak, and knew that he could not afford to allow the duel to drag on – he was too weak. His only chance lay in pouring everything into immediate attack.

Penda nodded to him. "You have done well – I did not think to have to fight for my throne. Now you can take revenge for your father and your brother."

Eadfrith sprang forward, using his shield as a ram, bringing all the hatred and rage of battle lost and captivity endured into his sword arm as he swung it down upon Penda.

And Penda met it. His feet did not slip back, his sword arm barely gave under the weight of Eadfrith's blow and then, face to face so that each might feel the other's breath, they strained against each other.

"You have… grown weak," grunted Penda, and he thrust Eadfrith back, pushing him across the cloak, and following it with blow after blow after blow, sending him down, slowly, beneath his fracturing shield, until a final shove sent Eadfrith sprawling upon the ground.

Penda stepped upon his wrist, holding Eadfrith's sword to the ground, while he held his own to the man's throat.

Eadfrith looked up at Penda.

"Go on then," he said. "Do it."

"Not yet," said Penda, and he kicked the sword aside, then stepped back. He looked around the witan.

"Who will you have for king?"

"Penda!" The chant started among some of the men whom Eowa had approached, but it spread beyond them, until all the men in the hall cried his name, and Penda stood, arms raised, warmaster no more but king of Mercia.

Amid the cheers, Penda looked to where Eadfrith sat huddled upon the ground, the shattered shield lying beside him. Bending to him, he whispered, "You failed."

Eadfrith looked up and tears streaked his face. His eyes were hollow and no words came from his mouth, for there were no words to say. When chance had come, beyond all hope, to avenge his father and brother, his strength had failed him. It had been as when an old warrior play-fights an eager boy.

"Yes," he said.

"Take him away," said Penda, standing again and raising his arms to receive the acclaim of the witan afresh.

*

The night crisped the air, but too little light came into the hut for Eadfrith to see his breath mist in front of his face. He sat tied to the centre post, surrounded by the waste of weaving and spinning: loom weights rolled beneath his legs whenever he moved them and dry teasel heads pricked his ankles. The sound of feasting had stretched deep into the night, but Eadfrith had barely heard it, for the blackness of his despair shrouded him as a sack over his head, deadening sound and smell and sight. In the dark, he spoke to his father, he spoke to his brother, telling his failure. But they were dead and answered him not.

Words exhausted, Eadfrith leaned against the post, mind blank and empty save for the wish for the death that Penda had denied him.

He was not alone in failure.

The thought, scratching at the side of his mind, would not go away. Another had failed before him.

He had tried to avenge his father and his brother. He had failed. His body was too worn down and broken to fight Penda.

"I can do no more," he said. "He is for you."

Eadfrith sat in darkness and said no more.

*

The light from the brand woke him. The flames, close wrapped around the waxed wound cloth, sent shadows dancing around the hut. Eadfrith blinked and went to rub his eyes, only for his hands to jerk against their bonds.

"Forget you were tied?"

The figure holding the brand sat down behind it, cross legged upon the hard-packed earth.

"I did the same once." Penda leaned forward, his face alive with flame light. "I decided then I would never allow myself to be captured again."

"We wouldn't have captured you," said Eadfrith.

"I know." Penda fell silent, and in the silence Eadfrith listened. The night held the watchful silence of the late night, when men, in their sleeping, skirted the kingdom of death, and the watchdogs held peace against attracting the attention of the creatures – wight, elf or ghost – that roamed the dark land.

"The feast is over?"

Penda nodded. "I am king, and content." He nodded at Eadfrith. "You spoke well – well enough to sway the witan to your account."

Eadfrith sat back. "Are you here to kill me?"

"No. Not this night. If you would swear yourself to me, not ever."

"Do you think I would?"

"No. But I would try. There is a new king in Northumbria, an Iding reigning over Deira and Bernicia. Swear yourself to me and I will bring him down and you will be king in his place."

"King under you?"

"Yes. Of course."

"I would rather an Iding rule than I bend knee to you."

Penda nodded. "As I thought." He began to get to his feet. "I will keep you yet, though. You may be useful in dealing with this Iding. Oswald is his name. Do you know him?"

"I know his name."

"I hear he has left the ways of our fathers and follows the new god." Penda looked down at the bound man. "The new god brought no fortune to your father or your brother. Or to you."

Eadfrith looked up at Penda. "Of a time, I thought that too."

A question formed on Penda's face. "And now no more? Though you lie here, tied and waiting on my will as to whether you live or die?"

"Yes." Eadfrith smiled. "It is true, I failed. I tried to kill you and I failed, as my father and brother failed before. The old gods, the gods of our fathers, they would turn their faces from me now, a broken, beaten man. But strength of arm fails, Penda. Victory ends in defeat. And only the new God understands that, for he was broken, he was beaten, he was set upon a tree and despised, and yet he had the triumph." Eadfrith sighed. "When I was a boy, all I wanted was to be a warrior, to wield sword and win fame like my father and the heroes of our tales, but now, now, how glad I am that the story is greater than sword glory." He looked up at Penda and his face glowed. "It is greater than I ever knew."

Against that burning face, Penda held his fingers up, making the sign against the eye.

"I will take the glory of the gods – and victory. I know our people, Eadfrith. They go after the new ways when they come with the mantle of the emperors of old, but most of all they will follow the gods who win. Come then: I will set my gods against your god, the ways of our fathers against the new ways come from over sea. We will see who brings victory, for what use is a god without power to bring victory?"

"What use are gods who cannot bring life?"

"They may not bring it, but they can take it."

"A life is a small thing, easily extinguished – as easily as blowing out a candle. But to light a candle, ah, that is no small thing. It makes light, and then the darkness is dark no longer."

Penda shook his head. "You do not understand. The gods give power and they take it as they will."

"Oh, I understand. What would we say of a king who did not keep faith with the men pledged him? You pledge yourself to the gods, yet they will as soon bring you down as raise you up."

"The gods require sacrifice. I provide it. So long as I do, they will give me victory."

"Do you believe that? Do you really believe that?"

Penda paused. "What of your god? What happened to the victory he promised you?"

"He does not promise victory. He promises life."

"He did not keep his promise to your father or your brother."

Eadfrith shook his head. "He did."

Penda grimaced. "That is the sort of promise I expect from priests – twisted and turned, so it means whatever they want it to mean. But here, I will give you my promise, and it is good: I will tell you when I am going to kill you, that you may be ready."

Eadfrith looked up at him and nodded. "Thank you," he said.

Chapter 3

"It is not often we wait here on people arriving by land. Even our gate faces the sea, yet now we pace upon the wall with our backs to the waves, looking to the mountains."

Oswald smiled at his brother. "I have not seen you so nervous before." They were standing behind the wooden palisade that topped the stone wall that itself was raised upon the rock of Bamburgh. They were looking landward, over the plough-scored fields sown with oats and barley, showing the first green of their growing, to the grasslands, speckled white with sheep and brown with cattle, that rose up to the line of hills beyond. The Cheviot, cloud-wracked, lay hidden, but the nearer hills glowed in the eastering sun, new risen from the sea.

Oswiu turned to him. "I have not awaited a wife before."

"But you have known many women; why should this one be so different?"

"Because she will not go away! Because she will carry my children. Because, as you have no wife as yet, she will be the lady of the hall and carry the cup to our warriors. That is no easy task, for she must encourage the men – they must love her – but she must remain above them."

"Mother did so," said Oswald.

"Did she? I do not remember. I was too young. But why do you not ask her to return, brother? Then she can be mistress of our hall."

"I have asked her. I do not know if she will come. Coll has been her home for many years, and she can see the Holy Island from there."

"She can see us here!"

"True. I hope she will come." Oswald turned back to scanning the land west. "But I hope Rhieienmelth arrives first."

"I'm not sure I do!"

"I do not think you will get your wish." Oswald pointed and, turning, Oswiu saw the glint of sun on spear point as riders breasted a hill, coming up the road that led to the Wall in the south.

"Oh." Oswiu swallowed. His face was suddenly pale.

"Come when you are ready." Oswald left him, staring out over the palisade, while he made his way down into the great space that the palisade enclosed upon the rock.

"How is the work going, Talorc?"

The Pict looked up from the drawing, scratched into the ground, that he and another man were crouched over, then he pointed to the building going up in front of them.

"They say they will start putting the roof on the church tomorrow."

"Good, good," said Oswald, heading towards the hall.

"Can't see what the hurry is myself," Talorc muttered to his foreman as the king went past. "It's not as if he's got a priest to use it – not since Corman went back to the Holy Island."

Exercising what he had found to be one of the most important aspects of kingship – selective deafness – Oswald continued to the hall.

"Acca," he said, seeing the scop there, stringing his lyre. "They are in sight. Is everything ready?"

The scop sprang to his feet. "Yes, lord. I have a new song ready, telling of how you slew Cadwallon after many grievous thrusts through the heat of the day, and only as night was about to set did he finally fall and breathe his last, surrounded by the bodies of the slain."

"It was not like that, Acca. Besides, this is a wedding, not a battle feast. My brother's wedding, not mine. Sing something appropriate and leave me out of it."

"But, lord, Cadwallon's ending is so pathetic – every man in the hall will be in tears."

"As I said: well for a battle feast but not for a wedding feast. Sing something of love and the duties of a wife. And seeing as it's my brother that is getting married, you had better add something about the duties of a husband. I do not think he is clear about them."

"I might know something that would fit…" A thoughtful look came into the scop's eyes and his lips began moving without sound. Oswald knew that when such a look appeared on Acca's face, the world serpent itself might rise from the sea and he would not hear it. It was similar to the battle mind that settled upon warriors, when all slowed and became precise and clear – he had known it himself a few times, but more often it was the battle fury that seized Oswald, the fire that killed, and laughed when it killed, but having burned itself out left him spent and shaking in its aftermath, half appalled at the death he had meted out and the pleasure he had taken in dealing it.

Leaving Acca, Oswald went in search of Coifi. When the old priest had first come to him, Oswald had needed a steward, as well as an almoner, a man to organize the household, to inform vills that the royal party would come to them next week, next month or next year, and to set aside provisions accordingly, and to supervise the wagoners. After a month of chaos it had become clear that Coifi was no steward – all too often, when clear head and cool memory were needed, he would be distracted by the fall of stream over stones, or the sight of a dead hare by the side of the road. So Oswald had found another man, with experience as a steward, and to Coifi was given the job of almoner alone. The harvest had been good, and the poor were fewer than they had been. Still, whenever they stopped upon the route through the royal estates that wound through Deira and Bernicia, each a day's march from the other, there would be the local poor waiting upon their arrival. Coifi would give food and drink each day they remained at the estate, hissing half-believed curses at those who returned for more when he had not yet fed the rest.

Oswald found Coifi by the kitchen, a building separate from the great hall for reason of its hearth, which might all too easily set flame to the hall if it were within it. Even so, the kitchen was built apart from the other wooden-framed and thatch-roofed buildings and, at feast, teams of slaves waited to rush the food to table.

The old priest saw the king coming and went to him, pointing at the kitchen.

"That man is holding all the food in store and refusing to give any up for the almoner. The poor are standing outside the gate, pointing to their bellies, and I have nothing to give them because this fat cook won't give me any, and this because I told him what the fate singers decree for him. Tell him, lord. Tell him to give me the food."

Oswald held up his hand. "I will, I will. But tell me first, what of the fate singers did you tell him?"

Coifi waved his hand. "Oh, little enough: that he will die coughing on a fish bone, and his children are some his but some the brood of his brother, whom he thought to leave with his wife while he went forth as king's steward." Coifi held up his hand to cover the side of his face and leaned to the king. "It was not hard to see that; all I had to do was ask the dates he was there and the dates when the children were born."

"Telling a man he will die and he is cuckolded by his own brother is not perhaps the way to get him to share the food in his charge with you."

Coifi blew out his lips, then shook his head. "It is what I have seen."

"But henceforward do not tell him what you see. Simply tell the cook what you need. That will be enough."

The priest looked doubtful, but he nodded. "What I need, not what I see." He paused. "But what I see is what I need."

"Yes... Are there any waiting for food now?"

"There are always people waiting for food, and whatever else we have to give." Coifi shook as an idea bit him. "If only there were some way to give food that they could eat when we are gone; we come often to Bamburgh, three or four times a year, but there are other estates to which we return only once a year. Many families from such places come to me to commit their children as slaves to you, lord, that they might have food."

Oswald nodded. "We take all that we can."

"More than we can – half your slaves spend their days sitting outside the kitchen, waiting to fill themselves with food and drink."

"But you are right; if there were a way we could give through the months we are away, it were better. For now, though, go to the people outside the gate and tell them to clear the way. A royal party approaches."

"Who is it, lord?"

"Princess Rhieienmelth of Rheged, my brother's bride."

Coifi's face went white and he reached for Oswald's wrist, grasping it convulsively.

"Send her away, lord. Send her away. I have seen – she comes surrounded with a great shadow, a darkness follows in her wake and the sun's face turns from this land. Send her back to her own land; scatter the clouds."

Oswald stared into Coifi's white face and slowly unpeeled the fingers from his wrist.

"You are my almoner, Coifi, not my priest. Keep to your task and I will keep to mine."

"But, lord, please, the fate singers…"

"If it is a matter of your fate singers, then there is nothing I can do, is there? But your fate singers do not weave our destinies – they lie in the lands of another, and he hears our prayers and answers them, Coifi. If you have seen these clouds follow in the wake of Princess Rhieienmelth, then pray for them to be diverted. For my part, I have given my word to King Rhoedd that my brother will marry his daughter, and I cannot turn my word on the say of a priest of the old gods."

"I – I know I am priest no more, lord, but the sight, the sight… It has come back to me, as it was when I first spirit-walked. I see these things; I see them."

"You might see them, but I do not. And unless I see with my own eyes what you have seen – and even then I could not go back on what I have promised – I would not change what is to happen. Rhieienmelth will wed, and be the mistress of my hall."

Coifi stepped back. He looked searchingly at the king. "If you will have it so, lord."

Oswald answered in silence.

The old priest shivered suddenly, and gathered his cloak around his flanks, the feathers rustling and creaking like old bones.

*

Oswald and Oswiu waited by the gate. As the wagons had lumbered closer to Bamburgh, their labouring teams pulling hard through the winter-churned tracks, the brothers had combed and dressed, hanging cloaks clasped with gold and garnet from their shoulders and pushing the thick arm rings up past their elbows, so they shone and glittered. Slaves bustled around the rock, and despite Coifi's words, none seemed to be sitting outside the kitchen. Bran, finding the rush overpowering, had flown up onto the palisade where he now stood, glowering down at the commotion while keeping a keen eye for the scraps from the kitchen. The castle dogs – small, alert beasts, unlike the great hounds used for hunt – also waited, whining eagerly whenever anyone emerged through the fire-limned doors, but Bran had imposed his place upon them; he had first choice of whatever the kitchen put out. Only when he had taken what he wanted could the dogs rush forward in a yapping, snarling scrap.

"Any sign of them, Talorc?" The Pict, dressed in the finery he had salvaged from the bodies of Cadwallon's men, went down and round the path to see. The gate to the rock lay at the bottom of a steep climb on the seaward side of the stronghold. Visitors by land had to come around the outside of the rock and then out upon a thin spit of land above the high tide line to come to the gate, set into rock and wall.

"They are nearly here." Talorc took his place beside Oswald and Oswiu with the other men in the guard of honour, their arms and armour a jangle of the treasure despoiled from Cadwallon's dead: Anglian brooches held Saxon cloaks, Kentish pendants and buckles from Francia took their place beside pins from Dal Riada and rings from Gwynedd. They had spent much time preparing, polishing and cleaning, brushing through hair and moustache and beard to remove knots and nits, until now they shone as burnished statues – somewhat fidgety statues, as each man craned around the next to see if the procession had yet come into sight.

And then they appeared. Coming round the edge of the rock, the first man, polished and painted shield hanging from his shoulder, spear serving as stick as well as weapon. He walked, for though horses might be led through the gate and up the path into the stronghold, they had to be taken one by one and slowly, lest one start and send the other beasts careering from the path. So they would come afterwards, once the royal party had entered Bamburgh.

With the guard lined up along the path, it was time for the king and his daughter to approach. Rhoedd came first, picking his way suspiciously over the steps, holding his robe up out of the way so that he would not fall over it. So intent was he that he barely lifted his eyes to the two waiting men. It was as well, for they were not looking at him but at Rhieienmelth, who followed behind her father. Where he walked heavily and carefully, she came with light step and head high. And though her face was veiled, yet everything about her bearing told of the smile that she wore behind the veil. Then a breeze, carrying in from the sea washing the beach below them, blew her veil aside and they saw her face.

"She is fairer even than I remember," Oswiu said to his brother. Oswald nodded, but did not speak. A hand clutched his throat and dried his tongue, and he turned his eyes from the princess and met the gaze of the king. Rhoedd stared up at him and his eyes gleamed. As father and daughter came up to the two waiting men, Rhoedd took Rhieienmelth's arm and twitched her veil aside for an instant.

"Do you agree this is Rhieienmelth, my daughter, for whom we made marriage settlement this past year?" King Rhoedd looked to Oswald.

Oswald cleared his throat. "Yes," he said, forcing the word through dry throat and lips.

"I sold her too cheaply." Rhoedd clapped his hands together. "But I am a man of my word. What I say, I do – even if I entered into the agreement with no belief it would come through."

"Father, you do not sell me. I go willingly, or not at all."

Rhoedd turned to his daughter. "Well, are you willing then?"

"Yes," said Rhieienmelth. "Yes, I am willing." But she was veiled and it was not possible to see where her eyes lay.

"We will talk on this later," said Oswald, "when we are within." He went to take Rhoedd's arm, but the king drew back.

"Wait," he said. "When we speak – later – think on this too. I bring you further gifts." And he turned and gestured back down the path. At his sign, a further group of men rounded the corner, but these were not clad in the cloaks and armour of warriors, but rather wore rough wool, belted at the waist, and their foreheads were bare of hair. Oswald stared down the path, then ran down it, stopping before the small figure that led the group of men.

"Abbot Ségéne," he said, and went down on one knee before him.

But the abbot laughed and raised him from the ground and embraced Oswald. Then, holding him at arm's length, the abbot looked at him.

"My son," he said. "My son, you have done well."

Oswald smiled in turn. "But why have you come? It is so far, and the Holy Island..."

"The Blessed One will look after the Holy Island in my absence. As to why I came, Bishop Corman gave me report of his time here. I thought it best to come to see for myself this ungovernable people. And I did not come alone." The abbot turned his head, and from behind him appeared Brother Aidan, smiling and blushing at the same time.

"Aidan! This is a day past all blessing. You came too."

"The abbot said I must. He told me I must come see how his hawk flew." The young monk looked around, at warriors and castle and sea and sky. "I see you fly very well indeed."

Oswald, beaming, looked from abbot to monk and back again. "That you should come on the same day as Rhieienmelth arrives – this is most wonderful indeed."

"Ah," said Abbot Ségéne, holding up his hand. "There is no chance there. After leaving the Holy Island, we stopped first in Rheged, and finding the king making ready to depart, it was no difficult matter to come with him." The abbot stepped closer to Oswald and whispered, "I think he was glad to have Brother Diuma and his men along too – the lands around the Wall have grown dangerous in past days." Stepping back, the abbot looked up at the stronghold above their heads. "But now all that will change. We have a new king in the land. And a wedding to attend." Abbot Ségéne rubbed his hands together. "I enjoy wedding feasts more than any other."

*

"We will have the wedding on the morrow." King Rhoedd slipped a glance at Oswiu. "Patience," he said. "Patience – she is worth the waiting."

"I know," said Oswiu fervently. "I know."

"But now I must speak to your brother alone, as one king to another. Here…" Rhoedd held out his daughter's hand. "Take her round, but no sampling the wares before market."

"Father!"

The old king laughed, and pushed Rhieienmelth towards Oswiu, who reached out to catch her. But the princess caught her own balance first, before taking Oswiu's hand and allowing him to lead her forth. As they went from the hall, Rhieienmelth glanced back to where her father sat beside Oswald, and both were watching her. She smiled, a small smile, and raised her hand before stepping to the door.

"I could sell her to you," said Rhoedd, his own hand raised but his voice lowered. "You could have her for yourself for another three white mares."

"No!"

Heads busy working to prepare for the wedding feast turned to the high table.

"Don't be a fool," said Rhoedd, still waving after his daughter and apparently not even talking to Oswald. "Keep your voice down."

"But you asked me if I wanted to take my brother's wife – your daughter."

"Yes, my daughter – so she is mine to give to whom I will. You want her. I will give her to you."

"I – I do not want her."

At this, King Rhoedd turned to look at Oswald. "Any man would want Rhieienmelth – I'd have her myself if she wasn't my daughter."

"I do not want her!"

King Rhoedd held up his hands. "I just asked. Look, I know you made the agreement for your brother, but we're kings. We can do what we want. Now, are you sure you don't want her?"

"Yes," said Oswald, tight lipped and looking away from Rhoedd.

"Very well. Now, about the price. I know we said five white mares, but that was before…"

"That is my price." Oswald turned to look at King Rhoedd and his face was grim. "Accept it or go."

Rhoedd met his eyes. "I'll accept," he said. "But I'll want to see the horses before tomorrow."

*

"I could have killed him." Oswald stood upon the beach, his cloak wrapped around his shoulders, looking to the low sea walls of the Farne Islands. Birds in their thousands wheeled around the rocks and isles – the local fishermen said the islands moved with each tide and moon, for it was impossible to count how many there were. He turned to the abbot and Brother Aidan. At the abbot's suggestion they had left the noise and preparations of hall and castle to come down to the sand, where they might talk without ears to hear.

"There have been few kings whom I have met and not asked God afterwards why he made them," said the abbot. "Some of the Uí Neíll, for instance, and King Congal – he was an appalling man. I could see no good reason for God to have made him."

"What did God answer?"

"He told me to mind my own business." The abbot shrugged. "It is good advice, even if, as abbot, I can seldom follow it."

Oswald laughed. "It is good to see you. Oswiu would have come with us too, but I could not drag him away from Rhieienmelth."

Now it was the abbot's turn to laugh. "I would not have thought ever to see your brother so – he runs after her like a calf. But then it is often the way with such men: they lead many girls astray and then themselves are hooked, flopping, upon the line."

"He is certainly hooked." Oswald looked up at the stronghold, lowering upon its rock above them. "Let us walk further – I have a restlessness upon me this day."

The three men turned north, walking the dark line of sand that showed the reach of high tide. Nets lay drying above this line, the air around them shifting with sandflies.

"I have heard Bishop Corman's account of his mission," said Abbot Ségéne. "Now I would hear yours."

"He put my people to the fire – them and their forefathers. After that, they would not listen to him further."

"Corman told me they are barbarous and obstinate." The abbot smiled. "What people of these islands is not barbarous and obstinate – and as for ungovernable, that certainly applies to all!" He shook his head. "I did wrong in sending Corman to you. I thought that his knowledge of the language of your people outweighed everything else. I thought he had overcome his hatred for the people who had taken him as slave. So, we will have to find you a new bishop, and men to help him."

"If you do send another bishop, let him be gentle," said Oswald. "I know my people – they can be broken to the kingdom, but as with a horse, it must be done with soft touch and quiet words rather than with bridle and whip."

The abbot nodded, then pointed ahead. "What is that land?"

"That is the island I spoke of before, Father Abbot. It is called Lindisfarne, and twice each day men can walk to it dry shod, and twice each day the sea claims it again."

"How long does it take to get there?"

"From here? On foot, a day, for the way goes far inland unless one risks walking across Budle Bay when the tide is out – but the mud and sand is treacherous there and many men have been lost while out hunting bird and seal. By sea, but a few hours, even if there is no wind."

The abbot nodded. "It will serve well. Is it yours to give?"

"It is mine to give. There are some families living upon it, making their living from fishing in the main, although there are sheep and some crops in sheltered places. Why do you wish it?"

"It will be the base for the monks I give you; a daughter house to the monastery of the Holy Island. And what better place for a daughter house than upon another island?"

"That is wonderful. I had not thought, after Bishop Corman left, to receive more help from the Holy Island."

"We set you to fly, my hawk. It is our duty and blessing to fetch the prey you bring down. Here…" The abbot pushed forward Brother Aidan, who had been following in silence behind them. "It is poor exchange, but in return for an island I give you Brother Aidan."

The monk looked in confusion at Abbot Ségéne. "Me? You want me to stay with Oswald?"

The abbot smiled. "Yes. I tried for authority and stern words and it failed; this time, let us see how friendship and a humble heart do with this obstinate people."

"B-but do you think I am able…"

"I wouldn't have chosen you if I didn't think you were able, Brother Aidan. Besides, you won't be alone: I'm leaving you the others I brought. Brother Diuma needs to spend more time on his knees and less time with a sword in his hand. Make sure you look after them."

"Me?" Brother Aidan looked around, as if searching for another monk upon the beach. "But I am just a monk. We will need a bishop, to teach, to consecrate priests and churches."

"As you said, you will need a bishop. The last one I sent did not work, so this time it will be you."

Brother Aidan stood looking at the abbot, his mouth opening and closing like a beached fish.

"B-b-but…" he stuttered.

"Yes, I know you are not a bishop. So we will make you one."

"A – a bishop?"

"I've sent messengers for the pallium; they should arrive back soon. When they get here, I will place the pallium upon you and consecrate you bishop." The abbot smiled. "Bishop Aidan. It has a grand sound to it, don't you think?"

"B-bishop Aid…" The words trailed away. Brother Aidan's eyes rolled up, his legs gave way and he fainted upon the sand.

Abbot Ségéne looked over the prone monk to Oswald. "Do you think he's pleased?"

*

"Acca, Acca, give us a song!"

The scop looked around the hall. The wedding feast was in full swing. Oswiu sat beside Rhieienmelth – Rhieienmelth unveiled – at the high table, and her beauty, and Oswiu's evident pleasure in it, filled the hall.

The feasting continued, but the beer and mead, and wine brought by boat from Francia, had flowed and the call went out for song.

Acca rose to his feet. He worked his tongue and throat, making sure they were supple and ready, while he tuned the six strings of his lyre and the men around him banged the tables in encouragement. Inwardly, the scop smiled. This was the way with an audience: tease them, make them wait. But what to sing? He looked around at the beer-bright faces and knew.

"*Hwæt!*"

The command to listen, underlined by the six-string chord he strummed upon the lyre, brought the hall to as near as it would come to silence this day: dogs snapped scraps, slaves slapped down cups, talk filled the corners of the hall, but around him faces were turned his way, waiting, expectant and quiet.

"What shall I sing?" Acca asked the question innocently, as if he honestly did not know what to do. Suggestions came, favourites were called out, but the scop held up his hand.

"When I sang for the wedding of King Edwin and Queen Æthelburh, they did not like what I sang – but then the queen had had her bride price stolen by Cadwallon. No wonder King Edwin was upset. Now, Princess Rhieienmelth comes without fear across the country because Cadwallon is dead!" At this, cheers resounded around the hall and men who had been nowhere near Heavenfield raised their cups and drank, although those few who had seen the bodies litter the ground sat quiet, and rather than raise their cups they stared into their depths.

"Now, it is meet that the slayers of Cadwallon, they who delivered our kingdom from him, should marry and enjoy the fruits of victory." Acca glanced pointedly at Rhieienmelth, who blushed and lowered her eyes, although she smiled at the men's cheers and, more, at the way her soon-to-be husband beside her beamed.

"Today, the younger, the more impatient, has wed. But how much longer can the elder's patience last?" Acca looked archly to Oswald, who looked away.

"Not long I think." Raucous laughter echoed around the hall.

Sitting together at the end of the high table, Brother – soon to be bishop – Aidan leaned to Abbot Ségéne. "What is he saying? I do not understand the language well enough yet."

The abbot looked at the young monk. "You will have to learn it, but perhaps it is as well that you do not understand all yet."

"For your wedding, I have a rare and precious gift," said Acca, bowing to Oswiu and Rhieienmelth, "and one that I shall give you whole and entire today, rather than making you wait. What say you to that?"

"I say get on with it, Acca," said Oswiu. "For we cannot leave the feast until you have sung!"

Even louder cheers greeted that, and Rhieienmelth blushed more deeply, but those near saw that she held Oswiu's hand.

The scop, in acknowledgment of Oswiu's sally, held his lyre high and strummed it, his hand a blur over the strings.

"Let us not keep the prince and his princess waiting. Here is my gift to you: a riddle! A new riddle, a fresh riddle, a wedding riddle."

Murmurs went through the hall; there were few things better for chewing over through the long nights of winter than a difficult riddle.

Acca dropped his voice, pulling his audience in closer.

"Riddle me this," he said, "riddle me this." And he pulled a single note from his lyre, leaving it hanging in the hall.

"Swings by his side a thing most magical!"

Acca strummed the lyre, fingers blurring over strings.

"Below the belt, beneath the folds
of his clothes it hangs, a hole in its front end,
stiff-set and stout, but swivels about!"

The laughter grew more raucous yet, and one or two of the drunker men staggered to their feet and threatened to pull down their trousers, until made to sit by the slightly less drunk men beside them.

"Levelling the head of this hanging instrument,
its wielder hoists his hem above the knee:
it is his will to fill a well-known hole
that it fits fully when at full length."

This time, Acca was taking care to watch the reaction of the people for whom he had composed the riddle; he had made the mistake with King Edwin and Queen Æthelburh of looking too much to the rest of the audience to realize that they were furious with his ribaldry. But seeing the delighted grin on Oswiu's face and the sidelong glances Rhieienmelth cast towards him, Acca knew that this time he had judged correctly.

"He has never filled it before.
Soon he will fill it for the first time!"

Acca finished with a final triumphant strum upon the lyre, then held it up above his head as cheers and laughter filled the hall.

Brother Aidan turned to Abbot Ségéne, who was delightedly applauding along with everyone else in the hall.

"What did he say?"

"Oh, you really don't want to know, my son," said the abbot, mixing the odd cheer into his applause. "You really don't want to know."

Acca held up his hands and the applause and shouts slowly died away, although occasional bursts of laughter could be heard coming from outside, as slaves passed on the riddle to those working outside the hall in the kitchen.

"It is not meet, today of all days, to keep anyone waiting for the answer to this riddle. So here it is!" And from a string around his neck, Acca held up the gleaming metal of a new key, and gave it to Oswiu.

"Now use it," he said.

And grinning, Oswiu stood up, waving the key to all in the hall, and then taking Rhieienmelth's hand he raised her to her feet and led her from the hall, accompanied by delighted cheering.

As they left, Abbot Ségéne looked at the unguarded faces following them, and saw the hood-eyed calculation upon the face of her father – as he had expected – and the strain of smiling upon Oswald's face, which he had not expected. He turned to Aidan, and speaking in Latin so no one around could understand said, "When you are bishop and I have returned to the Holy Island, I think it best you encourage Oswald to marry as soon as possible."

Aidan looked at the abbot, taken aback that even when he heard something spoken in a language he understood he still did not understand.

Abbot Ségéne sighed. "Oswald will never join us on the Holy Island. I know of no king since the days of the emperors who has died in his bed. He must marry and have children, that the kingdom may survive him… and to keep him from testing."

"What do you mean?" asked Aidan.

"You have heard the stories of Arthur? Some tales say it was the witchery of his half-sister that destroyed him, but others say it was the enmity that flared between Arthur and his warmaster over his wife that divided his kingdom."

Aidan shook his head. "I do not understand."

The abbot shook his head. Although he said nothing, he appeared to be having second thoughts about the wisdom of making Aidan a bishop and putting him in charge of this mission.

"I do not know if he knows it himself yet, but there is a … tension between Oswald and his brother's new wife. I have seen such before, in Dal Riada, among the Uí Neill; a princess from a minor kingdom weds and though she means no harm, yet she charms the king as much as the prince she married, for she has been charged by her own people to smooth the way between the two kingdoms, and a rift opens between king and prince. I know Oswald: he will not, I think, yield to temptation, but the strain of it will be great until he is safely wed himself. So see that he marries, and soon, and all will be well."

Aidan sat gaping at the abbot. "Is this what being a bishop is all about?"

"You should try being an abbot," said Ségéne.

Chapter 4

"Come on, Aidan, you've been shut away on this island for weeks now." Oswiu circled his horse, stepping it between the stacks of worked timbers and piles of thatch. "Time for some rest."

The monk bishop stood up from where he had been kneeling, taking it in turns with Brother Diuma to plane wood.

"There is still much to do, Oswiu. We must have the abbey ready before winter, or we will be blown away."

"Could you not be spared for an afternoon?" The question came from Rhieienmelth, sat astride a roan horse.

"No. No, I do not think I can," said Aidan.

Oswald swung himself down from his animal and came over to where Aidan and Brother Diuma were working.

"Could you manage without the bishop for an afternoon?" he asked Brother Diuma. "We – I – have missed him since he was elevated so high."

"Of a surety we could manage without the bishop for an afternoon," said Brother Diuma.

"There, you see," said Oswald. "So you can come hunting with us."

Aidan stood looking at Oswald, the breeze from the North Sea blowing the rough wool of his habit against his legs.

"I – I gave away the horse."

Oswald looked blankly at his friend. "What did you say?"

"I gave away your horse."

"You gave it away?"

"They had so little and the child was ill – I could as easily walk as ride. More easily in my case."

"You gave it away?"

"Yes. Yes. I told you. Would you have me not help the poor? Would you have me go against God?"

"Yes. No." Oswald blinked. "The horse was my gift to you."

"Ah," said Aidan, "do not think I am like one of your warriors, giving loyalty for gold."

"I did not think to buy your loyalty but to give a gift to my friend. My oldest friend."

"Yes, well." Aidan looked away. "For my sins, and at your bidding, I am a bishop now."

"But can a bishop not have friends?"

Aidan looked at the king. "Among his monks, no, he cannot. But," he smiled, "maybe with a man he has known since he was a boy."

"Good," said Oswald. "I will give you another horse for the hunt. Do not give this one away – it is promised to the king of the Gododdin."

*

"How does it feel being a bishop?"

"It is... frightening," said Aidan. He tugged without thinking at the pallium, the woollen band that marked him as a bishop. He still found it hard to believe that such office had been placed upon him. Maybe it would have been easier if it had not all happened on one day. Abbot Ségéne, before returning to the Holy Island, had ordained Aidan a priest and consecrated him bishop too. By the end of the day, Aidan had not known whether to bow to himself, dance with joy, or hope that he would die in the night before he had chance to disgrace the office he had been given. Instead, the morning had come, Abbot Ségéne had departed, taking ship north to the great firth that cut deep inland, where the boat's master, having emptied the vessel, would then take the familiar portage route across the narrow belt of land and float the ship again in the western firth. The two days' labour, dragging the boat on rollers over the well-worn path, was quicker and safer than the long passage around the rocky, storm-wracked northern shores.

"It can't be as frightening as seeing you astride a horse hunting," said Oswald, pulling back his own animal as it chewed at its bit, eager to get after the hounds that had swarmed into the wood ahead. They had ridden back across the causeway from Lindisfarne – Oswald hoped that soon men might call it Holy Isle too – and sprung a boar from amid the copses that sheltered the fields from the worst of winter's east winds.

"Give me a boat rather than a horse," said Aidan.

"But you will have to get used to riding now you are a bishop," said Oswald.

Aidan looked at him. "Why?"

Oswald shook his head. "Well, because I have given you another horse for one thing."

"But you said it was promised to Gododdin."

"That was to ensure you rode it. Now you have, it is yours. Besides, a bishop, like an ætheling, should ride."

"A bishop is not a warrior. And sitting up here, it puts me too far above the people I must serve. Seeing me on a horse, they will fear me, as they fear any man they see upon a horse."

"But they should fear you and do your bidding – you are a bishop."

Aidan shook his head. But before he could answer further, the baying of the hounds reached a crescendo and the boar burst from the woods, its trotters pounding the earth as it ran towards the waiting horsemen. Then, seeing them, it swerved aside and made away towards the thick line of rushes that marked the salt mere that stretched inland from Budle Bay. Oswald made to urge his horse after the stag, but the huntsman held up his hand and whistled to the dogs.

"Why do we not go after it?" Oswald asked, his horse circling in its frustration at being pulled back.

The huntsman pointed to the mere and the mound that rose from its heart. "The old king sleeps there – it were best we not wake him."

Oswiu, impatient also at the delay, rode up behind the huntsman. "What old king? What was his name? What did he rule?"

The huntsman looked up at Oswiu with calm eyes. "He ruled all this land," he said.

"Ach, you've lost us a good hunt." Oswiu pulled his horse back and looked into the mere. There was no sign of the boar now. He turned to his brother. "See if Bran can find it."

The raven was standing, one eye closed, behind Oswald. Oswald shook his head. "Bran is only interested in animals when they are dead. He won't search for a living boar."

"Pfah," said Oswiu, "why don't you get a hawk? The Lord of the Isles has an eagle. You have a big crow. What's more, it lets others do the killing and then expects all the choice bits afterwards."

Hearing him, Bran opened his other eye, regarded Oswiu, then decided he was not worth contemplating and shut both his eyes.

"Oh, I'm sure Bran would look for the boar if we asked him nicely," said Rhieienmelth, as she trotted her horse up to the brothers. She reached forward and began to tickle Bran under the beak. He did not open his eyes, but twisted his head from one side to the other to bring her finger where he wanted it, all the while making the mewing sounds of a raven's pleasure.

Rhieienmelth leaned forward from her horse and put her mouth near Bran's head. "Will you look for the boar, Bran? For me?"

The bird opened its black eyes, stared at Rhieienmelth for an instant, then croaked and took wing, accompanied by the sound of the princess's delighted laughter. She looked up after the bird and saw Oswald, turning to look at her, and she smiled at him, as beside them Oswiu laughed too.

"See? Even Bran melts when my wife asks him favour."

The raven, seeking the wind waves, rode them high and began to circle above the mere, until, as rough as rock, there came his cry echoing over the marsh.

"He's found him," said Oswiu. He looked down at the huntsman. "Come on. If a raven does our finding, you're not going to let a sleeping king stop us, are you?"

The huntsman pursed his lips. Bran called again. The huntsman smiled, and let slip the dogs. Freed from check, the pack set wind and made into the marsh, splashing through the shallow brackish water, Oswiu urging his horse after them, and the huntsman running to keep up.

Oswald looked to sea. "I don't like the look of the weather," he said.

But Rhieienmelth pulled her horse alongside him. "You're not going to let your brother get to that boar first, are you? Or me?" And she pushed her own light-footed horse after Oswiu.

Aidan, the last, sighed and suggested to his own animal that it might like to follow into the mere. The horse disagreed, so they settled for walking around the marsh, where they met the hunting party coming out again.

"He went that way," Aidan said without enthusiasm, pointing up the wide channelled creek that fed into the marsh.

"We've got him!" said Oswiu. "There's no way he can escape the hounds there."

*

"I thought you said there was no way he could escape the hounds," said Aidan.

They had been searching for an hour. Even the hounds had lost voice and enthusiasm.

"There isn't," said Oswiu. "He must be here somewhere. We just need to keep looking for him."

That was when the rain started, swiftly followed by the fog descending, so that everything disappeared behind a shifting curtain of wet. Only the bedraggled hunting party, taking stock in its small patch of sight, remained in a world gone grey.

"That's the old king," said the huntsman. "He'd not be brooking anyone disturbing his sleep." He looked to Oswald and Oswiu. "The day's turned. Best we get back."

Aidan leaned over to Oswald. "What did he say?"

"Ah, I forgot you do not yet understand our speech so well, and besides, he has an accent so thick I bare understand him myself. He said we should go back." The king looked around at the wall of rain that surrounded them. "That is, if we can find our way back."

They couldn't. The cloud was too thick and the rain too heavy – it had washed all scent from the ground, so even the hounds could not find the path.

"Isn't there somewhere we can shelter?" Oswiu pointed to Rhieienmelth. "I would not have her take chill."

"I am all right," she said. "I am of Rheged – we get rain there."

"Well, even if Rhieienmelth is all right, I am wet and cold and fed up. Let us wait for the worst of the rain to pass; then we can try again."

Oswald agreeing, they searched, following tracks, until they came to a low, round hut, water slating off the turves that made its roof.

The huntsman called at the entrance and a man emerged blinking, a sheepskin over his shoulders. Seeing the men on horses he quailed, but the huntsman spoke to him and he brightened a little, then gestured them within.

"Will you translate for me?" Aidan asked Oswald as the shepherd pressed cups of milk into their hands. The inside of the hut was rank with man and steeped in smoke, making their eyes run and their throats ache, but it was relatively dry, and warm.

"You want to speak to him?"

"Yes. Of course."

"Oh. Right."

"What is your name?" Aidan looked to Oswald. "Well?" he said and repeated the question.

Oswald shrugged, turned to the shepherd and asked the question.

*

The clouds finally lifted and they emerged to a world gone green again. Their horses steamed gently, cropping the grass, while the hounds bickered among themselves. The huntsman sat among them, his cloak wrapped around his shoulders, for he had remained outside with his dogs – there were too many sheep to leave them untended.

Most of the hunting party mounted, but Aidan remained on foot.

"Why don't you get on your horse?" Oswald asked him.

The young bishop patted his horse's neck. "When I speak to a man, I do not want to be looking down at him, but to talk at his level." He turned to the huntsman. "What is your name?" Aidan looked over his shoulder. "Well?"

Oswald sighed, and started translating again.

*

The rain followed them, on and off, back to the stronghold at Bamburgh, the clouds dipping low then rising for a while before descending again.

The hounds trailed miserably after the horses, their fur plastered to their skin, and even Bran appeared bedraggled, the water dripping from the tip of his beak. The waxed cloaks Oswald, Oswiu, Rhieienmelth and the rest of the hunting party were wearing kept the rain off well, but beneath them they were clammy from sweat and the sweet rising smell of wet horseflesh. Aidan, though, was as bedraggled as the huntsman, his woollen cloak sponging the water and sending it in a slow and steady trickle down his back.

"There," said Oswald, pointing. "We are nearly there."

Aidan stopped his plodding and peered ahead. In truth, his conversation with the huntsman had died away into the wet misery of this long march home. He had tried to tell him the news of new life, but the rain washed his words away, and Oswald, as tired and miserable as the rest of the hunting party, after a while refused to translate any further, leaving Aidan to proceed with his limited language and through gesture and expression. In the end, he had given up and simply trudged in silence beside the huntsman. But the sight of the stronghold, perched atop the great rock by the sea, cheered them all, and, man and beast, they lengthened pace and quickened stride to reach it.

"There's a new boat moored there," said Oswiu as they drew closer and saw, among the little cluster of boats pulled up upon the beach, a craft with the unmistakable lines of a vessel of the Lord of the Isles.

Leaving the horses for the young boys to unsaddle and groom, the hunting party, still wet and in Aidan's case starting to sneeze, entered the hall. Most of Oswald's household men were away on patrol or answering summons for help against brigands, so the building was clearer than usual. Being near empty, it was clear as soon as they entered who sat near the fire waiting upon them.

"Mother," said Oswald.

"Sister," said Oswiu.

"Oh no," said Rhieienmelth, throwing her cloak back over her hair and fleeing the hall.

"Was that your wife?" Æbbe asked a few minutes later, after the initial greetings and embraces were over.

"Yes," said Oswiu. He looked to the door. Still no sign of her. "I don't know why she ran away."

"She would not want our first sight of her to be like that: wet through and looking as if she had been dragged from a river," said Acha.

"She didn't look that bad," protested Oswiu.

"Go to her," said Acha. "Tell her to come to us when she is ready."

As Oswiu went in search of his wife, Oswald looked to his mother and sister. "Will you stay?" he asked.

The two women looked to each other, then smiled at him.

"We'll stay," they said.

Oswald went to embrace them, but Æbbe held up her hands, laughing. "Wait! You have not heard our conditions yet."

"Whatever you ask." Oswald took his sister's arms and held them.

"It is simple really. But difficult too." She looked to her mother, then back to Oswald. "Land. I need land to build a monastery, and the hides to provide for it."

Oswald swept his arm wide. "I am king – I will give you land."

"It is not as easy as that, brother. This is not a gift as you give to your thegns, land that they earn but that their sons must earn again if they are to keep it. A monastery is not as a warrior – it must have roots. It cannot move. Therefore, the land must be made over to the monastery, beyond the reach of memory and forgetting."

The king looked to his sister and mother. "How may we do that? When a warrior serves me well, I give to him land, that he may raise a hall and family; but the land is mine and reverts to me when he dies. How may I give to you beyond your deaths – and mine?"

"There is a way. The land must be made over into bookland and entered into a great ledger, which the abbey may keep and show to kings and lords in future, saying that Oswald granted the land to them, and granted it forever." Æbbe pointed to Aidan, standing steaming by the fire. "Brother Aidan could do it."

"He's not a brother any more. He's a bishop."

"A bishop?" Æbbe stared. Aidan blushed. Acha clapped her hands and went to the young man.

"At last," she said. "Ségéne saw sense! I told him to choose you from the start, but he insisted upon sending Corman. I am glad."

Aidan's flush deepened, and he had no ease from his embarrassment as Æbbe came to him. She took his hand.

Aidan jerked it away. "What are you doing?" he asked.

Æbbe looked at him. "I was going to kiss your hand. Bishop."

Aidan's flush turned puce. Seeing that, Acha poked her daughter in the ribs. "Æbbe," she warned. "Don't."

It was Æbbe's turn to look embarrassed.

"Besides, now there is a bishop, we must ask him for permission to found a monastery. Will you grant it, Bishop Aidan?" Acha bowed her head to the young man.

"Y-yes. Of course."

"There. That is settled." Acha turned to her son. "The ideal place would be Lindisfarne; then we could keep our eyes upon you as well as our prayers."

It was now Oswald's turn to flush.

"I cannot, Mother. I have already given that land to Aidan, although he did not ask for it to be put into a great book."

"Very well. Some other land then – though for myself, I would have sight of the sea."

"I will find a place for you, Mother."

"Good." Acha looked around. "Oswiu is a long time returning. I would meet his wife." She looked to Oswald. "Rhieienmelth of Rheged? I knew her mother. A slave that Rhoedd raised from his bed to his throne. Rhoedd still reigns, does he not? An oafish man, ruled by greed. Although it was many years ago, I doubt such a man would change."

"Mother, she is beautiful and fair," said Oswald. "Do not speak of her so."

Acha looked at her son closely. "I was not speaking of her, whom I do not know, but of her parents, whom I do know."

The door to the great hall opened and Oswiu entered with Rhieienmelth by his side. She had changed her clothes, and rich clasps held her gown upon her shoulders, while gold gleamed about her throat and on her wrists. Oswiu brought her in and presented her to Acha and Æbbe.

"Rhieienmelth of Rheged. Is she not the fairest woman in the land?"

Acha looked Rhieienmelth up and down, and nodded. "Fair indeed – without. I hope you are as fair within." She stepped forward and took her hands and looked into her face. "I was as you are once. But you have a better, kinder man as husband than I. Serve him well."

"As well as my mother served my father," said Rhieienmelth.

Acha looked again at the princess, but Rhieienmelth smiled sweetly at her, and Acha nodded. Before she could say further, Rhieienmelth turned to Æbbe and held out her hands.

"Oswiu has told me so much of you."

"I hope he spoke well of me."

"He has nothing but praise for you: for your beauty, your wit, your goodness. Ah, if only he would speak as well of me."

"But I do," Oswiu protested.

"So you say. Mayhap my new sister will tell me how you speak on me when I am busy with women's work and you are alone. But for now, you must tell me all the news of the small islands whence you came. I, for my part, shall try to find some interest among the matters of kings and thegns for you – but it is wearisome stuff. I would much rather hear of fishing and weaving and suchlike." Princess Rhieienmelth smiled brightly at Æbbe. "Will you tell me?"

"If – if you wish."

"I do. Come, let us speak." Taking Æbbe's hand, Rhieienmelth led her across the hall to be nearer the fire. Acha watched them go, then turned to Oswiu.

"Be careful with her," she said.

"Mother," said Oswiu. But Oswald looked across the hall and saw the glance the princess cast back upon them as she patted Æbbe's hand, and he was troubled.

Chapter 5

The raven was coming closer. It walked stiff-legged among and over the slain men, pulling at flesh, picking and swallowing with its sharp beak. The slaughter bird. Its black eyes glittered.

He struggled to get free, to get away from it, but he lay among the dead, and their weight crushed him, holding him immobile. They lay in heaps about and above him, but his face was free and the raven saw him, saw the movement of his eyes, and it stepped up upon the mound of bodies, climbing towards him, its head turning but always, always, turning back to him. The raven was coming for his eyes.

He strained and pushed, but there was no movement in his limbs. The dead did not move and nor did he: only his eyes. He looked around, saw the faces as still as the bodies, eyes as thick and still as winter ice. Only his eyes moved, searching, looking, but all he saw were the bodies covering him and the raven, picking its way towards him. He tried to close his eyes, to hide them, but they would not close. The raven stalked closer, climbing the body hill, digging its feet into the arms and legs and bodies sprawled in the heap of the battle dead. It turned its head this way and that, as if looking for rivals, but there were no other animals yet on the battlefield. Not even the human scavengers, who were normally first, had arrived. Only the raven, and it was coming for him.

The raven stopped and stared down at him, cocking its head from one side to the other. He tried to turn his face away, but he could not move. All the movement he had was in his eyes, and they were locked now, helpless, staring at the bird standing above him, its thick, heavy butcher's beak clacking, once, twice.

And then it stabbed downwards…

*

"I dreamed."

Penda turned to the man standing silently by the bed upon which he sat. Waking, screaming, he had recovered enough, when he saw the dim light from the tapers filtering into his room, to know that he still retained his eyes. The woman, whom he had woken with his waking and who had tried to calm him, he had pushed away, unable even to remember her name.

"Get me Wihtrun."

As she reached for him again, to comfort him, he sent her sprawling on the floor.

"Go!" he had screamed at her, and such was her terror that she did not stop to dress, but ran unclothed from the room.

Penda had sat, waiting, listening. Wihtrun did not keep him long. Penda heard him running, his feet slapping against the rushes, then slowing sharply at the door.

"Lord?"

"Shut the door."

Now Wihtrun stood waiting, silent. Penda glanced up at him. The priest looked bare without his wolfskin about his shoulders. The woman – her name was Frithburh he remembered now – must have impressed him with the urgency of the summons for Wihtrun not to have pulled on his wolfskin cape. Without it, his shoulders appeared scrawny and weak; a runt. But the priest's strength did not lie in his arm, nor even in his mind, but in his eyes; he could see the workings of wyrd and the spinning of the fate singers. He could walk the path of dreams where gods spoke to men.

"I dreamed." Penda did not look at Wihtrun as he described it. He made his voice as flat as he could, seeking to drain the horror of the dream with his tone, but this was not as other dreams. No man could be king, and see what he had seen, without suffering sometimes in the dark watches of the night. Waking banished dreams. But this one did not diminish. It remained fixed and bright in memory; wherever he turned, he saw again the black button eye of the raven fixed upon him.

"What does it mean?" Penda looked up at Wihtrun. "Tell me."

And the priest smiled.

"Each day and each night, Woden sends forth the ravens that perch upon his shoulders, Thought and Memory, and they bring to him in his hall what has transpired in the world and in men's hearts. That he should send one of his ravens to you is honour, glory beyond any gold."

"It pecked out my eye!" Penda was on his feet, screaming into the face of Wihtrun, but the priest did not flinch.

"How many eyes has the Lord of the Slain?"

As Penda took the priest's shoulders to shake him, the import of the words passed through his anger, passed through his fear and entered into his heart. He did not let go, but held the priest, face to face, their noses all but touching.

"What did you say?"

"How many eyes has the Raven God?"

And Penda let go, sitting back on the bed as the import of that simple question drained the strength from his legs. For Woden had but one eye.

"The Hanged One spoke to me?"

"Yes." Wihtrun the priest knelt beside Penda. "He has come to you; he has spoken to you. He has favoured you, lord."

"But what does it mean?"

"When the gods speak, their words take many meanings, lord. Woden sacrificed his eye that he might drink from the well of wisdom; mayhap he requires sacrifice from you?"

Penda nodded. "That is as may be. But I am not a god – I cannot give an eye for wisdom, nor hang upon a tree for nine days. I have given him much gold and weapons and slaves in the past; what more can he want from me?"

"Something of value. Something, or someone, that you do not want to give."

"Who is that?"

"Only you can answer that, lord. But also, there is another way to read this dream. Does not the king of the Northumbrians have a raven? And are we not hemmed in, constricted by the kingdoms around us rushing to make alliance with him? For has not news reached us that to the east the kings of the East Angles, Sigeberht and Ecgric, have made joint cause with Oswald, taking him as their overking against Mercia? And in the south, the king of the West Saxons, has he not sent to Oswald seeking alliance too? Only in the west, among the Britons, with the men of Gwynedd, do our old alliances hold firm, for they hate the slayer of their king. Is it not clear what the Lord of Battles is telling you?"

Penda stared at the floor. "It is what I have been telling myself. I have let others dissuade me. No longer."

*

"This is not wise." Eowa stared at his brother across the high table. "We – you – are not yet secure upon the throne, and yet you would leave our kingdom and our backs unprotected and attack Oswald. That is madness."

Penda leaned across to Eowa. "I will tell you what is madness, brother. Madness is waiting, suffocated with fear, while your enemies draw the hobbles tight around your legs and slowly bind your arms, and then stuff your mouth with gags. That is madness. While we have been in Mercia, trying to get thegns whose mothers were slaves and whores but who fancy themselves Iclingas to accept me as king, going from one hall to another, giving gold, giving promises, Oswald has been tying the other kingdoms to his belt, until all but a few dangle from it like keys. If we do not act, and soon, he will strangle us without even trying – we'll die like pigs."

"We'll die like pigs if we attack him alone, brother."

"Not alone, Eowa, not alone. There is a new king in Gwynedd; Cadafael will march with us. And there are others among the kingdom of the Britons who remember the Twister all too well: they will be eager to strike down the Twister's son. If we act, and soon, we can beat him."

"The blood moon rises in but a few weeks; winter is coming."

"Then we attack in the spring, before he is ready."

Eowa shook his head. "I do not like this, brother. We have worked long and hard to gain this throne and held it but a short time; the

Lord of Battles is fey and his favour passes to whom he will; we know not where it will lie."

Penda smiled, his teeth showing sharp behind his lips. "Ah, but I do, brother, I do. Woden came to me in dream, and took my eye from among the piled-up slain."

Eowa stared at him. "And you want to go into battle with Oswald after such a dream?"

"Wihtrun the priest told its meaning for me: my enemies are all around, suffocating and close." Penda stared at his brother as another meaning of the dream occurred to him. "Very close, perhaps."

Eowa paused as he took Penda's meaning. "No, brother, no. I am not your enemy."

"It is ever told in tales how two brothers, great in arms and founders of thrones, fell to each other."

"This is not a tale, Penda."

Penda stared at his younger brother. "Let it not become one."

"It is the task appointed to a warmaster to speak when the king is too bold."

"I can get another warmaster."

"You cannot get another brother."

There was silence between them for an instant, then Penda smiled. "That is true and it is as well. One is enough."

"And for me too."

"As my warmaster, go to Cadafael of Gwynedd, ride to all the kingdoms of the Britons to our west; give them gifts and promises, give them whatever they need, but let them ride with us in the spring, when the frosts still come and the willow is breaking leaf."

"Very well, brother. I will go. But before I leave, answer me this: why do you keep Eadfrith alive? I do not understand. As long as he lives, you will not be secure upon the throne, for there will be an Iclinga for the witan to call upon, should enough thegns grow jealous of your glory. So why do you not kill him?"

"I – I cannot. Not yet." Penda sat back and looked down at the hands he now held clasped in front of him. How many men had they killed? He could not count. More than he knew, most likely, as there were men who crawled from the battlefield whom fever and the rotting sickness later took. Sometimes, in the dark, some of their faces came to him, but in the light they cast no shadow upon him. The dead were dead, and though their ghosts might claw at him from the dark places, they had no substance: they could no more cut him than he could cut a shadow. So why could he not bring himself to dispose of Eadfrith?

"At first, there was reason: we could use him against any other king that rose in Northumbria. That stays true: Eadfrith is Yffing, of the line of the kings of Deira, and Oswald is Iding of Bernicia; there may yet be chance to use him against Oswald. But it is true; he has become a danger to me now that the witan knows he lives. Maybe that is reason enough to kill him." Penda stared at his hands. So much killing. Death was the measure of glory and already scops sang his deeds, reciting the list of the slain and their kin. There was no glory in killing a captive, but that was not the reason he stayed his hand – he knew well enough that sometimes death must needs be dealt by knife and in silence as by sword and in battle.

"He does not fear death." Penda looked up from his hands and to his brother. "Truly, he does not fear it. I have spoken to him, I have held knife to him and seen his heart through his eyes. He no longer fears death – but not in the way I have seen other men overcome fear, through battle madness or beer courage or the fear of fear. He does not fear death, for he no longer fears anything. I have seen this change in him over the months I have held him captive. He has gone from rage and revenge, through the hope that came when he stood against me in the witan, to a peace I do not understand. He is in my power and yet he does not fear me. I would know whence this peace comes before I kill him."

Penda looked back at his hands. He could see that they shook. Ever so slightly. Yet they shook. With a sword his hand was still, but without, it had begun to shake.

"I need it."

Eowa nodded. He got up. "Very well. I will make ready. But I do not understand."

Penda stared after his brother as he left the hall.

"Neither do I," he said.

*

"It is you." Eadfrith looked up from where he lay shackled to the centre post of an old hut. "Why do you keep torturing yourself?"

"Torturing myself?" Penda sat down, cross-legged, in front of Eadfrith. The young man squinted against the light pouring into the hut through the door thrown wide. The king of Mercia took the seax from its sheath and stropped it on the whetstone he carried in the pouch on his belt. "I think it is you that is being tortured."

Eadfrith tried to smile, but his lips, cracked and dry, barely moved.

"I can but endure what you deal to me. But you. You come here, again and again, like an ox scratching for an itch it cannot reach. There is nothing I can give you, no knowledge or power, so I ask you again: why do you torture yourself?"

"I do not torture myself!"

"Then why do you come to me?"

"To hurt you! To make you feel pain, to make you scream."

Eadfrith tried again to smile, and this time he succeeded. It was a sad smile. He held out his hands, as far as the shackles would allow, towards Penda, and his hands and arms bore signs of the ill usage done to them.

"Why do you not hate me? You used to hate me. I saw it when I faced you across the duelling cloak before the witan. But now, now… " Penda reached out and pulled Eadfrith's head back and stared into his face. "Now. Pah!" He pushed Eadfrith's head aside, and so little strength did the man have left that it hit against the hut pole before he could stop himself.

Penda grabbed Eadfrith again, holding him by his throat. "Tell me."

Eadfrith, being throttled, pointed to the hand upon his throat and Penda let go.

"Tell me," he repeated, and this time his voice was a whisper.

"If we had won, if we had taken you, then I would have been the one with the knife and you would have been the one shackled."

"And do you not wish that?"

"I did. I dreamed of what I would do to you, of the slow ways of killing I would invent to draw out your pain. But now... No. I would not be the one with the knife; though I would rather not be the one shackled."

"But why not?" Penda, without thought, scratched his nails over his face in the intensity of his asking, and drops of blood leaked from the skin.

"Because you are in more pain than I."

Penda stared at Eadfrith, and his eyes clouded with hatred. He leaned towards the bound man and whispered, "Not for long."

*

"You should give him to Woden." Wihtrun the priest was sitting outside the hut when Penda emerged. The king of Mercia looked back into the stinking shadows whence he had emerged; Eadfrith lay slumped against his shackles, unconscious finally.

"You heard him?"

Wihtrun stood up. "Everyone heard him." He pointed to the sky, where cloudbanks were massing in the west. "Even the gods heard him."

"There is something in him I want. I will not give him to anyone until I have cut it out."

The priest bent down and looked curiously into the hut. "He will not live long if his wounds are not given chance to heal." He stood up and looked at Penda. "Nor would he make a worthy sacrifice as he is."

"I am not sacrificing him." Penda pointed towards the hall. "I have many slaves. Take one of them if you need a sacrifice."

"The Tricker is not so easily tricked, nor so cheaply won over. Any man might sacrifice a slave, for he is his to do with as he pleases. But the son of a king? That is sacrifice worthy of the All-Father. That is meat to his table and matter in his sight. The Hooded One will take such a sacrifice and he will honour it, and honour you, its giver, beneath the branches of the Tree of the World, hanging your gift upon its boughs as I hang mine upon the blood oak." Wihtrun leaned towards the king. "There are many ears about. I would speak a word with you where they may not hear."

Penda looked around. In the compound that surrounded the hall, men were plying their crafts outside the tents and huts that sprang up like mushrooms whenever the king's household stopped to take the render from the farms and villages of the district. The men of his household, the hearth warriors who had earned the right to eat in his hall and sleep beneath its roof, sat in the autumn sun, while others ran through sword and spear exercises, or talked, or simply slept. With Eowa having left on his mission, there was less urgency about their training, and Penda noted that he would have to appoint another man to Eowa's role while his brother was away. But it was true; there were few corners indeed where a man might speak and not have others waggle their ears to hear.

"Where would you have me go?"

Wihtrun pointed. Standing a few hundred yards from the gate to the compound was a dark copse of trees.

"There?" asked Penda.

"None will follow us in there."

"Very well." Penda signalled to some of his nearer warriors. "But I will have men follow us to it. Let us go."

They walked to the grove in silence, Penda's men following close behind, but as they reached the boundaries of the grove, the king told them to wait before passing, with the priest, over the blood-marked line that separated the world of men from the world of the gods.

As the trees drew dense and dark around them, Penda slid his seax from its sheath. He felt, he sensed, eyes upon him, a watching presence, and his eyes and other senses shifted about, seeking, searching.

"He knows you come."

"Who does?"

"The Hanged One."

Wihtrun pointed through to the blood tree, standing alone in the centre of the grove, its boughs hung with the corpses of sacrificed animals. The air, even in this late season, buzzed with the heavy thrum of flies. Penda tasted iron in the still air. A battlefield tasted the same when the slaughter was done and the dead lay exposed and helpless.

Penda looked up at the tree. Upon it hung the fruit of the knife. Gifts to the God of Battles, supplications for his favour. It was sacred ground.

"The old ways are dying."

Wihtrun the priest turned to Penda. "The kings of our peoples, the kings of Kent and Essex, of Northumbria and the East Angles, they are turning away from the gods of our fathers." Tears glittered in his eyes. "It is bitter to me to hear of the sacred groves fired and the altars cast down. Why do they do this, lord? Why do they scorn the ways of old?"

"For victory." Penda nodded as he thought further on the question. "That is why they have taken this new god, even though he is the same god as the Britons serve, from whom our fathers took this land. But now, some have won battles by his hand, and so they cleave to him, and others, unsure, look to the new ways and think on them, watching with watchful eye. That is your answer, Wihtrun. Their new god has given victory to the kings of Kent and Essex, the East Angles and Northumbria."

"But Edwin was cast down."

"The new king, Oswald, is a follower of the new god as well, and his strength grows the greater. If you would have the old ways come back, Wihtrun, then have the gods give me victory! The kings will follow the god of battles – but for now they are not sure of his name."

"Lord, give me a gift for the Battle God, and he will favour you."

Penda looked at the priest. "Tell the Battle God, if he wants gifts, then to give me victory, and I will give him gifts: I will give him so many gifts the branches of the blood tree will break."

"But you have the son of a king…"

"I will not give him." Penda stopped, feeling his chest contract, as if ropes were tightening around it. "Not yet." He looked up at the blood tree. "Was it such a tree Woden hung from?"

"Yes, such a tree."

Penda nodded. "So I thought." He turned to the priest. "I feel it too. I feel the old ways, the ways of our fathers, slipping away. I would not lose them." He pointed up at the tree. "Tell them, tell all the gods, but most of all tell the Slaughter God, Woden, Lord of Battles, that if he would have the old ways remain among our people, then he should give me victory. Tell him that victory will bring him sacrifice, rich sacrifice in gold and red. Tell him that, Wihtrun, then ask the fate singers what wyrd they have woven." The king sheathed his seax, which he had been holding loosely the whole time he had been in the grove. "Even the gods are bound in wyrd, Wihtrun. That is what you learn in battle, in the clash of shieldwalls and the screams of men. The gods too are caught in its thread." The king tapped the end of his seax, eyes downcast as he thought. "If I could find a way to cut its web, then I would fear nothing. Nothing."

*

"You ask if we will make alliance with you against Northumbria?"

The king of Gwynedd, Cadafael, rose from his throne, where he had sat to receive the visitor from Mercia. "You ask if we will carry sword to the killers of our king, to the murderers of our priests, to the despoilers of our land?"

Eowa stood before him, travel-stained and weary. The winter was rolling north – it had not yet arrived in full force, but the ways were hock deep in mud and all he had seen for the last few days' travelling was rain.

"I come from Penda, king of Mercia, and yes, I ask this."

"Then I say yes. I say yes, as sheep upon our hills, as streams in our valleys. I say yes for the sake of Cadwallon, my cousin, the furious stag who drove our enemies from our land and fell far from it. I say yes for his father, Cadfan ap Iago, who sleeps alone when beside him should sleep his son. I say yes for his sister, Briant, who sleeps now too. I say yes for all my people. We will ride with you and kill this son of the Twister."

Eowa looked around the hall, all but bare of men.

"How many will ride with you when you come?"

Cadafael gestured to the winds. "There are many not here now; they have returned to their households, to their fathers and their wives, but they will ride with me in the spring."

"We will go against Oswald as early as the first greening of the willows. How many of your men will come then?"

"There will be many men," said Cadafael. "Many."

Eowa nodded, as if satisfied. "How many?"

"Enough," said Cadafael. He came down to Eowa and stood in front of him. The Mercian stood a hand's breadth taller than the king of Gwynedd. "I will send word to our brothers across the sea, to the Lord of the Isles and the kings of the north. With you, with Mercia at our side, we may finally drive the sons of Ida from their stronghold; a thing that Urien of Rheged would have done if not for the treachery of Morgant. Now, together, we make alliance and destroy the Idings for good and all." Cadafael smiled. "With the kings of the north and the Lord of the Isles, there will be more than enough men to destroy the Idings and take back our land."

*

"Where are they?"

Eowa rode to Cadafael, king of Gwynedd. He pointed past the king to the warband that followed him: some fifty men astride the wire-haired ponies of the hills, their spears held aloft and glittering in the bright spring light.

"You said you would bring the kings of the north and the Lord of the Isles with you. Where are they?" He glanced back to where Penda waited, at the head of the warband they had brought from Mercia. With the contingent Cadafael had brought, they numbered some two hundred and fifty men. It was a good-sized army, but not what he had promised his brother when he returned from his mission to the kingdoms of the Britons.

Cadafael pushed his horse alongside Eowa and he leaned to him. "They will come. They sent word that they will take ship and meet us without the walls of York, for it is better for them to take the grey road, the blue path, than make their way through land that Northumbria controls."

Eowa turned his horse's head and rode back to Penda. When they had seen the approaching horsemen, Eowa had ridden ahead, for he alone knew Cadafael's face and could give guarantee that it was the king of Gwynedd that rode to intercept them.

"Not that it's likely that fifty men would attack two hundred," said Penda, as Eowa made to urge his horse forward. "But find out where the rest of them are."

"York," he reported back. "They will meet us in York, Cadafael says."

Penda nodded and sat back upon his horse, looking searchingly at the approaching riders.

"That is all he could bring?"

"Gwynedd must have lost many, many men at Heavenfield," said Eowa. "There's bare sufficient there for a group of bandits."

"We have men enough of our own, so long as Oswald does not hear of our approach. What king has two hundred warriors in his household?"

"I have heard tell that the kings of the Franks take five hundred, a thousand men to war."

"That is Francia. This is here," said Penda.

"Let us hope they do not cross the Narrow Sea, then."

"Yes." Penda was not listening. "What of this king, this Cadafael? Is he the match of Cadwallon?"

"In words, yes, and more so. I spent two days with him and scarce a moment passed in his presence when he did not press me with words. But in deeds? I do not know. Any man of battle would have been with Cadwallon when he fell. A man of words? Maybe not."

"Well, let us greet this man of words and hope he is a man of battles as well." Penda pushed his horse a few steps forward so that it stood alone at the front of the men of Mercia. They were travelling fast and travelling light, so no slow, ox-drawn wagons laboured up the road behind them. Each man carried food for the journey, a cloak for the night, and what weapons he had earned or received. Penda had spent the winter drilling the men of his household, dressing them in the shieldwall so each knew his place exactly, by the very feel and weight and smell of the men pushed in close to either side of him.

As he sat waiting for the king of Gwynedd, Penda glanced idly to the sky, where he saw the familiar shape of a red kite, soaring upon the wind. It held in its talons the body of some animal that it had scavenged. But then, from above the red kite, a black dagger plunged, a raven croaking its challenge through its butcher's beak, and the kite, alarmed, made to roll out of its way, but the raven struck the meal from the kite's claws and followed it. Seeing it fall towards him, Penda realized it was no animal. Then the arm, severed from below a shoulder, thumped dully to the ground and the raven, landing beside it, dipped its head over the meal it had won from the kite, while the men behind Penda pointed and whispered, even as a tremor of fear passed into his own bowels.

"What was that?"

Penda turned to see Cadafael, the king of Gwynedd, staring past him at the raven pulling flesh from the arm that had fallen from the sky.

"Somebody's arm," said Penda.

"Oh," said Cadafael.

"It's all right," said Penda. "It doesn't belong to any of my men."

"Yes." Cadafael licked his lips and glanced back to his men. "It is not exactly propitious."

Penda urged his horse closer to Cadafael. "It is if we make it so," he hissed. Then he turned to his own men and pointed. "See, the gods send us Oswald's arm. We just have to collect the rest of him!"

Nods and laughs, nervous but relieved, spread down the Mercian column. But heads shook beside those who laughed, and Penda saw many men making the sign against the evil eye whenever the raven raised its head to check that they were not approaching to steal its meal.

But when he turned to see how Cadafael was dealing with his men, he saw the king of Gwynedd was still staring with horrified fascination at the raven and his meal, as if he had never seen a slaughter bird gorging itself upon the battlefield. Behind him, the men of Gwynedd had clustered into pointing, whispering groups.

"They will break before we even see battle if you do not speak with them."

Cadafael's head jerked around, searching for Penda. "Yes. Yes, of course." He turned his horse and rode back to his men. Soon, the same message, although in a different language, was spreading among the men of Gwynedd. But there too Penda saw many uncertain glances to where the raven continued to make its meal on human flesh.

While he waited for Cadafael to settle his men, Penda gestured Wihtrun the priest to him.

"Did you see that in the wyrd before we rode?" he asked.

The priest shook his head. "It – it was not clear. I have never known the signs to be so hard to read."

"Then what of this? This is a sign from the gods, surely?"

"The best I can say is that it is as you said. The Raven God gives us Oswald's arm; it is to us to take the rest of his body."

"And the worst?"

"The worst?" Wihtrun looked around to see no one could hear. "Oswald steals from us that which we thought to take from him."

"His life?"

"An arm is a man's strength."

"Our strength." Penda pursed his lips. "We shall have to make sure the first is the meaning then. Later, when it is dark and our new allies cannot see or hear, make sacrifice for victory, Wihtrun."

The priest looked at Penda. "You want me to sacrifice the king's son? You brought him with us. I saw that he has recovered much from when I last saw him in the autumn."

"I did as you said: death would have claimed him if I had not let his wounds heal and given him to eat and drink. But no, I do not want you to sacrifice him. Eadfrith is here for other reasons. I have slaves. I will give one of them to you."

"Sacrifice in secret carries not the same weight with the gods as sacrifice in public."

"Sacrifice in public would lose us Cadafael and his fifty men. Do it in private and tell the Lord of the Slain I will give him as many sacrifices as he wants after the battle, as long as he gives me victory during it."

"Very well. I will make sacrifice tonight." Wihtrun looked to the sky. "There will be no moon; it will be dark. On such a night, the Shifter oft walks this middle-earth. It is a good night to make gift to the gods." The priest wheeled his mare away down the line of men, eyes searching for those men, marked by their lack of weapons, who accompanied the army as slaves.

"We will reach York tomorrow," said Eowa, pulling his horse up beside Penda. "We should send scouts ahead to see if Oswald is there."

Penda shook his head. "Scouts can be captured. Everything depends on surprise. And if he is not there, there will be people in York who will tell us where he is; once we know, we can get to him quicker than news of us can reach him."

Eowa pursed his lips. "I do not like riding to a place and meeting when I do not know what awaits us there."

"Nothing that two hundred and fifty warriors can't deal with, I'll warrant." Penda patted his brother's arm. "You are warmaster; it is your task to worry. But I am king, and my task is victory: that we might earn glory and gold for our men. All will be well. I have set Wihtrun to make sacrifice this night – quietly, so Cadafael and his men do not know of it – to the All-Father, that he give us victory tomorrow."

Eowa looked sharply at Penda. "Is that why you brought him? Eadfrith?"

"No, not him. Now he has largely recovered, it was not wise to leave him behind, a temptation to any ambitious thegn who thought to make a move for the throne while I was away. But I brought him for other reasons too, which you will see tomorrow."

"Glad to hear there is a reason. I have had two men to guard him the whole way."

"You will see," said Penda.

*

"Have you come to tell me why I am here?"

Eadfrith, hands and ankles tied, looked up at Penda. They had started no fires that night, and only the fading light trailing behind the setting sun lit the face of the king as he stood over the bound man.

Penda squatted down beside Eadfrith. His hands went to the ground and he picked up a pebble. He held it up in front of Eadfrith's face.

"You have endured. Like this pebble, you have endured and I honour you for it. I have given you time to heal; I have fed you." The king tossed the pebble from one hand to the other. "If you faced me across the duelling cape, you might even win this time." He threw the pebble back again. "Then again, probably not."

"I would not fight you."

Penda, in the act of tossing the pebble once more, dropped it.

"What did you say?"

"I would not fight you."

"But – but you would have to. You are bound to. I killed your father. I killed your brother. You would have to fight me." Penda held up his hand. "Ah, I understand. You fear losing to me again."

"No." Eadfrith shook his head. "Well, yes, maybe. A little. I would not want to lose again. But even if I were as strong as I once was, even if I knew I would win, I would not fight you." The bound man turned his face from Penda. "I have done with death."

"I do not think death has finished with you."

"I hope not. It would be good to leave this middle-earth; I am weary of it."

"But what if I gave you your freedom? What if I gave you a kingdom?"

Eadfrith turned his face back to Penda. "You can give me nothing I want."

"But I can." Penda put his hand out to the ropes that tied Eadfrith's wrists together. "I can cut these bonds. I can make you free. And I can give you a kingdom again."

"How would you do that?"

"Tomorrow, when we face Oswald, I will ask you forth. I will place you before the men of Northumbria, and then you may speak, and speak in freedom, for you will be unbound. Claim the throne for yourself, for it should be yours. We are in Deira; the men facing us will be the men of your house, the followers of the Yffings. Call on them to come to you, to acknowledge you as king. They will cleave to you, and you will be free, and king."

"What of Oswald, my cousin?"

"We kill him, of course. There cannot be two kings on one throne."

Eadfrith looked away into the dark. "I have no wish to be king."

"But do you want to be free?"

Eadfrith turned his face back to Penda, and tears lay upon his cheeks.

"Yes," he whispered.

*

"Did you do it?"

The morning sun had barely broken the horizon but the men of Mercia and the warriors of Gwynedd rode towards York, their horses' hooves rattling over the old road of the emperors. Penda had held his horse back so that the men might pass, until he saw Wihtrun astride his mare, and then he swung in beside him.

"Did you do it?" he repeated, leaning across the gap between the two trotting horses. "I did not hear anything."

"You were not supposed to hear anything," said the priest.

"How did you manage it? Even slaves cry out when they realize they are about to die."

"He never knew. I woke him and asked him to come with me. He did not wish to, but..." Wihtrun shrugged. "He was a slave, what could he do? So he came and when we were far enough from the camp, I gave him to the gods."

"But how did you do that? It is no easy matter, to kill without sound."

"I cut his throat. Blood is black by starlight. I poured it out in offering to the Lord of the Slain."

"Did he accept the offering?"

"H-he took it. But I do not know for certain whether he accepted it."

"He must. If he would have worship and sacrifice, I must have victory. He must accept our offering."

"Yes. Yes, that is what I hope." The priest turned to look at Penda and his face was pale. "But I do not know if my hope is justified."

The shout went up from the head of the column and was passed down the line.

York. The old Roman city, its walls still largely intact, was coming into sight.

"We shall know soon enough," said Penda and he urged his horse on, up the column to its head. There was the city, rising above the surrounding water meadows, the early sun catching the spires of smoke that rose from within its walls as new-risen wives set to cooking the breaking of the night's fast. He shaded his eyes against the sun and narrowed his eyes to slits, a trick he had learned from his father that brought greater clarity to sight. Cadafael had promised that the kings of the north would meet them outside York, and there, downriver, he saw the jagged spikes of masts, many masts, moving gently in the current.

"They have come." Penda pointed, and Eowa and Cadafael looked to where he indicated. "The kings of the north."

"There, I said they would be here," said Cadafael, and Eowa caught the relief that ran across his face. For his part, Eowa's relief was tempered; they still did not know if Oswald was in York. But even that anxiety waned as they rode closer, for one of the sharper-eyed men saw the flag of the king flying from the walls of the city.

Penda looked to his brother.

"We've got him," he said. "We've got him." He turned in the saddle and raised his arm, waving the men behind to hurry.

"Five white mares to the man who brings me Oswald's head," he shouted. "On."

As the column of horsemen streamed past, Penda stopped the priest. "He accepted our offering," he said to him. "The All-Father has taken our sacrifice."

Wihtrun nodded. "I think so."

"Of course he has." Penda wheeled his horse to catch up with Eowa. "When Oswald's sentries see us, what do you think he will do?"

"I know what I would do," said Eowa. "I would barricade the gates of the city and send my men up onto the walls. I would send messengers to any ally who might come, summoning them to my aid. And then I would wait, and hope that disease grows rife among my enemies camped outside my city. That is what I would do. But I do not think Oswald will act in such fashion." Eowa peered ahead. There was still no outward sign of alarm to the city, although surely any sentry would have spotted the approaching army by now. "I do not know what Oswald will do."

"We will know soon enough." Penda pointed downstream. Turning past the willow meads that filled the water meadows downriver from the city were the first boats, pulling upstream against the flow as lines of oars dipped and raised in unison, and voices, distant but clear, were lifted in rowing song.

"The kings of the north," said Penda. "The kings that Cadafael promised. They have come." He pointed. "They will land south of the city. We approach from the west." Penda clapped his hands. "We have him, brother, we have him. He either stands siege against us, and surely we have enough men now to drag him from his hole like a rat, or he flees; and the kings of the north have blocked his best chance for escape."

And even as they watched, they saw the first boats pull up on the riverside and the men within them disembarking and moving into formation, shields slung upon shoulders and spears raised, about the walls of York.

"There must be three hundred – four hundred men," said Penda as the boats arrived and the ranks thickened.

"I make it close to five hundred," said Eowa. Behind them, they could hear the excited, elated chatter of their own men. This was a huge host; together they made an army more than seven hundred strong. Such a force had not been seen on these islands since the days of the emperors.

"Who has come?" Penda rode to Cadafael. "Can you read the banners?"

Cadafael squinted. "We are still far from them. I am not sure. Perhaps Strathclyde and the Lord of the Isles?"

In his excitement, Penda sought out Eadfrith, who rode with his hands bound together and a guard holding a rope looped about his neck. Should he try to urge his horse into flight, a simple pull on the rope would jerk him from the horse and break his neck.

"Mayhap I will not need you to speak to Oswald's men. Together, we shall be such an army that he will quail before us. But do not worry, I will keep my promise. When Oswald is dead, I will give you his kingdom."

Eadfrith gave no answer, but stared ahead at the city.

"Did you not hear me?" asked Penda.

The captive, without taking his eyes from York, said, "I wish for no throne, Penda of Mercia, but I thank you for this: the chance to see again the land of my birth, and the city of my new life. For that, I thank you indeed."

Penda stared at him, but Eadfrith made no sign that he noticed his scrutiny; all his attention was directed to the city ahead of them. Few of the cities of the Romans remained as intact as York. Even fewer were as striking. Eadfrith had seen the ruins of London, the once magnificent but now broken-down city shunned by the traders who had founded a new settlement upriver from the Roman city on the strand, where merchants from distant lands would beach their boats and lay out their wares. He had wandered the empty streets of Chester, the dark eyes of the empty windows staring out at him, and looked into the swirling, steaming waters of Bath. But only Carlisle, where the kings of Rheged held their court, still functioned as a town – the king's men had taken him once to see the water, still flowing into the town along the great bridge the Romans had built.

York took a middle place; not entirely abandoned – its walls made it a better refuge than most places – what inhabitants there were had pulled down houses and shops and sown the ground in between with seed, that they might grow crops within the walls, and pigs rooted amid the ruins, excavating with their sharp teeth the seed crop from the trees establishing themselves in untrodden roads and untended gardens.

Of all the royal estates of Deira, his father had loved York best, and Eadfrith had spent more time there than anywhere else on the ceaseless royal circuit. So it was he who first saw the change in the city: the smoke streams dammed as cooking fires were extinguished and the signs of movement on wall and turret.

"You have been seen." Eadfrith pointed, and Penda, head jerking round, saw the movement upon the walls.

"Ride!" He urged his horse forward to the front of the column, picking the speed up to a canter. Although he did not think Oswald would dare issue from the city, he wanted to get to his allies, forming up outside the walls, before there was any chance of the two forces being separated.

But even as he reached the head of the column, the gates of York opened and men began to march out, shields on shoulders and spears held high. And at their head, carried upon a high pole, the gold and purple banner of the Idings.

Penda held his hand up, slowing and then stopping the column of riders, while he waited for Eowa and Cadafael to ride up alongside him.

"He has come out of the city." Penda shook his head. "Why would he do that?"

As they spoke, he saw the gates close. The last man had emerged. Penda pointed.

"I make that, what, one hundred and fifty men? Why would he do that?"

Eowa scanned along the line as Oswald's men formed into a wall, his lips moving as he counted silently. "Maybe two hundred. A match for us."

"But not for my brethren!" said Cadafael. He pointed at the far line of men. "We have Oswald between us, caught in our vice." He turned to Penda and held up his fist. "Let us squeeze him."

But Penda shook his head. "This makes no sense. We are missing something."

"Whatever that is, we should dismount and form line," said Eowa.

"We men of Gwynedd prefer to fight on horseback," said Cadafael.

"Easier to get away," muttered Eowa as he dismounted and signalled the army to follow suit.

While the horses were gathered and picketed, and Cadafael gathered his riders around him with orders to wait until the clash of shieldwalls and then to harry the flanks of Oswald's line and to pick off the stragglers and the injured, Penda sat yet ahorse, staring at the shieldwall slowly forming across the main gate to the city. Maybe Oswald did not think he could hold the gate from within and had decided to defend it from without. That at least made some sort of sense.

Behind him, shifting along the line of waiting men, Penda heard the whispers and questions. These were experienced men. They could not understand what Oswald was doing, and it disturbed them as it disturbed him. There was, in their chatter, the uneasy sense of having missed something vital.

It was quiet. Penda turned his head to listen. It was unnaturally quiet. Usually, at this stage, with the opposing armies forming up against each other, the air would be thick with boasts and threats, calls and insults, as each side strove to bolster its own courage and to break that of their enemy. But barely a voice rose above a whisper.

In this silence, the croak of a raven sounded clear and solid. It sounded again, and then Penda saw it circling above them all, and some of his men saw and heard it too, and pointed. The slaughter bird, the eye of the Lord of Battles had arrived to witness the slaughter and to carry the dead away. Further whispers spread among the ranks behind him, and Penda saw many men, and not just the least experienced, make the sign against the evil eye as the raven circled above them.

But then it began to descend. In long, slow sweeps the raven flew lower and lower until finally it landed in front of Oswald's army. Then, stiff-legged, it marched towards the line and from the shieldwall a man stepped to meet it, a man armoured and helmed in such fashion that Penda knew he must be Oswald, and the raven lowered its head to the man, who bent to it, and the bird climbed up his arm and stood upon his shoulder. The raven turned towards the watching men and lowered its head and croaked its call, and cries went up from behind Penda – cries of shock and horror at what they had seen.

"The slaughter bird."

"Woden's herald."

"The Battle God has turned against us."

Penda turned to look for Wihtrun, but the priest stood with face pale and hands held to his cheek.

The Mercian turned to his men, riding up and down the line, pulling their sight from the terrible bird back to him.

"Oswald has delivered himself into our hands. The Battle God has dazzled him, Woden has fuddled his wits. He has come out, and we surround him on either side." Penda pointed beyond Oswald's line to where the kings of the north were forming their battle line. "We will crush him, and then we'll see why the slaughter bird stands upon his shoulder: it did not want to be late for the feast!"

The laughter that greeted his sally was weak, but at least some men laughed. Penda looked to Eowa, who silently nodded his assent. This was no time to wait. Waiting would only test the men's nerves and send them looking for further omens.

Penda dismounted and sent his horse through to the rear, then made his way to the centre of the shieldwall. That was his place, with his sword fellows around him, sworn to protect their lord with shield and sword and life.

But before he could take his position, Eowa came running to him from the right wing.

"The kings of the north are advancing." He pointed, and Penda saw the shieldwall of his allies had already covered half the distance between them and the waiting line of Oswald's men.

"They want all the glory," said Penda.

"The glory comes to those who finish the battle, not those who start it," said Eowa. "This is better than we could have hoped for, brother. Let them bleed Oswald's strength, and their own, and then we will finish the job. There will be many men the richer tonight."

"And even more dead. Order slow advance, warmaster. Let us be late, but not too late."

Beating the step on the rim of his shield with his sword hilt, Eowa set the shieldwall of Mercia forward. The riders of Gwynedd walked beside them, half the horsemen on each flank.

As they advanced, every man watched with eager eye the march of their allies, closing with Oswald's shieldwall. But as the lines neared, the picture grew blurred. For Oswald's shieldwall did not turn to meet the advance of the kings of the north, but remained where it was, in front of the gates of the city. And the advancing men, they did not beat the rhythm of their approach on their shields, nor did they call down insult and death upon the men facing them, but they approached in silence. And then the silence was broken by cries. Cries of welcome. And instead of engaging, the two armies merged, the battle line of the kings of the north joining to the end of Oswald's shieldwall, and both turned together to face Penda.

"Halt!"

Penda gave the order, but there was no need to issue it. Everyone had stopped already. They stared in shock at the army facing them, now three times the size of their own. He looked to the flanks and frantically gestured Cadafael to him.

"What's happening? They're supposed to be our allies. They're your brethren. What's going on?"

The king of Gwynedd shook his head. "I – I do not know."

"Find out!"

Cadafael swallowed, glanced at the waiting line of men, then rode his horse forward, stopping it in the empty ground between the two armies.

"Kings of the north," he shouted. "I am Cadafael, king of Gywnedd, your kin by blood and tongue and faith. I summoned you here, yet now you form line against me. For why do you break your trust?"

A man stepped from the battle line and signalled for a horse to be brought to him. Then, alone, he rode to meet Cadafael.

The king of Gwynedd tightened his grip on the reins, ready to jerk his horse into motion, but the approaching rider kept his sword sheathed and his shield slung over shoulder.

"Who are you?" Cadafael called as the rider approached.

The horseman slowed his animal to a walk.

"Rhoedd, king of Rheged." The king twitched the reins and his horse walked in closer to Cadafael – close enough so that they might talk without the men in either battle line hearing.

"You said you would join me in fighting Oswald. I sent messengers."

Rhoedd gentled his horse to a halt. For a large man, he sat easily on the beast and his hands were light upon it. "I said I would be here, outside the walls of York, and here I am. But I did not say I would fight Oswald on your behalf."

"Not on my behalf. With me."

"With you or without you. My daughter is wed to Oswald's brother; why would I fight him? He has the favour of Iona; why would I fight him? He has the blessing of the Blessed One; I would be mad to fight him." Rhoedd leaned towards Cadafael. "Why do you fight him, Cadafael? Through him you came to the throne. Enjoy it for many years to come. Live, and bring your men to us, or have them ride aside. For else the Baptized will battle the Baptized, a thing most grievous to God – and most unlikely to win glory with the bards or renown for a new, untried king." Rhoedd put his hand out and took Cadafael's arm. He leaned to him.

"Stand your men down, Cadafael, and live, and enjoy your throne."

The king of Gwynedd swallowed. He looked back to where Penda stood watching him with the intensity of a hawk. He turned to Rhoedd.

"Men will call me battle-shirker. The bards will mock me."

The king leaned closer to him. "I have been king near twenty years now. Listen to what I have learned. The bards sing songs of Cadwallon, they call him the 'furious stag' and lament him, but he lies with his eyes pecked out far from his homeland and they will never find his bones and lay them by his father. Let the bards sing, and feed them and lade them with gold, and you know what? They will find glory for you too. So which do you prefer, Cadafael of Gwynedd: to die, and never hear the songs the bards will sing of you, or to live and to hear your song sung in your hall, with your children about your feet and a woman in your bed?"

Cadafael slowly removed Rhoedd's hand from his arm. He turned his horse about and walked it back to Penda's battle line, stopping it a safe distance from the king of Mercia.

"Kin shall not fight kin; cousin will not slay cousin."

"You…" Penda charged from the battle line, drawing his sword, but before he could reach Cadafael, the king of Gwynedd turned his mount and urged it away, across the battle line, signalling his own men to follow.

Penda stared after the horsemen of Gwynedd. They cantered away, heading back the way they had come, before stopping when safely out of range and turning. They were going to watch. They were going to watch him die.

A cold, hopeless fury settled over Penda. He turned back towards the battle line, his face set. This was the day he was going to die. The Battle God had spurned his sacrifice. He sought out Wihtrun's face in the battle line. The priest turned his face away from him. Penda went to him. The priest looked up, his face bloodless.

"This is the Battle God's blessing? Our allies desert us?" Penda grabbed his throat. "I should kill you."

Wihtrun choked, his eyes bulging. Penda let him go and the priest sagged, but the men to either side of him held him up, their support immediate and instinctive. He stood beside them in the shieldwall; therefore they supported him.

"You're not worth my knife." Penda turned away.

"Eadfrith," Wihtrun gasped. "Eadfrith."

Penda stopped. Of course. He looked around. Oswald's shieldwall had not moved; there was still time. He pushed through the shieldwall, signalling Eowa to follow him.

"Get us horses," he said to his brother, as he sawed through the ropes tying Eadfrith's ankles and wrists.

As Eowa fetched the horses, Penda pulled Eadfrith to his feet.

"Here it is," Penda said, holding Eadfrith up, his face all but touching Eadfrith's face. "Here's your chance for freedom. Do to Oswald what you did to me at the witan. Make them want you as king, and you will be free."

"I do not want to be a king," said Eadfrith. He stared at Penda. "I have seen what the throne does to a man."

"There's — there's no time for this now. Come on." Penda pushed Eadfrith ahead of him, then swung up onto a horse, with Eowa following on his own mount. "Make way."

The shieldwall parted, men squeezing up against each other, and the brothers rode through, one after the other, with Eadfrith walking in between.

They rode into the gap between the two armies. Still Oswald's shieldwall stood in silence, guarding the gates of York but not yet advancing upon the Mercians. For their part, the Mercians stood firm, shield to shield, and though whispers of their betrayal by Cadafael passed up and down the line, yet no man fell back from it.

"Men of Northumbria!" Penda reined his horse to a stop. He searched the line, looking for his enemy, and thought to have found him standing near the battle standard at the centre of the line: a warrior with purple and gold cloak over his shoulders and a helmet that told the face it covered. But if it was Oswald, still he made no move, nor gave a sign.

"Men of Deira! Hear me." Penda pointed to the man standing silently beside him. "Here is your true king! Here is Eadfrith, son of Edwin, son of Ælle, of the house of Yffi. Men of Deira, you allow an Iding to claim your throne when an Yffing yet lives."

Penda saw a ripple pass up and down the line, whispers passed along relaying to the men furthest away what Penda said. Still the man he took to be Oswald made no move.

"Here is the man who should be your king, men of Deira. Hear him!" Penda leaned down to Eadfrith. "This is your chance. Take it. I will let you go. You will be free." He leaned even closer. "Don't try to run, though. Do you think Oswald would make you welcome?

Your father killed his father – he will kill you in turn."

Eadfrith stood rubbing his wrists, looking up and down the line of men in front of him, searching for faces he knew. There were none he could see, but simply being on the land he had known as boy and man gave his heart ease.

"Speak," said Penda.

Eadfrith bent down and placed his hand upon the ground. He felt the grass, the rich soft grass of spring.

"Speak," said Penda.

Eadfrith stood, and calmly, steadily, he began to walk towards his home.

"Speak!"

Eadfrith did not look round. He did not run. He spoke no word. He was going home.

Penda looked to Eowa; nodded. His brother swept forward on his horse and struck the back of Eadfrith's head heavy and fast with the hilt of his sword. The man dropped, and Eowa leapt from his horse and threw Eadfrith over the animal. Penda pushed his own horse forward, as a growl, feral and ferocious, came from the men watching in the shieldwall.

"That worked well," said Eowa as they retreated back to their own line. "I said you should never have kept him alive."

Penda stared at him, his eyes cold. "If you have any ideas of how we can survive this, tell me. Otherwise, shut up."

"I advised against this attack."

"And I will kill you – if we live – if you do not shut up."

But before Eowa could answer, a shout went up from their own line. The brothers turned to see two men, under flag of truce, advancing from Oswald's battle line. Above them circled a raven.

"They want to talk," said Penda. "Maybe we can get out of this after all." He turned to his brother. "Take Eadfrith back and then come to join me. I will go to speak to them. Give orders: if they kill me, make sure Eadfrith's throat is cut before battle begins."

Then Penda dismounted and went alone to meet the two men.

Chapter 6

"Tell me again why we are doing this." Oswiu spoke without taking his eyes from the man approaching them.

"To save the lives of our men and to save the life of our cousin," said Oswald. Above them, Bran croaked mournfully. Oswald looked up and laughed. "I am sorry, old friend, but I would not have you feast today."

"We have twice the men he has; ours are rested and eager; it will be an easy fight."

Oswald shook his head. "Men without hope sell their lives dearly, and it will be the blood of our men that buys them. If we can gain victory another way, I will take that victory."

"Acca won't like that much – no glorious deeds to sing about."

"Bran is already cross; but many children will give thanks to have their fathers return to them." Oswald checked to see how far they had come. "We will wait here. Let him come to us."

Oswiu pointed. "There's another coming from their line."

"I wondered why Penda came alone."

"Do you think the man they paraded in front of us really was Eadfrith?"

"I had not thought he could yet live. But men who knew him said it was indeed Eadfrith."

"Then why did he not speak? There are still many in Deira who would wish an Yffing as king."

"Maybe he would not speak for Penda. By the look of him, Eadfrith has been ill used."

"Penda would have offered him his life and freedom if he could peel some of our men away from us," said Oswiu.

"Then let us try to earn it for him ourselves," said Oswald.

Oswiu looked at his brother. "Do you think that wise? Eadfrith has claim, true claim, to the throne of Deira and Northumbria. Do we really want him back?"

Oswald turned to answer his brother. "Yes," he said simply. "Do you not?"

"Of course. He is our cousin. But it might have been easier if he had died with his father and brother."

"In truth, I agree. But Eadfrith is alive, and he spoke not against us, as his father raised no hand in our pursuit while we were in exile. Therefore, we will keep him that way."

"Very well." Oswiu nodded in front of them. "They will soon be here."

The second man had caught up with Penda and they walked together towards the waiting brothers.

"Let us make ready," said Oswald. He drew his sword, then thrust it, point down, into the earth beside him. Oswiu did the same.

Seeing their actions, the approaching men stopped and did likewise, leaving their swords quivering in the earth's sheath.

The two groups of men stood some twenty yards apart, eyes fixed upon each other.

Oswald nodded and stepped forward, Oswiu by his side, and the two men they faced advanced, measuring step for step, until they stood facing each other, at equal distances from their swords.

"I am Oswald, *Lamnguin*, son of Æthelfrith, Iding, king of Bernicia, and son of Acha, Yffing, king of Deira."

"Oswiu, brother to Oswald *Lamnguin*, warmaster."

They waited in silence.

"Penda, king of Mercia."

"Eowa, brother to Penda, warmaster."

Silence again as the four men measured each other, eyes skilled at judging warriors marking each other for height and weight and strength of arm; for grace of movement and the bluster that masked fear.

"Why do you come into my land to make war upon me, Penda of Mercia?"

Penda stared at Oswald, then spat upon the ground.

"War is what kings *do*. Do you not know that, Oswald *Lamnguin*?"

"War is not all that I do. But I will answer war with war, sword with sword, cunning with cunning. Did you think to catch me unaware and unprepared?" Oswald indicated the men of the kings of the north. "They assured you they would meet you outside the gates of York. They have kept their word. But they kept their pledge with me as well, for the kings of the north have acknowledged me as king over them; they stand by me as I stand beside them."

"Send them away. Then let us see who will win between us."

"Would you have sent Cadafael away, if he had not left rather than fight his kin?"

"What do you want? You come forth to speak, but all I hear is your prattle."

Oswald stared at Penda, his eyes narrowing. "I want to give you your life."

"It is not yours to give."

"Now it is."

Penda's eyes locked with Oswald's. The two men fought with sight. Penda, teeth grinding, began to shake his head, but then the raven, Bran, descended in the darkness of its feathers and landed next to Oswald. It dipped its head towards the king of Mercia and croaked, its black eyes black fire.

The sight of the slaughter bird shook Penda's gaze from Oswald. He stared at the raven, his face paling. Eowa looked at his brother, the tightening of his lips betraying his alarm.

Penda fought to stop himself swallowing, but he could not prevent a traitorous tongue flicking nervously over his lips. He turned his gaze back to Oswald, striving to ignore the raven, but the bird croaked again, its head turned up to the king, and Oswald bent down, extending his arm, and the bird climbed, forearm, elbow, upper arm, to his shoulder. It stood there, its black eyes upon Penda, and the king of Mercia saw again the bird of his dream stepping upon the bodies of the dead, stalking closer as he lay immobile under corpses.

Eowa laid his hand upon his brother's arm. "We can live," he said, whispering to his brother. "We can live. Give them what they want."

"If we fight, many of your men will not return to their hearths," said Penda.

"If we fight, none of your men will return home," said Oswald. He reached up and stroked a finger over the raven's feathers. "Bran will take your eyes, Penda."

The bird croaked, turning its head from side to side to see Penda the more clearly.

"What are your terms?"

Oswald nodded. "Good. Now we speak true. These are my terms, Penda of Mercia. Accept them and you and your men will live. Refuse, and when battle is over I will send the pigs from the city to eat your bodies."

Penda waved his hand. "A dead man is a dead man: food for fire or worm or beast. Think not to scare me with such."

"Very well. Pledge yourself to me; take the new life that flows from the Holy Isle. Give up your captive, Eadfrith, to me. Hack from sword and buckle and shield the silver and gold and jewels. And give hostage to me, as surety of your faith. Those are my terms, Penda of Mercia. Accept them, and live."

Penda made no answer. The silence grew between them.

"What is your answer?"

"I will give silver and gold and gems, but our swords I will not give over, lest you then slaughter us."

"I did not ask for your weapons; only your wealth."

"I will give pledge to you, never again to march against you, unless you march on me first."

"I will not march on you without reason, Penda of Mercia. But what of the new life I offer you? Will you take that?"

"I – I would have further knowledge of that. Send to me such as might instruct us on this matter. But I may not go against the ways of our fathers without word to the witan of my people."

"Very well. I will send to you one who will instruct you in these things, that you might understand and accept them."

"You would have Eadfrith back? You would have another who might claim the throne?" There was a thread running through

Penda's question, a question within the question, but Oswald could not read what it asked.

"Yes, I would have him back," he said.

"I will give him over to you. But not until we are horsed."

"I would have him back now."

"I will not give him until we are ahorse."

"Then why should you give him?"

"Why should I not? What further use is he to me? He would not speak."

Oswald thought a moment. "Very well." He looked askance as he saw a thin smile, bleak and cold, cross Penda's face. "What of the hostage?"

"Who will you have?"

Oswald pointed. "I will have him."

And Penda turned to his brother.

Eowa stared at Oswald, then to his brother.

"No," he said.

"As you advised, warmaster, I am giving them what they want."

"No," Eowa said.

Penda turned to Oswald and Oswiu. "Take him."

Eowa leapt for his brother, hands reaching for his throat, but Penda stepped aside and Eowa tumbled past, falling over the foot that Penda stuck out. Before he could move and get back up, Penda was on him, pinning him with his knee and wrenching his arm behind his back.

"I'll break your arm," he whispered into Eowa's ear. "Keep still. Listen." His brother stopped struggling and lay still beneath him. Penda looked up to the two watching Northumbrians. "Get your swords and take him," he said.

As Oswald and Oswiu retreated to where they had left their swords, they saw Penda bent over his brother, whispering urgently to him, but it seemed to do little to quiet him, for when they returned, Eowa was again struggling, like a boar caught in a net.

Penda hauled his brother to his feet, keeping the armlock upon him as he did so, and pushed him, struggling, towards the Northumbrians.

"Here, take him," he said, and he pushed Eowa forwards, so he fell at their feet. He made to spring up, then fell back when he saw the two swords poised to pierce his flanks.

"Get up," said Oswald. "Slowly."

Eowa rose to his feet, but he gave no glance to the men into whose hands he had been placed as hostage. Instead, he glared back at his brother.

"I will kill you," he said. "I will kill you and take your throne."

Penda shook his head. "Remember the stories of our people, Eowa. Think on how the brothers Icel and Ine first claimed a throne here, and yet they fought in the end and Icel killed Ine. I should have known from that: one brother is enough for any kingdom." Penda looked at Oswald and Oswiu. "I will leave Eadfrith by Ælberht's oak, where the roads cross." He turned to make his way back to his lines, then stopped and looked back. "Oh, I'll take Eowa's sword with me. I don't suppose he will need it again."

Eowa made to leap after him, but Oswiu struck out with the hilt of his sword and the man fell, his face smearing in the dirt. He looked back to Oswald.

"Are you sure about taking him hostage? Penda does not seem so sad to lose him."

Oswald stared after the figure of the Mercian as he walked back to his battle line, calling orders as he went.

"Who else could we have asked for?" He turned to Oswiu. "If he cares not for his brother, who does he care for?"

Oswiu shrugged. "I do not know. But brother, we have won a victory, a great victory, with no blood, much gold and even greater glory. For when the news of this goes out to the thrones and kingdoms in the land, they will stand amazed that you defeated Penda of Mercia with not so much as a sword raised."

"We."

"Pardon?"

"We defeated Penda, Oswiu. Not I alone, and with you also our allies: the kings of the north and the kings of the East Angles."

"We then. We defeated Penda."

But Oswald stared after the Mercian. As he stood among his men giving orders, he did not seem like a man defeated, but rather one retreating. Still, he had won all he could on the day without drawing sword.

"We'd better send some men for the hack silver. They are not to move until it has been delivered." Oswald pointed to Eowa, lying on the ground. "Let's get him back." Sheathing their swords, the two men grabbed Eowa under the arms and dragged him to the waiting battle line.

*

"Now that is what I call a victory!" Rhoedd of Rheged stood over the pile of hack silver laid out on the ground in front of them in the tent that had been set up for the kings while they waited the spoils. He bent down and pushed his hands into the pile as a man puts his hand into water, and then broke the surface, the silver cascading from his skin as water from a leaping fish. He laughed and scooped up more silver, throwing it in the air. He looked up to where Oswald and Oswiu stood looking down at the great hoard of hack silver.

"It was a good day when my daughter married you!" he said. Then turning to the other men standing around the hoard, Rhoedd pointed at Oswald. "I married my daughter to his brother, and see what it's brought me. You've got daughters, he's still not married; what are you waiting for?"

"Will you set about dividing the spoils?" Oswald asked Rhoedd. "I would speak with these others yet awhile."

Rhoedd grinned, and pushed his hands into the pile once more. "Have you ever noticed? Silver is cool, like water, on the skin, but gold is warm, as sun and a woman's skin."

"I will leave some men to help you."

"Oswiu?"

Oswald spotted his brother making frantic "no" gestures behind Rhoedd's back.

"No, I will have need of him. We must follow the Mercians when they leave, and ensure they do as promised."

"And you've got to pick up that other ætheling too." Rhoedd leered at Oswald. "Where's Penda leaving him?"

"Ælberht's oak. Where the roads cross."

"A good place." Rhoedd turned back to the hoard. "Let me not keep you from your speaking; do not keep me from my treasure."

Oswald signed a few men to help – and watch – Rhoedd while he divided the hack silver and gold and gems. He turned to the rest.

"Come," he said, holding out his arm.

They followed him from the tent. The men who had brought the hack silver from Penda were making their way back to his battle line. The men there had already formed into line, ready to march back to the waiting horses. The men of Rheged, the sons of the Lords of the Isles and some of the Northumbrians watched them from horseback, ready to shadow the Mercians as they marched back to their horses.

"It was indeed a great victory."

Oswald turned to the man who had spoken. He was older, and his hair was grey and gold, but he had the air that sometimes accompanied a man of many battles, Oswald noted: the sadness of comrades lost and the knowledge that the only thing worse than a battle won was a battle lost.

"It would not have been possible without you, Sigeberht of the East Angles."

"I do not think I and the few men I brought with me made much difference here."

"It was the knowledge that he faced so many kings, united, that persuaded Penda to give up his silver and gold, and to pledge allegiance to me."

"As have the rest of us, Oswald; as have the rest of us. But do you think his pledge will hold?"

"Honestly? No. But now he knows better how many kings stand ranged against him, he will think more carefully, much more carefully, before bringing war to any of us."

"That is as I believe." Sigeberht fell silent for a while as they watched the Mercians making their way back towards the waiting horses. He turned to Oswald. "And it gives me hope. Now I am here, I will tell you of something I have given much thought on, for I would have your counsel."

Oswald turned to the king beside him. "Let us go away from here, that we may speak on this without ears to hear." He called Oswiu to him. "Go with the riders; follow Penda from our kingdom. I will follow when I have finished speaking with Sigeberht." Then, taking the king by the arm, he led him down to the river.

"What would you speak on, Sigeberht? I have known you but a few days, when first you came to pledge allegiance to me, and then this time when you answered my call, yet already I call you friend."

The king of the East Angles looked over the glittering water.

"When I was a boy, I would hear the tales of war and battle in my father's hall, and that was all I wished for: glory and honour, and the scops to sing my praise while I lived and to lament me when I died. But then I came to know war, to know it for what it is." He turned to Oswald. "And it seems to me that if we did not sing songs and raise praise, it would be a thing too terrible for any man to face. So the scops sing deeds and we tell tales, and these are the lies we tell ourselves, that we may face battle when it comes and not shame ourselves. So I became known as a warrior and, after Rædwald's death, a king. So all that I had dreamed as a boy, and more, I had achieved. But I cared not for it." Sigeberht sighed. "It is a terrible thing, Oswald, to gain all glory and praise and riches, and to want none of it. Then news came to me. In the old estate of the king, there was a building raised in honour to a new god, and I sought to know more of this god. I see the same hope in you."

The Northumbrian nodded. "I know whereof you speak, Sigeberht."

"Then know that I would have more of this new life. When I return to my land and my country, I will put away the crown and step away from the throne. There is another, Ecgric, who is ready and able to rule in my place. And I will enter a monastery, the holy house at Beodricesworth, and raise sword never again." Sigeberht looked to Oswald. "What say you of this, Oswald, High King?"

"I say I would that I could join you, Sigeberht. I say I will raise no counsel against you, for there is no work greater than the work of prayer in the houses of the holy. I say, if God wills, someday I too will put the sword aside and join you in prayer."

The king nodded. "I thank you, High King. I have yet to tell any others what I plan, but now I have your blessing I will return and tell my people. Ecgric will make a good king, although he still follows the old ways." Sigeberht took Oswald's hand in his own. "But my heart tells me the days will be long, and the time may never come, before you can lay aside the sword."

"That may be so." But here Oswald smiled. "Yet there was less death today than I feared, far far less. Now I must catch up with my brother, for I have redeemed my cousin from Penda, and one who was as dead will live."

Sigeberht looked at Oswald. "You truly want him to live?"

"Yes," said Oswald. He stopped. "You are the third to ask me this. Is it so strange?"

"Yes, it is strange. Few kings would welcome back alive another who might claim their throne, particularly when there is blood, much blood, between your families."

"Nevertheless, I have redeemed him, and now we shall go to fetch him."

Sigeberht nodded. "I hope Penda realized your wishes."

"What do you mean?"

"It would be easy for him to think you wanted Eadfrith dead but sought to have another's hand do the killing, lest the guilt, and blood debt, incur to you."

Oswald stared at him. "But I told him I wanted him alive."

"Did you say alive?"

"Yes. Yes, I'm sure I did. Yes."

*

They found Eadfrith, son of Edwin, Yffing, lying by Ælberht's oak. He lay upon his back, and his arms were spread, as if in his dying he sought to embrace the sky. Oswald saw Oswiu standing beside him as he slipped from his horse.

"Penda left a message." Oswiu pulled a slave forward, a young lad who, seeing Oswald and the rage and grief upon his face, shivered back against Oswiu's side. But Oswiu bent down to him. "Do not fear; his anger is not for you. Tell him your message."

The boy stepped forward, his hands behind his back, as he had been taught when delivering messages from memory.

"Speak," said Oswald.

"Penda of Mercia leaves this gift for you. He has done as you wished. The only ætheling who might yet claim your throne is your brother, and Penda leaves him to you to deal with, as he has given his own brother into your keeping."

Oswald nodded, tight-lipped.

"Anything else?"

"Penda of Mercia says it is better to rule alone. He thanks you for your aid in securing his throne."

Oswald began to turn away, but the boy coughed. "There was one more message, lord. Penda of Mercia said that Eadfrith never gave him what was in his heart; he took it with him when he died."

Oswald nodded. "Thank you." He went and knelt beside his cousin. He saw there something of the face he remembered, of the young man who would play with his eager cousin, before their families had been torn apart in blood and death. Oswald drew his hand down over Eadfrith's face and closed his eyes.

The last of the sons of Edwin was dead.

PART 3

Rule

Chapter 1

"We could be sending Brother Diuma to his death."

Oswald looked to Aidan. He nodded. "I know."

The warrior monk, his spear laid aside for a staff that might possibly pass as an aid to walking rather than a weapon of war, sat in the curragh, bobbing high on the shore by Aidan's monastery.

"But if it is the red martyrdom he faces, Diuma goes willingly." Aidan raised his hand as the wind caught the small sail of the curragh and sent it skimming over the sea, down the coast towards Bamburgh and beyond: the great tidal flows of the Humber and then the long haul upstream, using every breath of wind along the way, as the River Trent took Diuma into the heart of Penda's kingdom.

"You're waving," Oswald said.

"Yes," said Aidan.

"You're his bishop. He might prefer your blessing."

"Oh, of course." Aidan added the vertical to his wave, now signing the cross over the departing monk. Brother Diuma, seeing the blessing, waved back.

"I keep forgetting," Aidan said.

Oswald looked to the slight figure standing beside him. Although outwardly he seemed the same as the hesitant monk he had known on the Holy Isle, inwardly the man had changed, and sometimes it was apparent to all around him. His monks on Lindisfarne harkened to his word, each eager to do whatever their abbot asked; Aidan appeared to not even realize that it might be different with a different abbot. So when he had asked for a monk to volunteer to go to Penda to tell him of the news of life, all had put themselves forward. The main difficulty Aidan had faced was preventing the competition from escalating to blows. In the end, Diuma had won, arguing that his background as warrior made him most suitable;

and that the blood guilt that lay upon him from his years of killing meant that he had most sin to expiate, and therefore most need of the red martyrdom, should it be granted to him.

Before the argument descended into a sordid competition to see who had killed the most men in their former lives – Oswald suspected that the tally for some of the men come from Iona would be large indeed – and with others, less bloodstained but more world weary, urging the inclusion of sins sexual, spiritual and corporeal, as well as martial, Aidan had decreed Diuma to be the monk he had chosen for the mission. Now they were watching him depart.

Neither monk nor king moved from the strand until the curragh was lost from sight among the dipping grey waves. The clouds hung low above their heads, but the rain that they promised did not fall, instead holding itself from the earth. Ducks, black and white, bobbed upon the swell. Aidan pointed to them.

"Eider," he said. "They have come in close to shore. There is a storm coming."

"When isn't there?" said Oswald.

"True." The monk smiled. "In one day I have been hailed upon, windswept, sun burned and snowed on, with the sea mist arriving to seal the day into grey."

"Oh, was this not the best place for your monastery?"

"It is perfect. All God's blessings, the sweet and the bitter, laid out for us near enough each day. Besides, it reminds me of home."

"Good. I had wanted to give you the right place, and one near to me."

"But you spend but a month or so in Bamburgh each year."

"A king must see the people, and the people see him. Besides, oft times when I have returned here, you have been gone yourself."

"A bishop must teach; I go into the hills and along the coast, speaking to every man I meet – now, at last, I speak your tongue well enough for people to understand me without someone else saying my words." Aidan smiled. "Although, it is true, I had no difficulty in getting a hearing when I had the king telling my words for me!"

"But they still hear you?"

"For the most part they do. The thegns and reeves, they listen with eagerness, for if they would know your mind better, they know they must understand the hope that moves you. The ceorls listen with half an ear and somewhat less mind, for as always their sight is tilted to their fields and their crops. But already, through prayer and by some knowledge that Brother Fintan has brought with him, their crops wax greater and their lives less harsh; so their interest grows. And the slaves, they are most open of all."

"You speak to slaves as well?"

"Yes." Aidan looked at Oswald. "Of course. Would you have me not?"

"No, no. But what of their masters – do they allow it?"

"I do not ask of their masters. I speak where and when I find men, in the fields or upon the road; there is no need to ask permission of masters there."

"Some masters might not agree."

"I do not ask them." Aidan looked at the king. "But mayhap it would be better if you did not speak of it."

"I will not." Oswald nodded. "Abbot Ségéne did indeed choose the right man to be bishop in my kingdom."

Aidan grimaced. "A man who still forgets he is a bishop and waves instead of blessing. But come, now you are here let me show you what has been done in your absence."

Taking Oswald by the arm, Aidan led him from the beach, studded with the upturned shells of curraghs and coracles and speckled with drying nets and fish traps, towards the monastery.

The church, its walls washed white, was the largest building. The roof was thatch, and three small windows in each long wall brought light, but not much light, into the nave.

Clustered around the church, and looking, Oswald thought, like chicks clustered around a hen, were the huts in which the monks slept and some slightly larger buildings: the refectory and, judging from the smoke rising from it, the kitchen. But these were not the buildings that Aidan wanted to show Oswald. Instead, he led him to another structure, built on the south-facing side of the monastery, its southern wall opened by two doors and more and bigger windows than he had seen before, although shutters, pegged back for the moment, meant that the windows could be closed should the rain and wind blow from the south. Outside the building, perched upon stools, were three monks with slabs of slate laid upon their knees and rows of long feathers, stuck into wax, by their sides, hunched over whatever lay upon their slates.

Aidan pointed. "A book is as vital to a monk as a sword is to a king. Books contain our Great Work, which is to call God's grace and blessing down upon this middle-earth, and your realm, as rain from clouds, and to offer to God our thanks and our praise…"

"You are God's scops," said Oswald. "The singers of his praises and the tellers of his deeds."

Aidan thought. "Maybe that is the case. But I would say we are monks: that is our work. And as books are necessary to our work, we have started to make them. The scribes sit out here, when the weather holds and the light is good. Abbot Ségéne, in his generosity, sent five books from Iona: a psalter, a gospel book, and three works of the fathers. These we must copy, the psalter and gospel book first of all, that others might have what is most necessary for all men to know." Aidan turned to Oswald. "For if you will grant it, lord, I would establish further monasteries, that those who are far from here may yet receive the news of life, and have it."

"Where? You have but to ask, Aidan, and I will give you the hides necessary to support as many monasteries as you have monks to fill them."

"It should not be difficult to fill them, for the abbot sends me more monks from the Holy Isle – so many that we can bare fit them all in here. So I would establish daughter houses, at Melrose first and then one or two other places." Aidan smiled. "In fact, that may be another reason Brother Diuma was so keen to go to Penda: at least there will be no lack of room for him there; here he had to sleep with his feet out of the door of his cell, so crowded had it become."

"Very well. Ask and it will be given you."

"You remembered. Very good."

Oswald smiled in turn. "It was not hard. It was given to me. Now, will you return with me to Bamburgh? Oswiu wants to see you, and I would wish you to speak with Eowa, Penda's brother. Now that Penda has given him into our hands as hostage, we must care for him; there is also the chance to tell him the news of life, that he might live and, in time, mayhap bring his people to such knowledge too."

Aidan shook his head. "There is much I must do here."

"But we are here for only a short time; after this we go to Ad Gefrin, to receive the render of the hill men. When I sought you as bishop from Abbot Ségéne, I thought in part to have my friend beside me in a land that, though that of my birth, had become strange to me through my years of exile. But now it seems I see you less than if you had remained upon the Holy Isle."

"Nevertheless, I have much work to do." Aidan paused, then turned to his old friend. "There is another reason. Abbot Ségéne warned me, when he left me here as bishop, to beware kings, even those who were friends – perhaps especially those who were friends. 'For their ways are not our ways, and their tasks are not our tasks; yet, being kings, they will of necessity seek to bend you to their will and their throne, that they might better accomplish what they set themselves to do. This you must resist, lest our work, which is the greater, become subsumed in their work, which is the less.' That is what Abbot Ségéne said to me before he left to return to the Holy Isle. Do you think it untrue or unjust?"

"I can think it neither; but I can also think it incomplete. Surely a king has need of counsellors, men of wisdom who will help guide him and, through him, his people. Should you not be my counsellor who is also my oldest friend?"

"I would that I might be so, yet the abbot also said that the risk of the great work being subsumed into the lesser work of kings is with a king who is a friend: 'For you will see him changed by the throne and you will wish to hold him unmarked, yet such cannot be, and to think so is foolishness.'"

Oswald held his hands to his chest. "Have I been changed by the throne?"

The monk looked at him. "Yes," he said.

"How so? Or would it be best that I not know?"

Aidan turned and looked down the coast to the rock upon which the stronghold of Bamburgh stood.

"I will come with you," he said.

"But what of my question? How have I changed?"

The monk turned to look at the king. "Once, you would not have had to ask me."

*

"This is as it used to be!" Oswiu's smile embraced Aidan and his brother. "When it was just the three of us on the Holy Isle."

"But let me remind you, it is not just the three of you any longer," said Rhieienmelth, flashing a smile to her husband and Aidan and, last of all, to Oswald.

"Well, that is true," said Oswiu. "But to have the three of us together again – it is like our days on the Holy Isle. And what is more, we have a new Holy Island too!"

"But no women were allowed on the Holy Isle of Colm Cille, whereas I have already been on your Holy Island, Bishop Aidan. Would you ban women from your Holy Island? Would you give him leave to do so?" Rhieienmelth turned her smile once again upon Oswald. He received it with no answering smile, but turned to Aidan, jerking his gaze from his sister-in-law.

"Do you wish to remove women from the Holy Island, Bishop Aidan?"

Rhieienmelth glanced at her husband and raised an eyebrow. "So formal," she whispered, loudly enough for all to hear.

"No, I would not remove women from Holy Island. Although, for some of the younger monks, it might mean less distraction, it would mean expelling the families of the fishermen and farmers who were upon the island before we came to it; and most all of these families have been baptized. That would not be just."

"So true," Rhieienmelth whispered again.

Oswiu stifled a laugh, then pushed it further down when his brother turned a disapproving glance towards him.

"Aidan is a bishop," said Oswald. "He should be respected."

"Aidan is our friend," said Oswiu. "He should be embraced." And, getting up from his place, he went to the monk and swept him into a hug. As he did so, slaves and servants began sweeping into the hall, carrying hastily prepared food and drink.

Oswald looked around. "Who ordered a feast?" he asked.

Eowa bowed before him. "I sent word to the kitchen, lord, that you would want food and drink for your friend. Did I do wrong?"

"No. No, of course not. Thank you, Eowa."

The Mercian made the courtesy and took his place at the end of the table, eating and drinking, but with restraint, through the course of the feast, until, as feasting gave way to conversation, a messenger came into the hall. Then Eowa rose again and approached Oswald.

"Have I leave to remain and hear what tidings the messenger brings? Now I am part of your household, it is only with your permission that I may learn what transpires in my home country."

Oswald pointed to the messenger; although his face was clear, swirling designs crept from his sleeves, sliding down his forearms. "I fear he brings no news of Mercia, but you are welcome to remain and hear what tidings he brings."

Eowa nodded. "I thank you, lord. I fear that if the fate weavers had spun their thread differently, you would not have received such courtesy from us."

"I am not you." Oswald waved the messenger forward. "Come, tell your name and tell your tidings."

"I am named Leith. I come with news and word from King Rhoedd of Rheged."

Princess Rhieienmelth sat forward. "My father? Is he well?"

"Yes, he is well."

"Oh." The princess sat back.

"But he sends word to his ally, Oswald, High King of Britain, and to his son-in-law Oswiu, that he is sore pressed by the warbands of the Gododdin, who harry his country and steal his animals and take his people, weeping and wailing, as slaves. He asks Oswald, as High King, to send aid, to send an army or, better still, to come himself, the *Lamnguin*, and drive these vermin from his lands and to take their ancestral stronghold, the great rock at Edinburgh." The messenger stopped and looked from Oswald to the other powerful men at the high table, then to the woman who sat between Oswald and Oswiu.

"Your father sends his greetings to you, princess, and reminds you that he has yet to receive all his wedding portion from you."

Oswiu stood up. "But I have given all we agreed."

"Not from you," said the messenger. "The king knows you have given all you agreed, and more. But from the princess Rhieienmelth. She will know whereof I speak."

Oswiu turned to his wife. "What is he talking about?"

"I will tell you later," said Rhieienmelth. Turning to the messenger, she said, "Tell my father he will get my portion when I am ready to give it." She stared at him. "Do you understand?"

"Yes. You will give the king your portion when you are ready to give it." When the princess nodded her approval of his rendering of the message, the messenger, with the skill born of years of practice, committed the words to memory, stamping them into his recall so that they could be pulled out again as sharp and distinct as when he first heard them.

"As for me, I will of a surety send help," said Oswald. "But wait before you return to Rhoedd of Rheged, that I might tell you when and of what kind." He looked to his brother. "Well, warmaster, what say you?"

"How large are the warbands that pray upon Rheged?" asked Oswiu. "And how many are there?"

"They are large and there are very many," said the messenger.

"But how large and how many?"

"The king said to tell you there were five hundred or more men in the warbands, and there were many, many warbands ravaging his country."

"Five hundred! That's not a warband, that's an army."

"Two or three armies," said Eowa.

Oswald, hearing him comment, nodded his agreement. "As Eowa said; so many men would be an army – and there would be no king left in Rheged to send a messenger asking for help." He glanced to his brother. "What do you think, Oswiu? Fifty men, maybe two warbands?"

"Probably just the one. But then, we have heard of raiders coming south from the lands of the Gododdin and raiding into our kingdom as well. Though King Medraut has pledged not to bear arms against us, either he has lied or he cannot restrain his young men. Either way, we may not let this matter lie."

"But I would not act as guard dog for another king, snapping at the intruders he will not take care of himself."

"He has not the strength." The words came from Rhieienmelth. Her eyes were downcast, but feeling their gaze upon her, she looked up, and her eyes went to Oswald. "He has not the strength," she repeated. "The warriors who flocked to my grandfather Urien, they have long taken ship, and my father has neither land nor gold to buy their replacements. Only daughters." She paused, but her eyes did not leave Oswald's. "I know he sold me to you like a brood mare, as bride for your brother, but have I not been worth the price?"

"Yes," said Oswald, and his voice was quiet.

"Then I ask you to take pity on my father, more pity than I can give him, and send aid, that he might yet remain king of Rheged."

Oswald looked at her, this dark-haired, pale-skinned granddaughter of the king who had all but driven his ancestors back into the sea, and his own face grew pale under her gaze.

"I – I would give you whatever you wish."

Oswald looked away, looked to his brother the warmaster, and his other counsellors, to ask their advice on what they should do. Rhieienmelth cast her gaze down again to the hands in her lap. Eowa, watching, looked to one face and another and another.

"We could spend months chasing around Rheged trying to catch up with one or two warbands," said Oswiu. "We would catch them in the end, but it would be weary work. I'm not sure what else we can do."

"Take their stronghold." Oswald looked around at his counsellors. "We can spend our strength chasing their warbands around Rheged – and I suspect that there will always be further warbands ravaging the parts of Rheged furthest from where we are – or we can remove the heart and let the limbs wither and die. Take their stronghold."

Oswiu grinned at his brother. "That is perfect. The Gododdin have been impregnable upon Edinburgh rock for so long, they will no longer give thought to any attack upon it."

"But if it is impregnable, how can you take it?" asked Aidan, looking from one brother to the other.

Again Oswiu smiled. "That is the great blessing of having a like stronghold ourselves. I have spent so long thinking on how attack might come against Bamburgh, and devising defence against it, that I know all the ways one might break into such a stronghold. But I warrant that the Gododdin, secure so long, have not given thought on this matter for many a year. There will be ways in. I am sure of it, brother." He clasped his fist with his other hand. "It will be like this: either we find the way in, or we suffocate them upon their rock. When do we leave, brother?"

"You will leave," said Oswald. He inclined his head in answer to his brother's expression of incredulous joy. "Yes, you will command, Oswiu. I have matters to attend to, and this will be your task, and its glory and gold shall be yours – and your wife's." Oswald nodded to Rhieienmelth. "If you wish, princess, when Oswiu has taken Edinburgh rock, you may take half the gold of the Gododdin for your father, that Rheged might have the warriors a kingdom of its glory, and the son of Urien, deserves."

"I thank you, brother; I thank you." Oswiu stood from table. "If you give leave, I will go and start to make ready."

"I will come with you," said Oswald. He put his arm around his brother's shoulders. "I would not have it be said that you went against the Gododdin without any thing of which you had need."

Oswiu turned to Rhieienmelth. "Will you come too?"

The princes rose and made her courtesy. "I will leave such as this to you."

"But you will come with me when I ride against the Gododdin?"

"I will go or stay as my lord commands."

Oswiu smiled at her. Then, taking his brother's arm, he left the hall. Rhieienmelth's gaze followed them as they went out.

Bishop Aidan made to rise as well, but to his surprise Eowa stayed him.

"Earlier, I heard you tell a story, which I would have you explain, if you have time."

"Oh, you mean the tale of David?" Aidan sat down again.

"Yes," said Eowa. "I have not heard it before."

"There are many stories you have not heard before," said Aidan. "But this one is of a king, a great and good king, who conceived a passion for the wife of one of his generals, Uriah the Hittite. Such was David's desire for Bathsheba that he ordered Uriah to be at the forefront of battle in such place that, when the army fell back, he was left exposed, and killed. Then David took Bathsheba for his own, and the prophet of the Lord came to David and, to his face, spoke of God's anger. And David repented."

"But did he keep the woman?"

"Er, yes, he did."

"I thought so." Eowa sat back. "Thank you." He glanced at Princess Rhieienmelth. "I'm sure your husband knows the story."

"He heard it today, as did you." Princess Rhieienmelth rose from where she had been sitting and went from the hall. Eowa turned back to Aidan.

"Tell me more of your religion," he said.

*

As they selected men, horses and weapons, and primed the steward to provide the necessary provisions for the expedition, Oswiu remembered what Oswald had said, and he asked him: "What matters do you have to attend to, brother?"

Oswald, hand upon the flank of the horse he was inspecting, did not look around, but ran his hand through the animal's short, thick hair.

"It is time I took a wife," he said.

Chapter 2

"Wessex is willing." Acca allowed himself a smile as he brought the news; he made over even the subtle work of building alliances into the pattern of song and tale.

Oswald, sat upon the mercy seat rendering judgment to the cases brought before him, looked to the scop standing beside him. Perched upon the back of the throne, Bran croaked, and turned his head to look down at Acca, his black eyes gleaming with interest. The scop stepped backwards under the scrutiny.

"When Bran looks at me like that, I always think he is wondering whether to peck my eyes out now, or to wait until I am dead."

"He is," said Oswald. "Wait, I will hear what you have to say after I have rendered judgment." Oswald glanced up at the sky. The clouds threatened rain, and he drew his cloak tighter around his shoulders to ward off the wind. The mercy seat, the throne of judgment that accompanied him on all his travels around the kingdom from one royal estate to another, now sat by the side of the road – thankfully one of the old roads of the emperors rather than one of the wheel-rutted tracks that criss-crossed the country, ways as old as the land through which they wound, invariably on exposed ridges. Up ahead, the wagons waited to cross a ford, while the steward, a man whom all welcomed after Coifi's disastrous spell in charge, assayed to make the crossing himself first to check if the water level was low enough for the wagons. While they waited, some of the local people who had come from their fields and houses to watch the royal procession go past, had made suit to the king's household, asking for judgment in disputes between them. Rather than call them to his estate at Tadcaster Oswald directed his judgment seat be brought from the wagon and set up by the side of the road, that he might render justice.

It was taking longer than he had expected. The steward had pronounced the ford safe, the wagons had crossed, and still Oswald sat upon the judgment seat, listening to the interminable workings out of a dispute over land, inheritance, outlawry and forfeiture. He was getting cold, and now Acca had come to him with this news. But he could not leave until judgment had been rendered. Oswald looked: there was another case after this – an anxious cluster of people waiting their turn for the king's justice. He sighed, and turned to Acca.

"Go on to Tadcaster. I will come to you there. When I have finished here."

So it was early evening, as the sun settled over the low line of hills in the west, by the time Oswald came to his hall at Tadcaster. But he had no need to call Acca to him, for the scop, seeing the king enter the hall, came rushing to him.

"There is further news, lord. The messenger arrived while you gave justice to those extraordinarily stupid-looking farmers you spent so many hours with this afternoon."

Oswald sat down wearily. "They were not as stupid as they appeared. That is why I am so weary; whenever I thought I had heard all the case, and was about to render judgment, then another would delve into the soil of memory and pull out a like case, settled according to the age-old custom of the law. In the end, I fear we went back, through the days of the emperors, unto the time before the emperors even came to this land. If I had not put an end to it, we would like as not have returned to the days of the sons of Adam themselves. But enough of that. What news have you, Acca?"

"A messenger arrived from your brother, lord."

Oswald sat up, looking with new intent at the scop. "What news?"

Acca held out his hand. In it was a lump of grey rock.

Oswald took and examined it, then looked at Acca.

"This is his message? I have never known Oswiu to be laconic before."

"There is a message to accompany it, lord." Acca cleared his throat and stood straighter, preparing to deliver the message he had taken from the exhausted messenger, whom he had sent to rest and eat and sleep.

"He sends the message as a riddle, lord. 'Rock of the rock, stone from stone; I have no voice, hear my song.'"

Oswald looked up at Acca. "He's taken it? He's taken Edinburgh rock?"

"Yes, lord, he has. This rock he took from it and sends to you, more valuable than the – very large – amounts of gold and silver he found upon the rock. For now, with Edinburgh rock taken, the chieftains of the Gododdin that yet remain have given pledge that they will render tribute to you, and hold your enemies as their enemies, and your friends as their friends, through all the years of their people."

Oswald smiled. "I knew he would succeed. Did Oswiu send word of how he did it?"

"Apparently, it was through Rhieienmelth that he gained entrance to the rock. As granddaughter to Urien of Rheged, she sought audience with the chieftains of the Gododdin, and they had no leave but to grant it, for such is the honour in which Urien is still held by the people of the north. Your brother accompanied her, and together they much charmed the chieftains of the Gododdin…"

"They would!"

"…so that when they had been with them for a few days, it was possible for Oswiu to steal away in the night and open the gates of the stronghold to let his men, silently, in. When the sun rose, they stood waiting, with swords ready, about and inside the great hall of the Gododdin, and the chieftains, with only their knives to hand, had a simple and easy choice: to accept as overlord a man they already knew, and one wed to the granddaughter of Urien, or to fight and die. They chose well, and in return Oswiu took only that part of their treasury they were most willing to give up."

Oswald grimaced. "What you are willing to give up always seems greater when a sword is poking into your ribs."

"That is true, lord. But Oswiu, though he is young, still had the wit not to take everything – although the princess urged it –

but rather to leave enough gold and silver that the chieftains of the Gododdin might yet hold their warriors to them and keep their thrones."

"Rhieienmelth wanted to take everything?"

"She is a woman of strong desires, lord; the Gododdin brought shame to her father and her family. If she had commanded the men, Oswiu said, the only Gododdin left alive upon the rock would have been those she held to sell as slaves."

"It was a great thing she did, though, to gain entrance to the rock through the reverence the Gododdin held for her grandfather."

"There is more of Urien in her than her father, lord." Acca smirked. "But not only Urien; Oswiu sends word that Rhieienmelth is with child."

Oswald nodded. He said nothing.

"Is that not wonderful news, lord?"

"Yes. Yes, wonderful."

"Oswiu therefore sends further word that he will go with Rhieienmelth to Ad Gefrin and Bamburgh and the estates in the north, until the princess is delivered of the child. He says that if it is a boy, he will name it for your father, Æthelfrith, giving the boy the same name root, Frith."

Oswald nodded. "He always worshipped Father. The great warrior, the Twister." He fell silent for a moment, eyes turned inward. "The child, if it is a boy, will be ætheling. Rhieienmelth will be pleased; her son, blood of the blood of Urien, master of Bamburgh, High King."

"But that is why you must hear my other news, lord. Cynegils, the king of Wessex, sends word, seeking friendship with Northumbria and offering his daughter in marriage, together with a rich bride price."

Oswald pursed his lips. "Cynegils yet follows the old ways?"

"Yes, lord; that is what I hear, although rumour says a priest named Birinus lives now in the land of the West Saxons with the permission of the king. He is mad, though."

"Mad?"

"God mad, lord. Everywhere, he sees spirits walking, and evil creatures, and he falls into fits."

"He sounds like Coifi."

Acca laughed.

"Does Cynegils listen to this Birinus? I will not have as wife the daughter of one who still follows the old gods."

"That he allows Birinus to live and teach in his kingdom suggests that Cynegils may be open to persuasion, lord, particularly if that would bring about so desirable a marriage for his daughter."

"What is her name?"

"Er, I do not know, lord. Cynegils did not send her name, only what he would give as bride price."

"The West Saxons, I hear, have the custom that the king's wife is not a queen, and reigns not beside him, but is his consort only. That is not our way. If I married his daughter, she would be queen here. How old is she?"

"She is of marriageable age, lord."

"Old enough to have children?"

"Yes, so I believe."

Oswald nodded. "Very well. We shall go to Wessex, then, and see the king there, and his daughter, and see what he is willing to bring to the marriage feast." He looked over to where Eowa sat by the fire listening to the talk of the hall, and called him over.

"Your brother still fails to send the whole render that is due to me as his overking."

Eowa shrugged. "That is of no mind to me now, lord. He has abandoned me; I answer not for him."

"But yet you send word to him, and he to you."

"The accounts of my lands, lands that are yet mine, lord. He sends to me of them, and I answer with judgments. Is that not to be permitted me while I remain your hostage?"

"No, I welcome it, for it enables me to send word, through you, to your brother. Tell him this: I still wait the tribute, the whole tribute that he promised me as his lord. And tell him this also, for it will be of interest to him: I travel, this six month, to the land of the West Saxons, mayhap to wed the daughter of the king there; of a surety to enter into friendship with him."

"That was ever his greatest fear, lord, since a fearful dream that was sent him, that his enemies would encircle him, tying him down with many ropes and leaving him as one dead upon the battlefield, helpless as the slaughter bird approaches."

As if he knew he had been mentioned in the conversation, Bran unfurled his head from wing and sleep and regarded the Mercian with cold eye.

Oswald held out his arm and the raven stepped down upon it from his perch.

"Make sure you send Penda this news; and that my brother has taken the stronghold of the Gododdin, and my writ now runs to the Painted People. Tell him that also."

"And that the princess Rhieienmelth is with child," Acca added.

Eowa looked to him. "Is she?"

Oswald glared at Acca, then turned back to Eowa. "That is not something I wish Penda to know. Send word of what I told you; no more."

"He will hear without word from me, lord," said Eowa. "Such news travels with the wind – an ætheling in Northumbria. All the thrones will know of it ere the babe ends his first wail. Besides, he oft spoke to me in the past that he well knew there was no more chance of putting mistrust between you and your brother than of splitting salt from sand."

"I did not mean that. But I do not wish Penda to know of such matters before they become common knowledge. Do you understand?"

"Of course. When will we see the young ætheling?"

"Sometime after the birth. Oswiu remains with Rhieienmelth in our lands in the north."

"Oh. So far. Still, they will be safe there. Even if five armies stood before Bamburgh, they could not take it."

"Yes." Oswald turned away from Eowa. "We will travel by sea, Acca, to the land of the West Saxons and see if this princess without a name shall be my wife."

"Cyniburh."

Oswald made the courtesy to the young woman standing in front of him, her face veiled, her father standing beside her. They were standing in the great hall at Easthampstead in the land of the West Saxons.

"Now I know your name."

The young woman made no response, and through the veil Oswald could see little of her expression. He glanced at Cynegils standing beside his daughter, then looked back to Cyniburh.

"Your father is willing to give you in marriage to me; do you accept freely?" Oswald waited. No answer came.

"Do you accept freely?" he asked again. Cynegils began to squeeze Cyniburh's arm.

Oswald held up his hand.

"Wait," he said. "We have yet other matters to discuss, King Cynegils, and for the princess Cyniburh, this is the first time she has lain eyes upon me; it is only natural that she should hesitate. Let us talk some more, and then we will return to your daughter. What say you to this?"

Cynegils looked at the woman beside him. For her part, Cyniburh did not turn her head to her father, but remained still, unresponsive behind her veil.

"Remember who is your father." Cynegils all but threw her arm down, then stepped towards Oswald. "Come, let us talk further. What do you need to settle in your mind before you can enter freely into marriage with my daughter?"

"Friends, kings, must needs have the trust of each other. I hear a priest of the new god has come into your land, and you have given him leave to remain and to preach to your people."

"Birinus? You mean Birinus? He is mad."

"I would meet him. And I would that you leave the old ways and be washed in the water of new life." They were walking together around the outside of Cynegils' hall now, but Oswald stopped and turned to the king of Wessex. "Cwichelm, your cousin, sent an assassin to kill my uncle when he was king. The murderer failed and Edwin destroyed Cwichelm's army and made Cwichelm kneel in the mud to him. I would not have such a thing happen between us, Cynegils."

The king of the West Saxons met Oswald's gaze, but his eyes were bleak. "If you would destroy me, I have not the men to stop you."

"That is why I ask this, for I would not destroy you. I would have you rule, my friend, my ally, my father-in-law, but for this to happen you must give up the old gods. Do you understand?"

"I understand. But before I give answer, I would have you meet Birinus."

"Very well. Where is he? Bring him to me."

"He will not agree to that. He will come to no man, even be that man king and lord over him, but remains in his hut, or comes raving into my hall when I least expect him and less want him."

"Well, if he will not come to us, then we will go to him."

*

"Birinus? Birinus, are you in there?"

Cynegils, king of the West Saxons, bent down to peer into the dark shadows of a lean-to cut from beech and hornbeam. It stood against the pollarded trunk of a beech, itself twigged and whiskered as a man grown old and hairy, covered in moss and ferns. As they had walked to it from the king's hall, Cynegils had told Oswald that Birinus followed the royal household as it made its way around the land of the West Saxons, never joining it but making always some rude dwelling when they stopped and emerging from it to talk to trees and rocks and, sometimes, people.

"No, no one there." Cynegils straightened up. "He is, as I said, quite mad, but mayhap it is the madness the gods bestow on those with whom they would speak."

"Mad?"

They looked up. From the whiskered branches of the beech a face peered, framed in green.

"Mad, mud, dumb, am I dumb, no, I am not dumb, I speak, not an animal, a man, a man, a priest, yes, a priest." The tumble of words stopped as abruptly as it had begun, and the face turned away from its regard of the men standing below the tree, to look into the green heart of the beech. "It's him, you say? Him, the one I've been waiting for? Why didn't you say so before? You were trying to, only I was talking too much? Hah, I'll take an axe to you if you're not careful, hear me now. Yes? Yes." The face swivelled back to them.

"You're him. Yes, yes you are. I can see it now. They told me to wait, but I couldn't help myself. I had to keep telling them, telling them, but would they listen, would they listen? No." Birinus pushed his head through the collar of leaves, then his shoulders and trunk, and climbed down the tree, hands splayed out upon it like a treecreeper.

On the ground, Birinus came towards Oswald, looking up at him and turning his head from side to side, before reaching out and taking his hand. He stroked it, then bent his head and kissed the back of the king's hand.

"You have come." He turned his head, as if hearing speech. "His raven? The slaughter bird? Yes, yes, where is it?" Birinus snapped his gaze back to Oswald, the film that sometimes covered his eyes dissolving in an instant as he stared up at him. "The bird. Where is the bird?"

As if in answer, Bran croaked and Birinus spun around, raising his arms as if to ward off attack, looking up into the heights of the tree from which he had crept. Bran croaked again, dropping his head and staring down at the men standing below the beech.

Birinus turned, facing Oswald and Cynegils. But this time, he fixed his gaze on the king of Wessex.

"Ah, you'll hear me now, will you? Ach, ach, ach. Offer men everything and they will refuse it; give them promises and they'll hand over their daughters. Ach, ach, ach."

"Wait, wait," said Oswald. "I have questions for you, Birinus. Cynegils says you are a priest: how come you here?"

"How come I here? How come I here? How come you here? Boat and horse and foot, you think, but I tell you, I tell you, you move with powers and dominions. They stand above you, like thunderclouds.

Can you see them? I can see them – they reach to the sky, up past the sky. The bridge. The bridge between heaven and earth sent me. I saw him, I spoke to him, I saw darkness all around, all around, and in the middle such a tiny light, and I said to him: let me go into the darkness and light a light there, that men might see, and he sent me. He said I could go, so I came."

"Who sent you?"

"He did."

"His name? If he has a name."

"Yes, he has a name. Honorius. Yes, that was it."

"What is he? An abbot, a bishop?"

"Oh no, none of these."

"What then?"

"A pope."

Oswald stopped. He raised a hand, then lowered it again. "You say – you say the pope sent you?"

"Oh yes, yes, ach, ach, ach. Of course. Yes." Birinus nodded, his head bobbing up and down like an apple in a fast-flowing stream.

"Right, right." Oswald looked at Cynegils. "The pope sent him."

"Yes," said Cynegils. He stopped. "Er, what is a pope?"

*

"There, there you are, all fresh and new and clean." Birinus lifted the newly baptized Cynegils from the river, and although he was much the smaller man, and slight of build, yet he picked up the king as if he were a child, and placed him on the riverside. The priest stared at the shivering, sodden king, his eyes bright and blue and hard, like the eggs of a starling. "All new, all new," he muttered. "A big baby, lovely, lovely." Birinus snapped his head up and around, as if following the escape of a startled animal. "Yes, yes, off you go, run away, back where you came from you turd of darkness: hah, hah! You thought you had him, but he's out of your hands now, and I'll be watching for you if you come slinking back. I'll be waiting for you, and I'll whack you and thwack you and send you back all over again."

Birinus stopped, chest panting, then slowly looked along the bank at the baptismal party, all staring at him.

"Yes?"

King Cynegils, still shivering, wrapped a cloak around his shoulders. But despite the sting of the cold, he felt a curious lightness, as if a load he had never known he carried had been lifted from his shoulders.

"My daughter," he said. "She is waiting."

"Ach, ach, ach." Birinus pounded his hand against his head. "Knock the words in with a hammer. Yes, yes. Please." He held out his hand and Cyniburh, small, slight, and unveiled for the first time in Oswald's presence, stepped forward. Seeing her thus, Oswald understood her silence: she looked bare old enough to have begun her bleeds. He looked askance at her father. Did Cynegils really think her old enough to marry?

"She is older than she looks." Cynegils came to stand beside Oswald as Birinus led Cyniburh down into the river.

"How many years has she?"

"After her mother died, it became difficult for me to keep track. But she was born when Edwin was yet king of Northumbria, so for sure she is old enough to wed."

"I have been king four years. I would not marry a five-year-old."

"She is older than four! Much older."

"How much older?"

"I do not know for certain – but her bleeds have started. She can bear child, so she is old enough to marry."

Oswald looked down into the river where the baptismal robe clung wetly to Cyniburh's shivering body. She had the body of a young boy.

"If I take her to wife, I will consider her as my betrothed until she is older."

"You will marry her?"

"Yes." Oswald looked down at the shivering little girl. In the years he had waited upon Abbot Ségéne, hoping that he might become a monk on the Holy Isle, he had held himself from acting upon the desires of the flesh. That he would, while wed, be able still to hold himself from such action seemed suddenly to him a blessing.

"Yes, I will marry your daughter, if you pledge to me."

Cynegils sighed.

"How much?"

"The produce of five thousand hides."

"Five thousand?" The words came out in a squeak, and from the river Birinus glared up at the kings.

"Shh, shh, shh," he said, holding finger to lips. "We conduct sacred mysteries here; take your money changing to the hall."

Abashed, they fell silent, and watched as Birinus brought Cyniburh up for the third and final time from the water.

With liquid still streaming from her face, she looked to her father.

"I am new, Daddy," she said. "I am new."

Cynegils smiled back at her, but his smile was uncomfortable, all too aware of the man standing beside him. Oswald remained impassive. Too much ranged upon this marriage for him to decline Cyniburh now, but in the silence of his mind he thought on his brother, rewarded for his incontinence with princesses and fishermen's daughters with marriage to Rhieienmelth, whereas he, who had remained continent through many years of testing, now stood ready to marry a girl who looked more ready to play tops than feed babies – or take the cup around the warriors in hall. But then, he had prayed for the strength to bridle his desires and bind them to his will, and God had given him the strength.

Birinus led Cyniburh to the bank and she stepped from the water. And though she was as wet as her father, and of such slight build, yet she did not shiver, but seemed to glow.

"Take the hand of your husband-to-be, daughter, for he has led us into this new life." Cynegils turned to Oswald. "Will you lead us back to the hall?"

So, holding Cyniburh's hand, Oswald led the procession back to the hall, and beside him Cyniburh skipped for her joy.

"A new life and a husband all so soon," she said to Oswald. "When my mother died, I thought I should never smile again, but now I think I won't stop smiling ever!"

Oswald turned to her. He smiled as well, but as he did so, he felt it to be the sort of smile he gave to children when they sat upon his lap or played about his feet.

"I pray that shall be true," he said.

Cyniburh giggled. "I can't believe it. I'm going to marry you."

"In truth, I find it a little difficult to believe myself."

Cyniburh's face suddenly fell. "You won't be like my father, will you? Even when my mother was alive, he had lots of other wives, only they weren't wives really, but he'd go to them rather than Mother."

"No," said Oswald. "I will not be like your father."

"Then I think I will enjoy being married to you."

"That is…good."

"I love babies. I want lots and lots and lots of them."

"Ah." Oswald stared ahead. "Right."

*

"What's wrong with me?"

Cyniburh stood beside the marriage bed that Cynegils had prepared for them. Outside, in the hall, they could hear the sounds of celebration, the drinking and boasting and singing, but the king of Wessex had given over to them his own room, that they might have privacy together. Now, Cyniburh stood beside it and tears streamed down her face.

"I am old enough," she said. "I have my bleeds; I can have babies."

Oswald took her thin shoulders in his hands and looked down at her.

"The fault is mine," he said.

"Can't you?" asked Cyniburh. "Some rams are like that – I've seen it. No good for mounting a ewe."

"No, it is not that." Oswald shook his head. "You are very young."

"Not that young." She began to reach for his waist, but Oswald took her wrist.

"No," he said. "You are too young and, besides, I am not ready." He sat down on the bed and indicated for her to sit beside him.

"Listen. If I were to have my life as I would wish, I would be no king, but a monk upon the Holy Isle. Although God has willed that I should be king, yet I strive to live as much as I can in the way of the Holy Isle and, in doing so, I have received many blessings – and many victories. I – I worry that should I leave the sacrifices I have made, then the blessings I have received will be taken from me also. Do you understand?"

"Oh, yes," said Cyniburh. "That's like if I want it to be sunny and it's raining, then I say I will be good if the sun comes out and it always does."

"Er, yes. Perhaps," said Oswald.

"Well, I understand that." The girl paused, her heels drumming against the side of the bed. "So, what should we do then? Shall we play?"

"Play?"

"Yes. Tops, or toss, or skipping?"

So it was that on his wedding night, Oswald of Northumbria played tops until his bride fell upon the bed and went to sleep in an instant, while he lay down beside her and stared up into the darkness and thought on whether he could indeed be husband to such a creature.

Chapter 3

"So, where is your wife?" Rhieienmelth, her baby son now near enough one year old lying sleeping in her arms, looked around the hall. "We have arrived without warning, but we wanted to get back in time for the Easter feast and we wished to present Ahlfrith to you, and to see her." She looked back to Oswald. "She must be in her chamber?"

"She is here." Oswald pointed to the diminutive figure sitting beside him, eyes downcast as she had been trained in the household of her father, but now blushing furiously.

"Oh yes, that is a fine jest, Oswald," Rhieienmelth began, but Oswiu took her arm.

"It is no jest," he said. "See."

And she saw. The colour had drained from Oswald, but it suffused the face of the girl beside him.

"I am so sorry," Rhieienmelth said, and giving her baby into Oswiu's arms she knelt down in front of Cyniburh and raised her chin. "Will you forgive me, please? I spoke without thought, with the eagerness of a mother keen to show off her baby to her brother-in-law, but I ask pardon. Will you give it me?"

Cyniburh looked out from under her brows, looking around the hall.

"Everyone is laughing at me," she said.

"No one is laughing at you," said Rhieienmelth. "No one. Tell her, Oswald."

"No one laughs at you, Cyniburh."

"Then why does no one look in this direction?"

"No one is ignoring you, Cyniburh." Oswald stood up. "Is this my nephew?"

Oswiu held the baby up, that Oswald might see him the better.

"Here is your uncle," he said. "Your uncle, the king."

"To him, may I simply be uncle."

"Come, look on your nephew in the light." Oswiu looked to Rhieienmelth and nodded towards Cyniburh, then he led his brother to the door and out upon the deck around the hall, where the sun bathed his son's sleeping face.

"He looks like Mother," said Oswald.

"So some have said. To me he looks like a little acorn."

Oswald put his finger under the baby's chin and he stirred a little in his sleep but did not wake.

"So, your wife. Daughter of King Cynegils."

"Yes. The produce of five thousand hides, sworn ally, and he has been baptized."

"She is very young though. Has she…?"

"Yes."

"Have you…?"

"No. Not yet."

"There is time. Do not worry about it, brother. Many a marriage starts as a long betrothal."

"We are already wed."

"Well, we wouldn't have the produce or the ally otherwise, would we?"

"No." Oswald shook his head. "She is not what I expected."

"I am fortunate. I married Rhieienmelth."

"Yes." Oswald turned and looked back into the hall where Rhieienmelth now sat beside his wife. Cyniburh was talking excitely to her sister-in-law and to his eyes it looked as if a mother spoke with her daughter. Rhieienmelth felt his gaze and looked to him. Oswald looked away.

"It is the Easter feast in a week. I have asked Aidan to join us for it."

"My mouth waters already, brother. It has been six weeks without meat."

"Do you abstain in other ways too?"

"What? Oh, no. Should I?"

"Perhaps."

"I might try next year. But it will be hard to persuade Rhieienmelth." In his arms, the baby shifted. "He wants his mother." Oswiu nodded towards the high table. A man had joined the conversation between the two women. "You have made a place for Eowa with us."

"Yes. Now his brother has betrayed him, he may prove most useful should we need to find a new king in Mercia."

"Penda should have known better. You should never betray a brother."

Oswald looked at him. "Yes," he said.

*

Through the night, they held vigil. The longest night, when heaven and hell fought over this middle-earth, and the prayers of the faithful battered at the gates of hell, that he who had been carried away might break them from within. Then the morning came, and light, and the doors of the church were thrown open and Aidan emerged, leading the throng in song and chant and bells.

The fast had been long and hard. The feast awaiting them was sumptuous, the accumulated produce of three of the king's estates brought to the palace at Ad Gefrin, where the kitchens had been busy through the hours of vigil, baking and cooking but never tasting, no – not till the sun rose and the Son rose.

Now they took their place in hall, processing in behind Aidan, and sat ready upon bench and stool, while silver plates were brought in, carrying all the finest food that the kitchens could make and the hunters, fishermen, farmers and trappers of the king's estates could produce.

But as Oswald sat down at table, Coifi came to him and took his hand.

"The poor are without," he said. "It was a bad harvest and a hard, hard winter. They wait beyond the stockade, by the gate, babes scarce able to lift head to mothers' breast, and nothing to suck there if they could."

"Have you nothing to give them, Coifi?"

"I have given all you gave over to me, lord, keeping none for myself. But it is not enough."

Oswald glanced around the hall. The food was still being brought in.

"Take me to them," he said. He looked to Aidan. "Come with us."

As they walked across the compound, Oswald drew his cloak about his shoulders against the wind that blew around the Hill of the Goats that stood above the palace. Snow still stood upon its summit, smoothing the rough stones that ringed the hill, the tumbledown fortifications of a long-forgotten king. The other hills, marching into the Cheviots, were also mantled white, and even in the valleys snow remained in those places where the sun came late, or not at all at this time of year.

They came to the gate to the compound, through which the cattle and sheep and goats, the render of the hill folk, were herded to the huge enclosure running down to the River Glen. The door warden, wrapped against the cold and dozing in front of a brazier, snapped awake when he saw who it was approached.

"Open the gate," said Coifi.

"There are even more without now," said the door warden. "More have come since hearing that you are giving food and drink." He glanced at the king and the bishop. "It might not be safe without guard."

"They are my people," said Oswald. "If I cannot walk among them without guard, then I am no worthy king. Open the gate."

"If you are sure, lord."

"I am sure."

The door warden opened the gate. As it began to swing open, a low murmur rose, growing louder as the gate revealed the men standing behind it. Outside, squatting or laying upon ground churned by the wagons that had brought Oswald and his household to Ad Gefrin, were people, in some cases whole families through three or four generations, in other cases all that were left after the

privations of winter and harvest failure. Children, big bellied with
the skin stretched so tight over their skulls it looked as if it would
burst; mothers holding babes, beyond crying, to dugs that held no
milk; fathers, eyes blank with the failure to provide for their families
and fighting the desperate need to grab what food could be found
for themselves.

"Bring them in." Oswald turned to the door warden. "Bring them
in. And never let me hear again that the starving were left outside my
gates." He turned to Coifi. "Go to the kitchens. Tell them to bring
food to these people: better pottage or porridge, something simple
for the moment; rich food would be too much for them."

Coifi began to nod, but then his eyes began to roll back into his
head.

"Oh no you don't," said Oswald, slapping a hand across the
almoner's cheek. "You cannot fall into trance now."

Coifi shook his head, his eyes slowly coming back to rest on
Oswald. "You stopped it," he said. "You stopped the god taking me."

"You are needed here, Coifi, here and now." Oswald pointed at
the crowd of starving people. "They need you."

Slowly, Coifi turned his gaze to the people, the families slowly
dragging themselves from the mud, and he nodded.

"Yes, lord. Yes, you are right." He turned back to Oswald. "I did
not think anyone could stop a god when he wished to take me, but
you have."

"Yes, yes." Oswald pointed. "The kitchens."

"Yes, lord." Coifi smiled. "At once." And pulling his raven-
feather cloak tight round his shoulders, the almoner ran towards the
kitchens.

"I will help you here," said Aidan. And with the door warden
they brought into the compound those who were grown too weak
to walk themselves, carrying them to the kitchens where slaves were
already beginning to put up tents for the people entering.

Many a hand reached to Oswald and Aidan as they brought the
people in, seeking by a single touch the blessing of king or bishop.
Seeing his mercy, and the provisions of his table, some families asked

Oswald that he might accept them as slaves, but for the moment he refused.

"Eat what you will for now. Then when you have grown strong, if you still wish me to take you as slave I will think on it," he told them, and the lure of the food rushed them on.

When all were within the compound, Oswald and Aidan finally returned to the Easter feast in the hall.

"We were beginning to wonder if you would ever come back," said Rhieienmelth. They had come together for this Easter feast, the households of king and his brother joining as they had not for a while. Since the subjection of the Gododdin, Oswiu had taken to making the circuit of the northern marches of the kingdom, while Oswald visited the royal estates of Deira and Bernicia south of the River Tweed.

"I was busy," said Oswald, taking his place at the high table.

"We missed you."

But Oswald did not hear Rhieienmelth. His mind was still full with the memory of the starving people he had helped into the compound, and even the flashing eyes of his sister-in-law, sparkling with their customary mischief, could not claim his attention. He looked down the hall at the mouths opened to receive the rich food brought by boat from lands where the sun held greater sway, or brought as tribute by hunters or fishermen who had taken unusual prey: the porpoise and the crane, defeathered, stuffed and then refeathered into a semblance of life, made centrepieces to the display of food, while silver and gold glittered in the plates that bore the food into the hall; he looked and he was filled with a profound disgust.

Reaching in front of him, he took his plate and tipped the food from it onto the table, then lifting the plate above his head he stood.

All around, the feasters slowly grew quiet, as eyes turned towards their king.

"We eat on silver." Oswald turned the plate in his hand, looking for a moment at the intricate design worked into it. "We eat on silver, while outside mothers have no milk in their dugs for their babies, and fathers offer their whole families to me as slaves if I will give them to eat. We eat on silver." Oswald turned the plate in his hands. He shook his head. "Wood will do for me." He signed a slave to him. "Take this to Coifi. Tell him to cut it up and distribute the silver to the people here."

At this, many of the people in the hall did likewise, sweeping food onto table or bread, and handing silver plate to slaves to pass to Coifi.

"Do you do this every Easter?" Cyniburh asked, wide-eyed.

Rhieienmelth, in the middle of handing her own dish to a slave, laughed. "Thankfully, no, or we would have no plates to eat upon."

Oswald grimaced. "Maybe it were best we did." He looked to Aidan. "What say you?"

The bishop reached over and took Oswald's hand, the one that had given the silver plate to be broken up for the poor.

"I say may this hand never wither with age."

Oswald laughed. "What about the rest of me?"

Aidan smiled back. "Yes, of course. The rest too."

"Well, as the time is meet for announcements, I have something to say as well." Oswiu stood up and went to stand behind Rhieienmelth. "My wife is with child again."

He looked, beaming, at his brother, only to see Oswald's face fall.

"What is wrong? I thought you would be pleased."

"I am. Yes, of course I am." Oswald smiled at his brother.

"Will you give Rhieienmelth your blessing?"

Oswald glanced at his sister-in-law, then looked back to his brother. "I give it you both, with all my heart."

"This will be number two; it is time you had children, brother, or I will have no choice but to take the throne after you!"

"Yes," said Oswald. He glanced at Cyniburh. She had grown much this past year. "Maybe it is time."

As if in answer, Cyniburh took the infant Ahlfrith from Rhieienmelth and held him, the baby settling upon her as she craned her head over his. Oswald looked away, his gaze settling upon Aidan.

"It is good to have you with us again, old friend. It has been near a year since last we sat down to eat together." Oswald paused.

"I miss your counsel. Now Oswiu sees to the northern marches and you remain upon the Holy Island, I make the round of judgment alone."

"Alone, apart from the forty men of your household who accompany you, and your wife, and scop, and almoner and steward, and wagoners and armourers, and hunters and farriers. Alone apart from them."

Oswald smiled, but there was a sadness to his smile. "You chide me justly, old friend. But these are all the companions of my new life, my life as king. The companions of my old life, when I was Oswald and might have been a monk, those companions have left me."

"You have Bran." The monk pointed to the bird, sitting upon a post that had been set for him behind the king, with a ledge where food from the feast might be set for him. The bird, busy with some of the crane, still turned a black eye in his direction when he heard his name spoken, but paid Aidan no further heed.

"Yes, I have Bran." The king swivelled and held to the raven a slice of tender meat. The bird inspected it, then took it delicately in a beak that could split bone, and tossed it into the air before swallowing it. He turned back to Aidan. "But I miss my other friends."

Aidan nodded. "There were other reasons, beside not thinking myself worthy, for me not wanting to be bishop. If I were still simply a monk, then I might, with the permission of my abbot, accompany you. But now my office and its duties stands between us, and whatever the love I bear for you, yet I must set it against the responsibilities I have to my community, and to the people we serve." Aidan sighed. "I remember Abbot Ségéne telling me how much of his time was taken with matters of this world, with settling the payment for cows and the disputes of farmers, with the jealousies of monks and the vagaries of the harvest, and I did not believe him, for all I saw was his great holiness. But now I know it to be true; even this all-too-brief time I spend with you a voice whispers to me that when I return, there will be matters to settle that will have grown great that I might have nipped if I had been there. That is the lot of kings and bishops, my old friend. We must be ever about our work, and in the end the only aid we may call upon is that of our Lord, for no one else can share our burden."

Oswald looked at him. A smile cracked at his lips, growing wider. Aidan, seeing it, smiled also, as the shared understanding between them grew. The smile grew into a great shout of laughter that went from Oswald to Aidan, setting the monk to laughter too.

"That...that was so pompous," Oswald said between hiccoughs of laughter.

"N-not so p-pompous as the lonely king," gasped Aidan.

As king and bishop held each other up, lest the helplessness of their mirth bring them to the ground, Eowa turned to Acca. The scop was eating with a singular ill grace, for he had been told that his stories and songs would not be wanted at the great feast of the new god.

"What do you think they are laughing about?" Eowa asked.

"How would I know?" Acca picked at a piece of porpoise. "I'm sick of fish."

"Maybe they laugh at the silver they give away." Eowa pointed to where the plates, some even of gold, were being hacked into small pieces.

"A great jest. And now I eat from the table." Acca picked up his cup. "With a wooden cup for my wine."

"It is a great jest indeed, for I know of no other kingdom so wealthy that its king might give such riches to the poor, rather than to his retainers and thegns."

Acca looked round at Eowa. "What about your brother? Mercia is rich."

"Not this rich." Eowa shook his head. "Not this rich at all."

*

"So you say your god said it is easier for a camel to pass through the eye of a needle than for a rich man to enter his hall?" Penda leaned across the table to Brother Diuma. "What is a camel? Is it like a fly?"

"No, no. It is an animal of hot lands, of dry lands where no rain falls and people may die for having no water to drink."

Penda glanced upwards, where the slating rain drummed upon the roof of his hall. "Not like here then?"

"No, not at all like here. I have heard there are other animals in these lands that are so fearsome to look upon that a single glance will turn a man to stone, while others spit poison or turn a man's wits to water."

"I would see such beasts – though not the one that turns men to stone! But still, you have not told me of this camel beast."

"Like all the creatures of these hot lands, it is strange and wondrous, somewhat like a cow, but with a great hill upon its back which it fills with water when it finds to drink, and then can go for a year and a day without further drink."

"But how big is it? It must be small if it can pass through a needle."

"No, it is large, as big as an ox, maybe even bigger."

Penda scratched his beard. "So how could this camel beast get through a needle?"

Brother Diuma beamed. "It cannot! That is the point. No more can a rich man enter God's hall than a camel pass through the eye of a needle."

Penda shook his head. "This makes no sense. Does not your god give gifts of gold and victory to those who sacrifice to him? If he does, then why would he give these gifts and then not take the men he gave them to into his hall when they die?"

"God gives victory to whom he will, but he gives his kingdom to the poor," said Brother Diuma.

"I am rich." Penda indicated his hall and the bored men making conversation or playing dice while they waited for the interminable rain to end. "I am rich and I am generous, giving gifts of gold to my men. How can I give gold if I do not have it?"

"Think on the dragon. It is rich, rich beyond compare: gold hoarder, treasure miser, the worm sits upon its hoard and gives gold to none, but slays any who come to try to take of it. Be not of that nature, cold and dragonish, but generous and open-handed, giving not only to your retainers and your thegns, but to the poor; then you will receive greater reward than any king."

"Ask any of my men: I am generous. But the poor? There are so many, if I gave to them it would be as if I poured my gold into Moseley Bog. That is stupid. And I am not a stupid man." Penda stood up. "Still, these are interesting matters whereof you speak, and I would hear more." He looked down at the monk. "It is as well for you that your talk is good, Diuma, or I would have sent you back long ago to your masters. Think you not that I know you pass word back to Northumbria?"

Brother Diuma stood up, and he was as tall as Penda. "While I am in your kingdom, I serve you and pass no account of your doings back home. Yes, I have received messages, but always I have told you of their coming, and most often those messages come from your brother. Should I not receive them?"

"My brother. From what I hear, he has become Oswald's faithful hound. You tell him, when next he sends a message, that Penda knows well what he does." The king stared at the monk. "You hear that? Make sure you send that message to him and the others who sent you." Penda turned away. "Now, Wihtrun, come." He gestured the priest to him. "This man has been telling me nonsense: that the gods prefer the poor, when it is only sense that they give favour to those they favour."

"It is the weaving of the fate singers, lord," said Wihtrun. "And the working of wyrd."

"I hope the gifts I give you for the gods, the animals for sacrifice, bring favour too; else why bother?" Penda pointed to the arm ring Wihtrun bore. "I give you gifts, you give me service; surely it is as such with the gods?"

"Yes, but we stand to them as a thegn stands to you, although the only service the gods require of us is sacrifice."

Penda nodded. "When this winter ends, we must see to gaining more gold, that we shall have more to sacrifice to the gods. It seems to me that the gods best favour those who win victory. And there is a kingdom that is ripe, waiting ready for us to pluck its golden fruit."

Brother Diuma, listening, could not help but blanch. Penda, seeing that, laughed.

"No, not Northumbria. I gave my word to Oswald not to attack him, and that word I keep. But I did not pledge to take his allies as my own, else there would be none I might ravage. And what better kingdom to ravage than one whose king has abandoned it to become a monk?"

*

"A son and now a daughter." Eowa rode beside Oswald as the royal party made the long, slow progress from Tadcaster to Leeds. "That is fine news indeed."

"Yes," said Oswald.

"Will we see the new baby?"

"Not yet. Oswiu sent word that it was a difficult delivery, and the baby is sickly. They remain on the marches, travelling as little as possible."

Eowa nodded. "Of course. It is what I would do."

"What do you mean?"

"My brother has not yet wed, although he has many concubines and there must I suppose by now be one or two whelps. If I had married and had children before he, I would have sought to remain upon the marches of Mercia, far from my brother, until I was sure of his intentions."

"Oswiu knows my intentions."

"But does the princess Rhieienmelth? Oft times a woman may change in heart when she has children of her own, and gives thought to their inheritance. Now, if you should die childless, it would be your brother who would take the throne, and his children after him. What woman, what mother, would not think on this?"

"Rhieienmelth is not like that."

"Mayhap she is not. But then she truly is as singular a woman as my lord thinks her to be."

"I believe she is. And my brother knows my heart."

"And you his, I am sure." Eowa looked back along the column of wagons. "Where is the queen?"

"She travels with her women."

"Ah, yes, I see them. They are playing."

"She – she likes to play."

"As is right in one so young."

"Cyniburh is not so young any more."

"Is she not?"

"No. No, she isn't."

"Of course, if you were to have a child, a son, say, it would make things clearer. Certainly your brother would be ætheling still, but the longer you reign – "

"You mean, the longer I live," Oswald interrupted, his glance bleak.

"The longer you hold the throne, then the more throne-worthy becomes your son. As he comes to manhood, first the warriors of your household and then the witan will get to know him and then, when the time comes, he will be able to call upon their support."

"Think you I do not know this?"

"Of course, lord." Eowa directed his horse closer to Oswald. "I have heard rumour that you, ah, yet wait, lord."

"Where did you hear this?"

"The queen's women, they talk, lord."

"Women's talk. You should know better than to listen."

Eowa nodded. "Of course you are right, lord. Still, it has been a while since you married."

"We will have children when God wills."

"Of course. Let us hope he wills for you to have them soon."

"Yes."

"Have you seen how she holds babies, ever since that time she held Princess Rhieienmelth's child? She is as one who longs to hold her own child."

"So she has told me. And she will, when God wishes and the time is right."

"Maybe – and I speak now as one who has come to think of you as friend as well as lord – maybe the time comes soon."

"Maybe. Maybe." And Oswald looked back along the column and saw his wife. She, feeling his glance, looked to him and smiled.

Oswald nodded and smiled in answer. As he turned back in his saddle, seeing the first sign of the royal estate, he felt the blood stir in him as it had not for her before. No, she was not so young any more. It was time he had a child. And Rhieienmelth was far from him...

Chapter 4

"I am sorry."

Oswald looked up from the squirming bundle of baby, still blood-streaked from birth, its mouth wide and howling, into the face of the midwife holding it. It was an old face, creased and weathered brown, with lines of laughter scored into the flesh. But there was no laughter now, only tears, running silently down her cheeks until they fell into the channels of her face and ran to her mouth. He held fast against the sorrow he saw, refusing to acknowledge it. He held out his arms and she put the screaming baby into his embrace.

"A boy," she said, and he held the infant to him and breathed into his face, and his eyes, wide and staring at this new world, rolled to him for an instant, dark, almost black.

"I am sorry," the midwife said again, and Oswald looked at her and the question came, though he would rather not have spoken it, not for anything in this world. "Whereof are you sorry?" he asked. "I have a son."

"The queen…"

And Oswald took his son and walked out into the night dark outside the hall and saw not the stars, nor the moon, nor the lights of his hall, but only the face of his wife, of Cyniburh, as she lay beneath him, hair spread upon the pillow, and she cried for joy that she was wife at last.

"You were not ready." Oswald looked down into the face beneath him, searching for Cyniburh in it, but he could not see her. "You were too young. I should have waited longer."

"Brother…"

Oswald made no move.

Slowly, gently, Oswiu came to stand beside him.

Oswald turned to him fiercely, his face afire.

"Swear to me," he said, "swear to me you will care for this boy as your own when I die. Swear it."

"Of course. Of course I swear it."

"Put your hand upon him, swear it; I want to hear you say it."

Oswiu put his hand as gently as he could upon the head of the boy, still wet from birth. "I swear to care for this boy as my own, should you die."

Oswald stared at him. "We all die, brother, we all die."

"It was not your fault. She was of age."

"If I had waited a year longer, she might have had strength enough to give birth and live."

Oswiu put his hands on his brother's shoulders. "It is not your fault."

"I am king, and her husband. Who else bears responsibility?"

"God." Oswiu held his brother tight as he seemed to jerk away from him. "No, hear me. He is the Lord of life and death. He has taken Cyniburh and we no more know why than we know what lies beneath the sea or beyond the stars or in men's hearts. He has taken her, who gave her. Would you call her back from her Lord?"

"Yes," whispered Oswald. "Yes."

The baby, quiet for a few minutes, sent up a thin, reedy wail.

"We must find him a wet nurse," said Oswiu. "Come. Come with me, brother." And leading Oswald like a child, Oswiu brought him back to the hall, where the midwife waited with a wet nurse, a cheerful, smiling woman whose cheer could scarce be quenched even in a hall where the queen lay newly dead.

"Give him here," she said, holding out her hands, and Oswiu took the infant from his brother and gave him to her.

"There, there, my poor little one," she said. "Now, let's be giving you something to drink."

Oswald stood, dumbly staring after his son as he nestled against the wet nurse.

"Come." A hand took his and Oswald looked round to see Rhieienmelth. He looked down. She was holding his hand. He looked up and saw that she wept too. And without thought, he stepped to her and lay his head upon her shoulder, and she folded him in her arms and soothed him.

Oswiu, seeing them thus, turned away.

"He will be all right?" he asked the wet nurse.

"He'll be fine," she said. "He's a bonnie little fellow."

Oswiu glanced back, but his brother still clung to Rhieienmelth, and he looked away once more.

"I – I will go and send word to Aidan. She will need to be buried."

As he stepped out of the hall, Eowa fell into step beside him. "May I come too? I may be of help; your brother will need you soon, and your wife, and I can send the message for you."

Oswiu looked back. "Rhieienmelth seems to manage well on her own at the moment." He stepped from the hall, Eowa beside him. "Come, let us find a messenger; he must set forth today."

They set out across the compound for the stables, which were housed away from the hall, and the enclosure where tribute animals – cattle, sheep, pigs – were brought before slaughter.

"I've promised to care for him as my own," Oswiu said.

"The baby?" asked Eowa, a note of incredulity in his voice.

"Yes. Oswald asked me."

"Already?"

"It was the first thing he asked of me."

"That – that is most forbearing of you."

"How do you mean?"

"That if the king should die you will be sworn to promote his son as your own for the throne."

"Yes," said Oswiu. "I know."

"Let us hope the king does not die for many years."

"Yes."

"Have you told the princess Rhieienmelth of this yet?"

"No! Of course not. What chance has there been for talk?"

"Of course. I am sorry. I could see she was busy."

Oswiu looked at him. "What do you mean?"

"She was comforting the king. As we all must do in his grief at the loss of his wife."

"It is not just grief. He blames himself for her death."

"The king takes everything upon himself."

"He does. Let's see if anyone is awake." Oswiu roused a sleeping boy from a snooze atop a pile of hay and sent him to find one of the messengers whose task it was, first, to ride ahead to the next estate that the royal household was due to visit to warn them of their arrival in plenty of time and, secondly, to be on hand to take messages to whomsoever the king wished to communicate with.

The message given and the horseman making ready, Oswiu and Eowa turned back to the hall.

"Of course, with the queen now dead, the king will be free to make alliance with another of the great kingdoms of the land."

Oswiu looked at Eowa. "I do not think that is what he thinks on now."

"No, of course it is not. But it should be uppermost in our minds, as his counsellors. Then when the king is more ready, we may speak with him and present our thoughts."

Oswiu stopped and turned, crossing his arms over his chest. "Since you already seem to have thought on this, what are your ideas?"

"I know." Eowa held up his hands. "I know, it seems I have the heart of a fox to be thinking on this and the queen barely dead; but it is the task appointed to a counsellor to keep cool mind when all around turn to grief, or joy, or some other emotion. Can you blame me for doing what is my task?"

"Speak then. Let me hear your thoughts."

Eowa held up his hands and began counting off with his fingers. "These are the great kingdoms of the Angles and the Saxons: Northumbria, Kent, the land of the East Angles, the land of the West Saxons, the land of the East Saxons and the land of the South Saxons. And Mercia, the kingdom of the Middle Angles. Although Cyniburh has died, the alliance with the West Saxons will surely remain secure. Any of the other kingdoms would be glad to make alliance with Northumbria."

"Any of the other kingdoms? Mercia too?"

Eowa shrugged. "Who knows? The humiliation you imposed upon my brother was very great but he still holds his throne, and seeks advantage for it. He has no daughter by a wife as yet, but soon he must take wife and, judging by the whelps he has sired, it will not be long before he brings forth children. But would you want alliance with him?"

Oswiu shook his head. "I would not trust Penda."

Eowa grimaced. "To my cost, I have learned that to be a wise policy. But if not Mercia, all the other kingdoms would want to join with you; and the more alliances you make, the tighter the net you draw around the only kingdom that remains a threat to you: Mercia."

Oswiu nodded. "It is a shame we can add only one more to us."

"It is indeed. If your brother had but waited before seeking marriage for you, you might have married the daughter of one of the great kingdoms yourself; for such is the fame of Oswiu, warmaster of Northumbria, that any king would as happily pledge his daughter to you as to Oswald. But," Eowa shrugged, "Rheged was once great."

Oswiu turned away. "We did not know the way of things then."

"No, that is true. No man knows what the fate weavers will bring…"

Oswiu looked back at Eowa. "There's a 'but' there. What is it?"

Eowa held his hands up.

"Well?" asked Oswiu.

"Only that since no man knows what the fate weavers will weave, it behoves a man to delay taking wife until he knows where he stands, and what advantage his marriage might bring. It is a shame your brother did not hold to this for you."

"I would have no other wife than Rhieienmelth."

"Of course not. Still, if it should ever prove necessary, it is not unknown for a king to put aside a wife for another, if she should bring greater advantage to his kingdom."

"I am not a king."

"No, so as long as you are not, it will not apply." Eowa smiled. "There is therefore nothing to consider."

"I wasn't considering it."

Eowa turned to the hall. "We should return. The king will have need of his brother. And we should find out the name of his son."

*

"Æthelwald."

Oswald watched as Aidan poured water over his son's head.

The monk had come as fast as he could when the message reached him. On arrival, Aidan had first buried Cyniburh, laying her in a stone-lined pit. Oswald had stood beside her as she was laid out in it wearing the clothes she had worn for their wedding.

Then, with due paid to the dead, came time for the living: the baptism of Oswald's son.

"*Ego te baptizo in nomine Patris...*"

The baby put up a scream as the liquid descended on his head, the cry ascending to anger, and then outrage, as the water flowed over his head again: "*...et Filii...*" and for the final time: "*...et Spiritus Sancti*".

Aidan handed the baby to his slightly startled godfather, Oswiu, who looked around to see who might take the screaming bundle from him. Rhieienmelth reached for the baby and Oswiu gave him to her, but though she soothed him, Æthelwald continued to scream.

Rhieienmelth looked up and saw Oswald looking at her. "He wants feeding," she said.

"Where is that wet nurse?" Oswiu looked around for the woman, but she was nowhere to be seen in the small wooden church that the king had had put up in the royal compound.

"I have milk," said Rhieienmelth. "I can feed him."

Before Oswiu could say anything, Oswald nodded. "Please," he said.

The princess turned aside and put the baby to her breast. Oswiu looked at her, saw his brother staring, then looked away.

"Daddy, Daddy."

Oswiu looked down to see his own son holding up his arms to him. He bent down and swept him up.

"Sasa?" he asked, pointing towards his mother and the baby she was holding.

"No, that's not your sister; that's your cousin."

"Sasa?" the child repeated.

"No, cousin. Æthelwald." Oswiu looked to his wife. She was still nursing the baby. "We will go to the hall," he said.

Rhieienmelth looked up. "Yes."

Oswiu's mouth tightened but he said no more, instead leaving the church, carrying his son in his arms. Aidan watched him go, then turned a worried gaze to Oswald. Going to the king, he took his arm.

"We should bring the baby to the hall," he said. "Rhieienmelth, it would be best that we find his wet nurse."

The princess looked up from the contented baby. "He's asleep now," she said.

"Then bring him," said Aidan.

As they walked across the compound to the hall, Aidan turned to Oswald.

"How will you raise him now his…"

"Now his mother is dead?"

"I would that it were not so."

"He is my first son. I would have him with me."

"Wait. Think on this." Aidan nodded ahead to where Rhieienmelth was about to enter the hall. "Already this child has brought strain between you and your brother."

"Oswiu swore to care for Æthelwald as his own should I die. And you see how Rhieienmelth cares for him too."

"Yes, I saw. And so did your brother. Old friend, there is danger in this. Ever the greatest strength of your kingdom has been the unity that exists between you and your brother. Should that unity be damaged or torn asunder…" Aidan shook his head. "To the days of our forefather Adam, there has ever been danger between brothers, but I had not thought to see such enmity arise between you who were always closest."

"There is no enmity between us." Oswald's voice was low and flat, and his expression brooked no argument. "None."

Aidan made to answer, then sighed. "Very well. I pray that you are right. But please, I ask you: do not place too great a burden for his upbringing upon Rhieienmelth."

"I will ask of her no more than she is willing to give."

"Oswald, I do not think this right."

"What do you know?" Oswald suddenly stiffened, the veins standing out at his temples. "You make of yourself a eunuch: you do not know what it is like to lose a wife, you have no children, no enemies who would spit your son upon their swords if they could. Think not to tell me how to raise my son, Aidan, nor presume overmuch on our friendship. I am king in this land, I and no other, and I will raise him as I will."

Aidan held up his hands. "I sought no offence, but I am a bishop, and I am called upon to give guidance."

"You, and my brother, and my thegns and my retainers and my counsellors, and my scop and my smith. Everyone thinks to give the king guidance. But, hear me: the king needs no guidance in this matter." Oswald's shoulders slumped, the anger draining from him as quickly as it had come. "Understand it is the custom among my people that a child be sent, once he is of age, to be brought up by an allied king, that he may learn different ways and forge friendships that will serve him when he is a man. But – but I do not think I can do that with my son. I could not give him to another to raise. But my own family, that is a different matter. He will be happy with Rhieienmelth; see, she already cares for him as if he were her own, and Oswiu has sworn thus to me. Let him be with family, and I will be king."

"A king should have his family about him."

"I did. She is dead now. Besides, I have Bran. A slaughter bird for the king of death."

Aidan shook his head. "Oswald, you take too much upon yourself. Cyniburh's death is not your fault."

Oswald held up his hand.

"You see this?" He splayed his fingers in front of Aidan's face. "This hand, the hand you prayed would never wither, is my hand of judgment. With it, I bring down vengeance upon the guilty and give mercy to the wretched. I judge the cases that come before me and pronounce innocence or guilt. But there is none to judge the king save the king, and I have given sentence." He dropped his hand to his side. "I thank you, old friend, for coming so quickly when you were called. But now, as you have oft told me, you have many calls upon you on the Holy Island; it were best you returned to it, and I to the tasks appointed me."

Aidan nodded and made to withdraw, but then stopped. "I will go, my lord, but not to Lindisfarne. I have a task before I return to my monastery."

*

Aidan heard him before he saw him. He heard him chanting in tones strange to his ear, calling to heaven and to earth one of the songs of David. And although the style was unknown, Aidan knew well the meaning of the words, so when the man singing them came into sight and fell silent, he continued as he rode towards him and dismounted.

"*Cantabo Deo meo quamdiu sum.*" Aidan stopped in front of the man. "I will sing to my God as long as I shall be."

"I too." The man looked long at Aidan. "I am James."

"Aidan."

James nodded. "Yes." He pointed at Aidan's shaven forehead and the hair hanging long down the back of his neck. "I thought it must be you."

"And I knew you to be James." Aidan pointed in turn at the circle of hair that crowned James's head, the skin within it leathered from sun and wind.

"*Nolite confidere in principibus,*" James chanted softly.

"Put not your trust in princes," translated Aidan and, continuing, he chanted, "...*in filio hominis cui non est salus.*"

"In the children of men in whom there is no salvation."

The two men fell silent, regarding each other.

"I have wished to meet you for a long time," said Aidan.

"I have not gone from here."

"I have duties…"

"As have I." James stood aside and gestured towards the framework of lashed branches that marked the entrance to his home. "Will you join me, lord bishop?"

"Right gladly." Aidan went ahead, as James bowed to him, and entered the low cave where the deacon made his dwelling. He saw a bowl and cup, a bed of branches and ferns, ashes marking a hearth, and a book. Placed in reverence upon a natural plinth towards the rear of the cave, far from the damp and cold without, was a book, and Aidan was drawn to it as naturally as the sea draws a stream.

Looking down at its rich leather cover, he put a finger to it, then looked to James – and saw him smiling.

"Please, my lord bishop."

Aidan opened the book and saw it to be a Gospel book, written in letters whose style was strange to him but which he could still read.

"This – this is wonderful."

"It was one of the books we brought, with much labour and more fear, from Rome. Bishop Paulinus left it behind when he went into exile with the queen, but I rescued it and brought it here."

Aidan bent and kissed the book, then turned to James.

"Will you bring it to me? We – I – have need for men, and for books. *Messis quidem multa operarii autem pauci.*"

"The harvest indeed is great, but the labourers are few." James came over to where Aidan was standing and placed his hand upon the book. "There are people who come to me to hear of God; in truth, not as many as I hoped, yet they come. If I go, there will be none to bring them God's word."

"You would return to them, when I could send you."

"But I would not be here." James stood back and looked at Aidan. "They are my people. I would not leave them."

Aidan looked carefully at him. "I could command you."

James blushed, but nodded. "You could. You are a bishop, I a deacon. Your word is my command. But you have heard me chant,"

James touched his scalp, "you have seen my head: my ways are not your ways."

Aidan could not help noticing that when James blushed, even the top of his head, where the hair was shaved clean, went red too.

"We follow the path laid for us by the Holy One, the Blessed Colm Cille."

James nodded. "Yes. At the witan…" He paused, his flush growing deeper. "At the witan, where Bishop Corman spoke, I heard of the Blessed Colm Cille for the first time. When I went from there, I asked of him, and now I know why you follow his path."

"Will you not follow it too?"

"Do you ask whether I would follow of my own free will, lord bishop, or under obedience?"

"Of your will, Deacon James."

"Then I would remain, following the practice of the Holy Fathers, and teaching those who would the Roman chant."

Aidan looked at the deacon. James met his gaze, and although he flushed, he did not lower his eyes and, truth to tell, Aidan felt his own neck grow hot under the steady eyes of the deacon.

"Very well. See to your people, James, and I will see to mine."

Chapter 5

The morning mist lay low upon the Great Fen in the land of the East Angles, spilling over from the marsh, creeping up towards the monastery that overlooked the endless miles of sedge and willow and black, stagnant water. Riding through the mist, so that it seemed from a distance they sat upon horses with no legs, a small group of riders approached the monastery of Beodricesworth.[2] They bore the marks of hard riding and recent battle: bandages and poultices cut from tree fungi covered wounds that were still far from healing but were not so severe as to stop them riding in haste. At this hour, the monastery's gates were still closed, but as the lead riders reached it, they pounded upon the wood with the hilts of their swords.

"Open! Open in the name of the king," they cried.

Within the monastery, a young monk charged with the duties of door warden ran to the church, which stood at the centre of the compound, and burst in.

The Great Work was being done; the monks of the community were at prayer, singing the office of dawn. The monk, trying to be unobtrusive but, in his anxiety, failing, made his way through the ranks of hooded figures to the man who stood at the far end of the choir, nearest the altar.

"Abbot Sigeberht, there are men without who would speak with you," he said.

The monk, who had once been king of this land, turned to the young man and lifted a finger to his lips.

"Shh," he whispered, and turned back to prayer.

"Abbot Sigeberht, they said they would break down the gate if you did not come at once."

---

2 This is the Old English name for the place that later came to be called Bury St Edmunds after St Edmund was buried there in the ninth century.

The abbot sighed. He turned to the monks next to him and indicated by gesture that they should continue without him. Then, gathering his robes about him, he stood and followed the young monk to the gate.

Opening the shutter, he peered without. "What do you want?"

A face appeared at the grille.

"We want the abbot, King Sigeberht."

"What do you want him for?"

"We will tell him to his face. And if he don't come to us soon, we'll come to him, right through this here door and anyone who tries to stop us."

"There is no need. He is here."

The man stepped back a little, then returned to the grille.

"It's you, is it?"

"I am Abbot Sigeberht. What do you want of me?"

"The king, King Ecgric, has sent us to fetch you."

"What does he want of me? I have given the throne to him. I want nothing more of the ways of this world."

"He wants your help in keeping his throne. And his life. King Penda marches against us. Already he has crossed the Great Ouse, and we were sorely beaten trying to hold him upon the further bank. Now he makes haste for the heart of our kingdom, and King Ecgric has not men enough to defeat him."

"I will pray for his victory." Abbot Sigeberht began to close the grille, but the man pushed it open again.

"You don't understand. The king does not want your prayers. He wants your sword; he wants you on the battlefield and at his side in the shieldwall."

"That is impossible. I have given up the wars of this world; I will not lift sword again. Please go. Assure King Ecgric that though he is yet a pagan I will pray for his victory." Abbot Sigeberht made to close the grille again, but this time the man forced it open all the way.

"Like I said, the king wants you and he said to come back with you, whether you were willing or not." The soldier stepped back from the gate. "Break it down."

The gate shuddered as axes laid into it. Abbot Sigeberht stood back and waited. His monks came running from the church to stand beside him, some brandishing staves and cudgels, but he placed his hand upon their weapons and bade them lay them down.

"Men may bring war into this house, but we shall not raise hand against them," he said.

The gate, weakened by the succession of axe blows, finally splintered, and men carrying axes or wielding swords poured through.

The man who had spoken earlier came and stood before Abbot Sigeberht. His left arm was bandaged, mud spattered his clothes, and the sword he held in front of him was notched.

"Right, you're coming with me," he said. He looked around at the monks standing by their abbot. "Anyone who wants to stop me?"

One or two of the younger monks made to step forward, but Abbot Sigeberht held them back.

"Stay, do not raise your hand," he said. "I will go."

"Get your sword. You'll need it," said the soldier.

"I have no sword; I gave it away when I became a monk."

"Don't matter. King Ecgric will give you one."

"I will not bear it."

"Tell *him* that, not me. Come on, let's go."

And with the man's sword jabbing into his back, Abbot Sigeberht went from his monastery to war.

*

"I hate boats." Eowa, having given his opinion of water transport, turned and leaned over the side of the ship.

Oswald laughed, and clapped the man's heaving shoulders.

"That is not helping," said Eowa, without turning round.

"Come, we are nearly there." Oswald pointed. "See that headland? Once we pass Lizard Point it is but a short way to Tynemouth, and then we are into the river; it will be smoother going there."

Eowa glanced in the direction Oswald was pointing and groaned. "Throw me overboard now," he said. "I won't live that long."

The sail cracked in the brisk wind, the raven painted upon it fluttering as if it were alive. Bran, perched in the midst of the boat as clear of the spray as possible, opened an eye, glanced as if with disdain, then went back to sleep again.

"You will get used to this," said Oswald.

Eowa, wiping his mouth but looking slightly less green, turned back into the boat. "I have not got used to it in all the years I have been your hostage."

"We have not been in boats all that time."

"Near enough," said Eowa, with feeling. "I am glad I am of Mercia, and far from the sea; the only time I ever went on boats was to cross a river."

"I have spent near enough my whole life by the sea." Oswald adjusted the tiller in natural response to a shift in the wind, not needing to think as he did so. "It is funny to see one so incapacitated by a little light swell."

"It's not funny for me," said Eowa. "Next time, could I not go with the wagons?"

"That is a long and weary journey. Besides, I would have you with me. Since Oswiu took command of the northern marches, and Aidan prefers to wander the land talking to farmers and slaves rather than his king, you are the only one left for me to speak with." Oswald laughed, but there was no humour in it. "You at least will not desert me, seeing as you are my hostage."

"It is strange to think that," said Eowa. "For I now think of myself as your friend."

"I too. And as my friend and counsellor, and seeing that you have nothing left in your stomach to vomit, I would have your advice. With my brother occupied, I have need of a new warmaster. Who do you recommend?"

Eowa nodded. "Let me think on this." He pointed ahead. "Is that the mouth of the river?"

"Yes," said Oswald, adjusting the tiller to bring the boat closer in to shore. He looked to the men sitting upon the cross benches – the boat carried twenty-five of his best warriors – and called them to make ready with the oars.

"It is indeed a shame that Oswiu so rarely joins us now. A king needs a warmaster he can trust. To that end, I recommend Bassus."

"Bassus? Why him?"

"I know he served your uncle and took into exile his queen and children, but since his return he has served you faithfully. Besides, he is no longer young, and he has no connection with the Yffings, so he will not be able to use his position as warmaster against you."

Oswald nodded. "I will think on that. You were your brother's warmaster, were you not?"

"I was, and would that I had used my position to act against him."

"Well, we will see what we can do about that."

Eowa looked sharply at Oswald. "What do you mean?"

But Oswald shook his head. "We will talk later on it. For now, I must concentrate: where river meets sea makes for choppy water."

Eowa looked round, saw the chaotic waves ahead, and groaned. "Will it never end?"

"There's clear water upstream."

"But a lot of rough waves to cross before we get there."

Oswald laughed. "That's not rough. You should see the storms in the west."

"No, thank you…" Eowa began, but then the boat's prow jerked up as it met the first of the waves, and just as suddenly plunged down. The Mercian's face as suddenly dropped, and he made a plunge for the side of the boat.

"Just in time," said Oswald as the first retch heaved through Eowa's body. The Mercian made no reply. He was far too busy.

*

"You came." King Ecgric looked up, his face tight and drawn as the wound in his shoulder was being stitched.

"Not by my will, but at sword point." Abbot Sigeberht indicated the man beside him. "Beonna would not accept my refusal."

Ecgric tried to smile, but the pulling tight of gut turned the smile into a grimace of pain. "That – that is why I chose him. Beonna is faithful to a fault; if I tell him to do something, he will not rest until it is accomplished."

"Nor care that he breaks God's commands in carrying it out."

"Another reason I chose him. Beonna follows the old ways, as do I."

"Old ways or new ways, it behoves a man to keep his pledge."

Ecgric winced as the gut was finally tied off. The leech made to bind it, but the king pushed him away. "See to the rest," he said. "There are others who need thee." The leech gathered his needle and gut, while Ecgric tried the arm for movement, wincing again as he did so.

"I would not have had you brought here without need," he said to Sigeberht.

"Your need would have been better served by my remaining in my monastery and offering prayer for you and our people."

"You know our need then?"

"Penda."

"Yes, Penda. He's pushed us back this far, Sigeberht. There's nowhere further we can go. We either fight here, or we run, or we die." Ecgric gestured for the other men, weary and war-torn retainers, and Beonna, to leave the tent. When they had gone, he waved the abbot to a stool, but when Sigeberht did not move, Ecgric sighed and got to his feet.

"You see me?" he said. "I can bare walk, my arm is useless, and in two battles against Penda all I've managed to do is extract most of my men alive. I'm desperate – we're desperate."

"Then send word to me at the abbey and we will storm God's hall with our prayers that he may listen to your pleas."

"Don't you think I've been praying and sacrificing the whole time? I've given twenty cattle and a hundred and more sheep, and have the gods listened? No, they turn their backs on us, and when I ask the priest he turns to me with bloody hands and says, 'It's wyrd,' or, 'It's the fate singers.' What use are gods that don't do anything when you wash their halls with the blood of sacrifice and smoke them out with burnt offerings?"

"My God has power over all gods."

"A pox on gods!" Ecgric grasped Sigeberht's arm, his face up close to his old friend. "They are faithless friends! That is why I brought you from your monastery. The men remembered – I remembered – the victories we won when you stood beside us in the shieldwall. All men had to hear was the name Sigeberht and despair would fall on our enemies and our own men would stand against the greatest foe without fear. Enough with prayers! Take your sword, stand with us; together we can defeat Penda and save our kingdom."

Sigeberht stared into the eyes of his friend of old and did not know them. He unpeeled the fingers wrapped around his arm.

"No," he said. "I made vow to put aside sword forever and take as my weapon only prayer and staff. I made no exceptions to the vow and I would be faithless were I to put it aside now."

"You made vow to gods who laugh upon us in our plight, who take our sacrifices and spit upon them. Such vows are worthless."

"I have one God and he is not faithless."

"Then why does he not guard your kingdom now you have given it up for his sake?"

Sigeberht shook his head. "That is not his way; he cares not for worldly honour, but for the spirits of those who turn to him – and those who turn from him."

"If he does not care for worldly honour, he will have none; men will not worship a god who brings no victory."

"He brings truth; that is victory enough."

"No." Ecgric shook his head. "No, it isn't enough. You look at Penda advancing across our land, ravaging as he goes, and then tell me truth is victory. Victory is truth, and you are going to help me gain victory whether you will or not. Old friend. Penda's men are close at hand. Even if I wanted to, I couldn't send you back to the abbey."

"I will bear no sword, but I will give counsel, if you would have it."

"Tell me."

"How many men does Penda bring with him?"

"More than I – than we – have. Sixty, maybe seventy or eighty."

Sigeberht nodded. "I saw, what, thirty men in your camp?"

"Forty, and most of those carry injuries, like me."

"Then I counsel that you seek not to meet Penda in battle again, but withdraw to one of the islands in the Great Fen, and take shelter there. He will not be able to bring his men to such a place. Then send word to our allies, to Cynegils of the West Saxons, to the kings of Kent and the East Saxons, but most of all to the High King, to Oswald, telling of our plight, that they may come to our aid, as they are pledged to."

"It will be at least two weeks, maybe three, before any could come to our aid at this time of year; the spring storms will stop Oswald arriving by sea, and those riding will be delayed, even once they have gathered their men."

"You may hold for two weeks, or even three, particularly if Penda knows not where you have gone."

Ecgric grinned. "I'm not going alone, old friend."

*

"Tell King Sigeberht and King Ecgric I will come."

The messenger made the courtesy, the smile that came with renewed hope spreading across his face, and he stuttered thanks to Oswald.

"I will leave a guide to take you to where King Ecgric has taken refuge; King Sigeberht takes the title king no longer, but he is our lord too, and gives wise counsel to King Ecgric, though he will bear no sword, but only a staff."

"Bid them have courage and endure; we will come as soon as wind and wave allow."

"You come by sea?"

"That is the quickest way."

"But less sure at this time of year."

"Speed counts for more in this matter – for you as for us. I will have my men prepare food and drink for you, that you may take upon your boat, but you must return forthwith."

As the messenger withdrew, Oswald turned to his counsellors: Bassus, his new warmaster, and Eowa of Mercia.

"Your brother could not sit content with his throne, but seeks to take another."

"My only surprise is that it has taken him so long to break his pledge to you," said Eowa.

"We can gather sixty men at once," said Bassus, "and leave upon the tide tomorrow. If we wait two days, that will rise to eighty or ninety. In a week we could have one hundred and twenty."

"I doubt Sigeberht and Ecgric have a week," said Oswald. "Nor even two days. No, we will leave on the morrow with all the men we have here." The king looked at Eowa. "We go against your brother. What say you of that?"

"I hope you kill him."

Bassus laughed. "Not much love for brother there," he said.

"My brother sent me as hostage that he might spare himself," said Eowa. "And though I have rich treatment here among the Idings, yet I remember that against him. And in giving me as hostage, he removed a threat to his throne. For there were many among the witan who said that I was the more throne-worthy." Eowa sighed. "But for my part, I held my hand from him and made no move against him, not knowing that my brother was plotting against me. It was ever thus: brother against brother."

Oswald made no reply, but Bassus nodded his agreement.

"Gather the men we have and tell them to make ready. We leave tomorrow with the tide."

Eowa groaned. "Not more boats."

Oswald laughed. "If you would have us strike against your brother, we must needs get there quickly, and there is no faster way than by boat."

"But I want to be able to raise sword when I get there. After two days in a boat, I will not be good for anything."

"That is as well. There is great blood guilt in slaying a brother – however much he deserves it," said Oswald.

*

"Where is he?" The seax, point deep into the side of the monk's neck, drew a welling bead of blood from the skin. "Where is your abbot?"

"I – I will not say," said the monk, his eyes swivelling from the man who held the seax against his throat to the one questioning him. Although the one with the knife was the one who might kill him, yet it was the other, the one asking the questions, who truly scared him.

"King Penda, I ask you, please, if I have done aught to please you, spare my brother monk." Diuma appeared, his robes hitched up to near his waist, that they might not catch his running legs. When he had heard that the acting abbot of Beodricesworth monastery had been dragged to the king, he had gone rushing to him.

"I am glad you have come," said Penda. "Tell this monk that I am a man of my word. If he tells me what I ask, then I will spare him and all his fellows."

"It may be that he can give no answer for the question you ask him, lord," said Brother Diuma. "There was a story when I was young…"

"I do not have two days," said Penda, "so you will spare me this story. Tell this monk to say where his abbot is, and I will spare him and all the others in this monastery. After all, I am not like the father of Oswald. Æthelfrith killed monks for his good pleasure; I allow one to speak of his god to me in my own household. Tell him this."

Brother Diuma looked to the men holding the monk, and in particular the one holding the seax to his throat.

"Release him," said Penda.

Released, the monk gasped, his hand going to his throat, but the skin there was merely bruised, not sliced.

Diuma looked at the man and saw the pale skin and dark hair of one of his own people. Speaking in the language of his fathers, he asked, "Whence came you here, brother?"

The monk started. "You are of the Baptized? I had not thought to hear the tongue of my forefathers from those who break down our doors and spill the blood of the brothers."

"I am of the sons of Ulster, sent from the Holy Isle to Northumbria and King Oswald, thence among the pagans and King Penda, that I might tell them the news of life and bring them to it."

The monk looked sidelong at the warriors standing ready and the grim king standing before him.

"I take it you have not succeeded?"

"Not yet. But King Penda makes no hindrance to my speaking; I may talk with whomever will listen. The king himself oft speaks with me of the faith, learning of it."

"No doubt that is why he wishes to speak to my abbot too," said the monk dryly, attempting to massage some feeling back into his neck.

"No, it is not," said Penda in the same language.

The monk froze. His eyes leapt from Brother Diuma to Penda and back again. "I – I did not know you spoke our tongue."

"I tire of this. Tell me where your abbot who was once king is, or I will do as the Twister did, and start killing monks in front of your eyes."

Brother Diuma placed himself in front of the monk. "You will have to strike me first, lord."

Penda shook his head. "Do you really think I would not?"

"No, lord, no I do not. But I would not live if I let such blood flow."

"There is no need." The monk pushed Brother Diuma aside. "There is no great secret to where the abbot has gone. I can show you." He looked questioningly to Penda, who nodded, and then led them through the broken gate and to the rise that looked over the black water and grey distance of the Great Fen. "He is there," he said, and he pointed to the fen fastness. From the heart of its immensity rose the wheeling black shapes of buzzards and hawks and kites, while the wind moved waves through the banks of reeds and sedge that crawled between the black waters.

"Where?" asked Penda.

"Who can say where anything is in the Great Fen?" said the monk.

From out of the immensity rose, in many places, the irregular columns of smoke that marked the dwelling of a fen family eking a living trapping eels and wild fowling in a world more water than earth. Any of those smoke columns might indicate the refuge of the kings. Within the untracked pathways of the fen, they were as unreachable as the emperor of the East.

Penda looked out over the fen. "It is not so easy for a king to hide," he said. "Less so for two of them."

*

"How long are we going to wait here?" Ecgric paced up and down by the mean fire that produced more smoke than heat and was the only source of warmth on the damp, low island in the Great Fen where they had taken refuge. To call it an island was to dignify it with a solidity it did not possess. Rather, it was a series of tussocks and humps of ground rising just above the squelching mud and black water, but more through the accumulated growth of many years of reed and sedge than through any depth of earth. It was a shifting, sodden world, and a single misstep would send the walker knee deep in stinking, clinging mud.

The men who had accompanied King Ecgric and Abbot Sigeberht into the fen lay about on what patches of drier ground they could find. Even the time-honoured pastimes of waiting warriors – talking, boasting, remembering and dicing – had grown tedious in the time they had spent waiting upon their allies to come. Of all the men, only Sigeberht seemed relatively content, and that was because he spent most of his day engaged in the Great Work of monks, praying the Office, most of which the abbot had committed to memory. But though the Latin phrases had first soothed Ecgric, they had come to annoy him almost beyond endurance, particularly when reports reached him, brought by one of the fensmen, of Penda's depredations.

"How long are we going to wait?" Ecgric repeated, this time stopping his pacing in front of the kneeling abbot.

Sigeberht continued the Latin phrase through to its end, then looked up at Ecgric.

"Until Oswald arrives," he said.

"If he was coming, he should have got here by now," said Ecgric.

"This is the storm season; it would be easy for him to be delayed, stormbound."

"He could have walked here by now. On his hands."

"But if he set off by boat to reach us the more quickly, and became stormbound, he would have to wait for it to clear. Still, it has been quite a long time."

Ecgric raised a hand. "Wait. How would he find us? We are hidden away in the middle of the Great Fen. Unless he has a guide, he will not reach us."

"I would expect him to send a messenger; it would simply be a matter of passing the news to one of the fensmen, and he would bring us the news. Then we would go out to meet him."

Ecgric shivered and drew his cloak tighter around his body. "I hope he is swift. This damp is in my bones and no fire seems able to drive it out."

As he spoke, the tell-tale sound of rushes compacting under foot – a squelching, fibrous noise – told the arrival of one of the fensmen, bringing tidings and meagre supplies. The man – a creature, to Ecgric's eye, who seemed all but made of the marsh he dwelled in – cringed in front of the king, tugging a finger through his matted hair.

"What news?" asked Ecgric.

The creature sidled closer, bringing a whiff of the marsh with him.

"He is here, master," he said. "He sent me to tell you, to fetch you."

"Who is here?" asked Ecgric, suddenly attentive. Beside him, Sigeberht got to his feet.

"The king," said the fensman. "The High King, the one you sent for. He is here. He waits outside and bids you come to him."

"Whereaways?"

"Yonder." The fensman pointed. Like all his people, he had only the vaguest appreciation of the geography outside the fen but the most minute knowledge of the shifting pathways within the marsh.

"Wait," said Sigeberht. "What sign or token did he give for surety?"

"Here it be," said the fensman, and he held up a single black feather. A raven feather.

The two kings looked to each other.

"It is Oswald," said Sigeberht.

"What are we waiting for?" said Ecgric. "Let's get out of this place." He turned to the fensman. "Lead us to him."

It was the work of but a few minutes to strike the mean camp they had made, and then the fensman took them, by narrow paths and uncertain steps, sometimes perforce wading through water still winter cold, towards the edge of the fen. As they went, the fensman pointed ahead.

"See, the masts of his ships." And rising up beyond the next line of dwarf alder were the tall poles and yards of Oswald's boats. No sail hung from them, of course, as this far upriver they would have been rowed or poled, but they were almost there, and the men, cheered by the prospect of finally leaving the bone-gnawing damp of the fen, splashed towards them, breasting through the final line of trees.

"There they be," said the fensman, pointing to the boats drawn up on the bank of the River Great Ouse. Tents were set up on the bank, and flying from a pole was the gold and purple banner of Northumbria.

As the Northumbrians saw the men emerge from the fen, the camp stirred into activity, men forming into an honour guard to welcome the kings of the East Angles as they marched towards the camp.

But as they approached, Sigeberht saw that the place of honour, where Oswald should have waited for them, stood empty. Looking more closely at the men of the honour guard, he began to see tension under the respect of the silence in which they waited.

"Wait," he said, taking hold of Ecgric's shoulder. "Stop." He looked around. Both ends of the honour guard were beginning to drift inwards. He peered more closely at the faces, and saw no man there that he recognized. Though he had not met all of Oswald's thegns and retainers, yet he would expect to see one or two faces he knew among the High King's men.

"What is it?" asked Ecgric.

As he asked the question, a man, armoured but with his helmet held under his arm, stepped into the gap at the centre of the honour guard.

"The High King," said the fensman, pointing.

"You know," said Penda, "he genuinely believed me to be the High King. That's why he made such a convincing messenger."

*

The river was grown too shallow for rowing now, so the men stood and pushed their oars down into the soft mud below the boat, poling the vessel along. Three boats, each holding some twenty-five men, moved slowly through the trailing grey willow fronds. In the lead boat, a fensman, his speech all but incomprehensible to Oswald but his gestures plain enough, pointed the way through the winding streams of black water. Each pole pulled up released an upwelling of foul gases, so they travelled within a noxious cloud, causing some of the men, seasoned sailors though they were, to gag and void their bellies over the sides of the boats.

The fensman brought them through the network of streams and channels to the broader waters of the River Great Ouse. He pointed ahead, but even without his indication, the circling cloud of buzzards and kites, crows and rooks, told the tale of what lay beneath.

"He said he be the High King. He said he be you." The fensman turned his face to Oswald, and tears tracked through the grain of fine silt layered upon his cheeks. "I not know. I think he tell truth."

"Did anyone get away?" asked Oswald.

The fensman pointed to himself. "The king, Ecgric, he wanted to kill me, but the other king, the holy man, he stopped him. He said I did not know what I did – and that is true. He put himself in front of me when Ecgric raise his sword against me, raising his staff to protect me. Then he told me, 'Run.' I run. I have children, wife, and no sword. I run into the fen and there I watch."

The boats, with enough water now to pull oar, made swift progress through the flat, turbid waters of the Great Ouse. The sound of the scavenger birds grew louder: the cough and caw of crows, the whir of rooks, the feather rush of buzzard and kite.

"The fight, it is not long, I think; but for me, I think it goes on forever. King Ecgric fight bravely, but he soon falls. Only the other king, the holy king, holds the battle together long, and he does not fight, but stands with his staff in his hand, praying and calling out until the last of the men around him fall. Then King Penda goes to him, and I hear, I hear…"

*

"You fought well without even raising a sword." Penda stopped in front of Sigeberht. "You should have stayed king."

"Seeing what kings become, I am glad I did not." Sigeberht held his staff in his right hand. It was notched in many places, where it had deflected blows intended for the men beside him, but now the last of them had fallen and he stood face to face with death. Sigeberht smiled. "I have taken the better part."

"You can live, you know," said Penda. "You don't have to die with the other one."

Sigeberht nodded. "That lies more with you than with me."

"No. No, it doesn't. All you have to do is acknowledge me as over-king, and I will leave you be, as long as you take back the throne of the East Angles. I will not have it occupied by another ally of Oswald."

"I have a new lord. One who is always faithful. I would not bow to another."

"Did he come to your aid when you called upon him in battle just now?"

Sigeberht looked surprised. "Of course he did."

"But you lost."

"No, I have won."

"What do you mean, you have won?"

"I prayed for the strength to keep my vow, to raise no sword, to be worthy of him who gave no stroke against his killers, and he answered my prayers."

"Those are not the prayers I want answered."

"You should." Sigeberht stared at Penda, and the Mercian saw upon his face an expression he had not witnessed for so long that at first he could not place it. Then he knew it for what it was. Pity and compassion.

"You would know peace," said Sigeberht. "You would be free of the fear that devours you."

"I am not afraid!"

"We are all afraid. Death takes, when it will, young and old, strong and weak, king and slave. Glory fades, deeds are forgotten. In a generation, who will remember our names? There is no hope in the old ways, Penda. But there is hope in the new ways; a hope of life, a hope in death, a hope even in defeat." Sigeberht held out his arms to Penda. "Take this hope, embrace it, and live."

The king stood staring at Sigeberht, and it was as if he was a ghost, for the blood drained from his face, and his hands shook. Terrible emotions ran through his eyes. Upon his form there appeared the shadows of the boy he once was and the man he had become, and they warred with each other.

Then, as Penda remained poised upon the point of his life, balanced, Brother Diuma, finally free of the man who had been detailed to keep guard on him through the battle, came running to him, calling on the king to spare Abbot Sigeberht. But as Penda turned towards the approaching man, Wihtrun came behind Sigeberht, none marking him, and he seized Sigeberht's hair and pulled his head back and ran his seax across his throat. As the abbot fell to his knees, hands to his neck, his eyes glazing, Wihtrun turned to Penda.

"The old ways are best. Cleave to them, and you will win many victories."

Penda stared at him. "Have you seen this?"

"I have seen this," said Wihtrun.

Abbot Sigeberht, the thread holding his will to his muscles breaking, fell upon his face.

Brother Diuma went on his knees beside the abbot, but the man was dead. He turned to Penda, holding Sigeberht's body in his arms.

"You promised to spare him," he cried.

Penda looked down upon him.

"I will cleave to the old ways," he said. "I will follow my fathers in this life, and feast alongside them in the next."

"You will feast in hell," said Brother Diuma.

"So be it."

Wihtrun approached Brother Diuma, seax in hand, but Penda shook his head.

"It is time he returned to his own people," he said.

*

They found Brother Diuma upon the battlefield. He was kneeling beside the body of Abbot Sigeberht, with the abbot's staff beside him and his eyes closed. As Oswald approached, he saw Brother Diuma sway, as if sleep was about to claim him, then, at the sound of Oswald's foot squelching into mud, Brother Diuma snapped awake and swung the abbot's long staff at him. It was only due to the fact that Diuma was upon his knees and Oswald on his feet that the blow missed, and Diuma was on the point of swinging again, when he finally heard Oswald's voice and he dropped the staff and, still on his knees, shuffled towards the king.

"You came," he cried, all but grasping Oswald's knees in the extremity of his joy. "You came at last."

Oswald bent down and helped the monk to his feet. Diuma stood swaying in front of him, the words babbling from his mouth.

"I have not slept for four days," he said. "First I buried the dead, then the last three days and nights I have been standing watch over the body of Abbot Sigeberht, protecting it."

"Protecting him from what?" asked Oswald.

"Those who would take holy relics from his body." Diuma pointed to where the earth was scraped away in a bowl-shaped depression. "They dig the earth from where he fell, and if I had not been here, they would have rendered him limb from limb. Already, when my back was turned or, God forgive me, I slept, they have taken three of his fingers and a toe, but no more. Now you are here, no more." Diuma stumbled and Oswald held him up.

"Who is taking relics?"

"Everyone." Diuma peered around blearily, as if seeing relic hunters hiding behind each tree. "All the people knew him to be a holy man and a king, and now he has died a martyr's death, they all seek his blessing and a piece of him for their own."

"We will take him back to his monastery. The brothers will care for him there. But as for the rest of this…" Oswald looked around the battlefield. Although Diuma had buried most of the bodies, still a few men lay scattered about it, and the debris of battle littered the field. "For the rest of this, Penda will pay."

Chapter 6

"Will you take the new god – my God?" Oswald asked the question of Eowa.

The Mercian, leaning over the side of the boat as it entered the mouth of the Humber, did not turn round, but said, "This... may not be the best time to ask." His shoulders heaved, and there came the characteristic sound of retching.

"I must have answer before we come to land," said Oswald. "For if you will, then I will make you king in Mercia."

Eowa turned to him. He was still pale, but the nausea that had settled upon him through their journey up the coast from the Great Fen had of a sudden left him.

"How?"

"By battle, if needs be. But that would leave you a poor kingdom, with few thegns to call upon in its defence. However, I do not believe that will be necessary. From what Brother Diuma has been telling me, there is little love for Penda among the thegns of Mercia; he is no Iclinga, and they accept him as king only because there is no one else. We will give them someone else. We will give them you; if you will accept baptism."

"But how will you bring this about? My brother will fight you and he is a skilful warrior and a deadly one, as Ecgric would testify if he yet lived."

"Now is the time to act. I will summon all my allies, in particular all those that lie about Mercia, and we will march upon the kingdom together, in such numbers that all will see the hopelessness of battle. But as we march, I shall send messengers summoning the witan of Mercia in your name, with promise of safety for all who attend; for you are ætheling and have such right. Then you shall speak, and offer yourself to the witan as king in place of Penda, with the promise also that I, and all my allies, will withdraw once you are king."

"And what of my brother, if the witan takes me as king?"

"That would be for you, and it, to decide."

"And for this you would have me follow your god in place of the gods of my fathers?"

"Yes."

Eowa smiled. "I do not feel sick any longer," he said.

*

Aidan turned to Oswald. They sat at the baptismal feast for Eowa, in Oswald's hall in York. The Mercian, clad in baptismal white, received with broad smiles the gifts that were laid at his feet.

"Your brother and Princess Rhieienmelth did not come?"

"They sent word. My son took ill, and they thought it best not to travel. But they have sent gifts." Oswald paused, looking north towards the distant hills of Bernicia where his brother was. "He is not coming when we march against Penda. He said there is unrest among the Gododdin and the Picts; he said he will guard the marches."

"Your brother means you no ill, Oswald," said Aidan.

"I have seen how affairs worked out between Penda and Eowa."

"Oswiu is not Eowa, and you are not Penda."

"That is true. But I have seen little of my brother these past two years."

"And he has seen less of you. Mayhap he fears you turn against him."

Oswald turned to Aidan. "He knows I would not do that."

"Does he?" Aidan paused. "But that is not what I would speak of now." He nodded towards Eowa. "I have baptized him, but I fear that he does not understand that which he has entered into."

"Did any of us?" Oswald smiled. "I know I did not."

"That is true. But I am concerned that Eowa has sought baptism to gain a throne and for no other reason."

"He has." Oswald looked at the Mercian, still receiving the blessings and congratulations of the Northumbrian thegns. "He would as cheerfully swim the Ouse in winter. My hope is that while the river would dry from his skin, the water of baptism will enter his soul." He turned back to Aidan. "At the very least, this will mean a king favourable to our faith upon the throne in Mercia."

"True. But Penda, though he is pagan, still permitted Brother Diuma to preach in Mercia."

"For a while. Long enough for him to learn much of the kingdom, but not long enough for him to win any to the faith."

Eowa, having received the blessings of Oswald's thegns and retainers, turned to the high table and came to stand before the High King and Bishop Aidan. He made the courtesy to them.

"While yet your hostage, you have set me free," he said.

Oswald glanced at Aidan, to see what he made of Eowa's comment, but the monk stayed looking at the Mercian.

"Now, though it seems I have no right to ask more of you, I have one further request of you both."

"What do you ask of us?" said Oswald.

"When I return to Mercia and sit upon its throne, I ask that I may take with me Brother Diuma, who already has knowledge of my people and their ways, that he may preach the new faith to my people and bring them to its light." Eowa looked to them. "What say you, my lord and my bishop?"

"For myself, I would be right glad," said Oswald, "but in this matter we must ask Bishop Aidan, for he is Brother Diuma's lord."

"If he is willing then I am willing."

Eowa made the courtesy to them both again.

"I thank thee," he said. "I thank thee, beloved lords of heart and soul." Then, turning to Acca, he cried, "A song! A song for my feast."

As the scop began strumming the lyre, Oswald took the chance to speak to Aidan further.

"Mayhap the Spirit has indeed entered into him. I have not seen Eowa in such light before."

"I trust that this be so." Aidan gazed at him, and his eyes were narrow. "At least there will be word of what he does from Brother Diuma."

"Eowa must know that too. Mayhap he seeks to allay our fears."
Aidan nodded. "It is a start."

*

The columns of riders, coming from north and south and east,
rode into Mercia, converging upon the great palace of the kings at
Tamworth. The armies of Northumbria, of Wessex, of the remnants
of the East Angles, and the men of the East Saxons rode against
Mercia, accompanied by small parties sent by the kings of the
north, riding with Oswald. And as they came, horsemen shadowed
them from hilltop and forest, watching, sending word, but making
no move against them. Oswald rode at the forefront of the men
of Northumbria, with Bran sometimes upon his shoulder and
sometimes upon his saddle, but most often flying above, circling
the column and announcing their arrival upon the wind. With
Oswald rode Bassus, warmaster, and Eowa, and wherever they
stopped, at farm or hamlet or village, they proclaimed Eowa king
to the people who stood silently watching, waiting beside plough
and loom, and none gainsaid his kingship nor opposed their
progress. Messages were sent to the great men of the kingdom,
the men whose halls dotted the land, nestled in valleys or stark
upon ridgetops, proclaiming Eowa king and summoning them to
witan in Tamworth, and as the columns progressed they saw, riding
before them, the concentration of the men of Mercia into the ever
decreasing circle made by their advance.

"I do not think he is going to fight." Bassus rode up beside
Oswald. Scouts had brought word that over the next rise the way
to Tamworth lay open, with the great hall gleaming gold by the
riversmeet, where it rose upon its high platform. Their sharp eyes
told further that the compound around the hall, surrounded by
ditch and high fence, seethed with men and horses, like an ant nest
poked by boys bent on mischief, but no ambushes or traps waited.

"That was the idea," said Oswald. His eyes narrowed. "It seems to
be working; mayhap too well."

"Word has come from Cynegils: he approaches from the south

without opposition. So too report the East Saxons and the East Angles."

Oswald nodded, then looked to his warmaster. "Have you ever known a plan proceed so well, Bassus?"

"No. But there must needs be a first time for everything. Mayhap this is the first time war goes to plan."

"I trust it not. Penda would not go so quietly to defeat."

"But has ever a king assembled so great a host in these lands?"

As Bassus spoke, they breasted the crest of the hill and saw before them the great bowl of land, crossed by the rivers Anker and Tame, in which lay the great hall of the kings of Mercia. And advancing upon it from south and west, riding down the further hill slopes, were more columns of riders, looking at such distance like dark snakes upon the hillsides, dark save for the fire glitter of sunlight on spear point and armour.

"Not since the days of the emperors," said Oswald. "My uncle had a standard bearer advance before him bearing the tufa as symbol of his power and authority. We must recover it from Penda and ride behind it in future."

"How do you know Cadwallon did not take it?"

"It was not among the treasures we recovered from his army. He sent little back to Gwynedd, no doubt fearing others might use it in his absence, and he would have kept such a sign with him had he taken it."

"But he was lord to Penda; Cadwallon would not have passed it to Penda."

Oswald nodded. "You are right. I wonder. Maybe my uncle's wife took it with her when she went into exile. It would be a token for her son."

"He died, did he not?"

"Yes. Far from home, among the Franks." Oswald shook his head. "How often we die far from our own lands. Maybe Æthelburh has the tufa still, and it is raised among the Franks across the Narrow Sea. Still, we will talk on this later. Now, we must deal with Penda." Heeling his horse, Oswald urged it on, down the hill towards the distant gleaming hall, and his men streamed behind him.

*

"I make this..." Bassus paused to count upon his fingers "...fifty days." He lifted his hood to peer suspiciously up at the sky. In the west, tears of blue appeared among tattered grey trailers of cloud, but above their heads the rain still fell, dripping off the wax-soaked hood onto his face. Around the camp, men took what shelter they could in tents and makeshift shelters made from poles of willow and alder and lashed bundles of rushes, while the horses stood flank to flank and steaming.

"My brother is a stubborn man," said Eowa. "And a cunning one. He thinks to outwait us, so while we advanced upon his hall, he stripped the land about bare of food, that we might starve while we waited."

"Just as well we thought of that, then," said Bassus, pointing through the mist of rain to the boat rowing upriver, set to join the other vessels moored up beside the camp. It would be bringing supplies: food for men and horses alike, loaded from the royal estates that lay upon the river routes from the Humber and the Tyne. "When I say we, it was the king who thought on this; I was certain it would all be over by now: a march, a battle, a king." Bassus shrugged. "I was wrong."

"I wish you had not been wrong," said Oswald, shaking the rain from his cloak as he stepped inside the tent. At least the drumming upon the roof was lessening, suggesting that the break in weather presaged by the clearing western skies would soon arrive. "But I feared you might be. Penda is not one to do what we want. But I do not think we shall have long to wait now." Oswald turned and gestured a man into the tent.

"Sidrac!" Eowa rose from his stool as the man, grizzled and scarred in the manner of an experienced warrior, entered.

Sidrac went down upon one knee in front of Eowa.

"Lord," he said, bowing his head and offering up his hand.

Eowa took it and, holding it, looked to Oswald and Bassus. "This is Sidrac, one of the great thegns of Mercia. He holds a hundred hides of land upon this bank of the Severn, another hundred at watersmeet, and more throughout the kingdom." Eowa, by his glance to the two other men, indicated how important a matter this was. "What reason brings you from the king's side, Sidrac? If my brother should gain knowledge of this, he would surely kill you, and like as not it would not be a pleasant death."

"I would have met death, and willingly, at your brother's side if he had done as I urged, as we all urged, and come forth to meet you in battle when you first set siege upon us." Sidrac looked up at Eowa. "But he would not come forth, telling us to let hunger and disease wreak havoc upon your armies first. But now nigh two months have passed, and it is we who starve, and shiver with fever, so that we bare have strength to stand, let alone fight, and yet Penda will hear no counsel from his witan." Sidrac looked around, to Oswald and Bassus. "If you had come to put upon the throne an outsider, a Northumbrian or a West Saxon, we would have fought you, however weak we were. But Eowa has as much claim to the throne as Penda, and all men say how he accepted the terms of the last peace, and offered himself as hostage for us. So now I offer myself for you, as messenger to the witan. Will you be our king, and hold true to the thegns of Mercia who are ready to give you this throne?"

Eowa looked to Oswald, then back to Sidrac.

"I will."

The thegn bent over the hands holding his own and kissed them, then rose to his feet.

"We will have a new king," he said.

"Hold." Oswald held up his hand. "What of Penda? He will not accept such actions, even should the whole witan turn against him, and I wager there will be some who keep pledge with him."

"You don't know my brother as I do," said Eowa. "He will not die if he might live. Let him ride forth with those men who hold to him, and go into exile, and he will stand aside."

"But would you have your brother an exile? Penda is an enemy to be wary of."

Eowa smiled grimly. "Who said he would reach exile?"

Oswald shook his head. "If I had given word, I would not break it."

"Nor would I have thee break it; for the pledge of the High King is sacred indeed. But the men of Mercia, the thegns taking me as king, they will not have made pledge in this matter." Eowa looked to Sidrac. "I think it would be as well to leave no vengeance to be taken in this matter. What say you, old friend?"

The warrior held out his hand, and Eowa grasped it.

"I will have men ready to pursue him once he has passed through the High King's lines," said Sidrac.

"He will head west, to Gwynedd. They are yet his allies, and would offer him exile."

"We will overtake him in the forest of the Wreocensæte. Not many men love Penda; there will be few riding with him on the iron road to exile."

Oswald held up his hand. "I would not hear this. I will give my pledge to Penda that he may have safe passage. If you would plot against him, do it not where I can hear, that my pledge be not tainted."

Eowa looked at him in surprise. "You have heard already."

"No more. Maybe it were better we let Penda go into exile."

"If that is what you wish, lord?"

Oswald paused in thought. "Yes," he said. "It is what I wish."

Eowa looked searchingly at the High King. "Very well," he said. "Sidrac, give pledge to my brother that he may pass unharmed through our lines and ride into exile." He looked to Oswald for confirmation, then added, "Tell him he has until the sun breaks through the clouds to leave."

*

The gates of the royal compound swung open as the first light of the sun to break through the clouds' defences streamed out over the plain of Tamworth. Through the gates, the great hall appeared, high upon its platform, the crossed beams of its roof making great gold-painted horns upon the sky. Without the gates, making a passage for those who would exit, stood two lines of warriors, the men of Northumbria to one side, the men of Wessex and the East Saxons and the East Angles upon the other, armed and shielded and glittering in the rain-washed light.

In the midst of his line, with the horses picketed close behind, stood Oswald, with Bassus to one side and Eowa upon the other. As the gates opened, the water-swelled wood creaking on its hinges, they turned to see what, and who, would emerge.

There, seated upon a horse with a guard of but a handful of men, was Penda, once warmaster then king in Mercia. The sun, shining from the west, cast deep shadows over his face. Behind Penda, arranged in a great half-circle in the compound, stood the witan of Mercia, faces blank and hard as they expelled their king.

Penda did not look back. Heeling his horse into motion, he rode forth, out of the gates, the few men remaining true to him following in line behind. He looked neither left nor right, but rode between the lines of warriors. They watched in silence, the only sound the hoof-fall of the horses and the stamp and snort of the tethered animals behind their own lines.

Riding level with Oswald, Penda drew his horse to a stop. He turned to look, but his gaze, heavy with hatred, settled not upon Oswald, but went to his brother Eowa.

"I will kill you," he said.

"You should have done so before. Brother."

"I will not make the mistake again." Penda glanced at Oswald. "I hope you trust your brother; then I know you shall fall."

"Get hence, while my pledge holds my patience."

Penda looked to his brother again. "How long, think you, until I come for you? Count the days, brother, count the days."

Then Penda heeled his horse, and it broke into a canter and then gallop; he and his men swept away, heading west, towards the distant line of hills that marked the marches of the kingdom and the land of his exile.

Taking his horse, Oswald mounted it and rode to the gates of the compound, but did not enter. Within, through the open gates, he saw the men of the witan, Sidrac among them, looking out upon him with all the tension of traditional enemies laying their stronghold and their lives open to their foes.

"Men of Mercia," he called. "Men of Mercia, come forth and greet your king. A man known to you, a man most throne-worthy, a man who brings you my friendship. Men of Mercia, come forth and bow before your king!"

And they came, some carrying the judgment seat of the kings, and they made courtesy to Eowa and placed the judgment seat before him and sat him upon it, while the acclaim they raised to him resounded over the plain even to the surrounding hills.

Chapter 7

The marram grass, brown tipped after its season of growth, whipped in the wind as Oswald climbed the steps from the beach to his stronghold atop the great rock at Bamburgh. The waves broke white against the Farne Islands, and fugitive birds flew past, seeking shelter from the coming storm. Oswald pulled his cloak around his shoulders and his hood down over his head. He was weary, and his head was bowed as he came to the top of the steps and the gate into the stronghold.

"Welcome, lord."

Oswald bare raised his head in acknowledgment before continuing the weary climb upwards to the plateau atop the rock, circled with walls and these surmounted by wooden pilings.

He entered the hall. Slaves, alerted to his arrival, rushed to raise fires and light tapers against the early winter gloom. The few men in the hall rose to greet him.

Coifi, squatting by the embers of the fire the slaves kept burning through all seasons, rose, pulling his raven-feather cloak tight about him to seal in the heat he had embraced. Acca, wrapped in a blanket and with a cup of hot ale beside him on the table, wiped a hand across red eyes and redder nose, and rose as well.

"Where is everyone?" Oswald stopped, looking around the hall.

"You – you sent them to their halls, lord," said Coifi.

Oswald stopped in thought. "Yes. I did."

"Dould dyou wand me to ding for dyou?" Acca asked, his voice thick with phlegm.

"No." Oswald went to warm himself by the fire. He held his hands to the flames and rubbed them together. "I can't get warm," he said.

"There is wine, lord," said Coifi.

"Yes. A cup of warm wine." Oswald sat down while Coifi went to fetch the wine. He gave it to him and watched as Oswald drank. "Do you need aught for the poor?" Oswald put his hands inside his cloak, holding them to his sides, that they might warm there.

"No, I have all they need; it was a good harvest this year and there is little hunger as yet." Coifi's head jerked sideways as he peered into the red heart of the fire. "But – but winter is coming." His head snapped to the ceiling, where coils of smoke roiled among the rafters. "It will be a bitter season."

"Dow are dyour mudder and dister?" asked Acca.

"They are well." Oswald looked into the fire. "Would that they were with me. But they have the house in Coldingham to set properly under their rule. And my mother grows old; frost whites her hair and she would remain in one place, not wandering the kingdom as I do." The High King returned to the silence of the fire, brooding upon its depths.

"Dhen I am dell, I will ding of your dlory, lord," said Acca. "I have a dew dong."

"He has sung it to me already, lord," added Coifi. "Many times. It is very fine. A song for the king whose rule stretches over all this land. From Kent in the south to the painted peoples in the north, all acknowledge you as king."

"Dore dan the demperors!" exclaimed Acca.

"More than the emperors…" Oswald looked up from the fire. "The emperors have gone from this land, and all they have left lies in ruins."

The scop and the almoner who was once a priest looked at each other. The king was in a dark and fey mood, and there was no one present to lift him from it.

"Des?" said Acca, eventually.

"All that they raised up, emperors over the whole world, moulders and decays, and I strive to emulate them who were as far above me in might as the Cheviot is above this rock where we sit. I would do better, much better, laying this aside and seeking a kingdom that does not fall to ruin. Seeking after the kingdom that Sigeberht laid aside his throne for…"

"... and you know what happened to Sigeberht." Aidan took his friend's hands in his own. They sat in the bare whiteness of his cell on the Holy Island.

"But that was Penda. I have dealt with him. Eowa has the throne now." Oswald looked up into Aidan's face. "Tell me I have not read the signs aright. My wife is dead. I have secured the kingdom, I have given you land and more to found houses throughout the realm, that the people might hear the news of life and live by it. My mother and sister raise further houses, and set rule over them. My brother... my brother rules the marches and I see him rarely now; but he will rule well. He has had much practice."

"There is one you haven't spoken of. What of your son?"

"My son. My brother raises my son, and he has pledged to take him as his own."

Aidan squeezed Oswald's hands tighter. "That I do not understand. Why did you give him so young? You could have had him by your side – it was no great matter to find a wet nurse to care for him."

Oswald pulled his hands from Aidan's grasp. "I – I could not see him. He had too much of Cyniburh about him. So I gave him into another's hands, that grief be removed from me." The king looked out of the window. The abbot's cell did not rate the luxury of a shutter, Aidan closing the small window against wind and rain with a square of sacking tied to the inside wall.

"I desired my brother's wife with a great desire, and I fear her heart was moved towards me as well. Lest in my grief I turn too much towards her, I gave into her keeping my son, knowing that she would keep him for me, as token of me, but knowing also that so long as she held him, I would not seek her out. But doing that, I have lost those that were dearest to me: my brother and Rhieienmelth."

The king barked out a laugh, short and bitter. "My scop sings of my glory, greater than any king of this land, but in my glory the only friend I found was a hostage, the brother of my bitterest enemy, and now even he has gone. I have set him to rule in Mercia and, setting the kingdom to peace, put myself alone." Oswald turned back to Aidan. "Would you have me know no peace, old friend?"

The bishop of Lindisfarne stood up. "When you came to us on the Holy Isle, you were young, wild. Abbot Ségéne, seeing you, said you were like a young hawk, and he set to teaching you, to training you, that when he set you to fly, you would fly high. He turned you loose, he set you to fly, and you have indeed flown high… But at what cost! No, I would not deny you the peace you desire, my old friend, and I believe you would find it here."

But Oswald shook his head. "I cannot stay here. Not within sight of Bamburgh, seeming ever a reproof to my brother and a temptation to those who would whisper against him. No, if I go, I must return whence I came, to Iona and the holy house there. Do you think the abbot would take me?"

Aidan smiled. "Not if you took Bran with you."

"He alone of my friends has remained ever with me. I could not put him aside now."

"There are other houses, deep inland, where a man might go and be forgotten by all the outside world."

"That is what I would wish. To go and be forgotten by men."

Aidan nodded. "I know whereof you speak. I would lay aside the bishop's staff and be done with farmers' complaints and fishermen's fears and the jealousies of monks. But some burdens may not be cast aside."

"I have made the way smooth for my brother. There is no reason he cannot be king after me – the witan of Bernicia will certainly accept him; I judge the witan of Deira would acclaim him too."

"Bernicia, yes. Deira, I am not so sure. There are other æthelings yet in Deira the witan may turn to; Oswine for one. He is loved by many there, and your brother is seldom seen south of the Tweed."

"Even more reason I should lay aside the throne, that Oswiu might claim it before Oswine has chance to further stake claim to the throne in Deira."

"Have you asked him?"

"Asked who?"

"Oswiu. Have you asked your brother if he would be king?"

"No."

Aidan smiled. "Don't you think you should?"

"No one asked me."

"If I remember right, you were asked many times and you did your best not to be king."

"Much use did it do me."

"Then let us send messengers to Oswiu; let us ask if he would be king, and then decide. What say you?"

Oswald fell silent. Standing at the little window, he looked out over the short-cropped grass around the monastery to the sea and beyond, where his stronghold sat at junction of earth and sea and sky.

"There's a ship coming," he said. It ran across the white-topped waves, sail recklessly spread despite the high sea. "It's in a hurry."

*

"My lord, King Eowa sends word." Bassus, chest heaving from his sprint up the beach to the monastery, stood in front of Oswald and Aidan.

"'King' Eowa. It still sounds strange to hear that." Oswald nodded towards the sea, now whipping to a storm. "You came fast, Bassus, outrunning the storm. It must be urgent."

"It is, lord. Penda has raised an army from his allies in Gwynedd and, taking Eowa by surprise, holds him besieged in his hall at Maserfield in the shadow of Selattyn Hill on the banks of the River Morda. He begs you to come to his aid, to come quickly, for he has not the men to hold for long in such a place."

"The fool!" Oswald pounded fist into palm. "He thought himself secure. How many men has he?"

"The messenger said but thirty."

"And Penda?"

"Not many more. Fifty or so."

"That is enough. How many days to get here?"

"The messenger took boat as soon as he might, and the winds have been strong. Three days."

"How many days did Eowa say he could hold?"

"A week to ten days."

"Then we have at most seven days, at worst four to reach him."

Aidan held out his hand and took Oswald's arm. "Are you sure you should go to him?"

"He is pledged to me and I to him." Oswald smiled ruefully. "And I am yet king."

Aidan squeezed Oswald's arm more tightly. "Send to Oswiu. Send to your brother: call him with you."

Oswald shook his head. "There is no time. Besides, he has been upon the marches these past two years. Why would he come?"

"He is your brother."

"He is a king in all but name. Why should he come? After this is over, I will give him the name too."

"Send for him. You were going to send to ask if he would be king. Send message also to ride with you to Maserfield."

"I cannot wait for him. But yes, ask him, if he would, to come after me." Oswald stopped. "It would be good to ride with him again." He shook his head, as if trying to shake it free of doubt. "I do not think he will come."

"He will." Aidan squeezed his arm. "He will."

Oswald smiled sadly, then unpeeled the fingers from his arm. "Maybe he will, but there is no time to wait for him. Send him after me, Aidan." Oswald's smile turned to the warmth of memory. "Tell him: when we were young I always had to clear up his mess. This time I am clearing up my own."

*

The courtyard of the stronghold seethed with activity: men sharpening swords and spears on whetstones, grooms rubbing down horses and cleaning harnesses, slaves storing food and the supplies necessary for a swift, lightly provisioned expedition. In the great hall, Oswald turned to Bassus. He had returned from the Holy Island but an hour ago, his boat racing the storm wind over the white-capped waves, and set all his household preparing to go to the aid of Eowa.

"Send word to every thegn within a day's journey to bring the men they can, horsed and armed, to be here for the first tide tomorrow. We sail then, and will not wait."

"We will miss a lot of men from such haste," said Bassus. "Can we not wait another day?"

"No." Oswald pointed around the hall, where his most experienced warriors sat upon benches, backs to tables and swords over knees, oiling blades and stropping them to their finest cutting edges. "We have enough men here, but any who can join us by tomorrow will be welcome. They must be ready to travel fast and hard though. We sail down the coast, take the Humber and then row as far upstream on the River Trent as we can, before cutting west to the River Morda and following that to Eowa's hall. If the weather holds, and no storms come, we can make the journey in two days. If the weather breaks, and winter storms may come at any time, it will take us a week or longer. I cannot wait."

"Very well. I will go and send messengers."

Oswald nodded. "Thank you, Bassus. You have been a good warmaster to me."

The warrior held his step for a moment. "And so I will remain, lord."

"Yes. Yes, of course."

As the warmaster set to his duties, Oswald went from the hall to the church that Edwin had begun and he had had completed within the stronghold. Going in, he found it empty save for a young monk who had been detailed from the Holy Island to match in the king's stronghold the Great Work the community of monks did on Lindisfarne. The monk sprang from his knees when he saw Oswald, but the king waved him back to his task.

"Stay," he said. "I would pray also."

And taking a stool, Oswald sat with his hands upturned upon his knees, and slowly found the peace that often came to him in prayer.

*

"Acca." Coifi tapped the scop on the shoulder, waking him from a doze.

"What? Yes?" Acca looked round wildly, then saw Coifi. "Oh, it's you."

"Doom. I see the king's doom." The priest's eyes rolled, threatening to turn up into trance, but he slapped himself viciously, once, twice, across the face. "No. No, I must stay," he said, and though the words were out loud, he seemed to speak to himself, or to some presence only he could see.

"Not again," said Acca, yawning. "Whenever the king goes forth, you always see his doom. Why don't you get some rest like me while all the warriors are busy getting themselves pretty for battle?"

"This is different." Coifi grasped Acca's arm and leaned to him, his eyes wild but steady. "The sight. It came to me again. I saw it, in the fire fall, in the wave crash, in cloud and rain and the whisper of men's voices and the call of ravens. If we let the king go, he goes to his doom. We must stop him."

"Do you really think he's going to listen to you any more this time than all the times previously?"

"That is why you must help me."

"Me?"

"Yes. In truth, the king might not listen to me, but if you speak too, he will give me hearing."

"What am I going to say to him? Coifi, who has prophesied disaster every time you've set forth with a warband, says that you're going to meet your doom; but this time it's different?"

"Yes. Say that. Say anything. He must listen. Please."

Acca looked up at the man staring big-eyed into his face, fingers convulsively clutching his arm.

"You really mean it, don't you?"

"Yes."

Acca sighed. "Very well. I'll try." He stood up, brushing down his tunic and pulling his cloak around his shoulders. "Where is the king?"

"He is in the church."

Acca nodded. "Let's go."

*

"Lord."

Oswald did not stir. And Acca, seeing him sitting thus, his eyes closed and his face clear of worry, did not speak again, but looked upon him.

Coifi nudged the scop.

Acca held finger to lips then turned back to the king.

"Lord, your pardon."

Slowly, Oswald opened his eyes, and there was a light in them that Acca had not seen before, as of the sun at the ending of a rain-soaked day, shining through the final break of clouds before the onset of night.

"Your pardon, lord, but Coifi would speak with you. I – I know he has oft times seen doom, but – but never before have I seen him like this. Will you hear him?"

Oswald slowly rose from the stool. The solitary monk continued his chant, the Latin words, seldom heard on this rock even in the days of the emperors, for their wall lay far to the south, now spreading forth over land and out to sea every day.

"Are the poor provided for, Coifi?"

"Yes, yes, lord."

Oswald looked at him, seeing the wildness in the priest's eyes, the film that came over them when he saw into the windings of fate and the weavings of the fate singers.

"What would you say to me?"

Coifi stepped forward, so his face all but touched the king's.

"Do not go," he said. "I have seen. Thy doom lies ahead. Do not go to it, lord. Stay with us. Live." He reached out, laying hand to Oswald's arm. "Do not go, lord."

Oswald laid his own hand upon Coifi's.

"If you have seen doom, then how may I avoid it? Stay, and it will surely follow me. Go and I go without fear and in fulfilment of my pledge."

"Then wait a while, lord. Gather more men, send for your brother; go as you went before into Mercia, at the head of many armies."

"Then Eowa would be dead, and I would have failed in my promise to him. Besides," and here Oswald smiled sadly at them, "kings do not live forever."

"Lord, please, I beg you." Coifi began to get down on his knees, but Oswald raised him up.

"You have served me well, Coifi. Do not be afraid. Should this be my doom, I will meet it. But for my part, I do not think it my end; Penda has but few men, the leavings of Cadwallon scraped from Gwynedd. It will be no great matter to defeat him and keep my pledge to Eowa. Fear more for the journey! We must hurry, so we sail tomorrow, praying no storm blows up to wreck us upon the coast before we can make the Humber. Is that what you see for me, Coifi?"

"No." The priest shook his head. "No, that is not the doom I fear."

"It is the doom I most fear." Oswald stepped from the priest. "I must go."

But Coifi stepped after him. "Take me with you. I would go as well; then if doom overtake you, I shall suffer it too."

Oswald shook his head. "No. We must travel fast; there is neither space nor time for any save my warriors."

"I would not hold you back, lord."

"I know that of your will you would not do so. But with you among us, my attention would be divided, and you are not the horseman I shall need once we leave our ships and strike across country."

"Lord…"

"No. I honour your faithfulness, but stay and pray for our return. I must go." Oswald turned and made his way from the church.

Acca stared at Coifi as the priest looked to where the king had gone.

"You truly believe what you told him, don't you?"

"Yes," said the priest.

"Well, we'd better follow him then."

Coifi, in turn, stared at the scop.

"You believe me?"

"I don't know if I believe you. But I do know one thing: I have no intention of becoming a lordless man once again."

*

"Whose idea was this?" Acca, his lips blue and his fingers bluer, looked out from the cape he held round his body to where Coifi sat on the other side of the boat, the wind blowing into his face as it blew against the scop's back. The shipmaster, snarling at the weather, held station on the steering oar, his face frosted, and when he was not snarling at the weather he was swearing at the passengers who had persuaded him to take to the sea in this season through the presentation of an unfeasibly large amount of silver. Now, as the waters of the Humber swirled around the boat, he was wondering if the silver would find its final home at the bottom of the estuary.

Coifi gave no answer to Acca's question. He accepted his position on the wind-lashed side of the boat – the master needed one of the passengers there to balance the light vessel – as he accepted the vision that had driven him in pursuit of the king. They had found the boat and the boatman not long after Oswald left with his men, and for the first part of the journey the sails of the king's boats were visible as they rounded headlands. But the king had drawn away from them, and the winter clouds had drawn in, blowing cold from the east until all feeling had left the further reaches of Coifi's body and he subsisted in a small core of vision, turned to the front of the boat and searching after the path taken by the king. The last glimpse they'd had of Oswald's boats was when they rounded Spurn Head and entered the Humber. Now they followed the king upstream, riding the inflowing tide and using the easterly wind, but the squalls of rain and sleet cast curtains over the upper reaches of the estuary, hiding Oswald's boats from their vision.

"Curse this for the game of a fool," said the shipmaster. "I'm landing." And he began to push the steering oar out, to bring the boat towards the nearer, southern shore.

"You will not," said Coifi, and he got unsteadily to his feet, movement burning his limbs. He leaned out over the side of the boat, bringing its low lip perilously close to the wave tops.

"What are you doing? Get back," cried the shipmaster.

"I will swamp this boat if you turn to shore." The priest stared straight and level at the shipmaster as he pushed even further outwards, heeling the boat over.

"Y-you're mad."

Coifi leaned further.

"Right, right, we go on." The shipmaster brought the steering oar back to the hull, and the boat straightened, heading up estuary after the king's vessels. "Mad."

Acca looked over to Coifi as the priest settled back down.

"Would you really have capsized us?" he asked.

Coifi looked to the prow of the boat.

"There," he said, pointing.

Between the squalls, far upstream, were the sails of Oswald's boats.

*

The messenger found Oswiu and Rhieienmelth in Carlisle. The king, Rhoedd, lay ill, and some whispered that he was dying, but for his part Oswiu would not believe the old man dead until he had been underground for at least three days. As he left the king's room, where Rhoedd wheezed noisily but where his eyes still flicked knowingly from his daughter to his son-in-law, Oswiu revised that to a week. The old man would cheat death yet.

Coming into the hall, he saw Rhieienmelth. In truth, he spent more time with her father than she did; after a few minutes, she would jump up and pace, then a few minutes longer and she would leave, saying the children, one of their own two or Oswald's, needed her, leaving Oswiu to hear the old man's talk of past glories. He had come to enjoy those times, for Rhoedd was a good storyteller and he did not let the reality of war – the slips on muddy ground, the vomiting with fear, the sheer fortune of it all – get in the way of the stories he told. And in between, when Rhoedd slipped into sleep, it gave Oswiu time he barely ever had otherwise: time alone, where he might think.

He often thought now of his wife, and how she looked upon Oswald, and held him, when he had turned to her. It was always Oswald. Always. He did not have to do anything; he did not have to seek people's love. It was given to him. Even Rhieienmelth's. Even his wife's.

Oswiu had not spoken of this to her. It was as it was. She could no more help it than any of the others; it was as inevitable as the sun rising. But, unspoken, it had raised a barrier between them, a barrier that had form and flesh: Æthelwald, Oswald's son. Rhieienmelth raised him as one of her own and so, in truth, did Oswiu. Now the boy was growing, able to walk and talk and even sit upon a small pony. He had his father's face but the temper of his mother, easily roused but swiftly abated, and he seldom asked after his father, for Rhieienmelth was his mother now and, being young, he had yet little need for his father. Already he could see his own son, a quiet boy, withdrawing from confrontations whenever Æthelwald demanded the wooden swords they played with, or to ride first when they made their way from one estate to another. Rhieienmelth treated them both as her own, showing no more favour to one than the other, but sometimes Oswiu wished he might see her favour the son of their flesh over the son of his brother.

"Oswiu." Rhieienmelth stood as he entered the hall. "A messenger from Aidan, from the king."

Oswiu nodded. That was how she always put it now. It was always "the king", never "your brother" or "Oswald". When had that changed?

He joined her, and the messenger, by the look of him a young man yet to profess his vows on the Holy Island, made courtesy to them.

"Bishop Aidan sends greetings and his blessings."

"What news?"

"Urgent news, lord. King Oswald goes to the aid of Eowa, king of Mercia. Bishop Aidan sends message that you go also to Eowa's aid, that you might there meet the king and help him against Penda."

"Penda? Where is he and when did Oswald leave?"

As the messenger explained, Oswiu glanced at Rhieienmelth. She sat forward, listening, concentrating intensely, as if through the messenger's words she might see Oswald's presence.

"It is too late," said Oswiu when the messenger had finished. "I would never catch him."

"But you must go," said Rhieienmelth. "The king has asked it."

"Did he?" Oswiu turned to the messenger. "Does this message come from the bishop or the king?"

"The bishop, lord. But as I understand it the king did ask for you to come to him."

Oswiu nodded. "Very well. As my brother asks, no doubt I should go, but I fear it will be in vain. We could hardly hope to get to Maserfield before he gets there, and if we are late then it will surely be over, and Penda's head will be on a stake."

"But you must go," said Rhieienmelth.

"You would have me chase from one end of the country to the other at my brother's command. But how to go. By horse from here, in this season, it would take us many days, and Oswald already has the start on us by three days. By sea – no, that would be too dangerous. And besides, once we entered the estuary of the Dee and made landfall, we would have to ride through territory the king of Gwynedd still lays claim to. That would be a perilous journey for the small party of men I could take with me."

As Oswiu finished speaking, the door keeper of the hall entered, with a travel-stained and snow-speckled man in his train.

"Lord, a messenger from King Eowa of Mercia has arrived."

The man pulled back his hood and, seeing him, Oswiu leapt to his feet in surprise and delight.

"Brother Diuma!"

The monk smiled in return. "It has been a long and difficult journey to find you, lord. But I have made it. And I have a message, an urgent message, from King Eowa."

"Though we delight in seeing you, you need hardly have struggled through the winter snow to get here with it," said Rhieienmelth, "for we received the message from Bishop Aidan. To join with the king and deliver Eowa from the siege that Penda has laid upon his hall in Maserfield."

Brother Diuma looked to Rhieienmelth and then to Oswiu, and his face cracked as if it were a pot.

"That is not my message," he said.

*

"Let me get this straight," said Oswiu. "When you left Eowa two weeks ago, he was at Tamworth, and he told you to seek me out and ask that I come to him there, for he had received word that Penda had raised an army and marched upon the great hall at Tamworth?"

"Yes, yes. I do not understand," said Brother Diuma.

"Did Eowa send other messengers, to my brother?"

"Yes, but I thought they took the same message."

Oswiu shook his head. "They did not. We got the message Eowa sent to Oswald, but we received it through Bishop Aidan. Eowa never thought it would get to me as well."

"But I still don't understand," said Brother Diuma. "Why would he ask you to come to one place and the king to another?"

"Oh, I understand," said Oswiu. "I understand all too well."

"Treachery," said Rhieienmelth.

"We go by boat," said Oswiu. "To Maserfield. Please God we can catch him before he gets there."

*

"There's a reason we don't fight in winter." Oswald rode at the front of the column, with Bassus beside him. They had rowed as far upstream of the Trent as they could before mooring the boats with a small guard and setting off cross country on horse. Oswald looked to the warmaster alongside him. "A good reason."

"You mean apart from the cold, the wind, the rain, the mud and," Bassus looked up as the first flakes spun through the air, "oh, joy, the snow?"

"Yes, apart from those. The day is too short. That is why we don't war in winter time."

Bassus pointed ahead. The land in the distance was already being smoothed away under the snow. The sky loured darkly overhead and, if sun there was above the clouds, there was no sign of it below them, only grey and the approaching white.

"Should we make camp?" Bassus looked around. "There is nowhere here for shelter."

"Then we ride on. We will be warmer on horse than afoot."

"How much further is it?"

"With good weather, we would be there tomorrow. But if the snow comes, then we will have to find our way when the tracks are covered and lost. Maybe two days then."

"That would get us to Eowa five days after his message reached us."

"Too long," said Oswald, "too long."

"What can we do? The weather delays us."

"Yes. It burns my heart, but there is nothing more we can do but press on."

Standing behind Oswald, and using him as shelter from the wind, Bran gave a mournful croak.

"By the sound of it, Bran would prefer to stop too," said Bassus.

"We will be out of the wind soon, Bran, soon," said Oswald soothingly.

Bassus stared ahead. "Can't see where," he muttered.

*

"They went this way." Coifi came back from the farmhouse shaking the snow from his hood. Behind him, from the door into the dark, smoke-wreathed interior, the farmer peered out, spear in hand, watching to make sure the strange man who called upon him in the storm left his land as promised.

Acca, snow mantling his cloak, squinted against the flakes blowing into his face.

"Where from here?"

Coifi pointed as he climbed back onto his horse. They were poor beasts, but the best they could buy when the shipmaster finally landed them, cursing his passengers from his boat.

"West," said Coifi. "There are old trackways, but they lie under snow. He said to follow the shape of the land – that would lead us aright."

"What does he mean by that?"

"We head towards the mountains. I suppose it would be best to follow the land where it rises."

"And get the full benefit of the wind." Acca paused. "Did the farmer say how long ago they passed this way?"

"This morning."

"Was there a morning?" Acca squinted around, looking into the white of the storm. "Is this an afternoon?"

Coifi urged his reluctant horse on. "We are catching them. Come on."

*

The landing had been as much a foundering as a landing, but Oswiu had got his men alive from the boats and, marching inland, they had bought extra horses from the local farmers, paying silver for nags barely worth slaughtering for food. Now the animals staggered beneath their riders, but at least the wind was at their back, blowing them onwards, and wherever they saw horses picketed by farms and hamlets pulled tight against the storm, they took them, leaving the weakest of their own beasts in return. A farmer might come to his door, spear in hand, but when he saw the group of armed men sitting silently on their horses, he would hold peace and take the beasts they left him, and thank his gods that they went.

Leading the column, Oswiu rode south and east, keeping the line of hills ahead and to the right. Maserfield lay in the wind shadow of the hills, sheltered from the westerly storms that blew in from over the sea. In the white of the winter landscape, with the trackways and drovers' paths fresh covered in snow, the mountains were all Oswiu had to navigate by. Squinting for some sign that he was heading in the right direction, Oswiu gave up and called over his shoulder for Brother Diuma.

The monk pushed his horse up alongside Oswiu.

"Lord?"

"Do you know this land?"

"Not this land, no. But I think, ahead…" He pointed. "Those hills look to me like the northernmost of the hills that rise above Maserfield."

"How far after that?"

"Maybe half a day's ride."

Oswiu measured distance by eye against the speed of the column and the difficulty of the conditions.

"We should get there tomorrow. Three days from leaving Carlisle." He turned to Brother Diuma. "Pray, and do not stop praying, that we are in time."

Chapter 8

"The storm is over." Oswald looked on to a world made white, all the roughness of it smoothed away beneath a cover of snow. First light greyed the black of the eastern horizon, but above stars glittered between the final tatters of cloud. Mist clouded around Oswald as he breathed and, above the horses, the air steamed as the beasts huddled together for the warmth they provided each other, and shifted in the cold before the dawn.

Beside him, Bassus clapped his hands together for warmth and tried to stamp some feeling back into his feet. They had gone numb in the night, when they had finally stopped, blind in the storm, and made what camp they could, taking shelter behind their horses from the wind.

"We will get there today."

"Good," said Bassus. He forced a smile. "Battle will warm us up, if nothing else will. But it will be impossible to take Penda by surprise. Against the snow, we will stand out clearly."

Oswald shrugged. "At least Eowa will know we are coming as soon as Penda does. Then we may catch Penda between us, Eowa issuing from his hall, us riding up to it. I would still have us approach as close as possible without him seeing us; that way, we shall force Penda to battle. If he were to see us from a distance, he might flee, and I do not think the horses have the legs to pursue him."

"Very well. I will order the men ready."

As the warmaster set to, ordering the weary men to their feet and to their horses, Oswald stood looking west to the hills. Bran croaked at his feet and the king bent down to him, allowing the raven to clamber up his arm and onto his shoulder.

"We are nearly there, old friend."

The raven croaked and ran its iron beak over his head.

*

"Wake up!" Coifi slapped Acca, but the man did not stir.

They had slept in a stand of trees, hoping to find under their boughs some shelter from the wind, but the cold had crept into their bones in the night, leaching in through the ground and sucking the warmth from them until the feeling had gone from Coifi's fingers and feet and hands, even his lips. Waking from a fitful doze, he had seen the sky clear through the branches of the trees and felt the air still. But turning to Acca, he seemed as one dead, unmoving, blanketed beneath snow.

"Wake up." Coifi slapped Acca again, and finally the scop answered, groaning as his eyes slowly opened. Coifi pulled him to his feet, the snow falling from him.

"What? Where…?"

"I thought you dead."

"I – I feel dead." Acca tried moving his hands and legs. "I can't feel my feet." He held his hands up in front of his face. "I can't feel my fingers either." Fear gripped, griping his bowels. "If I lose my fingers, I won't be able to play. Coifi, I won't be able to play."

The priest pulled the gloves from Acca's hands. He took the scop's hands in his own, moving the fingers, kneading, breathing on them.

"There. There is some colour in them."

"I – I can feel something," said Acca. He looked up, beaming. "I can feel something."

"Ah, that might hurt…"

Acca was still complaining an hour later when Coifi pointed ahead.

"There," he said.

Crossing in front of them and then turning towards the line of hills was a track, the churned and crushed snow made by many horses following in line after each other.

*

"I am lost." Brother Diuma turned one way and another, searching for a landmark he knew, but the snow had laid its hand over everything, smoothing away all the marks that he might have used to tell where they were.

"We cannot be lost. Not now we've come so far." Oswiu looked in turn for anything to tell their place, but there was nothing.

"If we cannot see, then we will have to ask. We ride on. The first farm we see, we take the farmer as our guide."

"What if he will not come?"

"He will," said Oswiu. "He will."

*

The smoke was the first sign. A column of smoke rising through the glitter of the snow-cleared air. Bassus pointed it out to Oswald. Turning to the riders behind, some fifty strong, he signed for silence, the sign passing down the column. The smoke rose against the line of hills, but its source was hidden from them by small woods, the trees coppiced and pollarded, and the land folding downwards into a final dip before the steady rise to the hills.

"Send a scout ahead."

Bassus pulled back down the column to select the right man, while Oswald rode them onwards, taking a steady pace now, eyes alert for sentries set against their coming.

The man selected, Bassus pointed him ahead, marking the possible places where sentries might wait, and talking over the best route to keep him clear of watchers.

"Don't go too close," said Oswald. "I just want to know if Penda still invests Eowa's hold. If there is a camp outside it, and the gates are closed, that will be enough to know."

Bassus gave the scout his final instructions and then he rode ahead, the horse barely making a sound over the new snow.

"At least they won't hear us coming," said Oswald.

Bran, taking pleasure in the contrast of the day's sun to the previous day's storm, took wing and flew above the column, croaking his greeting to the other ravens that rose above the snow fields. On such a day, after the storm, there would be carrion to be found. Oswald looked up to the slaughter birds. There would be more carrion for them by the day's end.

The column rode onwards, Oswald taking them towards the

wood that offered the final cover before they rode down upon the army investing Eowa's hall. He pointed to the trees.

"We will make battle plans there," he said to Bassus.

"We should be able to see Penda's army from the wood," said Bassus.

"Let us hope he is still there to see."

As they neared the wood, the scout appeared, riding towards them, dark against the snow-draped trees.

"He is there." The scout pulled his horse up beside Oswald. "There are many tents outside the ditch and fence around Eowa's hall, and I could see men moving among them. The gate to the hall is closed, and there are men within too, but I could not see how many."

"How many has Penda without the hall?"

"I counted thirty-eight, but there may be more in the tents."

Oswald looked to Bassus. "Not many. Not at this time. Eowa said he had thirty men. With our fifty, that is more than enough."

Bassus nodded. "Yes."

"To the woods. We will make final preparations there."

But as they were about to reach the woods, a shout, put up from the rear of the column, came to them at its head.

Riders, approaching from behind.

*

"What in the name of heaven are you doing here?"

Oswald stood in front of Coifi and Acca, glaring at them. The two men, who had dismounted, stared at the ground in front of them. Trees, layered on their western sides with white, surrounded them.

"Answer me."

Acca looked to Coifi. "You tell him."

The priest twitched, pulling his raven-feather cloak around his shoulders. Bran croaked disapprovingly. He knew too well where those feathers came from.

"We would share your doom," said Coifi.

Oswald's eyes flicked to the men gathered around Bassus and receiving instructions. Some ears would be tuned to the conversation their king was having with the two unexpected additions to the warband.

"Shut up about doom," he whispered. "Here, come with me. But keep quiet." Leading Coifi and Acca through the narrow strip of wood, he stopped in the shelter of a holly bush and pointed into the valley below. There, protected by the land folding down after the hills, was the great ditch and fence that surrounded Eowa's hall, standing stark against the snow. Around it, looking more like white mounds than tents, was Penda's camp. Men, distant shapes, moved desultorily around it. Within Eowa's compound there was similar movement.

"Snow stops even war," said Oswald. He looked to Coifi and Acca. "Penda is not ready. We will catch him between our forces and Eowa's, crack him between us. What doom do you see there, Coifi?"

The priest shook his head. "I – I do not know, lord. But I know what I saw. If you will not hold, then give me leave to come with you, that I may share your doom – whatever it be."

"No. You are not warriors. I will not give men – men I need – to keeping you both safe. You will stay here." Oswald smiled at Coifi. "You will have a fine view of Penda's doom unfolding."

*

They rode from the line of trees, down towards Eowa's hall. As they advanced, moving at an easy pace, riding two abreast with Oswald and Bassus leading, the camp beneath them began to seethe with activity, men running to and fro, shouts and orders resounding up the slope towards them.

The movement was mirrored within the besieged hall. Men ran to the palisade, staring and pointing up at the advancing column of riders.

"I think Penda has seen us," said Oswald.

"I think you are right, lord," said Bassus.

When they had advanced far enough, Oswald signalled halt.
"Dismount!"

The warmaster's voice, trained to be heard above the shouts and screams of the battlefield, easily passed to the end of the column. The men slipped from their mounts, slinging shields over shoulder and taking spears in hand, while the horses were picketed behind them.

Bassus glanced down the slope towards the camp. Similar preparations were being made there.

"We have the slope," Oswald said to Bassus as he dressed the men into line, forming the shieldwall. "Make sure we keep it."

"It slopes right down to Penda's camp," said Bassus. "We can use it to crush him."

Looking down into Penda's camp, eyes slit against the snow glitter, they could see the frantic efforts being made there to form the men into line.

"Let's not keep him waiting." Oswald signed the advance and, in step, shields tight together and spears bristling, they began to make their way down the gentle slope, the snow smoothing the ground beneath their feet and all but removing one of the great dangers for an advancing shieldwall: that a man might trip and fall, taking the men either side of him down too.

A ragged shieldwall began to form to meet them, desperate shouts calling the men into line.

Bassus measured the line forming against them.

"We have the advantage, lord," he said. "But not by much."

"Come on, Eowa, come on," Oswald muttered under his breath, as they moved down the slope towards Penda's line. The men had formed up quickly once the commands were given, showing themselves to be experienced warriors. Seeing the way they waited, spears bristling but held loosely, shields tight but not so tight that the men bearing them could not see the enemy, Oswald knew this would be no easy fight. These were Penda's own retainers and he had trained them well. They wasted no energy climbing a slope to meet an enemy, but waited.

Oswald, from his position in the centre of the line, glanced past the waiting shieldwall to Eowa's fortified hall.

"Come on," he said again. How much encouragement did Eowa need?

But then, finally, the gates of the enclosure opened, and men streamed out, bristling with spear and sword, fanning out into line in front of the ditch.

"We've got him!" Bassus shouted.

And they had. Penda was now trapped between two advancing shieldwalls, one bearing down on his front, the other approaching him from behind.

"Take the right, Bassus," Oswald ordered, "and start us up."

The warmaster peeled back from his place behind Oswald and ran behind the line of advancing men to take his place on the right wing, ready to try to roll around Penda's line and force it to disintegrate.

Reaching his position, the warmaster pushed his way into the line and then, matching the step of their advance, he began to pound the shaft of his spear against the rim of his shield. The men took up the beat, striking spear and sword on limewood, the sound hollow and resonant, rolling over the snow-covered ground and up toward the distant line of hills. Mist rose from the men's mouths as they began to shout and chant, matching the rhythm of their drumming with the sound of their voices.

Oswald, in the centre of the chant, made no sound himself. He looked around, taking in the glitter of the snow beneath his feet and the rise of smoke, untroubled by wind, from the hall. Squinting against the glare he looked around, searching for Bran, and saw him black against the sky, riding the rolling levels. He knew Coifi and Acca were watching them from the wood, yet he felt as detached as they, though he marched in the midst of his men.

Penda was making no move to reshape his line, even though Eowa was forming into shieldwall behind him. Oswald noted that and, unsure what it meant, he signalled down the line for Bassus to slow the advance. The warmaster, seeing the sign, held the rhythm of the march to the same slow beat, rather than speeding it up. Oswald measured the gap between the lines. They were still more than one hundred and fifty yards apart. More than enough space to increase the tempo and, using the slope, to crash like a rockfall upon Penda's shieldwall.

Slowing the advance also gave Eowa time to form his line properly. Oswald looked past Penda's shieldwall, trying to see what was taking Eowa so long, and then he saw Eowa's banner being brought through the gates, carried by three men, to be set up beside the Mercian's line. Oswald's eyes narrowed as he squinted against the snow glare. There was no wind, but it did not look like a banner hanging from the crosspiece of Eowa's standard. And he knew no standard that required three men to carry it.

Something was wrong.

The lines were one hundred yards apart now. Oswald signed down the line and Bassus, his voice rising even over the thump of spear on shield, called halt. The warmaster peered along the line and saw Oswald gesture him over, and again he ran behind the line to him. On either side of Oswald, men muttered, tension rancid in mouth and gut, while the jeers and cries of Penda's men ran up the slope to them.

"What's that?" Oswald pointed to Eowa's standard.

Bassus shielded his eyes against the snow glare, but shook his head.

"I – I cannot tell," he said.

"At last, Eowa is advancing. We'll be able to see it better soon."

"Shall I hold the men here?"

Oswald peered down into the glaring snow light. The sun, high risen now, turned all the snow fields into jewels – flashing, blinding jewels.

"Yes. We wait for Eowa to advance. At the moment, it looks like Penda is hoping to meet us one at a time."

The shieldwall of the new king of Mercia slowly began to advance towards Penda. Keeping pace with it, the three men bearing the standard advanced alongside the line. Oswald looked for Eowa. At such range it was impossible to be sure, but judging by the armour on show, Eowa marched in the centre, surrounded by his personal retainers.

"What is that?" Oswald asked the question of himself, under his breath.

The standard, a single straight pole with a crosspiece from which dangled a strange, thick banner, refused to resolve itself into anything he knew.

And then he saw it.

The shape had been there all along, but his mind had refused to see it. It was no standard, no banner; it was a cross. And hanging from the cross, his arms bound to the crosspiece, his feet bound to the upright, was a man.

The whispers, the murmurs, the shouts and cries going up and down the line showed that others too among his men had seen what he had seen.

"Who is it? Who is it?" Oswald asked, but the cross was still too far away for any to see who lay upon it.

"Can you see, Oswald?"

The voice came thinly over the snow, but it carried and Oswald knew it.

"Can you see now?"

"Eowa."

"It is Sidrac. Usually we hang traitors in Mercia but, for you, we hung him upon the tree you worship. He lasted longer than your god."

Oswald gasped. It was as if water, ice water, had been thrown over him. In an instant, he saw: he saw his folly, and his trust, and his betrayal. And his peril.

"Get the horses closer," he ordered Bassus. While the warmaster frantically signalled the two men detailed to guard the picketed horses to bring them closer – no easy task with so many animals and so few riders – Oswald measured the new odds they faced.

They were not good.

Penda's original line all but matched his, man for man.

Now, he knew that Eowa was advancing not to attack his brother but to fight alongside him. The two shieldwalls would outnumber his own by at least two to one.

He glanced back to the horses, gauging distance. To try to retreat to them was impossible; Eowa and Penda would catch them as they fled up the slope, and slaughter would ensue.

Looking down the slope, he saw the two lines beginning to form together. Behind them, looming over them, was the cross upon which hung Sidrac.

A cold anger gripped Oswald's heart.

"Penda!"

Oswald stepped forward, out of his line, and his voice rolled down the hill, huge in its fury.

In answer, a man came from the line in front of him.

"Penda, my anger lies upon your brother, for he is a traitor. Stand aside, and I will offer you no war."

Penda looked towards his brother's line then back up the slope to Oswald.

"Brothers cannot share a throne," he answered. "Neither in Mercia nor in Northumbria." He turned to his men. "Stand down. For now, we watch."

At this, Eowa sprang forward, calling over the snow to Penda.

"Brother, you promised, when I gave myself as hostage to save you, that we would work together to bring down Oswald."

Penda turned towards Eowa. "We have." He pointed up the slope to Oswald and his men. "Now fight."

"Quick," Oswald said to Bassus as Penda and Eowa traded insults across the field. "If we can destroy Eowa, we might yet live."

"Even if we do not, let us kill Eowa this day," said Bassus.

Oswald swiftly grasped his warmaster's hand. "Yes." He nodded towards Eowa's line. "As fast and hard as we can."

Bassus ran to the right wing, his armour jangling and flashing in the fractured sunlight, then, beating the rhythm, he started the men downhill.

Fast this time, and getting faster, the pace building so that soon it would be impossible to stop.

Oswald, in the centre, beat his spear against his shield, looking over its leather rim, searching for the point, the man, where he would hit when the shieldwalls met. With the slope taking them downhill, there would be no stopping at spear range, no jabbing at distance, seeking to bring a man down and use the opening. This was an all-or-nothing charge, a gamble that the sheer weight of running men would bear down and break Eowa's shieldwall, pushing it open in one united blow and then turning back to kill anyone who still stood after the initial impact.

"*Lam-n-guin! Lam-n-guin! Lam-n-guin!*"

The war chant of the men of Northumbria rolled in front of them, reaching down towards the waiting, watching men.

Oswald took a final glance at Penda and saw him standing in front of his line, leaning upon his spear, watching but not advancing. Then there was no time to look elsewhere. No time for anything but to search for the man he was going to hit, the man he was going to kill.

"*Lam-n-guin! Lam-n-guin! Lam...*"

The shieldwalls struck.

*

"Not far now, lord, not far." The farmer waved his hand ahead, but he was looking anxiously at the man riding beside him.

"Where?" said Oswiu. "You are not pointing at anything. Is it behind that next ridge of land? Or maybe the wood over there on the right? There is a dip beyond it."

"Yes, yes," jabbered the farmer.

"Which one?" snarled Oswiu. "You have been leading us since the sun came up, and the whole time you've been telling me it was just beyond the next rise, and we have not yet come to it. Where is it?"

"There, there," said the farmer, waving his arm, but with no more direction than before.

Oswiu pulled the seax from its sheath at his waist and held its point to the side of the farmer's head.

"As I asked before, where? The ridge, or the wood?"

The farmer licked his lips, not daring to turn his head.

"The wood," he said at last.

"Good. I hope for your sake you are right. If not, I will kill you and find another guide – someone who knows where to take us." Oswiu sheathed the seax and pointed his riders towards the snow-hooded wood at the far side of a broad valley.

Brother Diuma rode up alongside Oswiu.

"He is terrified," he said, glancing ahead at the farmer jiggling along on a horse, clearly uncertain of how to stay atop the animal.

"He should be," said Oswiu. "If this direction proves false, I will kill him."

"He is only a farmer, trying to protect his family."

"And I'm trying to save my brother." Oswiu turned on the monk, his face terrible. "If we are not in time…"

He spoke as they breasted the final ridge before the long dip into the valley. With his face turned to Brother Diuma, he did not see what was immediately obvious to the monk. Brother Diuma pointed.

"Look," he said.

Cutting through the snow that lay thick in the valley, heading straight to the wood, was the track made by many horses.

"Ride!" yelled Oswiu, heeling his horse into a frantic gallop. "Ride for the High King's life!"

*

"I don't understand. What's happening?" Acca turned to Coifi, watching beside him from the shelter of the wood. "The king is fighting Eowa? I thought he came here to save him?"

"He did," said Coifi.

"But the king is fighting Eowa, and Penda is just watching."

"We must go to him." Coifi turned to Acca. "Treachery."

Acca stared back at the battle. "No," he said. "Not Eowa. He loved my songs."

Coifi grunted. "He probably lied about that, as he lied about everything else." He began to get to his feet, but Acca held his arm.

"What can we do? The two of us. We have no armour."

For answer, Coifi pointed to where the horses stamped and steamed, nostrils flaring at the sudden iron tang that filled the still air: blood was being spilled and they could smell it, and it excited and scared them.

"I watched. The men guarding the horses ran to join the king when they saw that Eowa had betrayed him. If we can get to the horses, we can take some closer to the king, so he can escape."

Acca pulled Coifi back.

"Do you really think the king would leave his men and ride away?"

Coifi strained against the scop's grip for a moment, then slumped back.

"No," he said. He looked at Acca. "What would you have us do then? Just watch?"

Acca stared down at the battle. "It is my task," he said. "To watch, to see, to give praise to the brave and to curse the coward. It is all I am fit for." He turned to Coifi. "Pray to the gods," he said urgently. "Pray, make sacrifice, do anything."

"But I have nothing to sacrifice," said Coifi.

"Find something, promise them something, anything." Acca looked down at the battle. "Quickly."

*

"Eowa!" Oswald circled, searching, scanning. Around him, the battle had dissolved into small groups of men grappling furiously. The first charge had broken the centre of the Mercian shieldwall. The man he had glimpsed over the edge of his shield – the man peering up at him through the steam of his own fear – he had killed, his spear sliding through the gap he left when he sought to see how far the enemy was from him, only to discover too late that they were too close for him to be looking past the shield's edge. He had run over his thrashing body, hurdling the flailing arms and legs lest they bring him down, and, leaving the spear embedded in the man's eye socket, he turned, drawing sword, and started striking at the suddenly unprotected flanks of the men to either side.

The shieldwall cracked, broke apart, leaving him in the break as men peeled from the flanks, some running full tilt, others retreating more cautiously, pulling back towards Penda's waiting, watching line.

Oswald saw his own men fall, their blood reddening the snow, faces turned up to the sky but no longer misting the air; or gasping, grabbing at stomachs rendered, looking to him, the shock and accusation of their passing vivid in their eyes. They had not thought to die this day.

"Eowa!" Oswald screamed the challenge, searching, looking for him.

There, on the right wing, where Bassus struggled to roll up the remaining Mercian resistance.

"Eowa!"

Oswald ran, picking up his pace, shield tight against his left shoulder, targeting the tight knot of men that held their shields fast around their lord, turning himself into a human battering ram. The flank of Eowa's guard was exposed to him and he struck it, his sword slashing low as he crashed among them, targeting the knees and tendons of the men straining to hold the wall.

It collapsed. Eowa's guard fell away, the constant pressure exerted by Bassus and his wing finally pushing them back. Some fell and, exposed upon the ground, were dispatched. Others peeled away, trying to keep shields turned towards foe, but with eyes glancing ever to the rear, moving back, back, back.

And as his guard fled or died, Eowa was left exposed.

"Eowa." Oswald had no need to raise his voice now. The Mercian, hearing him, snapped round.

Oswald stalked closer, his sword balanced in his hand, his wrist loose and supple in the way he had learned ever since his father had first placed a wooden sword in his hand when he could barely walk. His eyes did not leave Eowa, but as he approached the Mercian he knew that Æthelfrith walked beside him, chanting the list of things that he had beaten into his son during his training: eyes tight, focus wide, knees loose, wrist loose, fingers tight. So he went now, his eyes not leaving Eowa but alive to every movement to left and right, his stance low and supple, the sword seeking its target as if knowing of its own will where it should strike.

Eowa stared at him. He licked his lips and looked past Oswald.

"Penda! Brother!"

All around, the battle was ending in the rattle of the death breath and the rattle of flight, armour clanking as men ran.

"Brother!"

Oswald stopped. He turned and looked back to where Penda waited, standing still at the centre of his shieldwall. A glance told Oswald that Penda's line had grown; some of Eowa's men had joined it rather than flee the field of slaughter completely.

"Brother!"

Penda stepped forward, but his shieldwall did not move.

"You are king now, brother. Fight like one."

Oswald turned back to Eowa. The Mercian's eyes flickered between him and Penda. He could see the fear in the way Eowa's gaze settled nowhere, but moved constantly, as a deer driven into a gully by the hounds rolls its eyes wildly as it searches for an escape.

"I did it for him," Eowa gabbled, pointing past Oswald at Penda. Oswald made no answer, but advanced, his sword hunting through the air for blood, his gaze steady.

Eowa stepped backwards, still pointing, although he pointed with a sword that he barely seemed to realize he held.

"When you asked for me as hostage, my brother told me to work towards dividing you from your brother. He said that was the way to destroy you."

Oswald shook his head, as if the words were blows raining down upon him, and, seeing that, Eowa redoubled his efforts, though still he slid one foot behind the other, working his way backwards. Behind him, Bassus signalled to Oswald, but the king shook his head. Eowa was his, and his alone.

"All these men," he pointed around at the twisted bodies of Oswald's men, locked in the intimacy of the death embrace with their foes, "they died because you believed me about your brother.

And he believed me about you!"

"Cursed one." Oswald advanced upon Eowa, but the man slipped backwards faster, gabbling accusations against Oswald.

"You call *me* traitor when I saw you – I saw how you wanted your brother's wife; you wanted her for yourself, and I told him. I told him."

"Damned one."

Oswald was nigh near enough to strike at Eowa.

"Fell one."

Eowa broke.

He turned and ran, his feet crunching over the snow, tight packed beneath the battle, its virgin whiteness stained with blood and bile, and Oswald pursued him, his breath rising as he ran.

Penda's men hooted and called, the remaining Northumbrians, gathered around Bassus, yelled their own abuse as king pursued king over the snow fields, Eowa turning, doubling back, as desperate as a hare, Oswald as relentless as a hound, gradually pulling back the distance to his quarry.

Eowa fell. Almost beneath the cross he had set up he stumbled and, twisting, fell, so he lay upon his back, staring up at the sky; staring up at the body tied upon the cross. His sword dropped from his hand as he fell, rolling over the snow to land at the foot of the pole upon which he had raised Sidrac.

Oswald stepped upon him, forcing Eowa back onto the snow as he attempted to rise. His sword went to the Mercian's throat. Eowa stared up at him, his eyes wide, and in them Oswald saw reflected the cross that he stood beneath. Slowly, keeping the point of his sword pressed into the base of Eowa's throat so that the man might barely breathe, and certainly not speak, he turned and saw the figure above him.

Sidrac's head had rolled forward. His eyes, filmed in death, stared lifelessly down upon Oswald. The High King returned his gaze and then slowly nodded.

"Yes," he said softly, as if speaking to the one upon the cross, then he signalled to Bassus and his remaining men. "Stand with me," he said. As they approached, their feet crunching over the snow,

Oswald stepped away from Eowa. He drew his sword back from the Mercian's neck. Eowa's throat worked, but he did not move.

"Get up," said Oswald. "Get up."

Eowa got to his knees, then to his feet, and stood swaying in front of Oswald.

"Go," said Oswald. He pointed his sword towards Penda and his watching line of men. "Go to your brother."

Backing away from him, as soon as he was out of range Eowa turned and ran across the snow to where Penda waited, floundering through a bank of snow until he came to him.

Penda and the men around him watched in silence as Eowa approached, gabbling, shouting for their aid, and they made no move to help him or approach him. Only when Eowa fell before him, crying his relief, his hands held out, did Penda move. He pushed his brother backwards, so he fell into the snow.

"I hoped you would take care of this for me," Penda shouted over the prone body of his brother to Oswald. He looked down at Eowa, lying at his feet. "But I shall have to take care of it myself."

"Brother..." Eowa held out his hand.

Penda shook his head. "You above all of us should know how hard it is to trust a brother." He looked to the man beside him in the shieldwall.

"Kill him."

The man stepped forward and thrust his sword into Eowa's stomach.

"Faster than that."

Pulling the sword out, Eowa's eyes opening wide in surprise, the warrior slid the blade in between the ribs. Eowa's eyes opened even wider. He stared up at his brother, trying to speak, but his words were drowned in the blood that filled his lungs. He reached up, hands trembling, but Penda stepped backwards and Eowa fell upon his face. Blood flowed, snow melting beneath it, making a red-branched scarlet tree that ran, all ran away.

Standing beneath the cross, Oswald saw Eowa fall.

Penda stepped forward.

"You said you would not raise hand against me, but I gave no such word myself." He signalled along the line and the men of his shieldwall clashed spear against leather and wood, yelling their war cry.

"Pen-da! Pen-da! Pen-da!"

As one, they began to advance.

"How many men have we?" Oswald asked Bassus, not taking his eyes from Penda.

"Twenty, plus three who can barely walk."

Oswald looked up the slope to where the horses were picketed.

"Do you think we can make it?"

But before Bassus could answer, the horses started to move. Three men were leading them away, towards the line of the Mercians.

*

"We've got to stop them!" Coifi pointed at the string of horses being led away by three warriors.

"They must have crept around the side of the battle," said Acca.

"Come on." Coifi ran from the shelter of the wood and floundered into the deep snow outside it, his legs disappearing up to his thighs in the drifts. The horses, skittish and nervous from the smell of blood and battle, were pulling at their traces, but the men leading them knew their business and mixed soothing words with judicious tugs on the tethers tying the horses together. Coifi waded through the snow, pushing through the drift until he emerged on its further side and the thin layer upon the upper flanks of the slope. Acca, following, ran after him as they made after the horses.

The crunch of their feet upon the snow alerted the men taking the horses to their approach. One remained at the head of the line of animals, urging them onwards, while the other two ran back along the line of horses towards them.

Acca pointed at the nearest animal.

"Take it," he shouted to Coifi. "Ride it to the king. I will stop these men."

The priest cut the rope to the last horse and jumped upon it, pulling its head round and heading it down the slope to where Oswald and his men stood gathered around the cross.

The scop, seeing him go, turned to the men advancing on him.

"Stop!" he called, holding up his hand and using the voice with which he might silence a hall of drunken men.

The men did stop, as surprised by a man facing them with but his hands and a lyre as Acca was that they had obeyed his command.

"I am Acca, the sweet voice, the scop, the teller of tales, the maker of history, the giver of glory! Do you wish glory? Do you?" He fixed the men with his eyes. "I can give it you." He glanced down the slope. Coifi had all but reached the king. "I will sing your names in the halls and all men will remember you – but I do not know your names. How can I give glory to the nameless? Tell me your names, and I will sing them."

The men glanced at each other, back to the scop, then charged.

Acca turned and ran, dodging back towards the trees, but as he went he saw Coifi pull the horse up beside the king.

"Take it, lord," Coifi said, making to jump from the horse. But the king stopped him. He pointed to where Penda's own horses stood, only many of them were already mounted.

"I would not escape when so many are ready to pursue me." Oswald looked at the men gathered around him. "Besides, should I live when these die?"

"Lord, you must take horse," said Bassus. "Flee. Let us buy you time with our lives."

"No. No, I will not leave you." Oswald took Coifi's hand. "Listen. Take word to my brother. Do not throw your life away, Coifi. Tell him he is king now; tell him to remember the promise he gave me; tell him I am sorry to have doubted him. Now go!" Oswald released Coifi's hand and slapped the horse into motion. "Go!" he yelled after him, as the horse sprang up the slope.

None of the mounted men set off after Coifi. Oswald had hoped that some might go, but Penda was not to be distracted. The king gauged the distance between his men and Penda's. There was still time before the battle began.

"Let us take him down."

With Bassus, Oswald cut Sidrac from the cross. He smoothed the man's eyes shut and eased his body upon the ground. Then, taking hold of the cross, he looked up upon its bare wood.

"Lord, you knew bitter death, as we will know it. Save my men and receive them into your hall. Do not hold my pride against them, but let them live, Lord; let them live."

As if in answer, Bran settled upon the head of the cross and, ducking his head, croaked his song over the battlefield. Oswald, seeing him, raised his hand.

"Farewell, old friend," he said.

Bran croaked.

"If you will, take word to my brother."

The raven turned his head, looking at Oswald with its black eyes.

"Thank you." Oswald slipped a ring from his finger and held it up to the bird. The raven regarded it, head to one side, then leaned forward and took the gold in its beak. Taking wing, Bran swooped low before heavy strokes of his wings beat him higher into the sky, circling up and up until the air bore the bird upon itself, and he flew away east.

"Pen-da! Pen-da! Pen-da!"

The shieldwall advanced upon them, thrumming spears against shields, while the mounted men circled round to the rear; there would be no escape for anyone breaking from the battle and attempting to flee.

Oswald came to stand among his men. Many among them took his hand and held it to their foreheads or kissed it.

"Why do you do this?" he asked, as another man pressed his hand to his lips. "I have led you to ruin and death."

"Don't you know?" Bassus asked.

Oswald looked to him. "No," he said.

"You are their good lord," he said. "And mine." The old warrior took Oswald's hand and, bending his head, pressed it to his forehead. "Edwin made me leave him; I will not leave you." Bassus turned to the ragged line of men. "Now, let's take as many of these Mercian bastards with us as we can. Right? Right." And as he lined the men up, Bassus turned to Oswald and grinned.

"This is where I would be, lord."

*

"Damn you! I thought you said Eowa's hall lay over this rise?" Oswiu gripped the farmer by the throat, squeezing.

The man choked, his eyes popping.

"He cannot speak if you are strangling him," said Brother Diuma, and Oswiu pushed the farmer away. Taken unaware, the man fell from the horse and lay upon the snow, gasping up at the sky.

"Do we need him any more?" asked the monk. "The way is clear enough." He pointed to the trail cutting across field and ridge, heading west.

"How much further? I need to know how much further."

"He clearly does not know."

Oswiu pointed his sword at the farmer. "Do not be here when we return." The farmer scrabbled backwards over the snow, but as Oswiu was about to kick his horse into motion, he stopped. He heard a low, croaking cough and, looking up, saw the raven, black against the blue sky. He knew that call.

"Bran?"

The raven circled down towards him, losing height as swiftly as Oswiu had ever seen. Straining his eyes, he saw something glitter in his beak. He held his arm up, in case for once the bird would settle upon it, and for a wonder it did. Bran dropped the ring into his hand and Oswiu knew it for what it was.

"Ride! Ride for my brother's life!"

*

"Why didn't you bring him?"

Acca grabbed the horse's head and brought it to a halt.

"He would not come." Coifi dropped from the horse beside Acca. "He gave me a message for his brother, else I would not have left him."

"What can we do? What can we do?" Acca stared past the horse. Already Penda's line was within fifty yards of the small group of men standing around Oswald.

"There is nothing we can do," said Coifi.

"If we could call for help…"

432

"There is no one to call. Only the gods, and they do not answer me."

"Try, Coifi, try." Acca pushed him back towards the horse. "Get on it, ride, see if there is anyone – maybe the king left some men behind; we didn't ask. Please try; do something."

Coifi pulled Acca's hands from his chest.

"There is nothing we can do," he said. "Nothing."

Acca fell to his knees. He looked up at Coifi. "Nothing?"

"All we can do is what we are meant to do: I will pray, you will watch, and we will honour the king by not turning away."

*

Oswiu urged his struggling horse towards the line of trees, limned in white, across the valley floor. The track they were following ran to the trees, two horses wide and cut deep into the surrounding snow – thirty or forty horsemen must have ridden across the valley. But their own animals, the nags they'd paid for when they landed, were blowing hard, their flanks lathered with sweat despite the cold. They could not go much further at this pace, and he could not risk any of the animals dying on them, for that would be to abandon a rider to following on foot, prey to riders and marauders.

They had crossed three valleys now, following the same trail, and each time, as they breasted the final ridge, Oswiu's breath had quickened as he looked down, hoping to see some sign of his brother or Eowa's hall. But each time the trail had simply continued, pushing towards the distant line of hills.

He looked up from the trail. The hills were not so distant now. Maserfield lay in the shadow of the hills. Surely it was not far?

Oswiu raised his arm and signalled his riders on; a final burst before they would, he knew, have to rest the horses a while.

The trees approached. Beyond them the land fell away. And then he saw it. A smoke column rising into the clear sky.

They were close. They must be.

Oswiu signalled the riders to slow as they approached the trees, then to stop. He listened, but could hear nothing. But the smoke rose thickly into the crystal sky. Steam rose from the horses' flanks and in billows from their nostrils. Oswiu signalled the dismount, then signed Brother Diuma and two men to him. He needed to see what lay beyond the trees before riding into it.

"With me. Quiet."

Following the track into the trees, the close-packed snow quieter beneath their feet than the unmarked snow to either side, they disappeared in among the stand of birch and hazel that marked the edges of the small wood.

Though he wanted to draw no attention, Oswiu knew that he must needs hurry, so he pushed on through the trees much faster than normal; any sentry standing still against a tree would see and hear them coming but he could not take the time for true stealth.

Coming to the end of the trees, Oswiu crept forward, looking, listening, all his attention directed into the valley below. So he did not see the men on his right.

"My lord."

Oswiu spun round and saw Coifi, raven dark in the shadow of a tree, and Acca, stepping forward, arms spread, as swords rasped from sheaths to point at him. And he saw their faces were pale and their eyes were red and he knew what they would say before ever they said it.

"My lord, you are too late..."

*

"Pen-da! Pen-da! Pen-da!"

The shieldwall advanced, a wall bristling with spears and swords, and Oswald searched along it for the man they chanted. There he was, in the centre. Oswald turned to Bassus, stationed beside him in what passed for their shieldwall.

"He's in the centre. See him?"

"Got him. Ready?"

Oswald took a deep breath. He tasted it deep within his lungs, feeling its cold fire.

"Closer," he said.

Bassus steadied the men poised on either side of him.

"Closer."

The Mercians were barely twenty yards away.

"Closer."

Penda was coming straight at him.

"Now!"

"Now!" yelled Bassus, his voice a bellow over the chant of the Mercians, and the Northumbrians sprang forward, making a wedge, driving on the man at its point, driving on Oswald, with all their strength.

He struck for Penda, pushing shield and spear and the weight of all the men behind him at the Mercian.

And Penda fell.

Caught by the charge, unable to shift his line or meet its ferocity, he went down, disappearing beneath Oswald's shield. Oswald went to stab down as the charge carried him onwards, but he stumbled over the prone man, staring down at him, and for a moment they saw each other, Penda helpless upon the ground, Oswald helpless before the fury of his own men as they carried him past the Mercian.

But the arms of Penda's shieldwall began to fold around Oswald's men, embracing them, sucking the motion from their charge, slowing them, stopping them, bringing them to a halt amid a mass of slashing, shoving, hacking, stabbing men.

"Bassus! He fell! Push back!"

Oswald turned to his warmaster, to see his eyes widen in surprise. Bassus looked down. A spear protruded from his stomach. He looked up into Oswald's eyes, and it seemed there was something he wished to say, something of great importance, but he could not force the words from his lips, and then his eyes glazed and he fell forwards.

"Back! Back!"

At the command, Penda's line pulled back, leaving the Northumbrians exposed.

Oswald, gasping, turned and looked around, but no one stood around him. They were all gone. He was the last of the Northumbrians. His men lay around, locked in death's embrace. The cross stood behind him. The surge and shift of struggle had pushed them back to its foot. He touched the wood, then knelt down beside Bassus and passed his hand over his face, closing his eyes. As no one approached, he bent down and kissed his forehead.

"Oswald *Lamnguin*. Oswald Whiteblade." Penda stepped forward. He held up his sword, the flowing lines upon it catching the snow light. "My blade is red today. I took it from your uncle." He held it up to his ear. "I hear it. It sings, Oswald; it sings the blood music. What say you to that?"

Oswald rose to his feet.

"I say: if you would defeat me, then fight me; fight me yourself. My sword against your sword."

Penda laughed, dropping his hands to his knees. When he had recovered, he stood up, still wiping tears from his cheek.

"Why would I want to do that? I have won; I will give you no last chance, Oswald Iding." Penda turned to the men gathered around Oswald. "My wolves, we have hunted our prey for long enough; now is the time to bring it down." He took a ring from his arm – a thick, richly worked gold ring – and held it up.

"This is for the man who kills him."

They fell upon him as wolves upon a wounded stag, and Oswald stood before their assault, wielding sword and shield and fist, swaying as a tree in storm. But then, as strength failed though will hardened, and blows cut through shield and mail and then into flesh, he went down to one knee. Seeing him down, they redoubled their attacks, using fist and foot and teeth, with sword and shield and axe, in their frenzy.

They battered him down, they buried him beneath their bodies, stabbing, biting, punching, and Oswald, helpless now, stared up past the screaming faces, past the bared teeth and raised fists. He stared up at the sky and knew that he had never seen it so blue. As the blades pierced him, he knew that he was dying and he realized why every man looked surprised when he died.

"So that is it," he said, and there was wonder in his voice.

*

436

Penda looked down into the face of his enemy. He stared at it for a long time, his eyes narrowing as if he saw something there behind the cuts and wounds that marred it. Around him, his men stripped the enemy dead of their weapons and jewels, working swiftly, for the cold was rising and fingers were growing numb and bodies freezing, making it all the harder to take valuables from newly stiff fingers. Many a scavenger resorted to the knife to remove rings.

Wihtrun came to stand beside Penda.

"The gods have brought him down," he said.

The king glanced at the priest. "I brought him down."

"But without the aid of the gods…"

"Without the swords of men, Oswald would still be High King and calling men to his new god." Penda poked the corpse with his foot. "Where is your god now, Oswald Iding?"

"Your sacrifice…" Wihtrun started again, but Penda held up his hand.

"No," he said. He looked to the priest. "This is wyrd, the weavings of the fate singers. Men die. The gods die. This middle-earth dies. The fate singers weave it all and they are blind. But now I am king – now I am High King – I will give the gods a gift." He looked down at the body lying at his feet, the shadow of the cross darkening it.

"Cut him up," he said. Penda looked at Wihtrun. "Cut him up and hang him on his tree," he pointed at the cross, "and we will give him to the gods and take his wyrd. His uncle had the tufa as his standard; I will carry Oswald before me."

Chapter 9

Aidan, taken from the Great Work to adjudicate a dispute between a fisherman and a farmer, stood listening patiently to them explaining how the case had divided their families for two generations. He felt a cold hand grasp his heart.

He gasped, but neither farmer nor fisherman heard, so intent were they upon rehearsing, for their own benefit as much as Aidan's, the story of their complaints. The hand squeezed again and sweat broke upon his brow. Aidan held a hand out to steady himself, but missed his hold and almost fell. The fisherman, seeing him sway, just caught the bishop in time, and seeing the sheen of sweat upon Aidan's face, he took him bodily and sat him gently upon the ground.

"Art thou all right?" the fisherman asked once he had Aidan sitting safely, his back resting against the wall of the church.

Aidan looked up at the concerned faces of the fisherman and the farmer leaning over him.

"He's dead," he said. "The king is dead. So, no, I don't think I am all right."

*

Hooves rattled over stone, the sound of a horse hard ridden. The rider, travel-stained and weary almost beyond standing, slid from his animal and stood swaying before the gate of the holy house at Coldingham. The panel in the gate slid open.

"Who calls at this holy house?"

The man almost fell, but he gathered himself and made it to the door, leaning against the wood.

"The – the king," he gasped.

The panel slid shut and the gate opened. Oswiu stumbled within and one of the nuns hovered about him, unsure whether to give an arm to help, but Oswiu forced himself upright. He would stand for this.

He heard footsteps, light and running, and then his sister appeared, a broad smile upon her face – a smile that died as soon as she saw him and she stopped, a terrible realization striking her. She put her hand to her mouth. She asked the question with her eyes.

Oswiu nodded.

Æbbe's face crumpled. She did not move, and Oswiu would have gone to her, but the strength was gone from him; he had ridden almost without rest from Maserfield to Coldingham.

"Oswald?" It was his mother's voice.

Acha appeared, coming from the church as Æbbe had done, her voice hopeful with the thought of seeing her son, the king. Then she saw Oswiu, and Æbbe's grief, and she stopped. Acha closed her eyes, and a shudder ran down her body, but when she opened her eyes again they were clear, and cold with acceptance.

"So, it has happened," said Acha. "Tell me…"

*

Feet moved slowly over the machair of Iona, the Holy Isle. In this winter season no flowers speckled the low-lying mat of grass and plants, but the snow that covered the hills of the mainland had passed over the Holy Isle.

One foot, then another, pacing out a life. Abbot Ségéne looked down as he walked, seeing the old toes, white now from the cold, poking from his sandals, but he did not return to the monastery to put on warmer shoes. Besides, he hardly felt his feet any longer. He walked over the machair to the northern tip of the Holy Isle, and he remembered. He remembered the brothers, the elder suspicious at first, looking around at sights and sounds new to him, the younger secure, as he always was, that his elder brother knew what he was doing. Then he remembered the long months of settling, as they learned the ways of the Holy Isle, and slowly began to cast off the burden of flight and exile and their father's death. He remembered them grow towards manhood, and the eagerness with which Oswiu left to fight among the warbands of the kings and princes of the sea kingdoms, and the reluctance of Oswald to take boat from Iona. He remembered the joy of each return, the radiance on Oswald's face as he came again to the monastery and heard the brothers' chant.

Abbot Ségéne remembered, and he came to the end of land and looked to sea, to the waves rolling from the west, and tears rolled down his cheek to be torn away by the wind.

"Oh, my hawk," he said, "my hawk…"

Historical Note

The facts of Oswald's life, as relayed in Bede's *Ecclesiastical History of the English People*, are few, although rich in implication. He was the son of Æthelfrith, the first king of a united Northumbria and one of the most devastating warlords of this violent age. His mother was Acha, a princess of Deira and the sister of Edwin, the man Æthelfrith had displaced to take the kingdom. With Edwin still alive and on the run, and thus dangerous, Æthelfrith spent a decade trying to hunt him down, alternating bribery and threats against the kingdoms where Edwin took refuge. But in one of the dramatic turns of fortune with which this time is replete, Edwin, cornered in East Anglia and about to be dispatched by the king who had given him refuge, found in that king, Rædwald, an unexpectedly ferocious ally and together they took Æthelfrith by surprise and killed him.

Edwin was now king of Northumbria. Rather than waiting around to see what her brother would do to the children of his usurper, Acha gathered them around her and fled into exile to Dal Riada. Unlike with Æthelfrith, there is no indication that Edwin sought to hunt down Æthelfrith's heirs, but neither was Acha sufficiently sure of his reaction to return with them. So Oswald grew up in exile, a stranger among people very different from his kin. The kingdom of Dal Riada straddled the Irish Sea, stretching from Ulster to Argyll, and its people were Gaels and they were Christian; growing up among them, Oswald and the rest of his family were altered fundamentally.

When Edwin was, in turn, killed, Oswald returned at the head of a small army and killed his uncle's killer, taking the throne of Northumbria. Having accepted Christianity in exile, once he was king Oswald sent to Iona, where he had received the faith, for missionaries to bring the new religion to his own people. The first bishop was a failure, but the second, Aidan, by his humble and simple approach, won many converts. Bede tells the story of the Easter feast, where

Oswald breaks his silver plate to give to the poor, and then writes of his death in battle, after an eight-year reign, at the hands of the last great pagan king of the Anglo-Saxons, Penda of Mercia.

That, in a nutshell, is it. Not much on which to base a novel. But the work of scholars and archaeologists over the last few decades has allowed us to flesh out the story and give it much more muscle. Where before the professors of Old English, Old Welsh and History had little to do with each other, now they fruitfully collaborate, allowing the collation of the poetic and allusive records of Old Welsh with the more prosaic chronicles of the Anglo-Saxons, to much mutual benefit. Years of work have been spent trying to work out which names in one language correspond to which names in the other, and I have shamelessly piggybacked upon this work. Through such painstaking work I have assembled the hints that suggest Penda had a brother named Eowa, that his kingship was contested and by no means certain, and that the monks of Iona were implicated in Cadwallon's defeat. This last deduction arises from the lines of poetry quoted in the story, when Cian laments his fallen lord:

> *From the plotting of strangers and iniquitous*
> *Monks, as the water flows from the fountain,*
> *Sad and heavy will be the day of Cadwallon.*

The lines come from the *Red Book of Hergest*, a collection of Welsh poems written in the late-fourteenth century but containing material that is much older.

This brings us, neatly, to J. R. R. Tolkien. For according to a learned authorial conceit, the source of his tales of Middle-earth was the *Red Book of Westmarch*. Tolkien was the Rawlinson and Bosworth Professor of Anglo-Saxon at Oxford University and one of his aims was to create a mythology for England, as the *Red Book of Hergest*, which contains the *Mabinogion* and other material, could be said to preserve the mythology of the Britons.

Many if not all the writers and scholars involved in Anglo-Saxon studies first came to the field through reading the professor's stories

– and I am one of them, so it is no accident that this story is called *Oswald: Return of the King*, in tribute and homage. Tolkien writes of Oswald in his seminal essay *Beowulf: The Monsters and the Critics* and the parallels between him and Aragorn – rightful king in exile returning to claim the throne – are obvious.

Oswald: Return of the King is imaginative history and, as such, it is as near a true story as I could write. Although the events of the story happened many centuries ago, there remain some surprising physical traces of those times. The inscription on the gravestone of Cadwallon's father, Cadfan ap Iago, can still be seen, taken from the churchyard and embedded into the wall of Llangadwaladr Church, near Aberffraw on Anglesey. And not just stone has been preserved: extraordinarily, Oswald's skull has been preserved and lies in St Cuthbert's coffin in Durham Cathedral. Bamburgh Castle has been much rebuilt over the centuries, but St Oswald's Gate survives, a stone testimony to the impregnability of the fortress of the Idings.

One point that needs comment is the use of human sacrifice by the pagan Anglo-Saxons. Although there is documentary evidence that Germanic tribes from the first century and the Norse of the tenth and eleventh centuries practised human sacrifice, there is no direct historical account of its use by the Anglo-Saxons. The excavations at Ad Gefrin by Brian Hope-Taylor found many, apparently sacrificed, ox skulls but no human remains. However, a number of graves, notably those at Sewerby, Finglesham and Mitcham, have bodies of people who appear to have been killed to accompany the main funeral, while at Sutton Hoo there are a number of bodies that appear to have been executed or sacrificed (possibly both at the same time). The consensus among scholars is that the Anglo-Saxons, while coming from cultures that frequently practised human sacrifice, only rarely resorted to rendering people to the gods, probably only doing so at times of crisis or opportunity.

I have tried throughout to keep to what we know or, at least, can reasonably infer. The only place where I knowingly break from the historical record is at the end, where I have Oswald's final battle taking place in winter rather than high summer as Bede records.

To be honest, this was because I forgot at time of writing that Bede records the battle as taking place in August, but the memory lapse became, I hope, a fruitful artistic decision: this is a winter's battle in implication if not time, and I decided to keep it as such.

Did Oswald really yearn to lay down his sword and become a monk? We do not know. Yet Bede, in the *Ecclesiastical History of the English People* (our key source for this poorly documented time), portrays Oswald as a saint very much for his life rather than for his martyr's death. That he was a convinced believer of the new religion is certain. Yet it is significant that when he turned for aid in building and evangelizing his kingdom, he sent to Iona and the people of Ireland, where Christianity had found its first secure footing outside the old boundaries of the Roman Empire. Oswald turned to a version of Christianity that was monastic, peripatetic and inclined to leave everything at the drop of a psalter and set off on wild peregrinations to lonely outcrops of rock set amid heaving oceans – the monks of Ireland were hugely influenced by the anchorites of Egypt but, looking around, they saw themselves sorely lacking in desert. So they settled for the next best thing: the sea (and, failing that, boggy islands in the middle of marshes). Through to the reign of Alfred the Great two hundred years later, it was not unknown for monks to set off in a coracle without thought of maps or even, sometimes, oars or sail, trusting to God to bring them to land, in this world or the next.

That there had been a profound change among at least some of the Anglo-Saxons is indicated by Sigeberht's abdication from his throne to take up the monastic life. Many more kings would follow his lead in the years to come, laying down sword and taking to their knees. Indeed, I suspect this was one of the reasons for the success of Christianity among the Anglo-Saxon warrior class: it offered hope beyond the walls of the world and a way out of the battle-defined limits into which they had been born. So, given Oswald's evident faith, I think it reasonable that he too hoped one day to lay down his sword.

The Britain of the seventh century was a violent place. Peace was established through fear: the fear of a king's strength. And a king could only maintain that strength by attracting new warriors to his side, men lured by the promise of gold and glory that a successful king scattered, open handed, to his followers. But this placed the kings of the time onto the treadmill of endless war; for only by waging regular campaigns could they reap gold and glory from defeated opponents and attract new men to their households. It was a brutal and bloody business, and not one of the kings of Bernicia and Deira before Oswald died in his bed.

The land was changing, melting and reforming as petty kingdoms rose and fell, but what it would become was at this time still far from clear. When the Romans left, the legions officially sailing home in AD 410 although Roman strength had been steadily drawn from Britain for decades before, they left a land that was quite thoroughly Romanized in the south, but far less so in the north – and of course, Roman rule stopped at the Wall. However, there is no doubt that the kingdoms that succeeded Roman rule saw themselves very much as Roman, maintaining a largely Christian civilization in the face of pagan pirates. The Romans had built a series of forts along the southern and eastern shores of Britain and northern France and Belgium, the Saxon Shore, to defend against these raiders, but as the army and navy withdrew, the local civilian populations were faced with coming to some sort of terms with these seaborne raiders. According to legend – and Bede, but he is writing about events that occurred centuries before – the Britons chose to employ Saxon warriors to keep the other Saxon warriors out. This proved to be a mistake. The Saxon mercenaries sent word across the grey sea that this land was rich, fat and fit for the taking. Others followed (according to tradition the Angles and the Jutes, although it is likely other peoples such as the Frisians also arrived), and Britain, unlike the rest of Europe, disappeared into a virtually prehistoric darkness. Not that the native British church was uneducated; Gildas, a bishop who lived in the sixth century, wrote the lament *On the Ruin and Conquest of Britain* that provides our only contemporary account of the desperate events of the fifth and sixth centuries. But the Angles, the Saxons and the Jutes were pagans and uninterested in recording the tale of these years in any other way than through the song poems of their scops – and those words, sung and recited over the thrum of a lyre to a hall of drunken warriors, are lost to us.

Whether the Angles and the Saxons displaced entire populations of Britons, pushing them into the more marginal, and definitely more mountainous, western parts of the island in a form of early ethnic cleansing, is still a subject of much scholarly debate. The majority view appears to favour the idea that warrior parties beheaded local principalities by killing the king and his warriors, and then installed themselves as rulers, taking local wives and concubines and forcing through a cultural and linguistic transformation at the point of their swords. If there had been major population displacement, we would expect fields to run fallow and then become forest, but palaeobotany finds little evidence that there was any significant reforestation in this period. According to this view, the elites among the Britons were killed or, as Gildas says, fled abroad, leaving the labour to continue to work the land for new masters.

However, many scholars, particularly those who look to the linguistic evidence and the dearth of place names showing signs of originating in the language of the native Britons, argue that there must have been significant population movement to explain the loss of local names. The idea goes like this. You are the new warlord ruler of a small kingdom at the head of the River Ouse. You've taken a local woman as concubine, you've still got the local peasants digging the fields to keep you in clover, and one day you're out riding when you come to a new part of your land and you see a hill with a distinctive summit. Naturally, you summon a convenient peasant and ask him, "What is that hill called?" He will give the local name and you, new master of this land and speaker of a different language, will take it, adapt it to your own ears and make it your own. What you won't do is give it an entirely new name in your own language, that none of the local people know, so when next you are round this way and ask for directions to the hill, none of the peasants will know where you mean.

But this is what happened. There are vanishingly few place names in what became England that bear the linguistic trace of the Celtic-speaking peoples who must once have named hills and rivers and valleys. Therefore, the argument runs, there must have been few speakers of the old language left of whom to ask, "What is the name of that river?" when the new rulers arrived, so therefore the land must have been cleared of its previous inhabitants.

The argument is set to run and run, and even DNA markers are unlikely to solve it in the short term. But whatever the answer, what is clear is that the identity of Britain changed profoundly between the fifth and seventh centuries. Where before there was mainly a division between Romanized and un-Romanized parts of the country, by the seventh century the Britons were well on the way to becoming the Welsh (and the Bretons, as many fled across the narrow sea to Brittany); the Irish, who were later to become the Scots, were spreading from Ulster across the Irish Sea to Argyll; the Picts (who were the Scots at the time, only there wasn't yet a Scotland because most of the Scots were still Irish) were fighting it out with the Britons (who were also living in Scotland, which wasn't yet Scotland); and the English were only getting the first glimmerings of an idea that they might, in fact, be English, but were for the most part still thinking of themselves as Angles or Saxons.

This was the cooking pot into which Pope Gregory sent his missionary delegation in AD 596 to the kingdom of Kent. From this mission came Paulinus, with the sister of the king of Kent, to Edwin in Northumbria, and a re-emergence into the light of history.

For that history, we are indebted to Bede (672/73–735) above all others. Writing about a century after the events of this book, he could speak to people who had themselves had the story from the lips of some of the protagonists. Monasteries in particular are memory institutions, carrying through the years the concerns of their brethren. In the Northumbrian church, Bede had a rich seam of memories, which he mined thoroughly, as well as corresponding with churchmen through the rest of the country.

Although he had his purposes, as do all writers of history, yet I am convinced one of the main ones was simply to do what it says on the cover: to tell the history of the English people. In this book, I hope to have done the same but through the medium of imaginative history, bringing to as much life as I am able the people of a time very distant from our own, but one whose battles and survivals played a crucial part in creating the country in which we live today. By the end of the so-called Dark Ages, Britain had become England, Wales, Scotland and Ireland, the peoples and languages had coalesced, and local boundaries such as counties had been formed for many centuries (can anyone born in Britain fail to delight in the fact that the county of Hampshire is a significantly older political entity than France?). These kings of small kingdoms, these leaders of tiny armies, played a critical part in the foundation of everything we are today, and, I would venture to say, few were as important as Oswald, *Lamnguin*, the Whiteblade that flashed for a few short years through the darkness of those times.

If you would like to read more about the kingdom of Northumbria, I would direct you to the first volume in *The Northumbrian Thrones* trilogy, *Edwin: High King of Britain*, which tells of the events before this book. The trilogy will conclude with *Oswiu: King of Kings*, which will tell of what happens after Oswald's fall. For a non-fiction account of the history and archaeology of Northumbria, see the book I co-wrote with archaeologist Paul Gething, director of the Bamburgh Research Project, *Northumbria: The Lost Kingdom* (published by The History Press) as well as *The King in the North* by Max Adams (a fine account and a truly wonderful, Tolkien-inspired map of Northumbria). For an overview of the Anglo-Saxon world there's no better place to begin than *The Anglo-Saxon World* by Nicholas Higham and Martin Ryan; and for the fascinating but seldom covered history of northern Britain, Alex Woolf's account in *From Pictland to Alba, 789-1070* is definitive.

Northumbria's pre-eminence among the Anglo-Saxon kingdoms waned during the eighth and ninth centuries, so during the Viking incursions of the ninth century it was left to Wessex, and its king, to save England. There is a reason only one ruler in English history has earned the title 'Great'. *In Search of Alfred the Great: the King, the Grave, the Legend* (co-written with archaeologist Katie Tucker) says why he deserves it.